Song of the Sisters

A FIVE DIRECTIONS PRESS BOOK

Song of the Sisters

A Novel

C. P. Lesley

Songs of Steppe & Forest 3

ISBN-13: 978-1947044296

Published in the United States of America.

A Five Directions Press book

Cover images: Sergei Solomko, *Declaration of Love* (postcard, 1890s), public domain via Wikimedia Commons; apple and cherry trees in bloom in the old orchard at Kolomenskoye, Moscow © Julia Mustivaya/Shutterstock

Book and cover design by Five Directions Press
Five Directions Press logo designed by Colleen Kelley

Five Directions Press

What are the wild waves saying,
Sister, the whole day long?
—Joseph Edwards Carpenter

BOOKS BY C. P. LESLEY

The Not Exactly Scarlet Pimpernel

Songs of Steppe & Forest
Song of the Siren
Song of the Shaman
Song of the Sisters

Legends of the Five Directions
The Golden Lynx (1: West)
The Winged Horse (2: East)
The Swan Princess (3: North)
The Vermilion Bird (4: South)
The Shattered Drum (5: Center)

Tarkei Chronicles
Desert Flower
Kingdom of the Shades

Contents

Cast of Characters

(in alphabetical order by first name)

Alexei Bulatovich: Maria's husband; a high-ranking Tatar, descended from Genghis Khan, in service to the Russian grand prince. As the son of a khan, he bears the title *tsarevich*.

Alya: Darya's maid.

Anfim Fadeyev: Government clerk, currently on leave and assisting Igor Bezzubtsev; father of Lara and Tolya.

Anna Semyonovna Kolycheva: Darya's twelve-year-old niece; daughter of Solomonida.

Darya Petrovna Sheremeteva: Younger daughter of the deceased Russian nobleman Pyotr Alexandrovich Sheremetev; heroine of *Song of the Sisters*.

Demian Pavlovich Bledny: A Russian prince, briefly suitor for Darya's hand.

Dmitry Ivanovich Vorontsov: Katya's younger brother; Nikita's friend and comrade-in-arms.

Ekaterina Ivanovna Vorontsova: Known as Katya; neighbor of Darya and Solomonida.

Father Faddei: Anfim's elderly father, a retired Orthodox priest.

Felix Ossolinski: Scion of a prominent Polish noble family; scholar and diplomat in service to King Sigismund the Old of Poland-Lithuania.

Fyodor Mikhailovich Koshkin: Maria's father, a high-ranking but incurably ambitious Russian nobleman.

Gavriil Timofeevich Vorontsov: Katya's uncle and, briefly, a suitor for Darya's hand; his sister-in-law Elizaveta Vadimovna also makes a brief appearance in the novel.

Igor Grigorevich Bezzubtsev: Second cousin of Darya and Solomonida; their father's heir.

Juliana Krasilska: Divorced wife of Fyodor Koshkin and consort of Lord Felix, formerly known as Roxelana.

Lara Anfimova: Anfim's seven-year-old daughter. Lara is a nickname for Larisa.

Lyuba Fyodorovna Koshkina: Maria's twelve-year-old sister and Fyodor Koshkin's youngest child; Anna's best friend. Lyuba is short for Lyubov.

Maria Fyodorovna Koshkina: Wife to Alexei Bulatovich, eldest daughter of Fyodor Koshkin, and a friend of Solomonida and Darya. Her marriage to Alexei gives her the title of *tsarevna* (khan's daughter or, in this case, daughter-in-law).

Masha: A kitchen maid in the Sheremetev household.

Mishka: Steward of the Sheremetev household.

Nikita Andreevich Monastyrev: Son of Pyotr Sheremetev's closest friend; hero of *Song of the Sisters*. His last name is pronounced Ma-na-steer-YOFF.

Pyotr Alexandrovich Sheremetev: Solomonida's and Darya's father, who died two months before the story begins, after a long battle with dementia.

Solomonida Petrovna Sheremeteva: Darya's older sister, formerly married to Semyon Kolychev (now deceased); Anna's mother.

Tolya Anfimov: Anfim's four-year-old son. Tolya is short for Anatoly.

Chapter One

Moscow, July 1543

"OH, DARYA, YOU *HAVE* TO SEE THIS. A STRUTTING PEACOCK just entered our yard!" Solomonida stood on tiptoe, leaning forward until I worried she might tumble right through the open window in her eagerness. The late morning sunlight glinted off her jeweled headdress and found an answering glow in the wisps of blonde braid that had worked their way out from under the rim as she sewed.

"Peacock?" I stared at her and sighed. It wasn't fair. My older sister was lovely, even at thirty-one. Not just beautiful, either, but vivid and charming—outgoing, outspoken, eager to interact with life beyond our courtyard gates. Next to her I felt like the quiet mouse she teasingly called me. "How would a peacock get into our yard?"

"See for yourself." She beckoned to me.

Sorely tempted, I glanced at the altar cloth I was embroidering, already well on its way to completion. I'd set myself the task of stitching the edge of the Blessed Mother of God's halo before I left for church, and I wasn't even halfway through. "I'll never finish this if I stop every time a bird flies by, Solomonida."

I rubbed the pure white rose I'd embroidered yesterday between my thumb and forefinger, imagining the flower's aroma—the scent of holiness. The thread, soft against my skin, reminded me of the real petals I'd stroked this morning on my journey through the courtyard. The sky-blue satin behind the flowers caressed my fingertips; the cloth-of-gold that formed the halo glittered with the light of Heaven. I liked nothing better than to watch my needle threading in and out, connecting one delicate stem stitch to the next, directing my thoughts and dreams along a clear, simple path.

Although I'd never seen a peacock outside a book. And a peacock on every corner would make the altar cloth quite unique. Why waste the chance to see what a real one looked like?

"Don't be silly," Solomonida said. "That altar cloth won't get up and walk off by itself. It will be there when you get back to it. Do hurry, or you'll miss him."

Temptation won, not for the first time. I dropped the altar cloth on a nearby table and ran to join her. When I saw what had attracted Solomonida's attention, thoughts of embroidery vanished from my mind as I too gave way to giggles. The young nobleman crossing our courtyard—the toes of his scarlet leather boots turned up; his brocade robe stitched with gold lions as long as my forearm, the full skirts held in place by a tasseled silk sash of a rich, bright blue; his high collar framing a face topped with reddish hair and a green hat; his long cane (obviously for show) tucked under one arm; his shoulders thrown back and his chest thrust forward—did indeed resemble nothing so much as a strutting peacock.

I whispered an apology to the powers above for my irreverence, but bright little bubbles of amusement continued to burst inside me.

"Who is he?" I asked. "I don't recall seeing him before."

A statement that meant nothing. How many noblemen had I met in the last seven years? I'd spent most of that time nursing Papa, rarely leaving his side and expecting every week to be his last, but he'd clung to life like a limpet until losing his final battle this spring.

Tending him had turned me into a hermit, to the point where I often wondered if I shouldn't forsake the world altogether and adopt the rough wool habit and simple prayer rope of a holy sister. As Matryona, who'd cared for me since babyhood, never failed to remind me, no man wanted a bride of twenty-five.

Although Papa promised to take care of us, didn't he? To find me a husband who would help Solomonida and me manage the estate. "You should be married, not stuck here wasting your youth nursing an old man. I have a plan. Trust me." I heard every word as if he'd said it yesterday, although I'd seen little evidence that anything had come of his vaunted plan. His promise had been the last words he spoke to me before crumpling over, gasping for breath, and I'd clung to it ever since. There hadn't been one moment between then and his death when I could safely question him, still less find out the name of the bridegroom he'd had in mind for me or whether he'd had a chance to put his plans into action.

I stared at the peacock, striding across the courtyard as if he owned the place.

Could Papa have picked this man, whoever he is?

No, that was impossible. Papa wouldn't have given me to such a pompous ass.

"I don't recognize him." Solomonida shook her head, and a few more blonde strands slipped free of their pearl-strewn bounds. "The peacock's a strange one, in more ways than I can count."

I put my fears into words. "You don't think it could be the man Papa chose for me, do you? The one who was supposed to help us with the estate?"

She turned toward me, my own shock mirrored on her face. "Oh, surely not!"

Again on tiptoe, she turned back to stare at the courtyard, as if assessing this dreadful possibility. I took a deep breath, seeking to calm myself. Through the open windows the scents of summer wafted, some pleasant—sage, thyme, lilies, ripening fruit, dried grass, the roses I'd buried my face in this morning—and some not, such as horse dung and refuse from the Moscow streets. On the whole, though, the pleasant smells conquered the unpleasant ones. The breeze from the river must be blowing in the right direction today.

The peacock continued to strut toward the main building, where we were. He seemed oblivious to the servants who clustered in groups of five or six—staring at him, giggling and pointing, muttering behind their hands. Some of the girls regarded him through eyes round with awe. The men, without exception, looked as if they hadn't seen such a good show since the last time traveling minstrels set up in the market square, surrounded by jugglers and dancing bears.

I had to admit, in this case I agreed with the men. Anyone but a nobleman, and they would have demanded to know his business when he first strolled through the open gates, but they seemed to see this visitor as more entertainment than threat.

"I don't understand," Solomonida went on, "why this young man, whom we don't recognize, is prancing through our courtyard without a care in the world. Does he not know we're here?"

She redirected her finger toward a second man, less ostentatious than the first, with a light brown beard and hair and a handsome, clever face. He trailed the peacock by a considerable distance and to my critical eye looked as though he sought to avoid any connection between the swaggering nobleman and himself. If so, his ploy seemed to be working. The servants, their gaze fixed firmly on the peacock, had no attention to spare for anyone else. "And who's that?" Solomonida asked, still pointing at the second man. "Are they together, do you think?"

"One the master, the other his servant, perhaps." I too stood on tiptoe, trying to make sense of this strange sight. The shutter I gripped for support felt smooth under my hand. Beeswax and oil coated the pads of my fingers and thumb, and when I sniffed them, they gave off a whiff of lavender. "Although even the not-peacock looks a bit well-off for a servant."

A leather sack swung from the second man's left shoulder. A cream-colored furl of paper peeped out of the opening, together with a set of quills. "Oh, look, I'd guess he's a clerk or something like that. For the peacock, I suppose. But why would a stranger bring a clerk here?"

Solomonida wrinkled her perfect nose. "We'll find out soon. They're heading this way. They'll be on the second floor before we know it. Let's go down and greet them, shall we?"

"I suppose we may as well." Wondering what I would find, I followed my sister down the stairs.

So much for my unfulfilled task. The Mother of God's halo would have to wait for its golden rim.

Once on the main floor, we walked from room to room, searching for our visitors. The dining room—its ceilings elaborately painted with curlicues and fantastic beasts, its long tables decorated with woven linen cloths and brass utensils, plain wooden benches lined up on either side—contained no one but servants preparing for the midday meal.

"Petka," I said to the closest of them. "Where's that boyar who came to call?"

"I don't know, Lady." He pointed to his right. "Mishka took charge of him. In the old lord's private chamber, perhaps."

Mishka, our steward, was not in the room, so the pointing must indicate my father's unused workspace. "Let's go, sister," Solomonida said. I followed her out.

The next chamber was a sitting area, and it too contained no one except ourselves. I straightened a cushion as I passed, brushed one of the roses I'd arranged in a vase that morning, and again held my fingertips to my nose, inhaling the scent. The table was highly polished, and I saw a blurry reflection in its sheen.

I made a face at the image. Hair straggled out from under my headdress, and my clothes were more suitable for a servant than a noblewoman. What would our visitors think of me? Should I have made them wait while I changed my clothes?

As we reached the third room, I pushed such thoughts aside and straightened my shabby dress. Whoever these men were, we hadn't invited them. Let them think what they liked.

Our visitors had mischief on their minds, I decided the moment I crossed the threshold. They must not have offered to pay their respects to anyone in the house, because Mishka would have announced them if they had. And it seemed safe to assume that they either didn't know that Solomonida and I occupied the women's quarters or, more likely, saw no reason to concern themselves with us.

All of which must mean that the peacock was *not* my intended bridegroom. A flood of relief washed over me at that thought.

The good-looking man I thought of as a clerk, despite the richness of his olive green robe adorned with twisted braid, had already taken a seat behind the table closest to the window and was laying out paper, quills, and ink. As I watched, the peacock propped his cane against the wall and picked up an enameled goblet covered with an embroidered silk cloth—work it had taken me a full year to complete because of its intricately patterned circles in shades of crimson and dark blue thread.

Without thinking, I reached for it, intending to tear it from the man's hands and put it in a safe place, but of course I was too far away. The goblet had belonged to my father. It sat alone on a shelf, a memento of happier days when Papa used to entertain his fellow generals, throwing the entire main floor of the house—even this private space—open for his guests to wander and chat in.

Our unwanted visitor lifted the covering and, without a second glance, tossed it aside. It hit the arm of a chair, then slid to the floor, where it pooled against the Turkestan carpet, the silk I'd chosen to match the underlying gold of the goblet clearly distinct from the cream wool beneath. My stitches found partners in the intricately intertwined medallions, dark red and gold and deep blue the color of the night sky, that formed the pattern of the rug. I'd chosen the silk and threads deliberately to mirror the effect; even the shapes of the emblems repeated the outline of the medallions.

The peacock gave no more sign of noticing me than he had of appreciating my work. It was as if his delight in mauling our possessions blocked any awareness of observers. He focused his whole attention on the goblet, holding it up to the sunlight to admire its beautifully chased thin gold wire, flicking the glass and jewels embedded in the center of each repeated pattern with his thumb, and running his fingers up and down the stem. The cup was as big around as his head and heavy, the stem as long as my two palms held side by side. I saw how he struggled to hold it up with one hand. I knew from experience that its weight would soon cause his wrist to ache.

I took a step forward, intending to dash across the room and grab the goblet from him, but Solomonida caught my elbow. When I glanced her way, she shook her head. I scowled at her. How could she permit this stranger to treat our father's cherished goods as his own?

But when she touched a finger to her lips, I realized she had something in mind. With an effort, I withdrew my foot and bowed quickly to the icons in the "beautiful corner," greeting them on entry to express my reverence for their sacred guardianship. Then I moved silently on slippered feet until I stood next to my sister. When I reached her, she gave me a wicked smile.

I smiled back. Wicked or not, I wanted to hear what she'd say next.

"Excuse me," she announced in a clear, carrying voice. "Are you lost? Can we help you find your proper destination?"

The intruder whirled, shock on his face. In his haste, he lost control of his captured prize. The goblet fell earthward as he waved his arms in wild circles and fought to keep his balance.

The cup hit the bench with a clang that made me groan. "You dolt!" I said. So precious an object, a gift from a former ruler to my great-grandfather—to be tossed about by a well-dressed robber?

The impact caused the stem, which had been loose for as long as I could remember, to separate from the circle at its base. The enameled base flew sideways, smacking our unwanted visitor in the stomach with impressive force.

"Good!" I said, before I thought better of it. It served him right, the brute.

The peacock howled and staggered three steps backward, colliding with the table where the clerk—if that's what he was—had set up his tools. The solid oak frame, sturdy enough that it took six men to move it, had no trouble surviving its assault by the peacock. I couldn't say the same for a single one of the objects strewn across its gleaming surface.

The clerk swore, leaped to his feet, and grabbed, too late, for the ink pot. It drenched his expensive stack of paper and tumbled onto the floor. The acrid smell made my nose twitch, and at the sight of that huge sooty blot ruining our beautiful carpet I was tempted to swear worse than the clerk.

"Mother of God," I yelled. "What have you done, you idiots?" Solomonida was shouting at them too. We sounded like fishwives at the market.

Groaning, the peacock dropped onto the window bench while the base joined the rest of the goblet on the floor. He rubbed his stomach and scowled at us. "What have *I* done?" he said. "You startled me! Is that any way to greet visitors?"

So it's our fault?

"Visitors—is that what you call yourselves?" Solomonida demanded. "How dare you storm in here without so much as a by-your-leave! Did it not occur to you to ask the steward whether the owners were in residence before you started pawing at our things?"

"Don't make me teach you manners, woman." He smacked the cushion at his side as if demonstrating what he had in mind.

"I'll have you shown the door first, you churl!" Solomonida told him, clenching her fists.

As I moved to support my sister, my beautiful cover caught my eye. I dragged it away from the spreading blot and held it up by the corners. A high, keening sound escaped me. I couldn't help it. A huge dark stain covered the center of the gold silk, with ink flowing in rivulets toward the edges and drenching the embroidered circles. The whole thing resembled nothing so much as a tick, with a rough circle forming the body and flowing ink representing the legs.

Tears ran down my cheeks. A year's work, ruined by a pair of thoughtless strangers. I'd made it for Papa, to show my love for him. Now Papa was dead. I could stitch another cover, but there was no point in putting in so many hours when I'd never again see the smile that creased his face when I gave him the cloth to celebrate his name day. The way he'd stroked the silk with his thumb, held it out to admire the stitching, laid it with care across the goblet before he moved the whole thing to the center of the display shelf, saying that's where it belonged because there he could look at it whenever he liked—all gone, all irreplaceable.

"I'll treasure it forever," he'd told me. It had been one of the few times I felt close to him, when I knew I'd done something that pleased him. And these ... *intruders* had destroyed everything but the memory.

Too distraught to talk, I rolled the cloth into a tight ball and threw it onto the sheets of paper scattered across the rug.

My hands were damp.

I looked down. Ink circles marked my palms, just like the cloth.

Wonderful. It needed only that to complete this dreadful scene. I grabbed a relatively clean piece of paper and scrubbed at the ink with it, to no avail. The stain dried on my hands. It would take the kind of soap the workmen used to get it off, and even then, I might have to wait for the ink to fade.

I muttered prayers for forgiveness, for a miracle that would turn back time. None of it worked. The angels withheld their aid from me, and my beautiful embroidery remained sullied, my hands dark with ink.

"Those marks will never come out," I said when I recovered my composure. What I saw on the carpet made me shudder. Getting ink out of wool—where to start? And while I watched, as if the two men hadn't already done enough damage, half a dozen quills settled onto blot, rug, paper, goblet, and cover, adding fluffs of feather to the mess.

The peacock stopped insulting Solomonida long enough to demand, "Who *are* you?" The other man watched the rest of us, his expression wary but not hostile. He folded his arms across his chest, his stance rigid, and didn't speak. Definitely a subordinate.

"Solomonida Petrovna Sheremeteva," my sister said in her haughtiest tone. I stared at the three of them, wondering what I'd missed while I focused on my ruined work.

When I failed to chime in, Solomonida sighed and tugged on my sleeve. "My half-sister, Darya Petrovna Sheremeteva. We live here, as you would know if you'd bothered to inquire before barging in and fingering our possessions. Who are *you*?"

The peacock looked me up and down as if he couldn't believe I was a daughter of the house. I definitely should have changed my clothes.

I gave him a hard stare, daring him to say so much as a stray word about my dress. "Yes, who *are* you?" I demanded. "What gives you the right to storm in here and wreck our things?"

"They wouldn't be wrecked if you hadn't startled me." Our visitor hissed the *startled*. Solomonida and I hissed back, and I saw his mouth tighten. He hadn't expected resistance. *Good.*

After a moment of silence, he put his hands together and dipped his head in our direction. If I felt generous, I might call it a bow. But a high official acknowledging a peasant would be closer to the truth. My hackles rose higher.

"My apologies," he said stiffly. "My tongue ran away with me. Blame my surprise." His companion—whose stiffness had given way to amusement, or so I guessed from the slight curve to his lips and the sparkle in his eyes—produced a far more respectful bow but again didn't speak.

"You haven't told us who you are," Solomonida reminded the peacock.

"Igor Grigorevich Bezzubtsev," he announced with the flourish I'd expect from a court herald. "Your father's heir."

"You are mistaken," I said. "Solomonida and I are our father's heirs. He didn't have time to name another. He had no living sons, so there were only a few cousins we haven't seen in years. Papa didn't want the estate to go to any of them." Only to my selected bridegroom, but it seemed obvious Papa had never had the strength to complete that arrangement.

Hearing the words leave my mouth, I stared hard at the peacock. Could *he* be a cousin? The Sheremetevs were an offshoot of the Bezzubtsev clan. He didn't much resemble Papa as I remembered my father from my childhood, but there was something about the eyes ...

If Igor Grigorevich told the truth about being Papa's heir, though, why had Papa not named him instead of talking vaguely about someone who would take care of us? Why had the priest who wrote the will not mentioned him?

I opened my mouth to ask the question aloud, then shut it without speaking. Father Hilarion, our former chaplain, had written Papa's will. Hilarion always insisted women's brains couldn't hold much information. He wouldn't have shared any provision with us except in response to a direct order. And he'd retired to a monastery three years ago. Who else would know what Papa had intended?

Father Job, maybe. He was the new priest, who used to live next door and now visited us daily from his house in the city. He might have little or no information about Papa's will, but he would certainly recall what Papa said on his deathbed.

"We should ask Father Job to join us," I said to Solomonida. "I saw him arrive about an hour ago, so I'm pretty sure he's downstairs in his study. He can help us figure out whether these men are telling the truth."

"Good idea." She walked to the door and called.

Mishka came running, shouting, "Lady Solomonida, there you are. I've been looking everywhere for you. We have visitors." As he entered the room, he gasped and clutched his chest at the sight of the mess Bezzubtsev had made. "Lady! What happened here?"

"Our visitors were careless," Solomonida said. "Send someone to clean it up as soon as possible. But first ask Father Job to come here. If he knows where to find our father's will, he should bring it with him." Mishka bowed, but I saw him shake his head at the ink-stained horror on the floor as he left.

Bezzubtsev ignored the whole exchange, although he waited for the door to close behind Mishka before signaling to his companion, who stepped around the table, avoiding the spreading disaster on the rug. He too bowed once more.

"Permit me to introduce Anfim Fadeyev." Bezzubtsev gestured at the other man. "He's on leave from the Treasury and, at the moment, working for me. I hired him to advise me as I take possession of this estate. Make sure the paperwork is in order. Things like that. He knows about documents. Tell them, Fadeyev, how things stand."

I glanced my sister's way and found her frowning at Bezzubtsev. Did she too suspect he might be our cousin and thus the rightful heir?

But I saw only annoyance on her face. At his presumption, probably.

I had no intention of letting two unwelcome strangers bully me. "Yes, tell us," I said, staring straight at them and using the voice I usually reserved for unruly servants. I'd been practicing that tone since the year I turned fourteen, when my stepmother died and I inherited responsibility for the household. As a result, I could summon it at will. "But don't think you can fool us because we're women. Papa promised he would leave us enough lands and goods to support ourselves, as well as the right to live in this house to the end of our days. He never mentioned you, in connection with this estate or anything else."

Bezzubtsev swore again and rubbed his brow. "And if you're truly our father's heir," I told him, "why didn't you ask to see us before barging into our sitting room and grabbing at our things? You must have known we lived here. You're acting more like a thief than a relative!"

He flushed then. "I wanted to get a good look at the place first."

"Nonsense," Solomonida said. "My sister speaks the truth. You have behaved abominably. You had no business showing up here without warning. So take yourself off. You're not welcome in our house, Igor Grigorevich, no matter how many papers you wave at us."

Bezzubtsev sighed, a false sound hinting at long-suffering and boredom. I could almost hear him wondering what sin he'd committed that led to him being burdened with these impossible females. "Why would I tell you? I assumed you knew," he said, waving a languid hand. "You should have expected me."

"How could we expect you when no one—including you—sent us a message saying you were on your way?" I demanded. "Were we going to see you in our nightmares? I don't believe a word of it."

"And how did you find out that Papa died?" Solomonida asked. "Did Father Job write to you?"

"He did, but not about the will. A former benefactor of my family contacted me about that not long after your father's funeral," he said. For the first time, he looked at the floor and blushed. Perhaps he recognized how ridiculous he sounded.

"A benefactor of *your* family," Solomonida scoffed. "Not our priest or clerks. That didn't seem odd to you?"

He shrugged. "What's his name, this benefactor?" I asked.

"No one you would know." His tone emphasized his lack of respect for us.

"Tell us anyway," Solomonida said. "We have a broader acquaintance among the boyars than you might expect."

"If you insist." Bezzubtsev sounded bored. "Fyodor Mikhailovich Koshkin. He's a high-ranking servitor at court."

I exchanged astonished glances with my sister. "Fyodor Koshkin?" I echoed. "We certainly do know him. He's the shiftiest man in Moscow. Now I believe you less than ever."

"It's true, though." Bezzubtsev nodded at the clerk. "Explain it to them, Fadeyev."

The clerk—who indeed was a clerk; I'd been right about that—looked apologetic, in contrast to his master. "Some of what you say is true, ladies. Your father's will gives the two of you control of specific villages and estates, which together yield a handsome income. You own the servants associated with this household as well as the movable goods—furniture, linen, dishes, and so on. If you husband your resources well, you can both live comfortably for the rest of your lives—not least because you have the right to remain in the women's quarters of this estate for as long as you wish. But your father left these buildings in Moscow—including the land on which they stand and the stables, carriages, horses, and military equipment associated with them—to his nearest male relative." He nodded to his right. "His first cousin's only son, Igor Grigorevich Bezzubtsev."

"Damnation," Solomonida said.

"Can you prove it?" I asked, fighting against the inevitable. "Because we don't know you, and our father did not tell us about you, as I said before. Nor have we seen the will ourselves, so why should we accept your story about what it says—or about who you are, for that matter?"

"I recognized your names," Bezzubtsev said. "I can't believe you don't recognize mine." Solomonida and I glared at him then, while he glared back as if he could force us to acknowledge his right to our estate by the power of his gaze.

That flicker of memory tugged at me again, but I refused to stop and probe it. I was too angry.

After a long and unpleasant pause, Fadeyev intervened. "Well, proof could be a problem. We have the bequest in writing, but ..." He bent and rummaged among the papers strewn across the carpet, picking them up one by one before scanning and dropping them onto a rough pile. At last he found one he liked the look of, plucked it from the floor, straightened it, and held it up for our inspection.

An ink blot almost as large as the one that had ruined my goblet cover saturated the lower half of the document. In the last two years, Father Job had taught me to read and write so I could entertain Papa with religious tales and literature. That training stood me in good stead as I stared at the paper, trying to decipher the letters. At the top, I could see written—in beautiful block lettering that reminded me very much of Father Hilarion's practiced hand—"In the name of the Father, and of the Son, and of the Holy Spirit, being sound in mind and body, I, Pyotr Alexandrovich Sheremetev, do bequeath my possessions as set forth in this will." A long list of goods and properties assigned to Solomonida and me followed, becoming ever more ink-spattered as my eyes tracked the words down the page. At the bottom, I saw my father's mark and seal, Father Hilarion's signature, and the places where he had written out Papa's name in full and another mark I didn't recognize—quite likely, that of the second witness. Any phrase that might identify Igor Grigorevich was obliterated by ink.

Unless our priest could produce another copy of the will, Anfim Fadeyev was right. We did have a problem. We might have no way to confirm or deny the claim that Papa had left the house in which we lived to this Igor Bezzubtsev. And how could we accept the word of two men we didn't know and had no reason to trust?

At that moment, Father Job entered the room.

Chapter Two

WITH A SIGH OF RELIEF, I TURNED TO GREET THE PRIEST. "Oh, Father, thank the Lord you've come. You can't imagine what these men are saying!" Behind me, Bezzubtsev made a disgusted noise.

At least, I assumed it was Bezzubtsev. His clerk had so far behaved with impeccable courtesy.

Solomonida echoed me. "Father Job," she said in greeting, "how kind of you to join us. Do you in fact have the will?" She stopped, bit her lip for a moment, then went on. "My apologies. I'm forgetting my manners." She introduced our cousin and Anfim Fadeyev.

"Our priest," she finished, with a gesture at Father Job. "He didn't write my father's will, but he has access to the papers of the man who did."

Fadeyev stepped forward to greet the priest with appropriate respect, bowing and accepting Father Job's blessing. As Fadeyev made way for Bezzubtsev, I noted the twinkle in Father Job's eyes. His lively sense of the ridiculous—here, no doubt, triggered by the peacock's haughty tip of the head—explained much of my very real affection for him. A kindly man in early middle age, of medium height and build, his dark hair starting to turn gray, Father Job combined significant learning with a genuine love of humanity.

"Unfortunately not, Lady Solomonida," he said. "I assume that so important a document must be in some obvious place, but it wasn't in the first few strongboxes I examined, and I didn't want to keep you waiting while I looked for it. I'll go back and search my study—your father's chambers, too—and will bring it to you as soon as I find it. Can you tell me why you need to see it? From what Father Hilarion said, I thought the provisions were quite clear."

"What *did* Father Hilarion say?" I asked. That would at least give us a place to start.

"That Pyotr Alexandrovich left everything he could to the two of you." Job frowned. "That's ambiguous, isn't it? Why everything he could, rather than everything?"

"Because he didn't include the estate," Bezzubtsev cut in. "The land belongs to the clan. He wouldn't leave it to a pair of girls who might marry into another family or pass it on to their daughters."

Solomonida stretched her arm toward the men. "As you hear, Igor Grigorevich insists that Papa bequeathed him this estate. But neither Papa nor Father Hilarion ever mentioned that to us. And our visitors have no proof of their claim, since they caused an accident that ruined their copy of the will." She made it sound as if she suspected them of destroying evidence on purpose.

I saw Fadeyev wince at that. Willfully wrecking a document probably counted in his book as the gravest of sins.

Holding the piece of ink-stained paper by the edges, he showed it to Father Job, who peered at the mess.

"It's impossible to decipher, Solomonida Petrovna." Father Job handed the paper back to Fadeyev, who flattened it between two sheets that had somehow escaped the ink cascade and set it to one side. "That looks like Father Hilarion's handwriting, based on the papers of his that I have to hand. And the beginning confirms that your father indeed left ample property to you and Darya Petrovna. But whatever he intended for the estate can't be read. Which means that the only way to verify the contents will be to discover our copy of the testament. Or track down Father Hilarion and the other witness and hope they have good memories."

My sister sighed. "And until then?"

"Igor Grigorevich is right about one thing," Father Job said. "It's a common arrangement to give various movable goods and even specific villages to the women of the household but keep the main estate for a male heir, so it can't pass into the hands of another clan. The only unusual provision is the statement that you and your sister have the right to remain on the property if you wish. I'm not sure what your father had in mind there, as it could easily become uncomfortable for all concerned. But the legible part of his will does state that. If this man is your cousin, can you vouch for his identity? That's not much, but it's a beginning."

Solomonida nodded—reluctantly, I thought—then turned to study our cousin with the same intent gaze I'd bestowed on him earlier. After a while, her head tipped to one side and her eyes widened. To my astonishment, a mischievous smile turned the corners of her mouth upward.

What on earth?

The men stared as well—Fadeyev and Father Job with alert curiosity, Bezzubtsev with something closer to alarm.

"Oh," Solomonida cried. "I *do* recognize him. It's Igrushka the Duckling! So many summers, so many winters! You only visited us once, because Papa and your father didn't get along, and we left you in the copse after you refused to climb trees with us. You deserved it, too—nasty little boy that you were, threatening to snitch on the rest of us. You *would* be the one to show up and try to take our home!"

"Igrushka the Duckling?" Father Job sounded as though he was trying hard not to laugh.

Anfim Fadeyev, too. A choked sound escaped him as he clapped both hands over his mouth. His eyes, as they say, danced. I expected him to guffaw at any moment, but he somehow managed to straighten his face while I gazed first at my sister, then at Igor Bezzubtsev.

By the saints, Solomonida was right. That's what I'd recognized as "something in the eyes." He looked different, of course: he'd been a boy of eleven the one time I saw him. But the reddish hair and light blue eyes and snub nose were the same. How could I have forgotten Igrushka the Duckling, even after seventeen years?

But of course, I hadn't forgotten him. I just hadn't connected the formal "Igor Grigorevich" with that silly childhood nickname.

"It's true," I said. "I should have known you right away. Igrushka the Duckling. Only now you're a peacock!" I burst out laughing, a vivid image of his outfit on that long-gone day as fresh in my mind as if it were yesterday.

"And how you hated it when we called you that," Solomonida said. "You got red in the face and chased us, but we were faster than you!"

"Shura and Dasha," Igor said, spitting out our childhood names as if he still carried a grudge against us. "You were pests then, and you're obnoxious now."

He sounded as if he hadn't aged a bit. He hated people poking fun at him, even after seventeen years. "Do you remember the absurd clothes you wore that day?" I asked. "Yellow brocade trimmed with brown velvet that matched your trousers? And those ridiculous blue leather boots with the turned-up toes? To play in the woods! You looked just like a duckling. An angry duckling, stomping about and muttering under your breath about how you'd make sure we paid for our sins."

"Absurd?" Igor stiffened and flicked the skirts of his lion-embroidered white robe. Today's boots were red instead of blue, and their turned-up toes seemed to quiver with indignation. "What do you mean, absurd? I've never worn anything that wasn't the latest style. And who are you to talk? Look at that sack you have on! Why, if your sister hadn't been here to introduce you, I'd have taken you for one of the maids."

My cheeks warmed as I glanced at my shabby skirts. He had a point, but so did I. Of all the things we'd said, his response told me he cared most about my criticizing his clothes. "At least I have enough sense not to go draped in silk and velvet while walking on muddy forest paths." I shook my skirt at him. "Or the vanity I'd need to worry about impressing my servants while they're sweating over steaming tubs of water filled with dirty linen."

I'd been embroidering, not supervising the laundry, but he didn't need to know that. I could tell from the twitch of my sister's lips that she approved of the way I was handling Igor. Beyond her, Anfim Fadeyev had given up his battle for self-control and was chortling quietly in a corner. Father Job wasn't much better off.

I kept going, determined not to cede the high ground to my beastly cousin. "I'll never forget that day. I was only eight, so they wouldn't let me climb trees because Solomonida worried that I'd fall and get everyone in trouble. I had to sit in the copse, feeling sorry for myself, while you, Igrushka, strode back and forth like a madman, threatening to tell the grownups how mean we were. In the end, I got tired of you and ran off."

"And the rest of us pelted you with acorns. Nikita pelted you harder than anyone. Do you remember me telling you about that, Darya?" Solomonida giggled as if she couldn't stop.

Nikita. That was a name I hadn't heard in a long time. An image of a tall, gangly boy with light brown hair and eyes and a delightful smile, who used to tease and joke with me but never failed to hug me when I got hurt. Who shared his drawings and stories with me, because no one else cared about them.

"I do remember," I said. I heard a certain wistfulness in my own voice, regret for a lost friendship. "I wonder where he is these days." He hadn't even sent us a message when Papa died.

Recalling that now, his omission surprised me. Papa loved Nikita, whose father was Papa's best friend, and I'd always believed Niki felt the same. Had they had a falling-out? The Nikita I'd known wouldn't bear a grudge, but life and hardship changed people.

Or perhaps Niki too had left the land of the living for a better world, and no one bothered to tell us. That our fathers had been comrades didn't make us family, although I had once seen Niki as closer than a brother. A heartbreaking thought.

Solomonida didn't answer; she was laughing too hard. After a while, she pulled herself together and held out a hand. "Peace, cousin. It happened long ago. How silly we were, in truth. Let's forgive and forget the past, shall we, so we can figure out how to handle the present? Why do you want to steal our estate? You have properties of your own—including a house in the city, as I recall. And don't you live with your mother?"

"No. But even if I did, this *is* my house in the city." Igor fondled a chair covering, as if assessing its quality. "It's a nice property, well maintained and situated in the heart of Moscow. Perfect for my needs. And your father left it to me. Just as Fadeyev told you. If you don't trust me, you can trust him. He's a government official. He has nothing to gain from lying."

"Of course he does," Solomonida snapped. "He works for you, so he'll do what you tell him. You said that yourself. Anyway, I know him even less than I do you. Why should I believe his recital of a piece of paper that can't be read?"

Fadeyev's laughter vanished. "It's the truth," he said. "I understand that you dislike hearing this news, but I'm a priest's son as well as an official. I don't lie just to make a kopeck."

When Solomonida huffed, I decided the time had come to step in. "We're not accusing you," I told Fadeyev. "Cousin Igor"—the name stuck in my throat—"what are your plans?"

"I'm moving in," he snapped. "And there's not a thing you can do about it, because I own the place."

"Over my dead body," Solomonida said.

"Don't tempt me," Igor shot back, glowering.

Fadeyev emitted an audible sigh, and for a moment Igrushka's head turned his way. Fadeyev shrugged, perhaps in apology.

"Lord Igor, Lady Solomonida, please control yourselves." Father Job stepped into the fray, arms outstretched to separate the combatants. "Enough insults. May I propose a solution?"

"Very well," Solomonida said after a pause.

"Please," I added.

Igor's mouth tightened. I wondered if he'd take out his anger on Father Job. An uncomfortable few moments passed before he nodded. "Propose your solution, Father."

"Thank you," the priest said. "This is something of a standoff. You have a claim that sounds reasonable on the surface but no proof to support it, not even a verbal statement from Lord Sheremetev warning us to expect you. Therefore we need to verify your right to live on this estate as its master. And since your cousins own everything but the land, as clearly stated in the parts of your document that *are* still legible, you can't simply assert your authority. You must secure their cooperation before you can move in. Solomonida Petrovna, Darya Petrovna, would you permit Igor Grigorevich to stay here as your guest?"

"Must we?" I didn't want him here. Who knew what tricks he would get up to? We'd be on tenterhooks at every moment.

Solomonida couldn't muster even that much of a response. After a short pause, Father Job said, "I think your father might expect you to extend such an offer to a relative."

Unfortunately, he spoke the truth. The laws of hospitality were strict, and Igor Grigorevich could claim the right of cousinship. "What happened to your house in Moscow?" I asked, wishing we could at least keep him away from our property.

Igrushka the Duckling pulled off his fancy hat and twisted it in his palms. A pained smile creased his face. "When my father died, his creditors took most of our property to cover his debts. There's a rural estate that my mother has gone to administer and not much else."

"You could stay there," Solomonida said.

"No, I can't." Igor mimicked her pose—both hands on his waist, elbows out. "Not if I'm to make my way at court and repair my family's fortunes. For that I need to live in Moscow. And whether you like it or not, I *did* inherit this estate."

"Although you can't prove it," I reminded him. "It's your word against ours."

"I'll find proof. But for the moment, if you need to pretend that I'm your guest, so be it." He glowered at us, and we scowled in return, but as the incendiary exchange continued, he gave a deep sigh. "Look, I'm sorry I took you by surprise. I had no idea your father hadn't told you about the bequest. It must be very unsettling. Thank you for accepting me into your home." He managed a perfunctory bow.

Lord above, was that a hint of humility? I could almost accept that Igrushka might be human after all.

Solomonida sighed, then stepped forward and took our cousin by the elbow. "Very well," she said. "Consider yourself our guest. I'll show you the general layout of the estate, and we can renew our acquaintance. Best that we get to know each other if we're going to be living in the same house—for now."

Father Job bowed. "That sounds like an excellent beginning. Meanwhile, I will search for the will."

"Will you let me know what you find?" I asked him. "I'd like to go over the provisions with you."

"Of course, Darya Petrovna. Let me look for it now." Another round of blessings and he withdrew, leaving us with a no-longer-smug Cousin Igor and his clerk.

The last thing I wanted was to wander around the estate trailing my long-lost and never-missed cousin. While my sister shepherded him and his clerk out the door, I muttered excuses about tasks I needed to complete.

Solomonida didn't insist that I come with them. I sent her silent waves of thanks for that.

Alone, I considered my options. When my sister and the men came back, the only acceptable behavior from me was to join them. But what should I do in the meantime?

I could wait for Father Job, but I had no idea how long it might take him to find Papa's testament. However important a document, it had been written more than three years ago under circumstances very different from those of today. Father Job might locate it quickly, but it could just as well take hours or days to discover. And there was little point in offering my assistance. With even less idea than Father Job of where to look, I'd be more of a hindrance than a help.

So rather than stand around fussing, I decided my best course was to take advantage of my temporary solitude to run off and change my clothes for robes suitable to my station in life. As I'd told my cousin when he challenged me, I'd dressed for comfort, not entertaining. My guests deserved better.

A small voice in my head warned me not to give in to vanity. I silenced it. The scorn on my cousin's face when he described the "sack" I was wearing made me yearn to show him I could dress well if I wished. I left a message with Petka, who happened to be the first servant I saw, to fetch me if Father Job returned, asked him to send my maid to join me as soon as possible, then set off for my bedchamber.

Once there, I headed for the cedar chest that contained the robes I'd worn years ago, when I still visited friends and kinswomen and attended various gatherings from christenings to weddings. Halfway there, I remembered my ink-stained hands and moved instead to pour water from the jug that always stood on a high table behind a carved screen. I was scrubbing the stains with soap, to no great effect, when my maid Alya entered.

I held up dripping hands, showing her the blots, less dark than before thanks to my scrubbing but still visible. "Do you know how to get these out?"

"I'll fetch the pumice stone the workmen use." She ducked out of the room.

Waiting, I wrapped cloths around my palms and went to look at the chest. But I'd not had the chance to do much more than lift the lid before she was back. She held out a small jar containing light gray powder.

"You found it," I said. "And so quickly too. Good work." I returned to the sink and attacked the stains. They didn't disappear altogether, but they did lighten to a point where I could imagine touching rich fabrics without leaving marks.

I pointed to the chest. "We need to unpack that, Alya, and find a robe for me to wear. I hope the moths didn't get them."

"I hope not, Mistress. It's ages since we opened those chests, but the cedar should have protected your clothes." She dove in, lifting one gorgeous gown after another and holding it out to me. Pink and yellow and emerald green and the soft blue of a springtime sky—silk, satin, and velvet flowed over my hands as I checked each robe for holes, then sighed in relief as I realized the cedar had done its work. One or two of the topmost robes had suffered damage, but that was slight. Most of the gowns were as fresh as the day I'd seen them stowed away. The woody, fruity scent called to me, and I pressed my nose against the pile of fabrics. It reminded me of incense.

"Which one should I choose?" I asked her, overwhelmed by the selection after so many years wearing drab homespun designed to resist the effluvia of sickness, the rough demands of polishing and laundering, and even the stray thread or pinprick that attended the embroidery I loved.

She stroked each robe in turn. "They're so beautiful. Soft and shiny. You'd look gorgeous in any of them, but I think ..." She returned to the chest and pulled out one more, from the very bottom. "This one, Darya Petrovna. I'll braid your hair with pearls and"—she bent once more and pulled out a pointed headdress—"you can wear this kokoshnik. Men will swoon when they see you."

The robe was scarlet brocade, adorned with pearl-encrusted cuffs the width of my palm and thick gold braid around the hem. I wanted to weep at the sight of it, because my father had had it stitched for what should have been my formal presentation to Daniil Kolychev—the boy next door to whom Papa had promised me but who had, in the end, married someone else. The contracts had never been signed, so no presentation had taken place, and soon after that my brother-in-law was disgraced and I stopped attending most of the gatherings that required such elaborate clothes.

I'd last donned the robe for Maria Koshkina's wedding, but that was already more than six years ago. I could have worn it at my own—it was that fine—but no one wanted to marry the sister-in-law of a criminal, however highborn, or the daughter of a man too sick to help his future son-in-law get ahead at court.

Remembering Daniil and that lost moment of possibility, I trembled. It wasn't so much that I'd wanted to marry him. I'd known him a little, contrary to custom, because he lived next door and sometimes visited my younger brother, who idolized him. But Daniil's amazing good looks and absolute assurance of his own place in the world invariably terrified me into silence. I'd clapped my hands with joy the day I heard the wedding was off. I hadn't known, then, how much the boundaries of my life would contract in the years since then or that another opportunity might never come my way. No wonder I'd become convinced that a women's monastery would suit me best.

"It's not too grand?" I asked the maid, thinking of that lost past, the monastery that might be my only future. My voice sounded choked, even to my own ears.

Alya shook her head. "It's perfect, Lady. You'll look like an angel. And it's lain in the chest too long. What good can happen to it there? Let's get you into it, and you'll see."

I didn't believe her. But I allowed her to do as she liked, thinking again of Daniil as she worked. He'd terrified me then, ten years ago, but now things might be different. And he'd been *so* good-looking, with that tawny hair and eyes that matched. He was happy with his wife, according to Solomonida. Would he have been happy with me, once we got used to each other?

Alya held up a brass mirror and turned it this way and that. She was done with her preparations. I stared at the pointed headdress, the matching robe, the cream satin tunic that went with the robe, and didn't recognize myself. She'd brushed my light brown hair until it shone, braided it with strings of pearls as she'd promised. How long had it been since I looked like the noblewoman I was?

When I took the hand mirror from her and gazed at the stranger who stared back at me fuzzily from the metal surface, she picked up a container of scent and dabbed it on my throat and wrists. The subtle scent of sandalwood pervaded the air. I blinked at the luxury of it.

Could I really give this up for life in a rough woolen habit? It would itch even in winter, and at this time of year I might as well be stuck in an oven. No perfume, no jewels, no delicious food or silken tunics against the skin. There were other ways to serve God. Why take vows myself, just because I'd spent the last seven years setting aside every pleasure that came my way to concentrate my energy on Papa?

I took a deep breath, held it, released it. These were dangerous thoughts. I'd chosen these clothes to make a point, not to decide the path my life should take. So what if Cousin Igor respected me more because I arrayed myself in brocade and pearls? It didn't change anything.

But try as I might, I couldn't convince myself. And when I thought of the impact my changed appearance might have, the image in my mind wasn't Cousin Igor or even Daniil Kolychev but Nikita, the last time I'd seen him. I was fourteen, just starting to think about boys as something more than a nuisance. He was only a year older, but in those days that difference, now so small, gaped like a chasm. At fifteen he was already a man in the eyes of the world. I could hardly put two words together, I felt so shy in his presence. For a few months I dreamed of him constantly, whether asleep or awake. Then he joined the army, as all boyars' sons did, and we girls didn't see him again, although Papa occasionally brought us news.

Not all of it was good news, either. I recalled Papa telling us—back in 1537, when he was already sick but not as addled as he became this last year or two, so he could still keep in touch with his former comrades-in-arms—how Niki had gotten into trouble with the government in Moscow for siding with the renegade Prince Andrei of Staritsa against his nephew Grand Prince Ivan. A stupid family spat that lurched out of control and led to the executions of thirty good men—of whom Niki, thank God, was not one. But he had fallen into disgrace for years, consigned to a punishment post on the southeastern border fighting off the Tatars. A dangerous post, which made his long silence even more ominous. Again I wondered if Niki still lived.

And if so, did he sometimes think about me, or had I dropped into a corner of his memory as he had into mine? Perhaps he'd cut all ties, believing that Papa failed him when he most needed help—or to save us from possible guilt by association. I didn't and couldn't know. Yet today, recalling the sadness on Papa's face when he delivered the news of Niki's disgrace, I experienced the same sense of loss I'd felt when I first heard it. Not just for myself but for them, because Papa never uttered Nikita's name again.

I was a fool. Reminiscing about Nikita made even less sense than mooning over Daniil, married close to ten years by now. What was wrong with me today? The shock of Cousin Igor's arrival had turned my brain to mush.

I thanked Alya for her efforts and went downstairs in an odd mood.

The sight of Father Job, waiting with scroll in hand, restored my spirits. "You should have sent for me, Father," I said, ushering him into the dining room, unoccupied except for the occasional servant stopping by to adjust a tablecloth or a place setting. "You had no need to wait. I told Petka to fetch me as soon as you arrived."

"But that was just now, Lady. And you look lovely. I see you spent your time well." He smiled. "Shall we sit on that bench, and I'll explain what's here?" A tip of the scroll indicated the bench he had in mind.

With a quick word of thanks, I took my seat. "You found it quickly then. That's good. We'll have an answer, even if it's not the one we want. Where was it?"

"Alas, this is not the will itself." He loosened the leather strip around the scroll and spread the paper out on the table, holding the ends flat with his hands. "I looked everywhere I could think of, including your father's bedchamber, but I couldn't find the equivalent of the document the clerk showed me. Father Hilarion may have taken the testament with him when he went to the monastery—for safekeeping or for some other reason. Or he may have put it somewhere I have yet to discover. Without talking to him, I can only guess. He could even have sent it to your cousin, if your father requested it. That may be the sole copy we saw today."

"What's this, then?" I squinted at the paper, covered with squiggly lines. Unlike the document Fadeyev had shown us, written in the neat block script used for church books, these letters had been scribbled in haste. It boggled my mind that anyone could make sense of them.

"Notes," Father Job said. "Probably jotted down during a conversation with your father in preparation for writing the will. Only after Hilarion felt certain that he understood every detail would he turn the statements into provisions and add the appropriate formulas, like the ones you saw in the actual testament. I'm surprised he didn't throw the notes away when he was done, but paper is expensive." He turned the unrolled scroll over, revealing more squiggles on the back. "These are instructions the good father left for me as he was departing for the monastery. But I didn't see them, because I didn't arrive for some months after he left. I knew nothing about this until I managed to pry open a strongbox that I thought might hold the will."

"So it came to you by accident, this paper." I stared harder at the notes, but the squiggles wavered before my eyes, refusing to divulge their secrets. "What does it say?"

Father Job turned the paper over once more. "Look, Darya Petrovna. Here we have 'estate,' 'girls?'" He touched a different spot. "And here, 'D. and S., servants, furniture, dowry villages.' Your father wanted to ensure you both had enough to support yourselves, just as he said."

I blinked back tears. "Is Igor telling the truth then? We have everything we need except the house we live in? And why him? What did he ever do for Papa?"

"He didn't have to do anything. He's your father's closest male relative." Father Job released the paper, which snapped back into its former scroll, and clasped my hand. "These are notes, not the will. And I don't see a name, only your sister's and your initials. I believe your father did consider alternatives; he mentioned them to me last year, and he promised to take care of you. But he was too sick by then to write another will. It seems likely that your cousin is telling the truth, but we should continue to investigate."

I nodded, unable to speak because of the lump in my throat. "What I do know," Father Job said in his gentle voice, "is that your father loved his daughters very much. If he could, he would have left everything he had to the two of you."

The tears spilled over. My father *hadn't* loved me. He'd avoided me whenever he could. Even my stepmother had shown more affection toward me, despite having borne a son of her own. Yet I mourned that father who hadn't cared for me, the father who had so recently gone to join the angels in heaven. I grabbed a cloth from the table and sobbed into it while Father Job patted my hand and murmured reassurances of God's abiding love.

After a while, I mastered my grief enough to set the cloth aside. "Are you sure, Father?" I asked in a small voice. "That he loved us, I mean. It never seemed that way to me. He was so uncomfortable with us girls—even at the end, when he sometimes confused me with my mother. He much preferred my brother."

"Of course I'm sure." Father Job released my hand. "It's difficult for men raised as warriors to know what to say to young women. But your father spoke of you with such pride, especially after you began reading to him. It didn't matter which story you picked; he loved hearing your voice, knowing that you'd chosen to stay with him when you could have spent time with your friends instead."

A renewed onslaught of tears threatened to break forth. "Thank you," I said when I could speak. "That means a lot to me."

"And what comes next?" He tipped his head to one side. "No more nursing duties. Will you renew your friendships? Let your sister find you a husband? Just because you *can* stay here in the house doesn't mean you have to."

He was the one person I could confide in, who would understand my doubts and not overreact to a decision not yet made. "I'm too old for marriage," I said. "I've thought of taking monastic vows, but I'm not sure I have a strong enough vocation." I rubbed the scarlet brocade between my fingers and my thumb, cherishing the softness and the sheen. "Every time I feel certain I've decided, something happens that shows me how worldly I am. Like this dress. I love it so much it's indecent."

He laughed at that, and I realized yet again that he was in many ways the father I'd wanted Papa to be. "And who would not? It suits you admirably. But what's this nonsense about being too old to marry? A daughter of the Sheremetev clan? You have a lineage longer than my arm. And you're young and pretty, healthy and good-tempered. Any nobleman would leap at the chance to wed you. *Bozhe moi*, any nobleman's *mother* would fall over herself welcoming you into the family."

Which was, as I well knew, more important than pleasing the groom. If a future mother-in-law came out against a potential bride, that bride would turn out to suffer from a previously unsuspected squint or hump, and the bridegroom—barred from invading the women's quarters himself—would never find out the truth.

His compliments warmed my heart. Still, I couldn't accept so rosy a picture without protest. "Not so," I said. "I'm twenty-five. Matryona tells me three times a week that no one wants a bride over eighteen. My brother-in-law died a traitor to the crown. And my father lost his ability to serve as a powerful patron years ago and certainly can offer no aid now. If Cousin Igor has inherited the estate, he's a better marital prospect than I am."

Father Job shook his head, still chuckling. "Silly girl. Twenty-five is nothing. I'm almost twice your age. And Matryona, much as she loves you, hardly holds the keys to the world's wisdom. Don't run off to the monastery yet. Plenty of time for that after you experience marriage and motherhood. How can you know whether you want to give up the secular life before you learn what it is?"

I sighed. He had a point—and one I'd heard before—but I wasn't convinced. I'd lived for so long without friends and parties and whispered conversations about boys, without beautiful clothes and jewels and cosmetics and extravagant confections adorning my braided hair: wasn't that evidence that I could fight the temptations of a worldly existence in favor of a higher calling? *Shouldn't* I fight those temptations rather than let myself be seduced by them once more?

"Why is everyone so set on getting married, anyway?" I asked. "My sister was miserable with her husband. My father lost three wives, two of them—Solomonida's mother, then mine—after such a short time it's hard to imagine the marriages meant much to him. I think he was happy enough with my stepmother Xenia, but then she died. He couldn't wed again, since a fourth marriage is not allowed. So much grief, and in the end nothing to show for it but a pair of daughters."

Father Job frowned, considering. He was a learned man and kind. I trusted him. We were lucky he'd joined our household after Father Hilarion left. Yet I wondered how much he knew of my family history. He must have heard some of it, having served the Kolychevs—yes, Daniil again—before coming to us. But my mother died at my birth. Even Xenia and my brother Lev left us eleven years ago—one after the other. Whatever Job said about being twice my age, he must have been a young man—perhaps not even a priest—in the year I was born.

"I can see why you might not have the best impression of marriage," he said after a while, "based on your sister's experience and your father's. But marriage exists to create a family, to nurture offspring. Your father survived his losses and brought three wonderful children into the world. Everyone dies, sooner or later. We can't refuse to live because someday we must die. Do you want to spend the rest of your life alone?"

"I'm not alone. I have Solomonida." I thought of my sister, how she'd always been there. Except for the two dreadful months after I lost Lev and Xenia, I could always count on her.

"Of course," Father Job said. "But a sister is not the same as a husband. Most men are not monsters like your former brother-in-law. By taking monastic vows, you would close a door on something you've never experienced: love and intimacy. My advice is to see what's on the other side before you hide yourself away."

"But how can I find a kind and caring husband? I'm not allowed to mix with men outside the family."

He stood, smiling once more, and gathered the notes he'd brought, tightening their cylinder before tying them. "Well, my dear spiritual daughter, I can only counsel you on how to behave as a good Christian woman. Your friends and relatives will find you a husband. And now, if you'll excuse me, I have parishioners awaiting my care." With that, he blessed my bent head and walked out of the room even as I murmured my thanks for his counsel.

Left to myself, I debated what I should do next. A lot of time must have passed since I went up to dress. Solomonida would finish her tour of the household soon, if she hadn't already. I'd better stop procrastinating and get ready to further my acquaintance with Cousin Igor. It wasn't fair to leave my sister to tackle him unaided any longer.

With a heavy heart and weighted feet, I stood and made my way to the women's quarters. Perhaps I could fit in a little embroidery before Solomonida summoned me to her side.

Chapter Three

I'd barely returned to the sitting room that Solomonida and I shared when Mishka appeared to announce more visitors.

When I saw who they were, my spirits bounced upward once more. Katya Vorontsova, whose family had taken over the confiscated Kolychev estate next door, had appeared at the same instant as our good friend Maria Koshkina. Maria had brought my niece, Anna, back to the house. Anna's best friend, Maria's younger sister Lyuba, accompanied them. Vociferous greetings ensued.

"Please stay," I begged as we finished. "We need as much company as we can get. The girls can amuse themselves here while we go downstairs. I'll ask one of the maids to sit nearby in case they need anything and send a message to Solomonida. She's showing our cousin Igor Bezzubtsev around the house. He arrived out of the blue with a clerk in tow and a plan to move in. Insists he's Papa's heir—and cites *your* father, Maria, as his patron. Such a nerve!"

"Exciting." Katya—a tall, slender beauty whose blue eyes contrasted with the dark brown hair visible through her gauze veil—clasped my elbow and turned me toward the door. "Insists, you say. Is he telling the truth? How could you not have known, in that case?"

"It's a mystery," I said. "Papa promised to find me a husband who would help us care for the estate, which suggests he meant to bequeath it to that man, whoever he turned out to be. But that was about a year before he died, and I have no reason to think he ever put his plan into action. He didn't tell us he'd left the property to Igor, although he may simply have forgotten. His illness robbed him of memory. Meanwhile, Igor and his clerk swear that Papa's will names Igor as the heir, but their copy has been damaged. Father Job is searching for the original will. Until he finds it, we won't know what to believe."

"My goodness, what a tale!" Katya clapped her hands, as if watching a skilled performer at the market. "I wouldn't miss this for the world. Can you trust your cousin?"

"No," I said. "I met him only once, and I didn't like him then. Solomonida and I didn't even recognize him at first."

"How amazing!" Maria leaned closer. "Suppose he's an imposter? It's been known to happen."

I shrugged. "If he's lying about the will, he *is* an imposter, cousin or not. But Solomonida did put a name to him after a while, and as soon as she said it, I knew him too." I told them about Igrushka the Duckling, which had them laughing as hard as our chaplain and the clerk. "Father Job convinced us to put Igor up as a guest while we sort out what happened. Don't you want to meet him? I'll order refreshments, nothing heavy, and we can sit and chat. Maybe among the four of us we can force him to confess that he made the whole thing up."

Maria, a glorious redhead, threw up her hands. "How can I refuse? Such drama. A missing heir, possible skullduggery, *and* a long-lost cousin. I can't wait to find out more!"

"Oh, good, we can stay?" Lyuba gave a little leap and hugged Anna. "More time together!" Anna dragged her friend toward the window seat, and soon Lyuba's coppery braid and Anna's blonde one appeared to grow out of a single double-headed twelve-year-old peering through the open shutters.

"Look at those two." Maria pointed at Lyuba and Anna. "I swear, they could be a mythical beast."

"A gryphon or a camelopard?" I asked, setting off another round of laughter.

"A girl-monster!" Katya clapped her hands once more.

Lyuba and Anna paid us no attention. I suspected they'd caught sight of Cousin Igor, because they burst into a spate of giggles and whispers and pointing, but I didn't stay to find out. "I'll be right back," I said. "I need to grab a servant, order those refreshments, and alert Solomonida that you're here."

"I'll come with you," Katya offered. "You can tell me the full story on the way."

"But that leaves Maria on her own," I objected.

"Not so," Maria said. "The girls are here. Go and do what you have to. I'll be studying this gorgeous work of yours." She picked up my altar cloth, lying on a nearby table, and unfolded it.

"Let me know how I can improve it," I told her. Much as I loved to stitch, I had no illusions that I could match Maria's skill. At times I thought she lived to perfect her art.

"It's beautiful." She held it up by the corners. "Look, girls, how neatly she's laid out the halo. And that white rose, with its hint of pink close to the center! The petals look so real I want to bury my face in them."

I stopped in mid-step. A warm glow ringed my heart at receiving such praise from one whose opinion I valued highly.

The girl-monster, as Katya called them, seemed much less impressed. Auburn and blonde heads indeed turned as one, but Igor or whatever held their attention outside exerted a pull like a lodestone, drawing them away from my embroidery even as Maria continued to admire it.

"I won't be long," I said. When she murmured a response without taking her eyes off the altar cloth, I moved swiftly from the room, and Katya kept pace with me. As we walked, I filled my neighbor in on the events of the morning, including the broken goblet and the damage it caused.

I'd known Katya since girlhood, but her sharp tongue and relentless focus on her own self-interest meant we had never become friends. In the last few months, since she returned home as a childless widow, we'd spent a fair amount of time together, if only because we both lacked alternatives, yet I still didn't feel close to her. But although as a general rule I hesitated to confide in her, it couldn't hurt to share this tale. My cousin's intentions would become obvious soon enough.

As we exited the side door and descended the two dozen steps between the second story and the courtyard, we saw Solomonida strolling ahead of a small crowd of people, gesturing at this building and that. From where I stood, I couldn't hear her words, but I assumed she was identifying each one and its purpose. Behind her, Igor strutted with his clerk close behind. I decided I'd been right about them being the cause of Lyuba's and Anna's giggles.

The followers were servants, most of whom should have been focused on preparing the midday meal. I counted about thirty, at least half the household.

Knowing my sister, I suspected her of deluging the men with details, hoping to bore them to tears. Perhaps it was working, for Igor gave no signs of listening. From where I stood, his strut seemed to occupy his full attention.

Anfim Fadeyev, in contrast, seemed interested in what my sister had to say. While I watched, he lengthened his stride until he walked at Solomonida's side. When she looked his way, he bent toward her, as if asking a question. She nodded, and he continued to tilt his head in her direction. To hear her better, I supposed, or perhaps to indicate respect.

Katya appeared not to notice Fadeyev. When I glanced at her, I found her gaze directed at Igor. "*Gospodi*," she said. "Is that fine fellow the one you're describing?"

I tried to guess whether she meant what she said or found Igrushka the Duckling as silly as I did. No, she wasn't laughing or even smiling; she couldn't take her eyes off him. How strange.

"Isn't he hilarious?" I asked. "Solomonida calls him a strutting peacock. Such finery, such airs."

"Yes, it fits." Katya spoke slowly, as if distracted. "He thinks a lot of himself, for sure. But he *is* rather good-looking, don't you think? And such wonderful clothes! Is he married?"

"I don't know yet," I said. "He didn't mention a wife. He was too busy making sure we understood that this property belongs to him. We'll find out soon."

"Well, if he can prove his claim to this estate, maybe he'll look for a bride. He'd have to give her a good allowance, wouldn't he, if she were to do him credit?" Katya plucked at the sleeve of my scarlet robe. "Speaking of which, you're looking fine today. It's nice to see you not imitating a scullery maid for once!"

A scullery maid? "Those clothes are far more comfortable than these," I said.

"I'm sure they are, for someone bent on mucking out a stable." Katya shook her head, turning the strings of pearls dangling from both sides of her headdress into a jingling quartet as they swayed in the noontime breeze.

She looked so offended at the thought that I burst out laughing once more. "You're exaggerating," I told her. "I like to keep the dust out of my fine robes, and no one cared how I looked when I was nursing Papa. But even I know that I can't entertain noblemen in clothes that the maids would toss in the rag bag. Look, there's my steward. Let me give him the messages so we can get back upstairs before Maria decides we've forgotten her."

"Mishka," I called. "Over here." Like the rest of us, he'd left the main house and was crossing the courtyard. At this moment, he was heading toward the kitchen, set well away from the other buildings in case of fire. At the sound of my voice he turned and hurried our way.

"Tell my sister we have more visitors," I said as he approached. "Tsarevna Maria and her sister as well as Ekaterina Ivanovna here." He bowed to Katya, and I went on. "Let Lady Solomonida know that we'll be in the main sitting room, awaiting her and my cousin."

"Yes, Lady," Mishka said.

"Good. We'll also need Alya to attend to my niece and her friend in the sewing room and refreshments for all. Something nice to honor our guests. That smoked salmon and sturgeon the cook prepared for our midday meal, perhaps. We'll be eating in the main sitting room, so you and the housekeeper should supervise the servants in the dining hall."

"Yes, Lady," he repeated. And with my errands taken care of, I ushered Katya back toward the house.

Katya and I retrieved Maria from the sewing room. As we left, Lyuba and Anna were having fun strutting around the room with their chests thrust forward and their shoulders back, kicking their skirts up in front in imitation of Cousin Igor.

"Alya will be here any moment," I told them. "She'll bring food. If you need anything else, just let her know."

They gave me distracted nods. I wasn't sure they'd heard me, but they couldn't get into much trouble up here, and I was sure they would eat if they were hungry, so I left them to their peacock imitations and ushered the others down the stairs to the main sitting room.

By the time we reached our destination, Solomonida had arrived with Igor. The clerk, Anfim Fadeyev, was not with them. A flash of disappointment assailed me when I realized he didn't plan to join us. I suppressed it. His looks and manner appealed to me, but I knew nothing else about him except that my family would consider him unsuitable because of his rank—or lack thereof.

We stood aside while the servants who followed close behind my sister carried their trays to the largest of the sideboards. As they passed me, I could see that the cook had produced a small feast: the cold-smoked salmon and sturgeon I'd asked for but also a bowl of glistening black caviar, baskets of sliced bread, porcelain dishes decorated with blue ducks and laden with pickled carrots and cucumbers, jugs containing apple juice and beer.

Something nice, indeed. I heard Solomonida tell the menservants to commend Mishka and the cooks.

Once they'd gone, Maria and Katya and I entered the room, where Solomonida stood in the midst of what, from the stiff set of her shoulders, I judged to be a rather awkward conversation with our cousin. I saw relief on my sister's face as she greeted Maria and Katya.

"Come in, come in. So lovely to see you. And look, we have a guest." Solomonida indicated Igor with a lift of her palm. "Tsarevna Maria Fyodorovna Koshkina and Ekaterina Ivanovna Vorontsova, permit me to introduce our cousin Igor Grigorevich Bezzubtsev. Maria and Katya both live nearby." She tipped her head at me and smiled. "You're looking lovely, Darya."

Indeed, Cousin Igor stared at me as if he didn't recognize me. For a moment, I experienced myself as the focus of everyone's attention. Their reaction both flattered and bewildered me. Were clothes so important? Did they change the essence of who I was?

Years ago, when I wore robes like these to attend parties and weddings, most people saw me as pretty but shy. I was young then, fifteen or sixteen, demure and well-behaved, so it wasn't hard to attain the status of pretty. Since Papa's illness I'd become a drab little thing, in the minds of others even more than myself. And despite my fancy clothes, I was still that drab girl inside.

Although I had to admit that a thrill ran through me as Igor swept his gaze from my head to my toes, awe visible on his face. He was still Igrushka the Duckling, more a figure of fun than a man I wished to attract. But if I could have such an effect on *him*, I might hope to do the same with a man whose admiration I sought.

Igor stopped staring at me and turned his attention to Maria and Katya, acknowledging my sister's introduction with a sweeping bow.

Maria, as the highest-ranking person present, dipped her head. "How lovely to meet you," she said. A hint of the laughter I saw tugging at the corners of her mouth tinged her voice. "I'm sure your relatives must be overjoyed by your visit."

Igor's jaw dropped for a moment, but he soon rallied. "I fear that my arrival was more of a surprise to them than I anticipated," he said. "I regret that, of course. I hope we will soon experience the joy you mention."

"Very gracious of you." Maria, her eyes still dancing, turned to Solomonida. "And of them, to entertain you despite their doubts."

Katya held out her hand to my cousin, returning the delighted smile he gave her in full measure. He clearly appealed to her. "But how fortunate that I stopped by today," she said. "To think that a man such as yourself will be staying right next door. Do you expect to be here long?"

Igrushka preened like the duckling we called him. "The pleasure is mine, Lady." He bowed low once more. "May God permit that I remain here for the rest of my life. With such a beautiful neighbor, how could I fail to rejoice to see every new dawn break, knowing it may bring you to my side?" He raised Katya's hand to his lips and, with a flourish, kissed the back of it.

I glanced at my sister and Maria, who weren't even hiding their giggles. I stepped back far enough to join them while giving Igor room to flirt with Katya. Which he proceeded to do, to the point where I thought he'd forgotten the rest of us.

"Look at him," I muttered to Maria and my sister. "Such airs! Does he think he's a Polish lord? I don't know anyone who kisses women's hands."

"No doubt he does think that. He seems to consider himself quite the ladies' man." Maria studied him. Her lips still twitched. "Katya appreciates it, though."

"You had him slavering over you, too," Solomonida told me. She caught the trailing false sleeve of my robe and waved it as illustration. "And so he should. See what you can do when you try?"

"Well, I don't want to have that effect on *him*," I whispered. "What happened to the clerk?"

Only when the words left my mouth did I realize that Solomonida might hear them as an expression of interest on my part—and directed toward the unacceptable clerk, at that.

Indeed, she turned her laughter on me. "He's good-looking, isn't he, that clerk? Seems nice, too, if a bit quiet. He went off to see whether he could salvage any of his papers. Our people are cleaning the room, so they'll keep an eye on him. Although I think that was an excuse. All this nobility scares him."

"I understand," I said. "Sometimes it scares me."

The mention of nobility caught Igor's attention. He stopped flirting with Katya and bowed to Maria once more. "Maria Fyodorovna Koshkina," he said, as if the idea had just occurred to him. "You're a daughter of Fyodor Mikhailovich Koshkin, then?"

"His eldest." Maria's voice held a slight edge, as it often did when she spoke of her father. He'd disillusioned her once too often with his crazy political schemes. But a moment later, she tilted her head and gave Igor her impish smile. "How do you know Papa?"

"My father served under his command." Igor rubbed his hands together, a smirk on his face that, oddly, increased his resemblance to a peacock. "Ten years ago, perhaps. He always spoke highly of your father, but I wouldn't have dared approach Fyodor Mikhailovich if he hadn't written to me first. He has kindly expressed a willingness to sponsor me at court. Naturally, I am both pleased and flattered by his condescension."

"Of course you are." Katya placed a reassuring hand on Igor's arm.

Maria paid no attention to this byplay. After a brief pause, she said, "Then I hope Papa's patronage brings you the success to which you aspire."

"Thank you." Igor hesitated, then asked, "Forgive me. Why do they call you tsarevna? Your father has not ascended beyond the rank of associate boyar."

Maria froze in place. The amusement that had radiated from her since we entered the room disappeared as if it had never existed. Her lips tightened, and she stared at my cousin the way she might stare at a cockroach crawling across her salmon.

"He has not," she said after that infinitesimal pause. The chill in her voice should have discouraged any further inquiries. "My rank doesn't come from my father. I married a Tatar tsarevich. Alexei, the eldest son of Bulat Khan."

Igor bowed, if possible, even lower than before. His nose nearly touched his knees. "My dear tsarevna," he said. "Would you consider introducing me to your husband?"

"What a good idea," Katya said.

Again Maria ignored the interjection. "Because a patron descended from the line of Genghis Khan would do an even better job of helping you advance at court?" She pulled herself up, every inch the haughty khan's daughter-in-law, and gazed straight into his eyes. "Alexei receives many such requests, but he seldom honors them."

Igor winced at the tartness in her tone, but he soon bounced back. "As you say, Tsarevna. Would it hurt to ask?"

Anger flashed in Maria's eyes. Her hot temper was legendary, and I waited, with quite un-Christian glee, to hear what she'd say next.

"Maria." Katya took two steps forward. Did she think she could restrain Maria's tongue with her bare hands? "Be kind!"

Maria turned her tsarevna glare on Katya, who spread her arms in front of Igor as if shielding him. "Good Lord, Katya," Solomonida said. "Calm down. She's not going to strike him." She sent a mischievous glance Maria's way. "Are you?"

"The thought never crossed my mind." Maria shrugged and waved a careless hand. "I can ask, Igor Grigorevich. Who knows, Alexei may agree. But I think you'd do better to cultivate your acquaintance with my father. If your goal is to advance at court, he plays the game there more skillfully than any of us."

"I see." I heard disappointment in my cousin's voice, but he controlled it well. "I appreciate every effort you and your father exert on my behalf. And your husband, of course."

"I'm sure you do, Igor Grigorevich," Maria purred. She treated him to a gracious nod, but the sparkle in her eyes spoke volumes. Whatever pique she'd felt at Igor's attempts to curry favor had dissolved, and she was again struggling to contain her laughter.

Katya tugged on Igor's arm. "Come," she said. "Would you not like some of this wonderful fish?"

With her usual aplomb, Solomonida grabbed the conversational opportunity Katya had created. "Indeed," my sister said, indicating the food and drink with an outstretched hand. "Friends and family, please accept our hospitality. Your presence here gives us joy."

Plates and cups in hand, we settled into a rough circle. Solomonida and Igor sat side by side with their backs to the door, Maria next to Solomonida and Katya at Igor's right. I completed the arc, facing my cousin and my sister. Since Father Job was not with us, Solomonida stood and spoke a blessing over the food while the rest of us bowed our heads. When she was done, I sat and watched the others, wondering what to say and whether to start eating. Conversation hadn't been a special gift of mine even before my long self-imposed exile from society.

Katya dove in without hesitation. "Will your wife join you here, Igor Grigorevich?" she asked.

"That would be impossible," Igor said. Again I saw a flash of humanity behind the pompous facade, as if he could indeed experience sorrow. I waited, curious. "She died two years ago," he went on after a pause that no one, I noticed, chose to interrupt. "In childbirth, with my son. God rest their souls."

"May you have life, cousin," I said to Igor. "I'm sorry for your loss." And I meant it. Whether he had loved his wife or not, I sensed that he missed her.

Father Job's description of marriage tugged at me. What would that be like, to experience a partnership close enough that even a fool like Igor grieved its passing? Shouldn't I give myself the chance to find out?

"And what of you, cousins?" Igor asked. "Where are your husbands?"

"Mine died seven years ago," Solomonida said, her voice curt. She didn't add "God rest his soul." Except for Anna, her greatest joy, Semyon Kolychev had given her nothing but grief. I recalled how she'd sung and danced the day she learned the government had divorced them and forced him to enter a monastery.

I expected Igor to probe for more information, but he didn't even produce the stock response I'd given him, "May you have life." I wondered if he already knew my sister's history—and if so, to what extent.

He must, surely. We were family, after all.

Igor gestured to me. "And you? What's your story?"

I stared at him, uncertain how to reply. As usual, my tongue tied into knots the instant I became the focus of everyone's eyes. Igor's question felt like an attack, although I had no reason to believe he wanted to disconcert me. After years of practice, I felt comfortable ordering the servants. Why couldn't I experience the same ease with men of my own station—as Maria, Solomonida, and Katya obviously did?

After an awkward pause I settled on a simple reply. "Papa offered me to one of the neighbors, but in the end he wed someone else. Then Papa fell ill. Now I'm too old to marry."

I must have chosen the right tack, because Igor stopped hassling me. "I'll make inquiries," he said. "Good marriages for the three of us could solve a lot of problems."

He assessed Solomonida with his eyes. "I'm not sure you can attract another husband, despite your looks. You must be thirty if you're a day. Better if you retire from the world."

While my sister spluttered her indignation, he ignored her and turned that assessing gaze on me. "You have some childbearing years left, whatever you think. There's hope for you."

"Excuse me?" Solomonida had recovered her self-possession. "You haven't yet established your claim to live here, and you're already telling us what we should do? Let's take one step at a time, shall we? I have no intention of entering a monastery, now or ever—whether that pleases you or not. *My* right to remain in this house is not in question, and I have every intention of raising my daughter here."

"Oh yes, your daughter," Igor said. "The best marital prospect of the lot, as soon as she comes of age. How old is she?"

None of your business," Solomonida retaliated. "She's mine to dispose of, not yours." This was untrue, as I knew very well (and assumed that Igor did too), but a noble effort on my sister's part.

"And it's too soon for you to marry me off as well, cousin," I reminded him. "You may be head of the family, but at present you're dependent on our good will. So slow down. We can rescind our invitation, you know, and then you'd be out on the street."

"Sorry," he said. "Didn't mean to offend."

A short silence ensued, until Katya jumped in to fill it. "Tell me, Igor Grigorevich, what kind of court position do you seek?"

"Perhaps an adjutant or a guardsman." For the first time, Igor sounded uncertain.

"As I mentioned before, you would do well to cultivate my father," Maria said. "And speaking of Papa, has he expressed any—how should I put this?—expectation of what he would like from you in return for his assistance?"

"Maria, really!" Katya gasped. "How can you suggest that your father would help Igor Grigorevich only in hope of a return?"

Maria laughed openly then. "Katya, you babe in the woods. When has my father—or any other grandee, for that matter—ever aided another man's career without anticipating some benefit?"

"Indeed," Solomonida said. "The goal can be as simple as keeping enough servitors in one's train to present a fine display when riding off on campaign or as complicated as lining up allies against a potential rival."

"Well, I will be happy to serve Fyodor Koshkin *or* Tsarevich Alexei out of thanks for whatever aid they can provide." Igor twitched his lion-embroidered robe. "And if called upon to present a fine display, I feel certain I can oblige."

"No doubt about that, Igor Grigorevich," Katya cooed.

"No doubt whatsoever," Maria agreed, the amusement in her eyes reflected in her voice. Igor, preening again in response to Katya's smile, seemed not to hear it.

"Please," Solomonida said. "Our servants laid out this lovely food, and no one has eaten a thing. Will you not enjoy yourselves while we talk of something less personal? Has no one heard any juicy court gossip?"

I certainly hadn't. While the others traded stories—even Igor had some information to share, although where he'd learned it I had no idea—I placed one slice of fish on a round of pumpernickel, admiring the dark pink against the pale yellow butter and black bread, and lifted the whole to my mouth. The salty fish with its hint of smoke, the creamy texture that the butter only enhanced, the rich texture of the bread—I closed my eyes for a moment to let the complexity of the overlapping flavors fill my mouth.

The food was delicious, yet the conversation left me stranded far out of my depth. Would I ever acquire Katya's skill at casual flirtation, Maria's wide-ranging knowledge of the world, or my sister's gift with words, which she plied with equal facility whether she was encouraging others to talk or puncturing Igor's more grandiose tales of his own achievements?

Before long, Maria announced that she had to get home and asked if someone could fetch Lyuba. My sister dispatched a maidservant to the third floor while Igrushka the Duckling exuded compliments and thanks. Anfim Fadeyev rejoined our group long enough to say farewell. When Lyuba arrived with Anna running beside her, Igor was still bowing over Maria's hand, cooing, "Tsarevna, I hope to see you again soon," over and over while she bobbed her head like a puppet at the fairground and repeated, "Yes, yes, Igor Grigorevich. I must go now, though." The fixed expression on my sister's face was almost a perfect match for Maria's glassy-eyed stare. Lyuba stood snickering in the doorway while Anna giggled next to her. Even Katya's lips twitched as the pleading continued. Was I the only one who saw our cousin's eagerness as pathetic?

Perhaps not. Anfim Fadeyev stared at the window, his expression unreadable. I experienced a flash of fellow feeling, a hint of connection to come, then brushed it off as premature.

At last Maria dragged her hand away. She and her sister said goodbye to Anna and headed down the stairs to their waiting carriage. Katya left the house with them, although her home lay in the opposite direction. Igor gazed after them like a lovelorn puppy.

"My daughter, Anna," Solomonida told Igor's back.

He turned, a dazed look on his face, and tipped his head in Anna's direction. "A beautiful child," he said. "How old are you, Anna?"

"Don't answer that," Solomonida snapped. Anna jerked as if she'd been slapped and put both hands over her mouth.

"I'm not angry with you, darling," my sister said. "Wait for me upstairs." Anna acknowledged Igor with a quick bow, then ran back through the door.

"Her age is none of your business," Solomonida told Igor. "Get that through your head. And don't you dare try to go around me again."

Igor opened his mouth, his stance challenging and his fists clenched. Then he sighed and relaxed his pose. "I apologize," he said in a grudging tone. "I forgot myself. Thank you for your hospitality. I will leave you now so that I can return tomorrow as your guest. A fellow soldier agreed that I can stay with him tonight, but not beyond that."

"When should we expect to receive you?" my sister asked in biting tones.

"Early afternoon," he said. "I hope you will permit Fadeyev to come here tomorrow as well to begin going through your father's papers. Whether you believe it or not, I *am* Sheremetev's heir. One day you'll accept that. And it can't hurt you to have everything in order. If your people could lose track of a last will and testament, who knows what else they've misplaced?"

I looked at my cousin. "You can't honestly believe we're that stupid," I said after a moment. "Your Fadeyev could do anything with Papa's papers. 'Find' a will that was never written but says whatever you want it to say. 'Lose' a genuine document that disproves your case. Discredit our servants, distort our accounts—"

"Darya Petrovna!" Fadeyev sounded shocked. "I wouldn't do any of those things. I want to help you by straightening things out. Your cousin's claim is genuine, and sooner or later we will prove it. I understand your doubts, but in this case they are misplaced."

And in truth, I believed him. Despite the brevity of our acquaintance I trusted him far more than I trusted Cousin Igor.

"Let him stay," Igor said firmly. "I'll prove my claim soon enough."

Solomonida bit her lip, as if wondering whether it made sense to argue, but after a while she nodded. "Very well. He can work with one of our clerks."

Igor dipped his chin, indicating agreement. I resolved to warn our own clerks not to leave sensitive papers lying about. They should keep an eye open for possible manipulation by our cousin as well.

"Thank you," Fadeyev said. "Will tomorrow morning suit you?" He sounded relieved.

"Yes," Solomonida told him. "So long as the sun is well up." He bowed and took his leave. Igor, alas, did not.

Solomonida turned her attention to our cousin. "So you are the only guest. We have grooms and manservants and artisans of various sorts. If you require their services, let Mishka or Darya or me know what you need, and we will order it done. Are there any other preparations we should make?"

"I have a man to care for my clothes," Igor said. That I could believe—more likely, an army. "My horse, which I hope can stay in your stables. And a dog."

"A dog?" Solomonida and I spoke together.

"What kind of dog?" I added. Dogs were not rare, by any means, but most worked as guards or hunters of various sorts. We had a few of our own, but they lived on Papa's rural estates. Why would my cousin bring one to the city, never mind into another person's house—even if he saw that house as his own?

"A Polish hunting dog," he said. "A scent hound. She's too young and playful to excel at the chase, so I decided she could stay with me until she's old enough to be trained or bred. Her name is Laika. She's very good-natured."

My mouth dropped open, and I hurriedly closed it. For the third time that day, I'd caught a glimpse of the real person hidden behind my cousin's irritating mask. Surprising enough that he kept a dog as a pet rather than relegate her to the kennels. But I also heard genuine affection in his voice—and for a dog. Many people felt defiled if they so much as touched a dog with their bare hands.

Yet Igor kept his dog inside. It was the first evidence of unconventional behavior I'd seen in him, and it made him a bit more interesting.

Solomonida's face mirrored my astonishment, but she rallied almost at once. "Bring her along, and we'll see."

He bowed. "Until tomorrow morning then." Then he, too, departed, leaving Solomonida and me alone in a world overturned by his arrival.

Back in the upstairs sewing room, we found Anna staring out the window. I folded my altar cloth and returned it to its basket. I'd come back to it on a day when I could concentrate. Today I'd probably stitch the Virgin's halo to her cloak, or worse.

From the same basket I pulled a length of linen embroidered with a daisy, more than halfway to completion. I pulled it taut across a wooden frame and handed it to my niece.

"It's lovely," I told her. "You do beautiful work. Two more leaves, I think, just like this one, on either side of the stem, and you can move on to a different design." I indicated the leaf I wanted her to use as the model, then passed her a twist of bright green silk. Smiling in response to my praise, she took fabric and thread, selected a needle, and retreated to a sun-bright corner of the room where two benches met.

I went to join my sister, who'd positioned herself near the window. From there we could watch the courtyard. With the men gone at last, we could talk freely.

"Igrushka the Duckling," Solomonida said as I joined her. "Who'd have thought it?"

"Not me. I'd forgotten ever meeting him until you said his nickname. Igor Grigorevich sounded like someone important." I made a face, recalling that moment earlier today when I'd grasped the truth. "But we're stuck with him now, if only as a guest. And although Father Job urged me not to give up hope, I can see he thinks Igor's claim is valid."

"The worst will be if we never find out for certain." She tapped a contemplative rhythm against the window frame. "How long do we have to put Igor up, do you think, before we've satisfied the demands of hospitality and can show him the door?"

I had no idea and said so. "You're wrong, though. The worst will be if he takes over the estate and starts trying to marry off Anna and me while forcing you toward the monastic life. He could make all three of us miserable at the same time, horrid man. And imagine what kind of husbands he'd pick!"

"As bad as Semyon." A shadow crossed her face, and I regretted reminding her of her dead husband. Papa, who according to Father Job had loved us both, had made *that* unsuitable match. The thought of the kind of man Igor would choose to improve his own prospects at court sent chills down my spine.

"Yes." I glanced at Anna, who appeared preoccupied with her needlework. I didn't know how much she remembered of her own father, exiled when she was three. Better not to risk scaring her with more speculation about Igor's potential for harm.

"So what can we do to render our cousin toothless in fact, not only in name?" I asked instead.

Solomonida laughed at that, as I'd intended. Bezzubtsev meant "toothless." Anna giggled too, so I knew she'd been listening after all. I was glad I'd turned the subject away from possible husbands.

"Hmm." My sister studied the courtyard beyond the window as she had that morning when Igor first arrived to disturb our peace. "There must be something. Refuse to accept his dog? No, it's not the dog's fault that her master is a dolt."

"We could insist she sleep in the stables. He'd dislike that. Improbable as it sounds, he loves her. Talking about her was the only time he seemed human, except when Katya asked about his wife. And then it didn't last long enough to boil an egg." I bit my lip, considering. "Let's see if the dog's as nice as he says, shall we? If she is, we can persuade the cooks to lure her with bones and spare meat. Igor would hate it if his dog liked us better than him."

"Oh, that's a good one. What else?" Solomonida resumed her study of the courtyard. I waited impatiently until she said, "Oh, of course." Her face lit up with mischief. "Let's arrange a few unpleasant surprises for him as well. I'd hate Igrushka the Duckling to feel *too* comfortable in his new surroundings."

"What? What are you planning?" I said.

Solomonida shook her head, laughing. "You'll find out in due course." And however hard I pressed her to elaborate, she refused to say another word.

Chapter Four

BY THE NEXT DAY WE WERE READY TO RECEIVE OUR unwanted guest, or so we thought. Solomonida had ordered a pleasant suite of rooms prepared, as far away from our own quarters as possible. Proximity to the outside staircase would permit the dog Laika to go in and out without disturbing anyone else, and we assigned several of the younger grooms to take turns exercising and caring for her.

When Anfim Fadeyev appeared as the church bells tolled the third hour after sunrise, we directed him to a room on the first floor, next to Father Job's study, where the good priest could keep an eye on him even when the clerk assigned to work with Fadeyev had other tasks. We were congratulating ourselves on our adroit handling of a difficult situation when life chose to hurl another piece of rotten fruit our way.

Igor arrived in early afternoon as promised, but he didn't come alone. He brought his manservant and Laika, of course, but we knew to expect them. Anna watched with a certain trepidation as Laika—a beautiful animal with chestnut fur mixed with black and yearning brown eyes that begged for a hug—sniffed at her feet. But when the dog settled on her haunches a respectful distance from my niece, Anna relaxed and took two steps forward. I thought they might soon become friends.

Trouble rode in not five breaths behind Igor, in the form of a middle-aged man of medium height who entered our courtyard as if he owned the place. The gold medallions on his horse tack caught my eye as I stood at the top of the stairs, where I had just finished greeting my cousin. The visitor's multicolored leather boots and elaborate robes, rich forest-green brocade trimmed with twisted gold braid and buttons the size of walnuts, caused me to hold out the skirts of my own robe to compare. I had worn the sky-blue silk today, less elaborate than yesterday's creation but perfectly acceptable for a noblewoman. It would do.

A second look as the man dismounted, and I recognized Fyodor Koshkin, father of Maria and Lyuba. I assumed he had come to pay his respects to Cousin Igor, although I found it odd that a man so senior in terms of both age and position at court would deign to visit Igrushka the Duckling instead of demanding that our cousin wait on him.

Should I go and greet Koshkin to remind him whose house this was? The thought had no sooner formed than Solomonida swept past me. "Come on," she said. So I followed her down the stairs.

"Fyodor Mikhailovich." Solomonida bowed, not deep. "Welcome to our home. Have you come to consult with our guest?" I matched the level of her gesture while murmuring a welcome of my own.

Igor looked put out at our arrival, but he didn't complain. "If you don't mind, cousins," he said. "I have business to discuss with Fyodor Mikhailovich. May we use your sitting room?"

"Of course," Solomonida said, oozing charm. "Shall I order refreshments?"

"That won't be necessary, Solomonida Petrovna," Koshkin said. "I don't intend to stay long. May I express my condolences to you both on the loss of your father? I don't believe I've seen you since his funeral."

"May his memory be eternal," Solomonida and I said, one after the other.

"Thank you for your concern," she added. Then, honor having been served, we withdrew to the women's quarters.

We didn't get as far as the sewing room, however, before my sister tugged me toward the back staircase, the one the servants used. "Come on," she said. "Let's not waste time. Don't you want to find out what Fyodor Koshkin has to say to our Duckling?"

When she put it like that, I couldn't resist. "How?"

She touched a finger to my lips. "Shh. This way." Holding my skirts in one hand to keep them from rustling, I followed her to a broom closet barely large enough to hold us both amid the mops and pails. She stood aside as I entered, then squeezed in next to me.

I recognized the space, although I hadn't visited it in years. When we were younger, especially after Papa started planning Solomonida's marriage, then mine, we'd slip in here and spy on him and his guests. It had once been part of the main sitting room, but our grandfather, while installing one of the new tile stoves, had cut off this corner from the rest with a screen. The cut-off part wasn't completely sealed, so anyone standing there could hear but not see what was going on in the main room. No doubt servants as well as curious daughters listened to discover what they could of the family's secrets. Goodness knew the household staff seemed, sooner or later, to learn everything that went on within our walls.

At eight and ten and even fourteen, the closet hadn't been such a tight fit, but Solomonida and I managed to get inside without making a clatter guaranteed to draw the attention of the men within.

After a while, I heard the oily tones of Fyodor Koshkin. "And what caused you, Igor Grigorevich, to request that I visit you today?" I exchanged glances with Solomonida, who smiled.

Good. They were getting down to business. "Your presence honors me," Igor said. "I owe you a debt, too, for notifying me of my cousin's death and sending me a copy of his testament. I'm most grateful."

"Think nothing of it," Koshkin said. "I rejoice to know that the property is in good hands. What more can I do to ensure your success?"

I wanted to whisper to Solomonida. Shouldn't Igor, if he had any sense, ask what price Koshkin demanded for his support? Maria had warned him yesterday that her father wouldn't act without anticipation of a reward.

But I could say nothing, for fear of being overheard. So instead I listened to my cousin, who expressed no doubts of Koshkin's motives.

"As luck would have it, I made the acquaintance of your daughters yesterday." Igor said. "I wondered if you might introduce me to Tsarevna Maria's husband."

"Hah." Koshkin snorted. "Much good that would do you. Alexei would turn you out on your ear just to spite me. You need a patron less convinced that his descent from Genghis Khan puts him on a tier higher than the rest of us."

"It does put him on a tier higher than the rest of us," Igor said, his tone gently chiding. "That's why I'm asking for the introduction. But if you think he won't respond, can *you* help me advance at court, in memory of my father's service?"

"I'll do what I can, naturally." I imagined Koshkin waving a careless hand, as I'd often seen him do. "But my long allegiance to the Shuisky family is working against me at this moment. A newcomer from the Vorontsov clan has been luring young Grand Prince Ivan to favor the Vorontsovs at the Shuiskys' expense. That limits what I can do for you until the situation changes. I'm sure it will, but who knows when? In the meantime, what you need is a father-in-law who can improve his own situation by promoting yours. You did say you were widowed?"

A newcomer from the Vorontsov clan? Katya was a Vorontsov by birth, and from what I'd seen yesterday, she wanted Igor. The newcomer must be a relative of hers; whether close or distant didn't matter. That might help her convince our cousin that she would be a good match for him.

Katya as the mistress of this house? That seemed more burden than boon. I hadn't forgotten the many slights she'd dealt me over the years, although she seemed friendly enough these days.

If Katya moved in, Solomonida and Anna and I might do better to find somewhere else to live.

Not yet, though. Igor had not proved his claim to the estate. I released a relieved breath, careful to make no revealing sound. But the thought of Katya as mistress of this house intensified my determination to ensure that my cousin never did prove that claim.

I settled in to listen once more. "I am widowed," Igor confirmed. "And looking for another wife." No surprise there. Noblemen rarely chose to stay single for long.

Koshkin continued. "You shouldn't have any trouble finding a suitable bride. I expect many fathers are eager to match their daughters to a young man of exalted lineage such as yourself. I'll look around for you—and I can advise you on who might be the best choice."

He paused, and I could imagine his catlike smile. Certainly I heard calculation in his voice. "But don't forget you have a potential bride right here in this house. No helpful father-in-law, of course, but her property will nicely complement your own. And from the little I've seen of her, Darya Petrovna is a lovely young woman, quiet and biddable. Not too old to bear you several sons, God willing. She'll suit you quite well."

Suit him? I'll drown myself in the Moscow River first!

With great effort I managed to keep from pounding my fists against the wall. I didn't even break down and sob. Instead I looked at my sister and slowly, steadily, shook my head.

But Igor, it seemed, disliked the idea of a marriage between us as much as I did. "It won't happen," he told Koshkin. "For one thing, we're too closely related for the Church to sanction our match—"

"That can be arranged." Koshkin interrupted him mid-sentence. "A word in the right ear, and you can get a dispensation. Why, half of Moscow is related to the other half, at least among the nobility."

"I'll keep that in mind," Igor said, his voice so dry that I concluded—or was it hoped?—that he meant nothing of the kind. "But before I can look for a wife, I have to control this estate. Otherwise I have nothing to offer."

"And you don't control it? That document I sent you should have removed any doubts. Why did you ask me to visit you, if you're not the master here?" Koshkin didn't conceal his impatience, and I rejoiced to hear it. *Why waste my time?*—he might as well have said the words aloud.

"My cousins dispute the inheritance." Igor explained the mishap with the will. "Until they accept that their father did leave the house and the lands to me, even though he bequeathed most of the household goods and even the servants to them, they insist on treating me as a destitute family member in need of a place to stay." It took no leap of the imagination to identify his emotions: exasperation, even a sense of affront.

How did he think *we* felt, with him barging in and taking over our home?

"Are they looking for it?" Koshkin said, more amused now than impatient. "The will, I mean. They won't find it."

What? What makes him so sure?

Igor asked the questions I could not. "How do you know that? Where is it?"

"At my house," Koshkin said. "Father Hilarion brought it to me before he went off to the monastery. He didn't want to leave anything so important lying around when it wasn't clear who would succeed him. I had a scribe copy the original and send it to you."

I glanced at Solomonida, who gazed at the opening with eyes as round as pebbles. Of all the possibilities we'd considered, this one had never occurred to us. But why had our former priest given the will to Fyodor Koshkin, of all people?

"Lucky for me that you kept it," Igor said, "even after the new priest arrived." It was a statement, not a question. His tone had reverted to smug, and I imagined him rubbing his hands together in joy. "May I have it?"

"Of course. I'll order one of my men to fetch it. Tell your cousins to join us, and we'll soon straighten the matter out."

"Should we not invite that priest of theirs too? He's the only one among them who can read."

Igor was wrong about that, but I had no intention of correcting him, even if I hadn't been listening at the equivalent of a keyhole. Father Job was our ally. If Koshkin didn't agree to invite the priest, Solomonida and I would refuse to meet with him until he did.

"If you insist," Koshkin said in weary tones. "I've never trusted him. He worked for an enemy of mine. That's why I didn't hand the will over to him when he joined the household. But he is a priest. I'm sure he'll tell the truth about what he sees on the page. And if he doesn't, my own priest will vouch for you, and you'll have an excuse to get rid of Father Job."

"The clerk I hired can swear that the text matches the copy I had," Igor noted. "If both he and the priest support me rather than my cousins, they'll have to accept the truth, whether they like it or not."

Solomonida and I didn't wait to hear any more. We got out of the closet as fast as we could without making a noise and raced back to the sewing room so we'd be ready to answer Igor's summons.

As it turned out, the summons didn't come for a while. We should have expected that. Even though Koshkin lived not more than two streets away, it would take time for a man to ride there, find the will, and return. I had stitched another section of the edging to the Mother of God's halo before Mishka appeared to convey Igor's request for a meeting with us. With a certain reluctance I set my altar cloth aside once more and accompanied my sister downstairs. On one hand, knowing the truth had to be better than living in uncertainty. On the other, every indication pointed to the news that Koshkin planned to deliver being far from what my sister and I wanted to hear.

Anfim Fadeyev was already in the room that had once been Papa's workspace when Solomonida and I reached it, although Igor and Father Job had yet to arrive. I checked the carpet, which still bore traces of yesterday's upset but had cleaned up better than I would have imagined possible. The broken goblet and ruined covering were nowhere to be seen. Just as well: the constant reminder of my lost work of art would have further undermined spirits currently lurking somewhere in the deepest underground cellars in response to my fear that Cousin Igor might prove his right to our estate after all.

Koshkin was harassing Fadeyev when we walked in. "You're the clerk from the Treasury," he said. "The one accused of conspiring with the Tatars."

Conspiring with the Tatars? What is this?

I exchanged glances with my sister. As one, we stopped near the doorway and waited to hear more. Koshkin faced the window, with his back to us. Fadeyev's eyes flicked our way, but he didn't acknowledge our presence. Instead he addressed Koshkin.

"I didn't conspire, Lord," he said in a steady voice. "I was captured along with the rest of the envoys."

"But you escaped, and they didn't. I don't blame your superiors for wondering how you managed to make that happen." Koshkin struck Fadeyev on the shoulder. "But don't despair. I have influence over your state secretary. Perform this task for me, and I'll be happy to speak to him on your behalf."

Paper rustled as Koshkin held up a single sheet. "It's the original," Koshkin said. "You recognize it, right? The text is the same."

My stomach tightened at his words. *Is it?*

Fadeyev took the paper and skimmed it. "The words, yes. The priest's hand looks different, but the other was a copy—made years later, from what you said. Everything appears to be in order. Lord Sheremetev's seal, in particular, looks genuine."

"Good. Convince Sheremetev's daughters, then make an additional copy for me and keep this one in a safe place. Once that's done, I'll consider urging your supervisor to return you to his service." Koshkin turned his head in response to a noise from the corridor and frowned when he saw us.

"How long have you two been standing there?" he demanded. Neither Solomonida nor I chose to answer. He cast a suspicious glance Fadeyev's way, but the clerk stared woodenly back and said nothing. I hoped his silence meant he felt some sympathy for us.

I didn't place much reliance on that hope.

"Where's our cousin?" Solomonida demanded. "Did he walk out and leave you alone? That was very rude of him."

"Not at all," Koshkin said. "A momentary absence to send someone for your priest, I believe. Igor Grigorevich will no doubt be here in a moment."

As he spoke, the noise outside the door resolved itself into our cousin. He strode into the room, his peacock strut fully restored, triumph radiating from him in waves. My already low spirits sank farther, even when Father Job placed a comforting hand on my arm as he entered the room right behind my cousin. Solomonida maintained a surface calm, but the way she clenched her satin skirts told me she looked forward to the rest of this meeting no more than I did.

"Everyone's here," Koshkin said. "Ladies, Igor Grigorevich tells me that you have questioned his inheritance of the land and buildings that together constitute this urban estate. I hate to bear bad news"—his self-satisfied expression belied this assertion—"but your cousin is speaking the truth. By great good fortune, the original of your father's testament found its way to my household, and I have now returned it to its rightful owner, Igor Grigorevich." He waved a hand at Fadeyev, who had not met our eyes since we walked in. "Fadeyev, read the will."

Fadeyev looked as if the order pained him, but he read the document from beginning to end, his tone flatter than before. The pompous phrases rolled on and on, each one unraveling my slim thread of hope that a mistake had been made and would be revealed by the reading. When he finished, he handed the document to Father Job, who scanned it from top to bottom, then flicked the seal with his thumb, as if testing it, before handing it back.

"Everything seems to be in order," Father Job said, just as Fadeyev had earlier.

"Wait," I asked. "When was it signed?"

Fadeyev glanced at the document again. "On December 15, 1537."

That was when I knew we were in deep trouble. Because although Papa was already ill in December 1537, he had not yet lost touch with reality. He had indeed been sound of mind, if not of body, so we could not oppose his written wishes, whatever plans he might have made in his final days. I remembered, with the clarity of despair, every word that Fadeyev had uttered yesterday, each one another pinprick piercing our sense of a safe, secure world. This document matched his recital of the ruined one in every particular.

I still didn't know how the will ended up with Fyodor Koshkin. But I did recognize that, in the absence of a miracle, Solomonida and I would have to stand by and watch Cousin Igor take his place as the master of our estate—with all that implied for our futures, most notably his ability to contract marriages for Anna and me.

And himself. In which case, staying in this house might not be a choice either my sister or I wished to make.

Although Igor gloated a good deal whenever we saw him—and we avoided him as much as possible—he didn't insist on moving into Papa's rooms. The advantages of keeping Laika where we'd placed her appeared to outweigh those of physically occupying the master's quarters. More than a week passed in complacency on his part and evasion on ours, punctuated by various domestic mishaps that affected only our cousin and his belongings and that I understood to be pranks orchestrated by my sister, despite her exhibitions of shock and dismay whenever Igor complained.

I had to admit that it gave me a guilty pleasure to watch him stomp around—furious because the boots he wanted to wear had developed a hole overnight, the bed he planned to sleep in had lost its linen since the morning, the beer he served a guest had gone flat, and the sugar plum he popped in his mouth might better be called a salt plum.

After a while, though, he shifted to taking his frustration out on the servants. At that point, the accidents stopped as mysteriously as they had begun, and I was glad. As much as I shared my sister's dislike of Igor's presence, it comforted me to know that she would not let our dependents pay the price of her revenge.

The best part of life with our cousin was Laika. The dog was a darling, sweet-tempered and loving, so gentle that Anna's fears dissolved within days. Laika had a soft mouth, floppy ears, and silky fur that I couldn't resist stroking despite the many warnings I'd received in childhood that some ill would befall me if I touched a dog. We took turns throwing a ball or stick for her to fetch. She couldn't be more than a year old—a big, frolicking, wide-eyed puppy—and she loved to run. Her long, loping stride took her across the courtyard and back in an amazingly short time. The grooms assigned to exercise her had their work cut out for them. And as a scent hound she loved treats. Often we combined games and food, hiding pieces of cooked meat in corners and letting her hunt them down.

Which is how, two weeks after Cousin Igor's invasion of our household, I came to be perched on the stone wall lining the duck pond, rubbing Laika's ears between my hands. I aimed to distract her as much as anything else. I'd soon discovered what Igor meant about her being too playful to make a good hunting dog. She kept dodging around me or raising herself up on her hind legs to yip at the ducks, who obliged her by setting up a storm of quacks and flapping wings every single time.

Igor had left the house in mid-morning, and no one expected him back before nightfall. Where exactly he went during these many outings, we didn't know. He didn't confide in us other than to throw off the occasional boast about having met this grandee or that. I gathered Fyodor Koshkin was fulfilling his promise to introduce Igor to people who could reward our cousin with lucrative government positions or offer him a highborn bride, but more than that Igor refused to say. Solomonida and I seldom asked. The less we saw of Cousin Igor, the better. In any case, he wasn't here now, so he had nothing to say about my decision to play with his dog.

I doubted he'd care even if he found out. He hadn't objected to our plying her with treats (had he even noticed?), and our half-baked plan to woo her away from him had foundered on the reality that Laika loved everyone, just as Igor had said. Adding two women, a girl, and a stable's worth of grooms to her circle of adoring humans hadn't diminished Laika's affection for her master by a hair's breadth, so far as I could tell. It was to my cousin's credit that he didn't mind that she enjoyed spending time with the rest of us as well.

"Shall we go for a walk?" I asked her. She wriggled with delight, and I laughed at her eagerness. Even for a dog she seemed guileless. When she was happy, her entire body rippled from nose to tail. Scold her, even a single harsh word, and she drooped, chin on her crossed paws, eyes downcast, quivering with sorrow and shame. I didn't scold her myself, because I hated to see her so dejected, although

Igor sometimes did when she muddied his clothes with her paws.

"Clever girl," I told her. "You knew just what I meant. Let's give the ducks a rest before you drive them crazy."

From the corner of my eye, I saw the solid figure of Matryona, who long ago had been my nanny. Another reason to make a quick departure. Much as I loved Matryona, it irritated me that she still believed I required constant supervision. I could tell from the expression on her face that she disapproved of my petting Laika and was on her way to, as she saw it, bring me to my senses.

I could order her to stop, of course, but arguing with her would leave me in a bad mood, and I wanted to enjoy the day. Better to escape a confrontation. I stood and tied the dog's leash. I had learned to move fast under circumstances like these. If Matryona didn't chide me for touching a dog, she'd complain that I was risking a cold in my nether regions by sitting on the stones that lined the duck pond. No matter that it was the middle of August, and the stones retained enough heat to bake bread on them. Or that at least three layers of fabric lay between me and contact with whatever miasma they exuded. Matryona insisted that I'd never bear children if I didn't act right (yes, despite my being too old to attract a husband in the first place). And if I did somehow avoid the curse that was, in her view, an inevitable result of sitting on stones, stroking Laika would ensure that my future son or daughter ended up hairy and barking.

"Let's go," I said to Laika. "We'll visit Katya. She's right next door."

Laika set off at a rapid pace for the main gate. I tugged on the leash and directed her the other way, toward the smaller gate that led to the kitchen garden. Matryona called to me as I passed her, but I waved and smiled and pointed to the trotting hound.

We reached the herbs and vegetables before she could catch us. Pleased with myself, I was laughing as I headed for the Vorontsov household. It was time I checked in with Katya. We hadn't seen her since Cousin Igor moved in. Perhaps she'd given up on the idea of chasing him, which would be much the better outcome from my point of view. We could enjoy each other's company again, even if we weren't exactly friends and never would be.

I had told Laika "next door," but getting there wasn't as simple as that sounds. Our house and the Vorontsovs' lay within the great brick wall surrounding the region of Moscow known as the Kitaigorod. These days we were well protected, but before the great wall was completed a few years ago noble families built their homes for defense against possible invaders from the south, east, and west, surrounded by thick oak fences that left only the roof tips visible from street level. Armed guards monitored residents and visitors as they passed through the sturdy gates—open during the day but barred from twilight to dawn. No one would stop me going in or out, but when the estates were connected, as ours and Katya's were, it was more fun to take the back way, especially when strolling with a dog.

So Laika and I, reveling in the warm bright sun and the smell of ripe fruit, took our time as we made our way through our own kitchen garden and orchard, then through a small lattice gate that led to the Vorontsovs' orchard and garden, before we reached yet another gate that led to the various outbuildings and, beyond them, the main house where Katya and her family lived.

By the time I reached that last gate, I had relished entire handfuls of raspberries pulled from bushes and cherries plucked from trees. Laika ran happily from one pile of greenery to another, crushing dandelions beneath her paws and investigating the roots of every tree we passed. Every so often, a startled bird or small animal broke out of the thick grasses, and she barked and lunged to the full extent of the leash while they flitted or dashed to safety. She couldn't do any damage besides scaring them. I knew better than to release her. I'd made that mistake once, in our own yard, and she'd been halfway across the orchard before I had time to clap my hands and call her back.

With so much noise, our arrival couldn't have come as much surprise to the man stationed at the gate between our neighbors' kitchen garden and house. I doubted he'd been paying close attention, because the chances of danger approaching from the direction of our yard were so low he could have fallen asleep waiting for it. But Laika's antics must have alerted him to our presence.

I made this short journey to visit Katya at least once a week, so the guard recognized me as soon as Laika and I cleared the trees. He smiled and waved us through. "Greetings, Darya Petrovna. The mistress will be glad to see you."

"Wonderful day for a walk, isn't it?" he added in response to my nod.

"It is indeed," I said as I passed through the gate. "Laika, come."

The dog joined me, then stopped to greet this new and, in her mind, no doubt friendly human. I stopped too, turning to face him while I waited. I had plenty of time, so I saw no reason to drag Laika away. I'd bring her here again, so she might as well make the guard's acquaintance—and he hers.

"Aren't you a pretty girl?" he asked Laika. "I haven't seen you with a dog before, Darya Petrovna. When did you get her?"

"She belongs to my cousin," I told him. As usual, the thought of Igor crushed my high spirits for a moment, but I rallied. It was a beautiful day; I'd had a lovely walk; I'd enjoyed delicious fruit; I would soon sit and chat with Katya. Who cared about Igor? "You've seen him about, I'm sure. Igor Grigorevich Bezzubtsev."

"I have, Lady." The guard, who'd extended his gloved hand for Laika to sniff, abruptly straightened. "The new lord of the estate, they say."

Laika, perhaps feeling rebuffed, abandoned her investigation of his boots and moved to press against my side, looking beyond me into the yard. Her ears lifted, and the tip of her tail wagged.

What does she see?

Another servant, maybe. We stood at the far edge of the courtyard, close to the kitchen and icehouse. I doubted any family member would have noticed us yet.

I was turning to find out what—or more likely who—had attracted Laika's attention when a man spoke right behind me.

"Igor Grigorevich is *not* the master of that estate," a vaguely familiar male voice said. "And I'll prove it, if it's the last thing I do."

Chapter Five

I SPUN TO FACE THE UNKNOWN SPEAKER. AND STOPPED. THE man before me had light hair, warm brown eyes, and a smile I'd never forget. His voice had deepened; the contours of his face were stronger and leaner than I remembered, the high cheekbones more visible; and his frame—although still slender—no longer appeared lanky. Yet there was no mistaking the boy I'd loved so long ago. And he was very much alive. "Nikita Monastyrev," I gasped. "Where did you spring from? I haven't seen you in ages!"

The man in front of me laughed and held out his arms. I walked into them, relishing his hug and amazed at my own boldness. As a child I'd have turned red and run.

The arms that circled me gripped with a strength that pointed to hours spent training with weapons. He'd been a good head taller than I the last time we met, but I must have grown more than he had since then, because my nose was at about the level of his chin. I pressed my face against his chest, inhaling the aroma of cedar that emanated from his robes, mixed with a hint of leather and horse. The mingled scents suggested he'd changed not long ago, from riding clothes to this tawny satin robe embroidered with gold thread. I reveled in the warmth that lit his eyes as I raised my head to greet him and the softness of his lips as he brushed them across my right cheek, then my left, then the right once more.

"You grew up, Dashenka," he said as he released me, using the affectionate form of my name. "You were always pretty, but who knew you'd become such a beauty?"

Pretty? He'd thought me pretty? Why did he never say so?

My cheeks burned, but rather than stand silent as I used to do, I pulled myself together enough to untie my tongue. "You too, Niki. You've filled out. Remember how Papa used to call you a beanpole? Now you look like a warrior!"

He winced. "Well, I don't have much choice, do I? I've spent enough time fighting this last decade."

"Oh, Niki, we heard. That business with Prince Andrei was dreadful." I gripped his hand. "But I'm so glad to see you—and especially to see you safe. When did you arrive, and why aren't you at our house? We'd love to have you stay with us."

Laika, who'd been sniffing at a pouch tied to his waist, stepped forward and gently butted her head against his thigh. I watched as he went down on one knee and stroked her. He looked as if he relished the silky feel of her fur and the adoring gaze she cast at him when he pulled a piece of dried beef from the pouch and held it out to her.

Yet he hadn't answered my question, and the attention he paid to the dog meant that he didn't have to meet my eyes. Did my knowledge of his disgrace bother him? After what I'd gone through with my brother-in-law, Nikita had no reason to fear rejection from me. *His* troubles, from what Papa had told me, had more to do with misplaced loyalty than criminal behavior.

I didn't ask. After more than a decade apart, it seemed too personal to dive straight into the pool of our deepest desires and frustrations. Still, I wasn't sure what to say instead.

So when Niki stood and treated me to his stunning smile, I ignored the city's worth of butterflies fluttering around my insides and gazed at him without speaking. Laika, preoccupied with her treat, had no attention to spare for either of us.

"Another beauty," he said, giving Laika one more pat on the head.

Did you just compare me to a dog? A dog I love, but still ...

"She is," I said, trying to hide my concern. "And sweet-tempered, as you see."

I must not have concealed my feelings as well as I hoped, because he gave me a quizzical glance. I realized we were both, in a sense, finding our way back to the friendship we'd enjoyed in childhood.

"I left Staritsa last week and reached Moscow this morning," he said, belatedly answering my question about when he arrived. "I came in response to a message I received from someone named Job—"

"Father Job! Did he reach you after all?" Then why hadn't Niki replied before now?

Nikita stared at me. "You know him?"

"He's our family chaplain." I frowned, pulling memories from a mist of grief. "He wrote to as many people as he could in the wake of Papa's death, but that was months ago. When we didn't hear from you, we thought the message had gone astray."

I thought you were dead. No, I couldn't say that. It was too pathetic, when he was obviously in perfect health.

"That note probably did," Nikita said, oblivious to my distress. "I didn't find out until I reached Dmitry's house that your father had died. I'd stopped off to say hello and find out what to expect at your place. But you misunderstand. Your Father Job wrote last year, while I was still in Serpukhov. He sent a letter on behalf of your father. I thought he must be the scribe who copied it out." He stroked my cheek, where tears dripped in response to sad memories of the last few months. "I wish I could have attended the funeral. Or at least the forty-day memorial service. May your father's soul find rest. He was a good man."

For a moment words failed me. "I wish you'd been here too," I said when I could speak again. My thoughts whirled. Father Job had never mentioned a letter sent a year ago. He had no reason to tell Solomonida and me about a commission he'd received from Papa, I supposed. But that left a lot of questions unanswered. "Why did Father Job write to you, then?"

The hand that stroked my cheek moved to my chin, and Niki tipped my head back. I saw sympathy in his eyes. "Your father asked that I come to your house as quickly as possible. I promised I would, but I couldn't get leave. Too many border raids and attacks from the east. As soon as I received my transfer to Staritsa, I pleaded to be included in young Prince Vladimir's escort. Fortunately, the prince has taken a liking to me, so he agreed. In fact, he insisted. Alas, when I arrived, I found out I was too late."

More new information. My head reeled as I tried to absorb it. "You received a message from Papa, asking you to visit. But you didn't. And then the second letter missed you. How odd!" But it was more than odd. A whole year. Papa had sent the letter a whole *year* ago, and Niki hadn't found the time to answer an urgent summons. I didn't know what to think. Could he really not leave his post, or had he just not tried very hard?

He shook his head. "I left Serpukhov in mid-May. Dmitry said your father died around that time. The messenger may have passed me on the road." His brief frown faded. "A good thing Grand Prince Ivan invited his cousin Vladimir to go hunting, isn't it? Otherwise I'd still be stuck in Staritsa searching for an excuse to travel to Moscow."

"And now you're stationed in Staritsa again," I said, struggling to put the pieces together. "I'm surprised the government sent you back there."

"It's not the same government. Or the same prince. Andrei Ivanovich is dead and gone, may his soul find peace." I heard bitterness in his voice and didn't wonder at it. Prince Andrei—manacled and starved at the orders of his sister-in-law, Grand Princess Elena, and her favorite—had undergone what could best be considered judicial murder. Even his three-year-old son, Vladimir, and Andrei's widow had spent years in captivity before being returned to their principality of Staritsa.

"Today's men in power don't fear Vladimir," Niki went on. "He's nine years old. They want someone to nursemaid him. Keeps me out of trouble and away from those who distrust me." He stroked my cheek once more.

I pressed my face against his hand, not knowing what to say. I'd already told him how glad I was to see him, but that was before I heard about his broken promise and my father's plea. "Will you stay with us, then?" I managed after a while. If we had to put up with Igor, surely Nikita had an equal claim on our hospitality. Papa had liked *him*.

"I think not." He coughed. "I meant to when I set out, but once I heard the news, including that your cousin Igor had taken over the estate, I realized it wouldn't work. I asked Dmitry to let me stay with him. We've been friends for years, so he agreed right away. I'll spend as much time with you and Solomonida as I can, but I won't give dear Igor the satisfaction of refusing to host me. Not to mention that if I catch so much as a hint of him gloating, I may punch him in the jaw."

And Igor *would* gloat if he saw a chance to lord it over Nikita. They'd hated each other on sight. "My cousin hasn't improved," I agreed. "He's still Igrushka the Duckling in every way that counts. I'd much rather avoid him myself, but for that I'd have to leave the house. This is his dog, Laika—the only good thing about him."

At the sound of her name, Laika perked her ears and barked. The piece of jerky was no more than a distant memory. When Niki laughed at her, she wriggled in joy.

I placed my hand on his arm. "Let's go inside. I came to visit Dmitry's sister Katya, so we can sit and chat for a while. And you can tell me why Papa wanted to see you." Belatedly I realized that *this* might have been his attempt to provide for me, undermined by Niki's failure to appear.

"I'd love a chance to talk with you, Dashenka." He gave me his delightful smile again as he spoke, and my fourteen-year-old self swooned. "For a while, your father at least told me about you and your sister, but then he grew so ill. I always intended to come and visit, but for too long I couldn't get away. Your father meant a great deal to me. I grieve for your loss."

Hearing anguish in his voice, I remembered that he hadn't gone to Serpukhov willingly; the government had sent him there as a punishment. Perhaps he told the truth, and he *couldn't* leave.

"It's our loss." I saw the tears that pricked my eyes reflected in his. "Papa regarded you as a second son. You meant a great deal to him, too."

He pulled me into another hug. "Yes," he said. "He told me that. That's how I know Igor is lying about the estate. Your father confirmed in his letter that he planned to leave the property to me, on one condition."

"What condition?" My voice sounded harsh, ragged, to my ears. Again I heard Papa's remembered voice in my head: *You should be married, not stuck here wasting your youth nursing an old man. I have a plan. Trust me.*

"That you and I wed." Nikita bent and kissed my forehead. "Shall we? I'm willing if you are."

Yes! the fourteen-year-old in my brain cried.

Embarrassed by my own eagerness, I crushed that girlish voice. It made sense that I'd loved Nikita in the days when I saw him often. But this grownup Nikita had a lot of explaining to do. Eleven years without a word, followed by a belated visit at my father's behest in return for an inheritance that any nobleman would value: a good-sized estate in the heart of Moscow—the source of all rewards, financial and otherwise, for highborn men. And a bride who might breed sons but could be ignored and set aside if she did not. To whom he'd just issued the most perfunctory proposal I'd ever heard. Even a stranger could do better than that.

I refused to stand there mute, like the child I'd once been. "Let's talk," I repeated. "Then we can discuss our future. There is, you see, a complication ..."

As it turned out, I had only the shortest of conversations with Nikita that afternoon. During our walk, I managed to explain the complication—that Igor could produce a signed and sealed will, with Fyodor Koshkin to swear to its genuineness, whereas Niki had at best a letter of intent. "And I have no reason to think Papa carried through with his plan," I finished as his friend Dmitry approached. "If he did make a new will, neither Father Job nor my sister and I know anything about it."

I greeted Dmitry, who took time to bow before dragging Nikita off to the stables to admire his new bay gelding—a miracle of horseflesh, according to Dmitry. Nikita apologized, mumbled something about pleasing his host, and departed with a promise to visit Solomonida and me soon.

Tempted to issue a tart comment that I'd appreciate it if he didn't wait a year this time, I bit my tongue. Whatever resentment I nurtured—would Solomonida and I be safe in our house now if he had not delayed?—his arrival offered us the best chance we'd had so far of ridding ourselves of Cousin Igor. It wouldn't do to offend a potential ally before discovering what assistance he could provide. Anything else, including that unanswered proposal, must wait.

Laika set off after Dmitry and Nikita, but when I pulled on her leash, she sat at my feet, gazing at their backs with yearning eyes until I led her toward the house and Katya.

"What's that about?" Katya asked as I settled into place on the window seat. "Until Nikita Andreevich arrived this morning, I had no idea you knew him, and here he's almost family, according to Dmitry. Why have you never mentioned him?"

I heard a note of envy, or perhaps pique, in her voice, which surprised me. I'd never considered myself her rival, nor had I seen evidence that she thought of me that way. And last time I saw her, she was flirting with Igor. When did she develop an interest in Niki?

I didn't *like* the sinking feeling the thought of her chasing Niki gave me, but I couldn't ignore it.

"I haven't seen him in ages," I said. "He's not family, although our fathers were best friends. We spent a lot of time together as children, but that was years ago. You might as well ask Dmitry why he didn't tell you. Niki says they know each other well."

She looked pleased, and I narrowed my eyes at her. What pleased her? As a challenge, I added, "You haven't visited us since Igor moved in. I thought you were considering him as a husband. Have you had second thoughts?"

"No," she said. "I've been busy."

Busy? With what?

But I had nothing to gain from contradicting her. "What do you see in Igor?" I asked instead. "He's not even pleasant, most of the time. And so shallow."

I was genuinely curious. The thought of wedding Igor, even to keep my family's estate, made my skin itch. I didn't much like the thought of Katya marrying him either, but only because I didn't want her taking over my house. If I understood what drove her, I might have a better chance of deflecting her away from me and my relatives.

And, if I could manage it, Nikita.

Katya shrugged her shoulders and raised both hands, palms up in an "isn't it obvious?" gesture. "He's been pleasant enough to me. Who cares whether he's shallow? I want to have children, so I have to remarry, and the head of a noble clan is a good choice. I like his clothes and his style. He's quite good-looking, he owns a nice property close enough that I can see my family whenever I want, he has a patron who's promised to help him, and he can be charming when you and your sister aren't poking fun at him or playing tricks on him. Why are you so dead set against him? You should be pursuing him for yourself instead of acting like an eight-year-old. He's not a bad person, even if he does fuss over his appearance more than most men."

"I'm not dead set against Igor," I told her. "If he hadn't inherited our estate, I wouldn't care what he did. He's not a suitable husband for me because we're second cousins. The Church wouldn't permit it."

"Unless you get a dispensation," she reminded me. She sounded like Fyodor Koshkin, and my gut seized up in just the same way. I'd die first.

"I may not choose to marry," I said, to deflect her from more arguments for why I should wed my obnoxious cousin. "I've thought of taking monastic vows."

"Monastic vows?" Katya couldn't have sounded more amazed if I'd announced I'd already lain with her desired groom. "Are you mad? You *have* to marry. You're a boyar's daughter. A virgin, I assume. Well-connected, pretty, healthy—and wealthy."

"But much older than the usual fifteen or sixteen," I reminded her.

"It was very irresponsible of your father not to contract you ages ago." Wisps of dark hair framed Katya's face as she shook her head.

"He tried," I said. "It's not his fault it didn't work out." She murmured agreement before plunging into a list of reasons why a women's monastery would be a terrible choice for me. I only half-listened, because I'd achieved my goal. I'd found out why she wanted Igor, and I'd stopped her from quizzing me about why I didn't.

While she rambled on, I reviewed my brief meeting with Nikita. Despite my doubts about his long absence and how his experiences might have changed him, I couldn't help wondering what marriage to Niki would be like. I recalled the sensation of his warm lips against my cheek, the strength of his arms, the press of his body against mine. Whether I wed him or another, what sense did it make to say no to such things without ever experiencing them? In that sense, Katya was right—Father Job, too.

I'd like to have someone I could talk to, someone I could trust with my secrets, such as they were. Niki had listened well when we were children. Wasn't that what Father Job had in mind when he spoke of a marriage of respect and affection?

Yet I hesitated. Niki and I weren't children anymore, and he'd waited a year to fulfill his promise to Papa, then proposed in that offhand way, as if he need only ask. I should wait and see.

Katya was still talking. "You're young enough to bear children, which is the only thing that counts. Your family's not going to stand by while you wreck its plans for a profitable alliance. Put the thought of a women's monastery out of your head and do your duty, like everyone else."

"Enough," I said, laughing. "You've made your point. I haven't decided about the monastery. But I'm sure I have no desire to wed Cousin Igor or one of his friends."

Laika, who'd lain quietly by the unlit stove since we entered the room, roused herself at the sound of her master's name and came to place her head on my lap.

She stared up at me with those liquid brown eyes, as if expressing sympathy.

I'd collected the information I came for, and then some. And the demands of Dmitry and his horse meant that I could expect no more conversation with Nikita today. No need to try Laika's patience further.

"I'd best take her home," I told Katya. "Come and visit us tomorrow. With Nikita, if you can drag him away from the horses and weaponry. He's well acquainted with our family and a guest of your household, so there can be no impropriety if you both join us." I tied Laika's leash to her collar once more and stood. "Shall we go home, sweetest dog?"

Katya regarded me with a keen expression, as if she were studying me. "Ah yes, Nikita," she said slowly. "Your childhood friend. Another handsome young man. Would you reject *him* for a monastery?"

Heat suffused my cheeks. "I said I hadn't decided about taking my vows," I reminded her. "As for Niki, today is the first time I've spoken to him in more than a decade. I told you that, too. A bit soon to marry us off, don't you think?"

Now she was the one laughing. "Of course, what was I thinking? Who could imagine a special relationship between you and *Niki*? Especially when the mere mention of him turns your face the color of borscht!"

I shook my head at her, then bent to kiss her cheeks. "Come, Laika," I said. "Let's leave this matchmaking mama to her plotting and go home. We'll see her tomorrow."

And with luck, she'd bring Niki with her.

As Laika and I re-entered our own courtyard, one of her assigned caretakers spotted us and ran to take her from me. I handed over her leash. He thanked me, then untied it right away. "To the kitchen," he told the dog. "Supper. Let's have a bite, shall we?"

He didn't have to prompt her twice. Laika made a dash for the kitchen, the groom in hot pursuit. It hadn't taken her long to learn her way around the house.

I planned to head for the women's quarters, not least because it would keep me out of Cousin Igor's sight if he'd already returned from whatever illustrious meeting had taken him into the city today. But as I reached the bottom of the main staircase, a casual glance to my left reminded me that here was the office occupied by Anfim Fadeyev, who knew more than anyone else, except perhaps Fyodor Koshkin and his copyists, about my father's will.

Fadeyev might, of course, not be at his desk so late in the day. Although the August sun would hang in the sky for hours yet, Laika was not the only creature with supper on her mind. I'd formed the impression that he worked late, though, so it seemed worth a try. With my cousin installed as master of the estate, Fadeyev was no longer under supervision by our clerks; I expected to find him alone, which meant I could pose a few pertinent questions without worrying about anyone else overhearing me. I passed through Father Job's study, now empty—I'd seen him leave for home around the time I set off with Laika—and pressed my hand against the half-open door on the other side.

Anfim Fadeyev indeed sat at the desk, laboriously writing out what looked like household accounts. Standing right across the desk from him, I could see the words for cucumbers, cabbage, and beets. He wrote a nice, clean hand—not the scribbles that Father Hilarion had produced in his notes—and I could read the text easily from where I stood.

Still, that didn't explain why he remained at his desk at a time when most people were thinking of their evening meal. Our household supply of cucumbers hardly warranted such devoted effort. Had he no family to go home to?

Accustomed to dealing with our own servants, I posed the question before stopping to consider that he might read my concern as intrusion. "Why are you here so late? Or at all, for that matter? I thought Fyodor Koshkin promised to put in a word for you with your supervisor."

"If he did, it hasn't helped," Fadeyev said, his tone sharper than I thought necessary. "I'm still on leave. As for *whether* he did, I have no idea. The authorities don't take clerks into their confidence—especially clerks whose loyalty they question. I'm lucky I haven't been dropped from the rolls altogether."

"I didn't mean to offend you." I realized then that he'd mistaken my intent. "We're pleased to have you here. You're obviously a hard worker, and you seem to know what you're doing." More than Cousin Igor, in truth, although I wouldn't win Fadeyev's confidence by criticizing his employer. "But you have no need to stay so long into the evening. Our household accounts aren't urgent. Unlike the diplomatic papers you must have handled before. Why do the people in the Treasury doubt your loyalty?"

He set aside his quill and sighed. "Did you know I was captured last year by the Crimean Tatars? The khan of another horde rescued me, but he wouldn't release me for a couple of months. That's what Koshkin was talking about the day he produced your father's will."

"I heard Koshkin, but I didn't know what he meant. Thank you for explaining." I sat on the bench opposite him, so he wouldn't believe he had to stand until I left. Indeed, he resumed his seat behind the desk right away and stared at the paper in front of him as if he couldn't wait to get back to it. Which couldn't be true, since I'd already deduced that he was gazing at a list of pickled vegetables from one of the storerooms.

Still, I didn't completely understand how his captivity led to his working for my cousin. "Is the government punishing you?" I asked. "Getting captured wasn't your fault."

He sighed once more, but he did raise his head to look at me. "I didn't ask to be captured. So you're right, it's not my fault. But the whole incident makes my superiors twitchy. You heard Koshkin: I escaped, the others didn't. The bosses think I must have made a deal—given away secrets, paid someone off. Nothing they can prove, or they'd have thrown me in jail already. But enough that they don't want me around. Maybe they'll take me back when I'm done here, maybe they won't. In the meantime, this is how I'm feeding my children."

So he did have a family to go home to, which made it even stranger that he spent such long hours here. "How many children?"

"Two," he said. "A son and a daughter. Their mother died last year. May she have eternal life."

"In blessed memory." I responded without thinking. "Did you lose her before you were captured, or after?"

"Before." Now there was no mistaking his discomfort.

Two children, no wife. My fleeting attraction to him vanished as I realized that he had problems of his own, a life he sought to avoid, in the same way as he avoided my gaze. I felt comfortable with him because he was not my equal; he couldn't tell me what to do—quite the reverse. But to probe into his affairs to satisfy my curiosity was cruel. His life outside our household was not my concern, only what he did within it. Time to get down to business.

"I came to ask you something else," I said. "You're one of the few people who saw both copies of my father's will before one was drenched in ink. The text is the same, you told us, but not the handwriting. As you noted, that in itself isn't surprising: a copy need not be made by the same person who wrote the original. But since Lord Koshkin insists that he gave Igor the original and the information in it contradicts what Papa told us, I'd like to look at the document."

"Look at it?" He rose from the desk in what I assumed to be an acknowledgment of my right, as the younger mistress of the house, to ask. Then he stopped, his brow creased. "What do you expect to see?"

"Whether there are signs that someone altered it," I said. "By scraping off the ink or in some other way."

"There are no such signs, Darya Petrovna." I saw compassion on his face, or was that pity? "Fyodor Mikhailovich swore that he handed us the original. I know your father told you something different, but we can rely only on the documentation we have."

"I understand that. I'd still like to see for myself," I said firmly. "I remember Father Hilarion's handwriting. And if Fyodor Mikhailovich lied, even by insisting that a copy was the original, that would hint at wrongdoing of some sort."

He nodded, accepting my determination, if not my reasoning. As I watched, he moved toward one of the strongboxes at the far side of the room, produced a key from his sash, and unlocked it.

While I waited, I surveyed the stack of paper he'd produced, which must stand as high as my forearm was long. Its size struck me as odd, because our household accounts had been in good order when he and Igor arrived. What made the stack so tall?

Fadeyev pulled a piece of paper from the unlocked box and handed it to me, and I stopped wondering about the stack. I scanned the testament, searching for the slightest incongruity. It was a single page, not in the least yellowed. Neatly formed letters, quite small, clustered in remarkably straight lines, laid out across the paper by a practiced hand. Nothing appeared to have been crossed out—Fadeyev was right about that—but nonetheless something struck me as odd about both the paper and the handwriting.

I struggled to name what made me uneasy. I picked up the list of vegetables that Fadeyev had been writing and rubbed both it and the will between my fingers. They were equally crisp. I sniffed the black ink; both pages smelled the same, metallic with an acidic edge. I held first one, then the other, up to the light that streamed through the window and saw the faint watermark of a crown on both sheets. The handwriting was different: Fadeyev's letters flowed across the page, joined one to another like the notes Father Job had shown me but more legible; those of my father's will were blocked out and separate, the way I remembered Father Hilarion writing. Everything was, as people kept saying, in perfect order. Yet something about the will troubled me.

Then I noticed that here and there, even on the list of vegetables, Fadeyev had struck through a word and rewritten it. And I knew what bothered me about the "original" of my father's will. It was perfect.

"Shouldn't this one feel and look older?" I waved the will to show which sheet of paper I meant. "And how could anyone produce such a clean text on the first try? Could you?"

He took the will from me and frowned at it. "Well, the copyist—whether your former priest or someone else—would redo it until he got it right, but I see your point." I handed him the list of pickles he'd written himself, and he held it up to the light as I had done. "The paper used for the will seems to be similar to my list as well."

"And the ink still smells of vitriol," I noted. "It shouldn't have such a strong odor after six years. Wait." I walked into Father Job's study, looking for any paper that I knew had been around for a while, and found Father Hilarion's notes lying on the desk.

As a test, I sniffed the paper. The only scent was the faint, musty aroma associated with old books. I brought the scribbled-on sheet to show Fadeyev, taking care to let him see only the notes that Father Hilarion had left for his successor, not the jottings made for Papa's will. "This paper is at least three years old," I said. "See how much browner it is than the will or your list. The ink has faded and has no distinct smell."

He glanced at the notes in my hand, then shrugged. "Yes, but we don't know how that piece was stored. A testament would be kept in a secure location, whereas that looks like someone's casual musings." Then he picked up the will from his desk, compared it to the sheet of notes that

I still held, and frowned again. "People keep paper around for years, if they don't have much need for it, and we can't tell when any of these sheets were purchased."

He picked up the list of vegetables and repeated his comparison with the will. "Still, if Fyodor Mikhailovich hadn't insisted that he sent for the original in order to present it to your cousin, I would agree with you. I'd say that sheet"—he tapped the page in my hand—"was years older than these two." He put the list of vegetables back on his desk and returned the will to its strongbox.

"Do you trust Koshkin?" I blurted out, when Fadeyev faced me once more. "It was awfully convenient, him being able to lay hands on a document that everyone else thought was missing. And at such short notice, too."

As soon as the words left my mouth, I wondered: Had I made a fatal error? Could I trust *him*?

But this time Fadeyev didn't hesitate. "The text hasn't been altered, Darya Petrovna. It's the same as the copy he sent us."

I frowned at the notes made in preparation for my father's will, willing them to reveal their secret. How Father Hilarion—never mind Father Job, who didn't have the advantage of having written the spidery mess in the first place—could make it out was a mystery to me. The words had initial letters that trailed off into long loops, indistinguishable as the threads I spun with my distaff or the individual stitches on my altar cloth.

I walked to the window and turned so that I stood with my back to it. The mica panes didn't allow for clear pictures of the outside world, but they admitted a fair amount of bright light when the sun was in the right spot. More than I'd had in the low-ceilinged dining room with Father Job—was it two weeks ago already?—even at midday.

I held the paper at an angle. Squiggles, curves, dots, empty spaces—some light, some darker brown against a background of beige. I looked for the places that Father Job had pointed out to me. "Girls"—yes, there it was. And our initials, D and S, directly beneath the "girls." With a bit of effort I found "estate," too.

Right next to that, I saw another squiggle that I'd missed the first time. Father Job must not have noticed it either, because he hadn't said anything. But then, when would he have had a chance to see a mark as faint as this? His study was even darker than the dining room, and the squiggle had been invisible there. It was almost invisible here, with the ink so faded.

I traced the squiggle with my finger, and the thrill of discovery raced through my body as I realized what it was. Not a word, and certainly not a whole name, but two individual letters. An N and an A, intertwined like lovers with my D.

N A. Nikita Andreevich. Niki.

Huh. That surprised me. Not that Papa had wanted Niki to have the estate (and marry me). Niki had said as much earlier today. But he'd received the news a year ago, or thereabouts. This note was older: three years at least, because that was when Father Hilarion retired to his monastery. And since Fadeyev was right that we couldn't confirm the age of the paper with any accuracy, Papa could have meant Niki to have the estate for much longer, even from the date of my brother Lev's death eleven years ago. That was only a few months after the last time I saw Nikita as a child.

I gripped the paper, fighting off a wave of bittersweet regret, a longing for that time when life had seemed so simple, when the harshest problems facing me were whether my embroidery pleased my stepmother, what silly trick Lev would pull next and how to avoid it, and whether Nikita would smile at me again.

Enough. The past was dead, the present far more complicated than I wished it to be. And this paper, such as it was, held the clue to my father's intentions.

I stared at the notes once more. Papa had told Father Hilarion that the estate should go to Nikita Andreevich, probably with some link to me—let's assume marriage, since Niki had said that and Papa too had sworn to find me a husband who would help me care for the estate. Father Hilarion jotted those and other provisions down in preparation for drawing up Papa's last will and testament.

Which said something quite different. Why?

Because of Nikita's disgrace, maybe. December 1537 was not a good time to ally oneself with Prince Andrei of Staritsa's men, even the son of a close friend.

Yet I didn't believe that was the reason. Papa had never been less than steadfast in his loyalties. And he hadn't expected to die right away. He'd worried about what might happen to his family if he became too weak to protect us; the will was a safeguard and nothing more.

Besides, even if Papa did waver for a while, he could have redone his will later. Although his claim to sound mind weakened as the years passed, he'd had moments of lucidity almost to the end—as witnessed by his ordering Father Job to contact Nikita. It was Niki's failure to keep his promise that scotched that plan.

So why did Papa leave the estate to Igor? And without the marriage provision (thank God)?

Like the letter Nikita had received from Father Job, the notes in my hand weren't themselves proof of anything except an intent. We had to discover whether they ever gave rise to a final document. The only person I knew who could answer that question was Father Hilarion himself.

"Did you find something?" Fadeyev asked. I must have been staring at the paper for too long without speaking.

I couldn't tell him what I'd seen. I'd already stuck my foot in the mire by asking him whether he trusted Koshkin.

"No," I said. "It's just an old piece of paper. I can't make heads or tails of it. I should leave you to your work. My sister's probably wondering what's become of me."

Fadeyev looked relieved. "It's been my privilege to serve you, Darya Petrovna." He hesitated, then added, "Igor Grigorevich is not such a bad master, you know."

About to leave, I stopped and stared at him. Hadn't Katya said almost the same thing?

I could have kicked myself. Why hadn't I thought of this before? It was the most obvious question of all. "How do you know him, anyway?"

"My father was the priest in his father's household when that branch of the clan still had a place in the city," he said. "In that sense, Igor Grigorevich and I grew up together, although he's a few years younger than I am. It was a blessing when he agreed to take me on."

"Were you with him, then, when he received the first copy of the will?" They couldn't have worked together for more than a few weeks before coming here to disturb our peace.

"I was not." The sympathy in his eyes caused my cheeks to flush, but I couldn't tell whether he regretted my predicament or his role in puncturing my illusions. "The first day I went to work for Igor Grigorevich, he showed it to me and asked me what it said, so I read it to him. It had reached him the week before, he told me. I had no reason to doubt its legitimacy, Darya Petrovna. I still don't."

"Yes, of course." I'd get no more out of him today, and I wanted to put the page I held in a safe place. "I've delayed you too long. Forgive me."

He seemed pleased to see me go. That made me sad, although I had no reason to consider him a friend. He was a clerk, hired to make my life and my sister's more difficult. I shouldn't even like him.

I walked out, determined to leave him alone from now on. Only at the last moment did I realize I should let Father Job know that I'd taken his predecessor's notes. I went back and jotted a quick message, then left one corner poking out from his edition of the Gospels, so it would be safe from unwanted attention but guaranteed to attract his notice early in the day.

Anfim Fadeyev didn't see me. His door remained firmly shut the entire time.

Chapter Six

I WENT BACK TO THE OFFICE THAT EVENING AFTER WATCHING Anfim Fadeyev leave for the day and verifying with Mishka the steward that Cousin Igor had gone off to visit yet another potential patron. Once safely inside, I positioned the candle I carried on Anfim's desk in such a way that its wax could leave no trace of my visit and examined his papers. I wanted to know whether that stack of his contained documents more controversial than our household accounts.

I wasn't looking for another testament. Fadeyev had convinced me of his sincerity when he assured me that the document he'd shown me this afternoon was genuine. I didn't believe he was right, but I accepted he meant what he said. So the real will would not be kept here, in his office.

Yet something was off. Fadeyev could have recorded every cucumber and beet that had passed through the house in the last fifty years, and he'd still have produced a stack half as high as the one he had on his desk. So what accounted for the rest of the papers? It had to be documents commissioned by Cousin Igor, because clerks follow orders if they want to keep their jobs. And so long as Igor and Fadeyev believed I couldn't read, I had a chance of finding out what my cousin sought to hide from Solomonida and me. I intended to make good use of my opportunity.

At first, the results were disappointing: the expected household accounts, intermingled with recipes for beer and bread, estimates of grain and hay required for the stables. Nothing odd there.

I suppressed a groan. What a waste of time! I could have stitched half a peacock tail in the hour I'd spent rummaging through these boring papers.

Well, in for a kopeck, in for a ruble, as they say. I didn't want to come back another day and search the pile again. Better to ensure that Igor had no nefarious scheme underway. A man willing to profit from a forged will could not be trusted.

I dug deeper and uncovered an extensive genealogy that showed the male members of the Bezzubtsev clan and its affiliated branches, going back to the fourteenth century and including the most important posts each man had held. If Fadeyev spent most of his time on this—it currently ran to at least thirty pages, and he had yet to reach the reign of the current grand prince's father—he had his work cut out for him.

Yet the genealogy was nothing unusual. Such records were common among aristocratic clans, whose members constantly monitored their standing at court and in the army against that of their rivals. Deciding there must be more to find, I continued my search.

After turning over what seemed like endless descriptions of vegetables and haunches of meat, I came across a description of our estate, together with a hand-drawn, brightly colored map illustrating the boundaries of the property, the walls circling the main house, and the various buildings that lay within.

How lovely! I didn't recall ever seeing such a thing, especially not one depicting a place that meant so much to me. I touched the document, rubbing my finger across the paper as I'd done earlier that day with the will. The paper used for the map, too, was not crisp or new, although someone had cared for it well, because it was in much better condition than Father Hilarion's notes.

But who drew the map?

I knew few artists. Maria and Solomonida and I might be considered artists with a needle—Maria especially—but not with a pen. The only person of my acquaintance capable of creating this map was Nikita, once upon a time. But I had no idea whether he still drew, and he hadn't produced this: the central image of Laika—tearing across the courtyard, ears flapping and legs at full stretch while a boy in servants' clothes chased her—underlined that however old the paper, the map itself must be recent. Recognizing her racing form from this very afternoon, when she'd dashed for the kitchen, I had to bite my lip to keep from convulsing with laughter.

Anfim Fadeyev, perhaps? He clearly demonstrated mastery of a quill, so perhaps he could do more with one than write. And whoever drew this had a sense of humor. In addition to Laika, I saw a horse marking the stables, blocks of ice near the icehouse, a miniature Father Job next to his study, and an embroidery frame signaling the women's quarters. It must be Fadeyev's work, as there were no other candidates in the house. With one last, long look at Laika, I set the map aside, smiling, and continued my search.

Next I uncovered a listing of court positions, those who held them, and their relationships to one another—with lines indicating alliances, including one connecting Igor (no position) with the complex web of lines leading to Koshkin. More lines linked Koshkin with the Shuisky princes who surrounded the young Grand Prince Ivan, represented by the letters IV inside a crudely drawn circle. I understood the purpose of that sheet: it plotted Igor's hopes for advancement through his connection with Koshkin and those associated with him. I felt a surge of excitement. Was I getting somewhere at last?

Then I came across a page that flummoxed me: the names "Anna" and "Ekaterina" underlined and separated, followed by short categories such as "Age" and "Beauty." Each row had a dash in one column or the other, as if someone had used it to assess the pros and cons of a choice. A third column on that page marked "Sophia" had a line drawn through it, so hard that the pen had left holes on both sides. There were no dashes under that name.

But who were Anna, Ekaterina, and Sophia? The names were common enough. I myself had a niece named Anna, a neighbor called Ekaterina, and an Aunt Sophia. The three on this list could be anyone. But the person who wrote down the names wanted nothing to do with Sophia—that aversion I could not mistake.

And there was another page listing the full names of noblewomen I recognized as either unmarried or widowed. A few Annas and Ekaterinas, to be sure, but many other names as well. Was this a list of brides my cousin was considering? And were the Anna and Ekaterina on the separate page the most desirable candidates or something else altogether?

I prayed that Igor had not set his sights on my niece, who at twelve was not even half his age. However firmly Solomonida declared her opposition to the match, Igor's rights as the male head of the clan would make it difficult to refuse him.

A list of brides was not illegal, of course, but it did hold an intrinsic interest for my sister and me, and Igor might therefore have a reason to hide it from us.

I glanced at the list of categories on the separate page once more. "Age," "beauty," "temperament"—and what was that? I peered at the page until my eyes watered. The word looked like "dowry." Those categories were ones a man would consider in choosing a bride. But if my cousin had settled on a particular Anna or Ekaterina, then the significance of the paper giving the women's full names was less clear.

It was a puzzle, and I didn't have time to stand around in an office that, at least in my cousin's view, I had no excuse for visiting, especially at this hour. At any moment, a member of the household might pass by and see light under the door. Most of the servants didn't like Igor and would protect me from him, but I'd still be better off if no one suspected me of prying.

I turned my attention back to the longer list. Katya Vorontsova and I appeared on the second page.

There was only one thing to do. I grabbed one of Anfim Fadeyev's quills, dipped it in the ink pot, and jotted down as many names as I could on a fresh piece of paper. I drew a small star on the list next to anyone called Anna or Ekaterina, including my neighbor. Then I copied the list of categories from the separate piece of paper and assigned an initial (A or E) to each one to match the check marks on the original sheet.

Lined up like that, I could see the scales were weighted in favor of Ekaterina, whoever she might be. She had age and beauty on her side, although "dowry" appeared in both columns and "temperament" in neither.

All of which gave me hope that Igor might not have set his sights on my niece.

I was running out of time. A noise from the courtyard caused me to blow the ink dry, fold the sheet, and tuck it into the sleeve of my tunic. I restored the pile of papers as close to the state in which I'd found it as I could, extinguished the candle, and darted from the room.

Fortunately for me, I encountered no one on the back staircase. I tumbled gasping into the sitting room of the women's quarters and whispered a grateful prayer that I'd managed to get in and out of Fadeyev's office without raising questions. I might have collected some useful information, too—if I could figure out what I'd found.

I hid my copied list in my sewing basket, under a pile of scarlet and orange silks that didn't match the various projects that Anna, Solomonida, and I were working on that month. Then, satisfied that the list would remain hidden until I could decide what to do with it, I went to bed.

The next day I was outlining the four peacocks destined to mark the corners of my altar cloth when the consequences of my evening visit intruded in the most literal way possible.

By then it was early afternoon. Nikita had not arrived as I'd hoped he would, and the lowering clouds outside suggested he would wait for another day, because anyone who set off on even such a short walk could expect a thorough soaking. Igor had left mid-morning, before the clouds rolled in, and taken Laika with him for once. So I sat in the women's sewing room with my sister and niece—the three of us, just like old times, stitching together on a gloomy August afternoon. Solomonida and I huddled close to the lanterns. Anna perched on the window seat, a brace of candles arranged behind her. Knees drawn up and face scrunched in concentration, she bent over her square of linen, diligently working on the leaves of her practice flower.

My sense of life restored to normal lasted perhaps a quarter of an hour before a knock on the door preceded the entrance of Anfim Fadeyev, looking annoyed.

I wasn't *entirely* surprised to see him. I'd heard him stomping around and swearing in his office when I'd gone down this morning in search of Father Job, hoping to share my discoveries of the day before. I must not have done such a good job restoring the state of his desk as I'd hoped.

But I hadn't expected Fadeyev to come here. He couldn't have figured out that I was the culprit, surely? I'd taken such care to hide my ability to read!

"What is the problem, Anfim Fadeyev?" Solomonida set aside her stitchery and motioned him into the room. She didn't invite him to sit, and he made no attempt to do so, instead standing near the door and glowering.

When she repeated the question, a note of impatience in her voice, he said, "Someone entered my office last night after I left, Lady Solomonida. He went through my papers, used my quill and ink."

He, not she. That was a good sign.

Although I saw him looking at me—my right hand, in particular. I glanced at it and saw a streak of ink at the far side of my thumb.

I cursed silently, recalling the haste with which I'd folded the list last night. How I'd managed to miss the ink when I washed my hands before bed and again on rising, I didn't know. But then I recalled the ink Fadeyev had spilled that first day, and how hard I'd had to scrub with pumice powder to get rid of it—without entirely satisfactory results. A simple application of water and soap wouldn't do much to remove that stain.

He didn't challenge me, but I saw suspicion on his face. He couldn't prove my guilt, or he would accuse me openly, but I'd done something that caused him to wonder. My many questions, or the length of time I'd gazed at Father Hilarion's notes, even my interest in seeing the will provided by Fyodor Koshkin for myself.

At that point, I was glad that I'd stayed and gone through the whole pile, despite the tedium of the search. He'd probably do a much better job of hiding his work from now on.

I stared at him, daring him to voice his suspicions aloud. He might work for my cousin, but I was still the younger mistress of this house. He met my gaze until Solomonida intervened, pulling him back to his statement that someone (male) had entered his office uninvited.

"And you suspect this person of nefarious intent?" My sister raised both eyebrows. "I had the impression you were verifying our household accounts. I find it hard to believe that anyone on the estate would sneak into your office to check whether we spent more on hay or pork last month. Nor can I imagine what you expect me to do about it."

Fadeyev blushed and lowered his gaze. "You're right, of course. But someone did disarrange my work. I thought I should alert you, as the person who oversees the servants, and request that a lock be placed on the door."

"Very well." Solomonida waved a dismissive hand. "Go, and I will order Mishka to see to it. Or was there something else?"

"No, Lady Solomonida. Thank you." Fadeyev bowed and departed in haste, as if eager to put the room behind him. My sister could be extraordinarily imperious at times. I was glad that today had been one of those times.

"Really," she said as soon as the door closed. "Did you ever hear the like? What does Igrushka have him doing in that office that they don't want people to know about?"

That was when I saw my chance. I went to the sewing bag, pulled out my copied list, and held it up. "This, for one thing."

Solomonida's mouth dropped open. She shut it hastily and said, "*You're* the one who raided the office? How very enterprising of you! What is that?"

"Well, I'm not sure." I unfolded the copied sheet, skimming it once more in the hopes that it might make more sense today than it had the day before. "It was two lists originally. One of women's names, including mine and Katya Vorontsova's." I pointed to our names, although I knew the letters meant nothing to Solomonida.

"And the second?" She didn't even glance at the words under my fingertip.

"A chart with three names, Anna"—I nodded at my niece, who was pretending not to listen, although I could tell from the tilt of her head that she was—"Ekaterina, and Sophia, the last crossed out. I have to assume they are potential brides—for Igor, most likely."

My sister's eyes narrowed. "He'll marry Anna over my dead body. That's worse than him making a match for her when she's only twelve."

I'd had time to think about that overnight. "I doubt he wants to marry our Anna, any more than he wants to marry me. He needs a powerful father-in-law or at least powerful brothers-in-law, remember? That's what Koshkin told him, and Igrushka agreed. His only reason for marrying you or me—but your name's not on the women's list—would be to keep us from pestering him about the estate. Marrying our Anna wouldn't even do that. It must be a different Anna he has in mind."

"If he wants to live, it had better be." Solomonida picked up her sewing long enough to stab the needle through the stiff fabric as though it were a stand-in for our cousin.

I silently cheered her on. The thought of Igor bedding my niece made me want to strangle him with my embroidery thread.

"What else did you find?" my sister asked.

I shrugged. "A family tree. A lovely map of the estate—I'll show it to you someday. The household accounts Anfim admits to writing. There's more, but nothing controversial except for those lists. Although I did notice something odd about Papa's will." I explained how the document Igor had shown us seemed too new, but I didn't tell her about the notes and Niki's initials—I wanted to discuss those findings with Father Job first.

As I talked, an idea came to me. "Could we not visit Maria?" I asked.

"May I come too?" Anna abandoned her stitching without a second thought, dropping it on the window seat and leaping to her feet. "I haven't seen Lyuba in ages!" Ages meaning, as I knew for a fact, two days.

"It's about to pour." Solomonida waved a hand at the gray sheet pretending to be sky, then at the half-finished work in my hands. "Why do you want to visit Maria?"

"I have two reasons. First, if our cousin marries, it affects us. I wouldn't want to stay here if someone else was in charge of the household. Even Katya, and at least we know her. Would you?" Solomonida shook her head, and I went on. "We can't prevent him from making an offer, but we can find out more about the women. How likely their families are to agree. Whether we can discourage the match by spreading rumors—that Nikita disputes Igor's claim to the estate, for example, which he does. Maria will know."

"And second?" Solomonida had perked up, I could see, at the chance to scotch Igrushka the Duckling's plans.

I laughed. The second reason had been my original goal, and I was particularly pleased to have thought of it. "And second, what our cousin wants most is an introduction to Tsarevich Alexei. He wants it more than a bride; he told Koshkin so. If anyone can arrange such a meeting, Maria can. If we get the credit for setting it up, maybe Igrushka will focus on that and forget about marriage for the moment."

Long enough for Niki to find Father Hilarion and the genuine will, I hoped.

"Hmm." Solomonida poked the tip of her ivory needle here and there in the cloth she still held. "It's a good thought. Except that I know Alexei—not well, but enough. One look at our Duckling, and he'll be hard put to keep from laughing. The best Igrushka could hope for would be cool courtesy, and a flat refusal to help would hurt his tender feelings even more than believing his goal out of reach. That would be salutary for him, no doubt, but it wouldn't do us much good. He'd be even more determined to wed then, especially if he realized that taking a wife would cause the three of us to find another place to live."

She set both needle and cloth aside. "Still, we should visit Maria anyway." Anna clapped her hands, and Solomonida added, "Not today. Look, the storm's started. We'd be drenched before we reached the carriage."

I couldn't argue with that. Rain pounded the wooden frame of the house. Thunder rumbled in the distance, silencing the usual cacophony of the courtyard—so familiar I often didn't notice it for hours on end. The occasional flash of lightning lit the sky, and I dropped my embroidery on a table as I crossed the room to close the shutters.

Anna slumped onto the window seat, the picture of dejection. "First thing tomorrow," Solomonida told her. "Or if not tomorrow, we'll go as soon as the skies clear." She produced her most mischievous grin. "We'll ask Maria what we can do to discourage our Duckling from even imagining that he needs a wife. I hope you're right about him not wanting to wed you or Anna, but then why are your names on his list?"

She had a point. "I don't know," I admitted. "I suppose I'm indulging in wishful thinking. I certainly don't want to marry him."

For all the good it would do me to refuse. I could see from the troubled expression in my sister's eyes that she knew I'd have little recourse if Igor in fact settled on me as his bride.

I could marry Niki.

I should tell her he'd offered for me. A rather perfunctory offer, to be sure, but a real one. And preferable to Igrushka the Duckling.

Why hadn't I mentioned it already? I'd told her about running into Nikita at Katya's house, that he planned to visit us, and even that he questioned Igor's right to inherit.

Because Niki still had to earn my trust. He hadn't visited us today, just as he hadn't kept his promise to Papa. I didn't dare count on his support, only to have him ride off without a care and leave me in my cousin's grasping hands. And I didn't want to share the news of the proposal, raising Solomonida's hopes, only to dash them because Niki failed to follow through.

Yet despite my best efforts to be sensible, the memory of Niki's smile sent shivers down my spine.

The thunderstorms lasted for three days straight, delaying our visit to Maria. Each morning Solomonida looked out the window, assessed the sheets of rain, and decided to wait one more day, despite Anna's protests. On the second day, Nikita sent me a written message via one of the Vorontsovs' servants, apologizing for breaking his promise, explaining that he'd been called to the Kremlin, and swearing that he counted the hours until we could be together again. After a flush of delighted relief, my doubts set in once more. I wanted to believe him, but I needed more evidence of his sincerity.

I did like having the note to read, though. With a few exceptions—Father Job, Anfim Fadeyev, and apparently Fyodor Koshkin—I didn't know many men who could read and write. And no one but Niki had ever sent me a letter expressing affection. I kept it near my bed and read it morning, afternoon, and evening.

Since Niki's absence meant that I couldn't share with him the scribbled initials I'd found on the paper Father Job showed me, I fulfilled my original plan and took them to the priest instead. I found him in his study and explained what I'd discovered about the notes his predecessor had jotted down and my suspicions of the will Cousin Igor had produced.

"I agree," the priest said when I held a candle close enough that he could see the faint lines as I pointed them out. "The N and the A, intertwined like that with the D, do suggest that your father intended, long before he dictated his letter to me last year, to bequeath the estate to Nikita Andreevich if the two of you wed. Alas, you're also right that the note has no significance unless it became the basis of a will dated later than December 1537. Your father didn't ask me to draw up such a document. Will you write to Father Hilarion?"

I traced the joined initials with my finger, considering. "I'm afraid a letter might go astray, as I'm not sure where Father Hilarion is now or which monastic name he chose. Did he tell you?"

Job shook his head. "I've had no contact with him in years. But I do know that he went first to Holy Trinity Monastery. I would start there. The monks will have records."

"I'll ask Niki to search for him, in that case. He can move about more easily than I can. Holy Trinity is not so far away. Perhaps he can ride there. If his duties to the prince of Staritsa don't interfere, that is." I sighed. I had no acquaintance with young Prince Vladimir and couldn't tell whether he would release Niki even for a few days. But I feared he would not. According to the message I'd received, it was the prince, as much as the rain, whose demands had kept Niki from fulfilling his promise to visit.

"Assuredly Nikita Andreevich can ride there." Father Job gave me his sympathetic smile. "A seasoned cavalry officer? He can get there in a couple of days, weather permitting. And what of you? Will you marry this young man, if it turns out that was your father's wish?"

I raised one shoulder, indicating uncertainty. "Cousin Igor insists he will select my husband, and he doesn't care what Papa wanted. So I may not have a choice. But if I do, I need more information before I decide. Nikita promised to come to Moscow, then waited a year before he did. He may have endangered Solomonida's and my future as a result. He has reasons, but I still wonder if he's telling me the whole truth. I adored him when I was a child, but what good is that? The last time I saw him, I was fourteen and so shy I could barely say two words in his presence. I don't expect undying devotion, but I'd like him to regard me as more than a path to the estate."

I'm willing if you are, Niki had said that day at the edge of Katya's courtyard. *Yes!* my soul sang in response.

My naive, fourteen-year-old soul. I'd left that girl behind long ago. Besides, what kind of proposal was that? Not even an "it would make me happy"!

I flushed at the memory of my misplaced delight, and I knew my reaction didn't escape Father Job's keen eyes. But despite my undeniable attraction to Niki, he had yet to persuade me that I could rely on him even to stop by for a visit.

"All valid concerns," Father Job said. "I'm glad, though, to hear you mull over possibilities that don't involve immuring yourself behind monastery walls at the age of twenty-five. I suggest you wait and see. There is time yet for your Nikita Andreevich to prove his worth."

"Thank you, Father." I bowed and accepted his blessing. But as I left the office, I wondered. *Would* Niki prove himself, and if so, how?

Chapter Seven

THE NEXT MORNING, THE SKIES CLEARED, AND SOLOMONIDA, Anna, and I set off in an enclosed carriage for Maria's house—an absurdly short distance away, but the streets were still damp from another round of storms and the sky overcast enough to hint at a possible recurrence. For me it was a grand adventure, the first time I'd left the estate on such a visit in years. At Solomonida's suggestion, I'd donned one of my best robes, so I knew I looked my prettiest in rose satin with ankle-length embroidered false sleeves over an ivory tunic.

While chatting with my sister and Anna, I gazed through the panes set into the carriage door, searching for buildings I recognized. But the effects of sunlight on mica, even the weak rays that managed to struggle past the still-menacing clouds, made it impossible to see anything but glare, so after a while I leaned back against the padded seat and recited the Jesus Prayer in my head to slow my rapid heartbeat and dry the sweat of anticipation that clung to my palms. You'd think me bound for a military campaign or imprisonment in a tower rather than on a simple visit to a house a few streets away from my own.

A few streets and a world away, I realized as I followed Solomonida and Anna through the doorway at the top of the outside staircase used by guests. Frequent visitors, they neither stopped nor stared, but I could hardly believe my eyes. The interior of the house was unlike anything I'd ever imagined: a clear light shone through transparent windows inset with colored patterns, illuminating wall hangings decorated with swirling lines, and carpets even more intricately designed than our own covered the floors. When the Russian housekeeper showed us into the sitting room where Maria awaited us, I stared speechless at brass tables on low wooden legs, inlaid screens and chests, and padded benches running the whole length of the walls with brocade pillows where a visitor's back would rest.

"You might have warned me what to expect," I whispered to my sister as we crossed the threshold.

"Sorry," she whispered back. "Forgot you hadn't seen it." Before I had a chance to respond, she stopped in mid-step and exclaimed, "By all the saints, where did *you* come from?"

I stopped dead as well and stared, trying to figure out what my sister meant. The room contained three times as many people as I'd expected, but Solomonida's question could refer only to a woman, because she'd used a feminine form, and she wouldn't ask it of Maria or Lyuba, both of whom lived in the house. Who else was there?

Anna had run ahead and was hugging Lyuba, who sat beside a lovely dark-eyed brunette dressed in sapphire silk with the full skirts, tight waist, low neckline, and puffed sleeves typical of the Polish style. She must be the person Solomonida had greeted, because the only others present were men. She looked familiar, too, although I couldn't recall where I'd seen her. I didn't know any Poles.

At that moment the Polish woman rose to greet us, spreading her skirts, bending her knees, and lowering her chin—the whole gesture one I'd never seen before, performed with extraordinary grace. Then she straightened once more and watched us, her head at an angle that struck me as challenging, as if she anticipated rejection.

What was that about? Why would I reject a woman I didn't know from a country I'd never visited?

The two men also stood as we entered. One I recognized, although I hadn't seen him in ages: Alexei—Maria's Tatar husband, in his mid-thirties by now but still uncommonly handsome, his dark hair as yet unmixed with gray, his upright stance and strong muscles proclaiming his status as a military commander. The other, dressed in the Polish manner, had warm gray eyes, chestnut hair, and a charming smile. If I had to guess, I'd say he was a few years younger than Alexei.

I definitely hadn't met the second man before. For one thing, he supported himself with a cane, which I would have remembered. For another, Solomonida didn't greet him by name either, although she went straight to Maria, then to Alexei, then to the Polish woman, embracing each of them in turn before stopping in front of the other man and beckoning me to join her.

Curious, I set off across the room. Maria intercepted me midway, kissing me on both cheeks. "Greetings," she said. "How wonderful to welcome you to my house. And perfect timing for a first visit, because our dear friends arrived unexpectedly this very morning. Come and greet my husband. You'll have seen him at our wedding, although perhaps not to speak to." By this point we had reached the far side of the room, and I bowed to Tsarevich Alexei, who dipped his head in response.

"Welcome," he said. "I've heard much about you, Darya Petrovna. I understand you've spent most of the last seven years nursing your father. May we all enjoy such devotion from our daughters." He had a rich, warm voice and a smile that touched my heart. I couldn't help smiling in return.

"And this is my former stepmother." Maria reached for the Polish woman's hand and drew her forward. I felt my eyes widen, and a small gasp escaped my efforts at self-control. So that's why she looked familiar!

I recognized her now. Roxelana was her name, and I'd never met another woman as outrageous in her behavior or as cutting toward those she disliked. Almost without exception, men yearned for Roxelana, and she encouraged them with seductive glances, cooing speeches, and sensuous movements; she had no interest in women even as friends, and few women had any use for her.

Including Maria, I'd thought, but that seemed to have changed.

"You saw her at our wedding too. You know her as Roxelana," Maria went on. "But she goes by Juliana Krasilska these days." While Juliana and I acknowledged our past acquaintance with wary nods, Maria extended a hand to the man with the cane. "She lives in Cracow with Lord Felix Ossolinski, whom you haven't met. Lord Felix, these are Solomonida Petrovna Sheremeteva and her sister, Darya Petrovna. The girl chattering over there with Lyuba"—she frowned at them, but I could hear laughter in her voice—"is Anna Semyonovna Kolycheva, Solomonida's daughter."

Anna, thus reminded of her manners, pulled away from Lyuba—who giggled, unabashed—and ran to join us. "Greetings, Tsarevna Maria." My niece put her palms together in front of her heart and bowed to each of the adults in turn. "Tsarevich Alexei, Lady Juliana, Lord Felix. Please forgive my discourtesy."

"You're excused," Maria told her. "Lyuba, come here and greet our guests. My goodness, child, were you born in a barn?"

Lyuba, a suitably chastened expression on her face (although I rather doubted her sincerity), did as she was told. But as soon as she'd welcomed Solomonida and me and received her release from Maria, she and Anna grabbed hands and ran from the room, chattering like magpies.

Watching them go, I sighed. Had I ever been so carefree? If I had, I'd lost touch with that feeling long ago.

Except when I first saw Nikita. No wonder I'd felt drawn to him. He sparked memories in me of that younger self—shy, yes, but fun-loving and lighthearted, secure among those I loved.

Where had that self gone during the dull years I spent caring for Papa? And how could I revive her if I shut myself away from the world? I should be doing the exact opposite!

Gazing around the room with a new sense of purpose, I surprised an expression of bemused regret on Lady Juliana's face. She was looking at the door that Anna and Lyuba had run through. She too gave the impression of wondering what she'd lost.

She was the last person I'd expected to feel a sense of fellowship with. I glanced at Lord Felix and saw him watching her, warm sympathy in his eyes. He touched the back of her hand, and she shook her shoulders quickly, like someone waking up.

Then she noticed me. She returned my gaze, the challenge again visible in the tilt of her head. I wondered at her defensiveness, if that's what it was, but then Solomonida caught my hand and pulled me to sit on one of the covered benches. The men excused themselves and left the room.

I turned my attention to the women, listening without interruption while my sister peppered Lady Juliana with questions about where she'd been and what she'd done over the last six years. I couldn't follow half of it, but I got the gist: Juliana had once been married to Fyodor Koshkin, Maria and Lyuba's father (which I knew), and now somehow was not; she'd met Lord Felix at the Polish court; and the two of them had grabbed the chance to accompany one of the many diplomatic missions that traveled between the courts of King Sigismund the Old and Grand Prince Ivan to visit Maria, Alexei, and Lyuba—for whom they had the deepest affection.

That last, in particular, sent a jolt through my veins. I didn't recall any love lost between Maria and Lyuba and their stepmother, so when had this great affection developed?

Before I could think of an acceptable way to frame that question, Solomonida launched into a long story of Cousin Igor and his latest exploits. As her story drew to a close, she produced, with a flourish, the list I'd copied and held it up for Maria and Juliana to view.

I yelped, drawing everyone's attention, and reached for the paper. "Solomonida! What are you doing?"

"Showing our friends the list." My sister switched the paper to her other hand so that I couldn't grab it away from her. "Isn't that why we came?"

I'd never wished more for Solomonida's quick tongue. Roxelana—Juliana, whatever she called herself—was *not* my friend. In fact, I didn't trust her as far as the door. I glared at my sister, who was laughing. Clearly, she didn't care a whit for my embarrassment, the wretch.

"If Darya Petrovna intended to share this with Maria and is now having second thoughts, I have to assume her problem lies with me." Juliana plucked the piece of paper from Solomonida's fingers, glanced through it, and handed it to Maria. "Forgive my ignorance, but I don't see what's so incendiary about a bunch of women's names. What's the significance of this document?"

I sighed. Let my sister answer that. This was her fault.

"Our horrid cousin," Solomonida said, "is scouting for a bride, a noblewoman with illustrious connections. Which would be awkward for us if he succeeds, since she would displace us in our own home. So we came to ask, Maria, what you know about these women. Whether any of them might agree to wed him, in particular."

Again I noticed Juliana regarding me with that assessing gaze. It made me uncomfortable, although I had to give her credit for figuring out that she was the reason I'd hesitated to share the list. To show her she couldn't intimidate me, I stared back, matching her expression to the best of my ability.

"Katya Vorontsova would accept him," I told Maria, since I saw no point in staying silent now that the horse had left the barn. Might as well get this candidate out of the way. "She's on the list, and I'm not sure we can discourage her. She knows what he's like, and she has her own reasons for pursuing him. He may be searching for someone with more powerful relatives than hers, though."

Or she's turned her attention to Nikita. Suppose she's the real reason he didn't visit me, and his letter was merely an excuse?

I pushed that thought away with a savagery I hadn't known myself capable of.

Maria frowned at the list. "The woman who lives next door to you? Your cousin should pray for such a match. Her uncles are in favor with the young grand prince, and have been for the last year." She flicked the paper with one finger. "These others are too high-ranking for their families to settle on an unknown young man. I don't think you need worry about them." As she finished, she placed the list in my hand.

Juliana pounced. I hadn't seen it coming, but I recognized it when it did. "And why is it, Darya Petrovna," she asked in the most casual tone imaginable, "that you don't want to marry your cousin Igor? Aren't you—forgive my plain speaking—getting on in years? Wouldn't a husband, even a silly one, be better than no husband at all? And if *you* married him, you and your sister wouldn't have to worry about someone else taking over your home."

I heard Maria's and Solomonida's indrawn breaths, but neither of them intervened. Perhaps they, too, wondered.

Tempted to tell Juliana to mind her own business, I again stared straight at her. I expected to see—actually, I couldn't have said what I expected to see—scorn, perhaps, or dismissal of another woman's foolish ideas.

But as I gazed into her dark-brown eyes, what I did see was knowledge, understanding, and, which surprised me most, empathy. For a wild moment, I believed she had somehow heard not just the history of my father's will, which Solomonida had revealed a short while ago, but that Nikita had proposed to me.

As soon as that last thought crossed my mind, I realized it was impossible. So far I had told no one except Father Job, not even my sister. But with Nikita again absent and my decision about him unmade, I would be crazy to share such news here.

I could tell the truth about Igor, though. "I don't like him," I said. "We have nothing in common. I doubt he would choose me anyway, since he needs a bride with powerful relatives, and our relatives are the same. But that doesn't matter. I'd take monastic vows before I agreed to marry him. Or anyone he picks for me."

Juliana's steady gaze didn't falter. I had the oddest sensation that she could read my mind. I braced for protests or rational arguments—the same litany Katya had produced when I proposed retiring from the world—but Juliana surprised me. "Men can be difficult to persuade," she said. "Especially if it means hearing that a woman doesn't want them. Do you have a refuge if you need one?"

"You could come here." Maria waved a hand, indicating the spacious room. "All three of you can stay with us if Igor proves intransigent."

"And abandon our home to him?" Solomonida leaped to her feet and paced, as if the mere thought made her restless. "I thank you for the thought, Maria, but I won't do it. Darya and I have as much right to live there as he does. I won't let him drive us away."

"Does Darya feel the same?" Juliana asked. Again I had the odd sensation that she read me as easily as she did the book she'd handed to Lyuba as we walked in.

And in fact, she did. I wished my sister would say yes to Maria's generous offer. From here my chances of scotching any scheme Igor developed to marry me off would improve considerably. He couldn't summon me into his presence and announce that he'd signed a contract for my hand. He could try, but if I refused to cooperate, he would have no way to force me.

Opening my mouth to respond, I looked at Solomonida's set face. I could see she was determined to defeat Igor on his home turf. And as her sister I owed her my loyalty. She'd always stood by me, and she would stand by me now, whatever Cousin Igor tried to do.

"It's early days yet," I said, repressing a sigh. "Let's not impose ourselves on your hospitality until we know what our cousin plans to do." A memory of him swaggering across the courtyard flashed before my eyes, and I giggled. "Igrushka the Duckling may have met his match in us."

"That's the spirit," Maria said. "But remember, my door is open if you need it."

Solomonida echoed my thanks, and with that the conversation turned to embroidery and other less fraught topics.

It was mid-afternoon by the time Solomonida and I summoned our carriage for the return home. In response to Lyuba's pleading and Maria's agreement, we left Anna to stay the night and departed feeling pleased with ourselves. We had succeeded in achieving both our first goal—at least to the point of identifying Katya as the main person who might interfere with our plans—and, more important, our second. Maria had promised to bring her husband and her guests to meet Igrushka the Duckling in person the next day.

Meanwhile, the carriage journey gave Solomonida and me a chance to talk without fear of being overheard by Cousin Igor and his henchman Anfim. I didn't plan to waste that opportunity. My sister, I felt certain, knew far more than she'd told me about Maria's mysterious guests.

"Who is Lord Felix?" I asked her. "Why haven't I heard about him before?" Roxelana—oops, Juliana—I'd at least met, although she seemed to have changed for the better since then. "And how is it that you didn't know that Roxelana was here last year or that she'd divorced Fyodor Koshkin?"

Solomonida stared at the opaque window, tapping her fingers against the side of the carriage as if beating a marching army into motion. I couldn't tell whether she was avoiding my gaze or concentrating her thoughts.

"I don't know how to answer that," she said after a long pause. "Maria didn't mention a visit from her stepmother last year, and I didn't have a chance today to find out why. There must be some mystery attached, because Lyuba didn't talk about it either, and she and Anna babble nonstop. As for Lord Felix, you saw Maria introduce me as well as you. So I hadn't met him before either. Based on what Maria said today, he's a scholar and a diplomat, a lover of the arts. He serves King Sigismund the Old and has visited Moscow several times. He's intelligent and charming—that's Maria's phrasing, because I barely exchanged two words with him, although he has a lovely smile. And he's the reason her stepmother wanted a divorce. There's no more I can tell you. Why did you invite them to accompany Alexei and Maria tomorrow?"

"It would have been rude not to include them. And I want to find out more about them." I sent her a mischievous glance. After so many years together, I could guess what would appeal to her. "Besides, won't you enjoy watching our cousin falling all over himself to please Roxelana—Juliana, I mean—and Alexei and Maria, for different reasons? He may underestimate Lord Felix because of the cane, and that would be a mistake. I suspect there's more to Lord Felix than meets the eye."

"What do you mean?"

I'd watched her delighted anticipation as she envisioned Igor trying and failing to impress his exalted guests shift into a frown as I reached the end. Now she looked puzzled.

It was my turn to stare at the upholstery and think. She'd said something about Felix that bothered me, simple as his story seemed. What?

The answer came in a flash. "Doesn't it strike you as odd that he's a diplomat serving the king of Poland, and we've been negotiating with the king of Poland for a year and a half, and he and Rox—oh, Mother of God, why can't I remember to call her Juliana?—came with the most recent mission, but we're supposed to believe that they traveled so far only to visit Maria and Alexei? Why would that make sense?"

"Why would it make sense for them to lie?" Solomonida asked this question in a reasonable voice, as if no one could accuse such a lovely couple of hidden motives. "Rox—yes, I'm doing it too; I mean Juliana—can't serve as a diplomat because she's a woman, so if they want to travel together, it's better for him to accompany her as her husband, even if he's not exactly that, than as an envoy."

"Yes, that's true," I said, struggling to solidify my inchoate impressions. "But staying with Maria and Alexei also offers him a different perspective. Official envoys see the house assigned to them and the palace, and then only for formal receptions. They can't visit people like us. They don't ride unescorted. They can't talk in private with nobles as high-ranking as Alexei and Maria. If I were the king of Poland and I learned that one of my diplomats had ties to a member of the court, I'd encourage him to stay with them. He'd bring me much richer information about what might help or hurt my cause than envoys stuck in a house and permitted to view only what my adversary wants them to view."

Solomonida considered the point. "I suppose," she said. "I certainly wouldn't put it past Juliana to spy on us. It fits what I recall of her. But we have no secrets, so it's not going to do them any good, is it? Let's talk instead about Igrushka the Duckling and how we can deflect him from marrying. Is Katya Vorontsova really besotted enough to accept him?"

"That's what she told me," I said. "She wants children and a handsome clothing allowance." Solomonida nodded, and for an instant I again considered telling her about Nikita's proposal and my fear that Katya might steal him away before I even had a chance to accept or reject him. But before I could find the right words, our household gates opened in response to a call from our coachman, and our chance to talk uninterrupted ended.

Indeed, a most unexpected sight met our eyes as we clambered out of the carriage and set foot on the smoothed planks at the base of the stairs.

Chapter Eight

KATYA STOOD IN THE MIDDLE OF THE YARD, DEEP IN conversation with Cousin Igor. From the way they laughed and gazed at each other, then blushed and turned their heads away, I concluded their courtship was proceeding apace.

My heart sank, then rose, and I scolded myself for being completely unreasonable. So long as Katya was flirting with my cousin, I could stop worrying about her chasing Nikita. And if I wanted to dissuade her from pursuing Igor, Maria had just handed me a perfect opportunity to reveal his true colors. I decided on the spot to invite Katya to tomorrow's dinner party. Watching him fawning over Juliana and Alexei and Maria might do the trick. And if it didn't, I might have to accept that the two of them belonged together and think about a new place to live.

Solomonida and I exchanged glances, then went to join them. Katya tensed as we approached, as if she'd prefer to continue her one-on-one conversation, although she soon banished the scowl and greeted us with hugs and kisses.

In response to a whispered query, Katya told me Nikita was again on duty in the Kremlin. I thanked her for the information, but inwardly I sighed.

With my plan to disillusion Katya in mind, I invited her to come upstairs. With a certain reluctance, she bowed to Igor and followed Solomonida and me into the house.

"I'll stop by as soon as I speak with Anfim Fadeyev," Igor said, returning the bow with a flourish and gazing meaningfully at her as we walked away.

She treated him to a gaze as yearning as Laika's and said in a sultry voice, "You honor me, Igor Grigorevich. That would be a great pleasure."

I heard Solomonida snicker. When I nudged her with my elbow, not wanting to arouse Katya's suspicion of our intentions, my sister pulled her face straight in a way that made her look younger than Anna, amusement still visible in her eyes. Fortunately, Katya didn't notice.

We escorted Katya to the sewing room, then reconsidered. If Igor followed up on his promise to stop by, the main sitting room on the second floor would serve the four of us better than the women's quarters. We wanted our cousin to see our part of the house as a space that did not welcome him, whether he owned the rest of the estate or not. The sitting room might not qualify as neutral territory, but if one half of the family had to invade the other half, better that Solomonida and I launch a raid into his domain than host an incursion into ours.

When Igor arrived at last, he brought Anfim Fadeyev with him. Behind him came menservants bearing jugs of frothy beer for the men and cherry juice for the women.

I accepted a cup of juice, using it to rid my mouth of the taste left by Maria's offering, an odd grassy beverage she called tea. Igrushka swigged beer with gusto, although Anfim cradled the ceramic cup between his hands, his attention firmly fixed on us women.

Once everyone was settled, Solomonida nodded at me, our pre-arranged signal that I should break the news to Igor. "I hope you have no business that will take you away from the house tomorrow, cousin," I said. Catching the wicked gleam in my sister's eyes, I forced myself to focus my attention on Igor instead. "Tsarevna Maria has promised to bring her husband to visit us. She has two quite illustrious guests who are eager to meet you as well."

Anfim Fadeyev wrinkled his brows, as if he heard the insincerity in my voice. Igor's face contorted into a mixture of shock and excitement that could only be considered comic. Beer spilled onto his hands as he clutched the cup, and he swore, grabbed for a napkin, and patted in vain at his elaborate robe. I managed to suppress my natural urge to giggle long enough to glance at Katya, seated between me and Igor. Like Anfim, she regarded me with a distinct air of skepticism.

"I don't know the exact time of day, but I'm sure they'd love to meet you as well," I told her, fulfilling my plan despite the astonished glance Solomonida sent me. "Could you come here around noon? I doubt they'll arrive before then. If you wish to bring that guest of yours who has promised to visit us"—I trusted her to know that I meant Nikita—"tomorrow would be the perfect time for that too."

"Of course." Her voice—cool, disinterested—was clearly designed to convey that she received such invitations so often that they had no special meaning for her. Her demeanor sent a similar message. Watching her, I had to suppress the urge to laugh.

I can't wait to see what you make of Juliana, and she of you.

Still, I had to give Katya credit for poise, especially when she darted a smile at the goggling Igor. "It's your cousin I look forward to seeing"—she paused long enough for his mouth to drop open at so obvious a compliment—"advanced to a position suitable to his lineage and his skills." She conferred another smile, this one lingering, on him before turning her head toward me. "Tell me more about these illustrious visitors. Tsarevich Alexei I have encountered while calling on Maria, but the others?"

"Solomonida knows more about them than I do." I swept my eyes across the company, from Katya to Igor to Anfim Fadeyev, whose mouth twitched as it so often did during these encounters, although he didn't force his way into the conversation. His reaction told me he guessed that we were manipulating the others. And that he'd either forgotten or overcome his suspicion that I'd invaded his office.

"Won't you tell them?" I asked my sister.

"With pleasure," she said, and I was sure she meant it, although not for the reasons Igor might imagine. "Lord Felix Ossolinski, the scion of an old magnate family and in personal service to the kings of Poland, and his beautiful consort, Lady Juliana Krasilska. She's fluent in Russian; she lived in Moscow for a year or so during her marriage to Fyodor Koshkin, your patron. They're divorced now. Lord Felix is less comfortable in our language, but I'm told he speaks enough to get by. You'll have no trouble entertaining them."

Igor looked as if he might explode from anticipation. A tsarevna, a tsarevich, and two foreigners—one well connected and the other lovely beyond compare—in his house at the same time? Only the knowledge that he owed this boon to us could cast the smallest cloud on his joy.

Katya looked taken aback. The plan was working.

The moment the door closed behind Katya, Igor plunged into an orgy of preparations that set the household on its ear. He ordered every dish and utensil washed and polished, every piece of linen pulled from its chest and examined, every corner of the second floor and the women's quarters swept, scrubbed, and dusted. You'd have thought the house hadn't seen a broom or a rag in decades. I excused myself long enough to change my fine clothes for plainer ones and dove in, ignoring Igor's tart remarks regarding my homespun linen robe.

"You should try it yourself," I snapped at him after the third barb. "I like to look good as much as you do, but if I'm to get covered in dust, I'd as soon not see it destroying brocade and velvet. I can still smell that beer you spilled on your robe, you know." That shut him up, and I went back to my work with vigor and a secret smile.

Solomonida remonstrated with him, too, pointing out that she personally supervised a full cleaning each Monday, the laundry on Tuesdays and Wednesdays, and intermittent sweeping and dusting the rest of the week. When she realized she might as well be talking to the wall for all the good it did her, she switched to calling him "Housewife" in the most sarcastic tone she could muster. He ignored that too, for a while, then raised his arm and yelled at her to check the kitchen and storehouses, plan the menu and instruct the cook. She glared at him, her hands on her hips, but I saw her lips tremble. When he turned away, she stalked out of the room without another word.

My heart sank as I took over the task of pulling table coverings from the closest chest to prove to our cousin that no speck of dirt or unraveling stitch marred their beauty. Solomonida was so strong in defense of herself and others, it was easy to forget that her by now long-dead husband had been an incorrigible brute. Papa hadn't laid a hand on any member of his family, and my sister had never once hinted that her husband beat her, but when I saw her quiver and back down as she had when Igor threatened her, I shuddered to think what secrets she might hold locked inside.

By nightfall, even Cousin Igor agreed we were ready to receive our guests the next day. I stood at Solomonida's side, struggling to keep my eyes open long enough to admire the glossy woodwork, the glittering goblets, the gleaming spoons and knives and carving forks, the pristine linen with borders my sister and I had embroidered ourselves. In the attic, no doubt, maids lay flat on their backs, staring blankly at the ceiling—if they still had the energy to stare. I imagined grooms collapsed in the stables, cooks napping in the kitchen, carpenters staggering home with bags of tools falling off one shoulder. At some point unknown to me, Anfim Fadeyev had slipped free of the insanity that swept up the rest of us: to spend time with his children, I hoped. If *I* had another house and family to go to, you wouldn't be seeing me here.

Igor stalked off, a wave of his hand releasing us for the night. Nothing so indulgent as praise, you understand, although he ought to have acknowledged that he owed the boon of Alexei and Maria's visit to the intervention of Solomonida and me. Most of the day's work lay to our credit as well—or at least our supervision of others' efforts.

By then, we didn't care. We wanted only to see him go, so we could make our shaky way to our own section of the house. There we could relax and eat the simple meal the servants had left out for us hours earlier, dishes protected by square cloths considered unsuitable for company. I'd seen them carried by while instructing some of the maids on how to rub beeswax into the dining table, but I could no longer remember when that was.

Once I reached our sitting room, I found another clean but ragged cloth, dipped it into a lacquered wooden bowl filled with water, and washed my sweaty face. I rinsed my hands, then passed the cloth to Solomonida. Not for the first time, I was glad of my own plain dress; it had survived better than my sister's finery, despite the once-white linen apron she'd tied around her robes.

I collected bread and cheese from the tray left by the servants and bit into it. Although I was almost too exhausted to eat, the salty taste and dark crust revived me to the smallest degree. "Did you ever see the like?" I asked Solomonida, who was drying her hands on the inside part of the apron before pulling it off and tossing it to land on the window seat. It promptly slipped to the floor, forming a dingy heap.

"Never." She sat on the bench next to me, then rested her head against the wall, rubbing her neck. "I swear, our Duckling should have been born a woman. He'd have been a housekeeper for the ages. This is the last time I ever agree to help him out. And what possessed you to invite Katya? I thought we were trying to keep them apart."

"So she can see him at his worst," I said. "Flattering and deferring to Alexei and the others. If that doesn't discourage her, nothing will. And I'm hoping she'll bring Nikita, who's guaranteed to annoy Igor by his very presence—although if Niki dodges this invitation as well, I suppose we'll have to give up on him too."

"Dear me, little sister, how devious you're becoming." Solomonida opened her eyes and laughed. "I'm proud of you! But are you sure you asked for Nikita only to annoy Igor?"

Sometimes she knew me too well. "Well, perhaps not *only*. You haven't seen him yet. He's become very handsome." Again tempted to tell her of his proposal, I refrained. I was too tired to go into that, especially when I wasn't sure he would visit us tomorrow.

I finished the bread and cheese. A yawn I couldn't suppress scrunched my eyes tight shut, and my forehead ached. "I'm for bed," I told my sister.

She groaned. "I understand," she said. "Pass me a cup of juice on the way out, will you? I'll be sleeping, too, before long."

"Take heart, sister," I said as I handed her the cup. "If we succeed in discouraging Katya or deflecting Igor, all this hard work will have been worthwhile."

It was good to be young, I decided the next morning—or at least not old. A sound night's sleep had restored me to my usual state of boundless energy. I wasted little time devouring the platter of bread and cheese I'd had the forethought to carry with me when I left the sewing room last night for my own chamber. When done, I called for Alya, who turned me out in a style that even my cousin and my sister would have to agree left no grounds for complaint.

When I reached the main sitting room on the second floor, I found Nikita staring out the window. He looked magnificent, his light brown hair glinting gold in the midday sun, his profile clean and strong. Laika lay at his feet, regarding him with an adoring gaze that I strove not to imitate. She must have followed him here, which struck me as curious in itself, since under normal circumstances she trailed Igor wherever he went, except when he left the estate altogether. Even then, he had to insist that she stay behind.

"Niki!" I cried, happier to see him than I had any reason to be given my uncertainty regarding his intentions.

He turned at the sound of my voice. "Dashenka! Don't you look lovely? Come here." He held out his arms. I rushed into them and was enjoying the way he whirled me around when I realized that women better at this seduction game than I would ever be—Katya, Juliana, my sister—would probably have advised me to hold back.

Well, too late now. And Niki was hugging me with enthusiasm and kissing my cheeks, so I saw no signs that my lack of restraint bothered him. Quite the contrary.

"I'm glad you decided to join us," I said, compounding my failures as a potential siren.

"It's my great pleasure." He released me, slowly, then reached out and pressed his palm against my cheek. "I'm sorry I didn't get here before. Settling Prince Vladimir in Moscow has been a nightmare. How can a nine-year-old boy be so demanding? And now I have to go hunting with him and his cousin Ivan."

"*Do* you have to?" I'd feared he'd say that. "I wish you didn't. I have so much to tell you, and some of it's important."

"Unfortunately, I do. Hunting, then visiting monasteries. When princes summon, the rest of us can't say no. But that doesn't start till next week. Until then I'm free."

"Monasteries. Which ones?" Would he have time to find Father Hilarion?

"I'm not sure. Holy Trinity, for certain. The grand prince goes there twice a year. Why?"

"I'll explain the whole when we have a chance to talk without interruption. But in brief, you may be able to find the priest who wrote Papa's will. He went to Holy Trinity, Father Job says, but that's as much as he can tell me. There's lots more, too."

"A mystery." His eyes gleamed as he spoke. "Can I steal you away right now?"

Flickers of delight ran through me. He was flirting with me, and I couldn't help laughing at the eagerness on his face.

"Alas, no," I said. "I'll meet you at Katya's house tomorrow. In the orchard, if it doesn't rain, so no one can overhear us. Today we won't be alone. And I haven't told Solomonida everything. I wanted to talk with you first."

I looked around. "Where *is* Katya?"

"She went to tell your sister we'd arrived. They'll be here in a moment. Tell me quickly how things are for you—with Cousin Igor and in general." He took my hand, and I let him lead me toward the window seat. As usual, Laika perked her ears at the sound of her master's name.

Nikita leaned sideways and patted her head without taking his eyes off me.

"Igor doesn't spend much time here," I said with a shrug. "So in that sense it's fine. Doesn't share his plans or where he goes. You'll probably learn more today from his conversation with Tsarevich Alexei than I've learned in a month. If you choose to eat with the other men, of course. You're welcome to stay and chat with us women if you prefer."

"Igor would like that, I'm sure." Niki laughed, and Laika responded with a bark. "But so long as I know I'll have a chance to talk with you tomorrow, I'll join the men. I can remind your cousin he doesn't in fact own the estate, whatever he thinks."

Footsteps sounded from the other side of the door, and he released my hand before I could respond. I wasn't sure what to say anyway. His pleasure in needling Igor had been one reason for inviting Niki. Yet I hated to lose his company after so short a time.

Solomonida bustled in with Katya. "What's that dog doing here?" my sister asked. "Darya, that dress is gorgeous. The turquoise suits you perfectly. And Nikita! *Bozhe moi*, look at you!" As I had done earlier, she ran lightly across the room on slippered feet and threw her arms around his neck. "You were always a handsome boy, but now ..." She stopped mid-sentence, as if no words could convey her pride and joy in seeing him grown up.

"Solomonida," he said, hugging her. "You haven't changed a bit. Lovely as ever. And don't blame the dog, please. She greeted us at the entrance and escorted me here as if I were an honored visitor while Katya went to fetch you. I could have sent her away, but she's so well behaved I didn't have the heart."

"Well, aren't we a credit to society?" Katya crossed the room and kissed my cheeks. "Your sister's right. You look gorgeous. You too, Nikita. That dark green sets off Darya's turquoise perfectly. The two of you belong together." She grinned, and my fears that she saw me as a rival for Nikita's affections dissolved.

What a relief! Perhaps I'd underestimated Katya, although I still preferred not to see her marry Cousin Igor.

Indeed, she was right about us being a credit to society. My turquoise satin, worn over a tunic in a lighter shade of the same color with cuffs embedded with pearls and semiprecious gems matching the emeralds woven into my braid; Nikita's green velvet, the color of a forest floor in midsummer shade, with an upstanding collar of black; Katya's silver brocade and Solomonida's lemon yellow—we would do my cousin proud, even in the company of a tsarevich and a tsarevna. Not to mention Juliana, possibly the world's most beautiful woman and likely to be clad in the revealing Polish style, to boot.

"Igor Grigorevich will have no grounds for complaint," Katya announced.

Speak of the devil, the country folk say, *and he appears*. Igor walked in just as that thought flitted through my head.

"Greetings, Igrushka," Nikita said, his voice dry.

"Nikita!" Igor reeled back in shock. "What brings you here?"

Niki shrugged. "Old acquaintance? I trust you're enjoying your new home."

"Very much," Igor said in a guarded tone. "My cousin Sheremetev was most generous." I waited to hear what Niki would reply to that, but he raised his eyebrows and didn't speak.

Laika rose to greet her master but stopped midway as he turned to usher Alexei, Juliana, and Felix into the room. The dog settled on her haunches and watched. The rest of us stared. Juliana wore a patterned silk gown the color of claret, cut low across her bosom, the neckline enhanced with a partlet of exquisite lace that drew attention to her ample charms rather than concealing them. Her tight sleeves, slashed to reveal an ivory chemise, extended to her wrists, where more ripples of lace spilled over the tops of her hands.

Most shocking of all, if one didn't include that neckline, was the way the top of the dress hugged her form to the waist, then belled out as it fell to her feet. A corded sash in the same dark red encircled her waist, and a brass pomander dangled from it together with a folding fan. She wore a single, stunning strand of pearls interspersed with garnets, from which dangled a small gold Catholic-style cross, and more pearls dangled from her ears. Her headdress was a simple band that matched her sash, and her dark hair flowed free from a tie at the nape of her neck. No one else in the room could match her exquisite simplicity. She dipped her head and bent her knees in that gesture that, when I asked Solomonida, I'd learned was called a curtsey.

I'd never seen an outfit like it, and when I glanced around the room, I realized I wasn't alone in my reaction. Katya fought back tears. Niki had a stunned expression on his face, although he recovered quickly when I kicked his ankle under cover of my robes. He bowed, first to Alexei, then to Felix and Juliana. Of the five of us, only Solomonida seemed unconcerned. Lord Felix regarded his consort with affection and pride, while Tsarevich Alexei watched our reactions with open amusement.

Igor resembled nothing so much as a besotted sheep. While we humans stood mute, Laika cautiously approached the visitors. Alexei held out a hand for her to sniff, and Lord Felix patted her head, but it was Juliana who surprised me. She went down on one knee and gazed into the dog's eyes. "Well, aren't you a beauty? What's your name?"

"Bella," Igor said. His voice sounded choked, and he looked at Juliana, not the dog. "Her name is Bella. She hails from Poland, like all beautiful creatures."

"Funny," Nikita said in the same dry tone he'd used earlier. "Most people call her Laika." At the sound of her real name, the dog barked, and everyone in the room except Igor burst out laughing.

Igor glowered at Nikita. "I don't even know what you're doing here. I didn't invite you."

"No, but your cousins did." Niki crossed the room and bowed to the visitors once more. "I'm Nikita Andreevich Monastyrev," he said to Tsarevich Alexei. "It's an honor to meet you, Alexei Bulatovich. My father had great respect for yours and for you, as did Pyotr Alexandrovich, the prior owner of this estate. I'm in service in Staritsa, which is why we haven't met before, but I know you by reputation."

Following Nikita's example, I took Katya's arm and walked her over to our visitors.

"But where is Maria?" I asked Alexei. "Did we not make it clear that we were inviting her too?"

He gave me his heartwarming smile. I sighed—gently, so no one would hear me. He was even more handsome than Niki, with those dark curls and warm brown eyes, that strongly boned face and perfectly proportioned body. Maria was a lucky woman.

"You did," he said. "She sends her apologies. She caught something from the children and doesn't feel well. Nothing serious, but it would make her poor company—and perhaps sicken others. We'll keep Anna at our house, if you permit, until we can be sure she won't fall ill as well. At least let her stay until tomorrow, since I didn't bring her with us today."

"I'm sure there can be no objection," I said. "But it's for my sister to decide, so I'll mention it to her. Please tell Maria I hope she feels better soon. Meanwhile, you remember Ekaterina Ivanovna Vorontsova?"

He promised he would convey my best wishes to Maria, and I moved on to Juliana while he greeted Katya. We exchanged various pleasantries as I waited for Alexei and Katya to finish so I could introduce her to our two Polish visitors.

While chatting with Juliana, I noticed a detail that had escaped me yesterday. Here, standing less than a foot's length away, I clearly saw, beneath the pink powder she wore on her face and neck, the indentations characteristic of smallpox.

That was new—meaning that she hadn't had the marks when I last saw her in Moscow, although they were faded enough that she must have recovered from the disease some time ago. I didn't remark on them; that would have been unforgivably bad manners. But Juliana must have guessed that I saw them, because she sent me that challenging gaze of hers. I shook my head as slightly as possible, hoping she would understand that the remnants of her illness changed nothing as far as I was concerned. And indeed, the pockmarks did change nothing: scarred or not, she was still the most beautiful woman I'd ever met.

"That gown of yours is fabulous," I told her. "I've never seen anything so elegant. You outshine the rest of us." Her mouth curved in a smile that touched me. I could see she was genuinely pleased. I caught Katya's hand, pulled her forward, and introduced her, then moved on to speak with Lord Felix.

After a while, I went to sit between Katya and Solomonida, waiting for Igor to order the meal be served, at which point we women could leave for our own part of the house. Juliana joined us, Laika at her heels. When Juliana sat, the dog rested her chin on her new idol's lap. Juliana didn't push Laika away but stroked her ears and cooed at her in a language I didn't recognize, full of liquid vowels. It sounded like poetry or song, and Laika lapped up every word, until I could believe the dog as smitten as her master. Then Igor summoned one of Laika's caretakers, and the dog, lured with a handy piece of chicken, departed amid a chorus of farewells.

"Send Mishka here," Igor told the groom as he left.

So it wouldn't be long now. I glanced around the room. While Igor mooned over Juliana, Nikita was deep in conversation with Alexei and Lord Felix. I couldn't hear what they said, but I could tell from their relaxed stance that the three of them liked one another. That made sense to me: in terms of experience and interests, they seemed to have far more in common than Igor would ever have with any of them.

Watching, I remembered my promise to let Solomonida know that Anna was still at Maria's house. I leaned close enough to my sister's ear to murmur what Alexei had told me. "Yes," she said. "He asked me if she could stay, and I agreed."

I turned toward Katya, staring disconsolately at Igor, who in turn couldn't take his eyes off Juliana. Definitely, the plan was working. After his initial greeting, Igor had barely acknowledged Katya's existence.

"He's a dolt," I whispered. "She cares nothing for him." Katya nodded without speaking, her gaze focused on my cousin.

Beyond her, Juliana cast the occasional sideways glance at Igor, whose resemblance to a poleaxed sheep increased with every breath he took. As I watched, she unsnapped the fan from her belt, opened it, and moved it languorously back and forth before her face, smiling her enigmatic smile. If I'd sent her written instructions, I couldn't have directed a better performance than hers.

During this byplay, Mishka the steward entered the room in response to Igor's summons. My cousin dragged his attention away from Juliana and pulled Mishka into a corner, where the two of them soon fell into what looked like a hurried and acrimonious conversation.

I tugged on Katya's sleeve. She turned her head. "What?"

Again I saw the glint of tears in her eyes, which sparked a flash of remorse at the success of my scheme. I didn't want to hurt her, only to discourage her from pursuing my cousin—and Niki.

"They're arguing." I jerked my head in the direction of Igor and the steward. "Why? Mishka's a servant. He wouldn't dare argue unless Igor proposed something outrageous enough to imperil the family honor. But Igor wants to impress Tsarevich Alexei, so why risk offending him?"

"How would I know? I think I'll go home." Katya pressed her hand against her forehead in dramatic fashion. "I have a headache."

That would never do, and once we women went off to a separate room, we could calm her down without undercutting the effect of Igor's bad behavior. "No, please stay. Igor has to stop acting like a moon calf soon. Besides, if you leave, Niki will think he has to escort you." I patted her hand, and she sighed but agreed.

Then Mishka departed, still grumbling, and I discovered that I'd underestimated Igor's capacity for idiocy. He extended both arms in a gesture as wide as his smile and announced, "In honor of our Polish guests, I have ordered my steward to set up a table for us in the next room, so that the women may eat with us."

He bowed in Juliana's direction, then—as if remembering his manners, or at least the reason he'd wanted to host this gathering in the first place—Alexei's. Beyond them, I could see Niki biting his tongue and the twinkle in Lord Felix's eyes. Alexei, too, looked as if he struggled to conceal his amusement.

So that was what had upset Mishka, that we women would share a meal with men of our own station, not all of whom belonged to our family.

"It will be a new experience for us," Igor went on. "And a salutary one, I feel sure. So, a moment's patience, I beg of you. We will go into dinner very soon."

"Oh, I don't believe it," Katya muttered. "Are you sure I should stay?"

"You must," I whispered, even as I wondered how to handle this new development. What would appeal to her without undermining our efforts?

A thought occurred to me. "I'll talk to Solomonida," I promised. "We'll position you right next to him."

Katya brightened even as I prayed that my solution would work.

Chapter Nine

A SHORT TIME LATER, I FOLLOWED MY SISTER TO THE improvised dining room, curious to see what our steward had produced. An oak table set up so that the eight of us could face one another stood surrounded by chairs. Not matching chairs: Mishka must have pulled them from throughout the house to replace the usual benches. Still, I was impressed that he had found so many in good condition.

In fact, the whole arrangement looked more comfortable than the usual high table, which forced diners to sit as if on display, facing front and unable to converse except with their immediate neighbors to left and right. The rest of the preparations were equally impressive. A fine linen cloth covered the table, and a full set of wooden trenchers, bowls, goblets, and utensils of various sorts marked the places each person would occupy. I decided on the spot that we should try this more often—except when it meant face-to-face exchanges with Igrushka the Duckling, of course.

Igor strode to the center of the table on the side nearest the window and invited Alexei, the highest-ranking guest, to sit at the head, with Juliana between him and Igor and Solomonida on Alexei's left. Nikita strolled to the foot of the table opposite Alexei. Igor glared at Niki for a moment, then gestured to Lord Felix, who moved into the central position next to Solomonida, and I quickly stood next to the chair between Felix and Niki. That left the final chair, on Igor's right side, for Katya. She grabbed it.

So far, so good. Whatever he chose to do, she would experience it firsthand.

Igor bowed to Katya, acknowledging her for the first time since she arrived. She rustled her skirts as she settled into place, but Igor was already staring at Juliana, who simpered and lowered her eyes as she sank gracefully onto her chair. Alexei pinched the back of her hand and whispered something I couldn't hear into her ear, and she tittered in response. I glanced at Lord Felix, wondering what he made of this exchange. He'd propped his cane against the wall and stood, one hand on the chair to support himself, waiting—for what, I couldn't guess. Except for Niki, who watched me with a steady gaze, the other men had already taken their seats.

I sat, wriggling a bit as I adjusted to the unusual sensation of the chair back and arms. Only then did Lord Felix join us. Had he been waiting for us women to settle ourselves first, then? How extraordinary! Niki took his place on my other side.

However unfamiliar, the new arrangement worked well from my point of view. In the midst of company, I couldn't say everything I wanted to Niki, but I could find out more about his life and his plans, and Lord Felix, with his intelligent gray eyes and calm demeanor and impeccable courtesy, intrigued me. Assessing him, I saw he had a smile every bit as charming as Alexei's, and his gaze as he surveyed me in turn was shrewd.

In fact, looking at the three of them—Alexei, Felix, and Nikita—one after another, I decided I'd been right yesterday when I made the choice to explore marriage rather than withdraw from the world. With a man like one of these, I thought I *would* enjoy creating a family—and a life.

Why had it taken me so long to figure that out? Most likely because, as Father Job pointed out, I hadn't met the right kind of man until now. I'd loved Papa, of course, but I'd spent little time with him until the last years of his life—and anyway, he was my father. Solomonida's husband hadn't appealed even to her. Igor left me reeling between laughter and irritation. And Daniil, although outrageously handsome, cared most about fighting and riding horses and chasing girls, which left me with nothing to say to him.

These men were different: they paid attention to me when I talked; they were knowledgeable and cultured; they cared about things besides war. If I could pick my own husband—if I could marry Nikita or a man like Alexei or Felix—I would welcome the prospect. But how could I ensure that Igor would let me choose?

Alas, I couldn't come up with an answer to that question, so I decided to take advantage of the opportunity that Igor's infatuation had given me. Leaving Solomonida to pursue the conversation she'd started with Alexei and Felix, I turned to Nikita. "How do you like being back in Staritsa?" I asked, to get him talking.

"On the whole, I enjoy it," he said. "It's far enough from Moscow to keep me out of the palace intrigues I detest but close enough for a visit now that I have another reason to come here." He tipped his head in my direction and smiled, and the flush I so often experienced in his presence warmed my cheeks. I struggled for a flirtatious reply and didn't find one. Maybe I should ask Juliana for lessons.

When I didn't answer, he went on. "It's a quiet place these days. You'd like it there too, I expect. Prince Vladimir's mother runs an embroidery workshop; her needlewomen produce beautiful pieces. But the city is a shell of its former self, and that makes me rather sad. Most of the warriors who served alongside me during the rebellion have either died or been reassigned, although the lesser servitors remember me. Even so, it beats Serpukhov, where you can't turn your back without Tatars howling up from Crimea or launching raids from Kazan. Nursemaiding a nine-year-old is easy compared to fending off the devil's own archers."

"Cousin Igor insists that the only way to a better future is through service in Moscow," I said. "You don't share his ambition to advance your career?"

Niki glanced at Igor and shook his head. His mouth quirked, and he said, "That's probably true—for Igor. I could advance on the battlefield if I chose. I don't choose. I had enough of that kind of attention six years ago." He looked straight at me. "If I can reclaim this estate and win you as my bride, I need nothing else."

"Nor do I," I said, hoping that his willingness to flirt meant that he wanted me for myself, not only because of the estate. His comment about not choosing the battlefield reminded me of the happier days of childhood, before his noble rank forced him to become a warrior, a time when he'd imagined a different path in life.

"Do you still draw?" I asked. "You used to show me the most beautiful pictures of ships and palaces and mountains." I thought of Anfim Fadeyev's map. "I have one I'd love to share with you, but I have to get hold of it again first. You might like my peacocks, too."

"Peacocks?"

"On the altar cloth I'm embroidering." I whispered a short summary of how the idea had come to me when I first saw Igrushka the Duckling strutting through our courtyard, and Niki burst out laughing.

"Very appropriate," he said, glancing at our cousin and shaking his head. "And yes, I still draw." He turned to gaze into my eyes once more. "Perhaps I'll sketch you, now that I have a week to myself. Then I'll have a memento to take with me when I go hunting. Would you allow that?"

I stared at him for a moment, bereft of words, then stammered, "Yes, of course." He wanted to sketch my portrait to take with him on his journey? *That* suggested I meant something to him, did it not? I knew that in the western lands people painted individuals, but with the exception of the map of our estate, every drawing I'd encountered was religious. "Is that a sin?" I added belatedly, as the thought occurred to me.

"Let's hope not," Niki said. "I much prefer art to fighting, but I don't want to paint icons. Too many rules. I found the most beautiful book in Serpukhov, full of pictures no bigger than this"—he made a rough rectangle with his index fingers and thumbs—"with scenes from daily life. That's what I'd like to do."

"May I see it?" This insight into him fascinated me. I hadn't forgotten his love of drawing, of course, and I remembered his bitterness when I described him as a warrior, but I hadn't suspected he might yearn to devote his life to so unconventional a pursuit (for a nobleman) as art.

"I'll bring it tomorrow," he said with a smile. "I carry it with me wherever I go."

Igor cut across our conversation. "What are you two whispering about?"

"Nothing important," I said. "Nikita was telling me about Staritsa."

Under the table, Niki clasped my hand and squeezed. I blushed again, sure everyone in the room could guess what he was doing. Such an absurd thought.

Although Juliana had a definite sparkle in her eye. Afraid she'd embarrass me on purpose, I sent her a pleading look. She smiled but didn't speak.

"Staritsa," Igor waved a dismissive hand. "A backwater. You'll never get ahead there."

"Getting ahead is your goal, not mine," Nikita said. "I'm happy where I am."

"Admirable." Solomonida beckoned to the manservant in attendance, and he bowed and left the room—to fetch the first course, I assumed. "I like a man who appreciates his place in the world rather than engaging in constant striving for little profit."

"Well, at least *I'm* not a traitor," Igor snapped, again glaring at Niki, from which I gathered that Niki's barbs—and Solomonida's, no doubt—had gotten under my cousin's skin.

"Nor am I a traitor." Nikita surged to his feet, fists clenched at his sides. "I was assigned to serve Prince Andrei. I took orders and went where I was sent rather than abandoning him at the first sign of trouble. Would you have had me stab my lord in the back?"

Alexei intervened in the brewing quarrel. "Sit, Nikita Andreevich. Your honor is intact. I served on the Moscow side of that campaign. I watched your lord surrender to prevent further unrest that could only damage the country. It wasn't the first travesty I've witnessed, but it may be the greatest—not least because the government then punished the loyal and rewarded the disloyal."

"Thank you," Nikita told Alexei before resuming his seat and turning to Igor. "Has Moscow fulfilled your hopes, Igrushka? Have you found the exalted patronage you seek?" Niki's voice was still dagger-edged.

Again Alexei intervened. "Igor Grigorevich has an exalted patron in my father-in-law. Speaking of whom, you didn't encounter him in Staritsa, did you, Nikita Andreevich?"

"Your father-in-law?" Nikita looked puzzled. "I don't think I know him."

"Fyodor Mikhailovich Koshkin. He visited Staritsa at least once while you were there. Rumor has him staying with Prince Andrei for a week or more."

"What?" Igor interjected. "Why was he there?"

"I've heard the name," Niki said, addressing Alexei. "And if he's the man I'm thinking of, I did see him once or twice. He came on a mission from the court in Moscow. I don't believe we ever spoke. I rode east with Prince Obolensky, on orders from the grand prince, as soon as that diplomatic mission ended. But when we returned a few weeks later, Koshkin was still there, even though the other envoys had gone back to Moscow. He left a few days later. I don't recall exactly when; nor do I know where he went. Does it matter?"

"Not in the least." Alexei glanced at Juliana, and I recalled that Koshkin had abandoned her in Moscow when he fled. They were married then, and the government punished her in his stead. She'd never forgiven him for that, Solomonida told me. It was a major reason, in addition to Felix, that Juliana had insisted on a divorce. "I'm sure he's the right patron for Igor Grigorevich."

"Indeed," Juliana drawled. "My ex-husband has a finger in every pie, from what I hear. And even without him, how could a man of Igor Grigorevich's talents do other than succeed?"

Servants arrived with borscht, which they ladled into bowls and distributed at each place. They put a basket of rye bread at our end of the table and a second in front of Solomonida, who murmured a blessing over the food before passing the basket to Juliana, then Alexei and Felix. "Please, eat," my sister said. "Your presence honors us."

I followed her guidance, offering my basket to Katya, then Niki and Igor before taking a slice for myself and dipping my spoon into the soup. The borscht was thick and tasty, the bread dense and chewy, redolent with the smell of caraway. Yet, focused on the conversation, I noted the mingled flavors without stopping to savor them.

"How tasty," Katya told Igor, who simpered as a girl might do. As if he'd prepared the soup himself, in fact. "I must have your cook give mine the recipe."

Well, he'd stopped gazing dumbstruck at Juliana for a moment. Would Katya realize how absurd this whole situation had become and have second thoughts about my cousin?

Solomonida shifted her conversation with Alexei to include Juliana, and Lord Felix turned to me and asked a question about how I spent my time. His voice was so kind and his manner so charming that for once I didn't feel threatened by a man's interest. I told him about the book

I was reading and my altar cloth. But as I was talking, it occurred to me that if I asked the right questions, I might find a way to include Nikita and thus continue to find out more about him without attracting Igor's attention.

"Tell us about the court in Cracow," I asked Felix. "How does it differ from our own?"

He laughed. "In every way you can imagine, Darya Petrovna. And probably a few that you can't."

I turned to Niki before responding. "Do join in," I said. "You must know more about what goes on at our court than I do." When he nodded, I turned back to Felix. "Is Igor right? Is it common for men and women to eat together there?" I was genuinely curious. Did the Poles not worry that men and women might form attachments that interfered with their families' marital plans? That seemed to be the main concern of every Russian parent. Even husbands obsessed nonstop over the possibility that their wives might fall prey to the wiles of other men.

"And to sing and dance and court one another," Felix said.

Well, that answered my question. Apparently not!

Felix was still talking. "Men and women are not equal in Poland, any more than they are here. But when our king married an Italian a quarter-century ago—do you know about that?—she arrived with a whole train of ladies who weren't accustomed to sit in silence in corners while the men caroused and had fun. A big fuss it caused in the beginning, or so my father says. I'm too young to remember what it was like before. Everyone's used to it now."

I glanced at Juliana, flattering and teasing my besotted cousin. She must fit right in. "Queen Bona," I said in response to Felix's question. "I didn't know *that* about her. But I've heard gossip. She's the power behind King Sigismund's throne. She bullied him into having their son crowned during his lifetime. The Polish nobles hate her. She's a witch and a poisoner."

"Not a witch or a poisoner, although she has that reputation," Felix said. "All the Italian royals do, whether they deserve it or not. Not the power behind Sigismund's throne either. She'd like to be, no doubt, and she did convince him to have their son crowned when the boy was only nine. But Sigismund is a canny old bird; he dislikes confrontation, so he says whatever will shut people up, including Queen Bona. Then he does exactly what he pleases while the rest of them fume and plot. Rather different from your Grand Prince Ivan."

"Ivan's still a child, although he turns thirteen at the end of this month," Nikita said. "He'll come into his full power within a year or two."

"Will he seek a foreign bride?" Felix asked. "Or hold a bride show of the boyars' daughters, as his father did?"

"Your guess is as good as mine." The stiffness of Nikita's pose suggested he knew more than he was saying. "We soldiers in Staritsa don't attend the conclaves of the inner circle."

"I see," Felix said. "Forgive my curiosity."

I studied them, hearing undercurrents I couldn't define.

"Grand Prince Ivan?" Before I could think of a question that might expose those hidden layers, Igor leaped into the conversation like Laika chasing a bone. "Well, he's too young to decide, isn't he? The boyars will handle the negotiations. I have it on good authority that they are indeed considering a Polish princess, although some members of the court favor a bride show, especially the nobles who have eligible daughters."

"Although they also prefer to conduct their deliberations in private." Alexei's voice dripped acid. "I'd have thought my father-in-law, being a master of duplicity, would have taught you that lesson, young man."

Igor's face turned the color of the soup, and he hunched into himself. "I'm sure Igor Grigorevich meant no harm," Katya said, earning a grateful smile from my cousin that made me sigh. Every time I thought our scheme to drive a wedge between them was moving forward, another obstacle appeared.

"Of course not," Solomonida put in. "We know Cousin Igor is the soul of discretion."

"Oh, it's no secret." Lord Felix nodded at Juliana, who dipped her chin in response. I wondered what they knew that I didn't. "Do you think King Sigismund is unaware that he has three unwed daughters, or that an alliance between our nations might secure a peace that would benefit both sides? With your Ivan approaching adulthood, rumors are flying around the painted halls of Wawel Castle like so many bees. But the answer depends, surely, on who stands behind the throne in Moscow." He tipped his head toward Katya. "Some say your Vorontsov clan is rising, to the Shuiskys' discontent. Have you seen evidence of that, Ekaterina Ivanovna?"

Ah, so that's what he wanted to find out: who held the reins at court and whether that group favored a Polish bride. Niki had sidestepped the question, whereas Cousin Igor, eager to make a good impression, confirmed the existence of conflicting views on the council and opened the door to this new question of whose views might prevail. No wonder Alexei snapped at him.

Now Katya was the one in an uncomfortable position, since Felix had asked her directly. I watched, curious to see how she would respond.

Unlike Igor, Katya was no fool. She must have heard Alexei's warning to watch what she said in front of a foreign diplomat loud and clear, because she produced a light laugh worthy of Juliana and a graceful shrug of her shoulders. "I can't say I have, Lord Felix. One of my uncles became a boyar not long ago—as I'm sure you know—but that was a reward for loyal service. The Shuisky princes guard their power as a miser hoards gold. Only the unwise challenge them. Don't you agree, Tsarevich?"

"Without a doubt," Alexei said smoothly. "That's why I prefer to keep my distance from court politics. It's so easy to ride into a ditch before one understands where the boundaries of ambition lie. I applaud your good sense, Ekaterina Ivanovna."

"Don't be rude to our host, Alexei." Juliana rapped the tsarevich's knuckles with her fan. "As Katya said earlier, Igor Grigorevich meant no harm, and indeed he said nothing we hadn't heard already. Shall we talk of something else?"

"Yes." Solomonida gestured to the head servant once more, and his men removed the soup and replaced it with a joint of beef and a large pie which, when they cut it open, revealed flaky pink salmon bathed in sour cream. "Since we're talking about marriage, what of your kings? Did the younger King Sigismund not marry recently? How confusing that he and his father have the same name!"

"Isn't it, though?" Felix said, laughing. "At least you have patronymics to separate your Ivans and Vasilys. We call them Sigismund the Old and Sigismund Augustus, but that's still a tongue twister. And yes, our younger king married Elisabeth of Austria a few months ago."

The servants sliced the beef and the salmon pie and distributed them among us, then placed bowls of buttered noodles and carrots on the table and withdrew to the corners of the room once more. I sampled the beef, which I found tender but too salty for my taste, then focused my attention on the salmon. Its combination of sour cream, mushrooms, and onions smelled and tasted like something angels might eat in heaven. The noodles and carrots added their own delicious flavors to the mix.

"But the couple has already separated," Juliana added. "The young king has fled to Vilnius while his wife travels the country with his parents. To escape the plague, supposedly, but they aren't escaping the plague together. The court gossips are beside themselves with glee."

"Why do the young king and queen dislike each other?" Solomonida signaled to the closest servant, who in response to her quiet command fetched flasks of claret and Rhenish wine, which they poured into glazed cups and distributed among the company—even the women. I sipped my Rhenish cautiously, since I rarely drank alcohol. It had a pleasant, fruity taste: sweet but a little tart, like the apples that grew on our estate.

I glanced at Niki, wondering if he too was thinking about that morning I walked through Katya's orchard and found him again after our decade apart. He looked at me, laughter in his eyes, then lifted his cup in a silent toast and drank. I took it as an avowal, a promise that we might be together someday.

My throat felt dry. I permitted myself a sip of wine, then another, trying to appear calm despite my churning stomach and lips that tingled as I remembered the strength of his hug and the warmth of his cheek when I kissed it.

I turned my head away, hoping no one noticed the blush I felt certain suffused my face and neck. If I shut out everything but the conversation ...

"No one knows," Juliana said. With an effort, I recalled Solomonida's question about why the young Polish queen and her husband had already parted ways. "Elisabeth seems nice enough, although not strong. Very young and inexperienced, which Sigismund Augustus no longer is." She gave the sultriest smile I'd ever seen, and Alexei cleared his throat in an admonitory way.

I could guess that Juliana, whom I knew had once been Sigismund Augustus's mistress, had contributed a good deal to enlarging the young king's experience.

I glanced to my left, where I found Nikita still gazing at me. He saluted me once more with his cup, and a flurry of butterflies took flight in my stomach. So much for my resolution to focus solely on the conversation.

Again he clasped my hand under the table. His touch settled and unsettled me at the same time. I couldn't think of a single word. Instead I stared at him while the conversation flowed around us. And I knew, in my heart of hearts, that I wanted to find out what Juliana did with Felix or Maria with Alexei, and I wanted Niki to be the one to teach me.

"Is it true, Lord Felix," Katya asked in the lull that followed Juliana's provocative statement, "that Cracow is full of Italian musicians? What do they play?"

"Beautiful music—madrigals and ballads," Felix said. "Juliana knows dozens of them by heart and even writes her own, although she didn't bring her lute today. Perhaps she'll sing some of her favorites for you before we leave Moscow."

"Now that's something I'd like to hear." Cousin Igor had stayed remarkably silent since Alexei's rebuke, but the chance to flatter Juliana caused him to rally at last.

"You won't be disappointed," Alexei said, sounding almost friendly. As if he'd forgiven Igor for his careless remark. "She has a lovely voice. If you ask her nicely, she might sing for you in Persian. A language even more beautiful than Italian."

"Persian?" Surprise caused me to blurt out the question without thinking. "How do you know Persian?"

Juliana spread open her fan and held it in such a way that the pattern faced me. Pink roses joined by green stems and leaves rioted against an ivory background. "It's my native language." She tapped the flowers with one long graceful finger. She certainly had the hands of a skilled musician. "I was named after the wild rose, but only Felix calls me that now."

"Were you talking to Laika in Persian?" I asked her. I'd heard a note of sorrow in her voice when she spoke of her past, and I wanted to distract her.

It worked. She laughed softly. "Yes, indeed. Dogs speak all languages, so one might as well use one's own."

"It *is* beautiful," I said. "I would love to hear you sing in Persian—or Italian."

"Then I will make time for that before we return to Poland," Juliana promised.

Solomonida jumped back into the conversation. "Have you visited Italy?"

"Oh, yes," Felix told her. "We go as often as we can, don't we, my love?" From there the conversation veered into a discussion of the various Italian city states and what differentiated one from another. I listened for a while, then resumed my murmured conversation with Nikita. Who knew how long I'd have with him before his tasks called him away? I didn't want to waste a single moment.

When the meal ended, I was sad to rise from the table. Juliana, Felix, and Alexei said their goodbyes, our wishes for Maria's recovery wrapping around them like a cloud. Katya and Nikita soon followed them out, although before leaving he whispered a reminder in my ear of my promise to visit the next morning. Igor walked around, rubbing his hands and repeating "a good day, an excellent day" for quite a while after he bade farewell to his guests, so he must have been happy with the results of his impromptu dinner party despite Nikita's unwanted appearance and the conflict it provoked.

Solomonida and I listened for a while, murmuring the occasional compliment—deserved or otherwise—to keep Igor in a good mood. Then she ordered Mishka to supervise the cleanup, and we withdrew to the sewing room. Although much of the conversation involved everyone, there had been times when the table split into halves. It made sense to talk over what we'd learned.

Although not my exchanges with and thoughts about Nikita. I wanted to savor those in private for a while.

Once we were settled, I dug out my altar cloth, found the brilliant blue thread I needed, and set to work on my peacock. His long tail was not held high but spread in swooping curves that spilled over the branch where he sat, like the bird in the bestiary Father Job had found for me.

I started the conversation with the most obvious point, to deflect attention from the things I wanted to conceal. "Katya certainly is determined. Did you see how our cousin ignored her at first? I thought it would discourage her, but I saw no signs that it did."

"They're a pair, aren't they?" Solomonida leaned back against the window frame and sighed. "She seems intent on winning him no matter what. And he's a knock-in-the-cradle, if you ask me. To spend the whole afternoon yearning for a woman who's involved with another man when Katya lives next door, has the powerful relatives he claims to need, and has expressed an interest in him? I don't want him to marry, it's true, so I suppose it's good that he's a dolt. Still, I shudder to think how his mind works."

"Who's to say it does work?" I asked. "But I agree, he's a complete ninny. And so is she, for that matter. If it didn't mean that she would take over our house, I'd throw them at each other on the grounds that they'd spare the rest of us."

Solomonida burst out laughing at that, and I moved toward my real interest. "What did Juliana want from him, anyway?"

"Entertainment, perhaps," Solomonida said in a dismissive tone. "She may be beautiful, but she has no morals to speak of. She likes nothing better than being the center of male attention."

I'd thought the same myself when Juliana first arrived at our house, but after watching her on and off throughout dinner, I'd drawn a different conclusion. "I get the impression she loves Lord Felix, whether she announces it to the world or not. Did you hear the sadness in her voice when she said that only he uses her birth name? And it's because she has no morals to speak of that I think she had another reason for flirting with Cousin Igor. I can't imagine a woman with her experience at seduction wasting her time on our cousin. What did she want from him if not information?"

"You have a point." Solomonida wrinkled her nose, considering. "But without knowing what brought her and Lord Felix here, it's hard to say what she might have wrung out of Igor that would be useful. She spent a lot of time praising his cleverness, I recall. Asking him about the various clans, expressing an interest in his search for a bride, wishing him luck in finding a suitable patron—nothing unusual."

Alliances and brides again. That matched my observations of Lord Felix. It made sense that King Sigismund the Old would take an interest in conflicts within the inner circle of a foreign government, whether he wanted to marry one of his daughters to our grand prince or not. "Why did she stop, then?"

"He bored her to tears, I assume," Solomonida said. "His mooning over her probably amused her at first, not least because it upset Katya, but as a rule Juliana doesn't put up with fools for long—which, now that I think of it, is the best evidence yet that she did have something to gain from their conversation."

"Yes," I said. "Our cousin played right into her hands. And he was so smitten he forgot about his plan to impress Tsarevich Alexei, so I didn't see much progress there. Alexei rebuked Igor twice. And he emphasized more than once that Igor had a patron in Koshkin, implying he didn't need another."

My sister shrugged her shoulders up to her ears, then released them. "Well, I didn't expect Igrushka to impress Alexei, did you? They're a study in opposites. Alexei came to please Maria. He liked Nikita better, I thought—which is no surprise."

Hmm. I respected Alexei, the little I'd seen of him, but I didn't take him at face value any more than I did Felix or Juliana. "What makes you think Alexei came only to please Maria?"

Solomonida straightened her spine and stared at me. "Why else would he put up with our Duckling?"

It was my turn to shrug. "I'm not sure," I admitted. "He sat closer to you than to me. But remember when he asked about his father-in-law's visit to Staritsa? He brushed it off as unimportant, but I had the sense it wasn't an accident. He didn't ask any other casual questions about Koshkin's plans? Or what Koshkin expects in return for his help? Maria has mentioned that last point at least twice, so I know it concerns them."

"Come to think of it, he did ask what results Igor had seen from his connection with Koshkin." Solomonida gazed at the courtyard, visible through the half-open shutter. Although the meal had lasted much of the afternoon, the sky was still light outside. "There may have been more. I didn't hear everything they said, because I did talk to Lord Felix some of the time, although he seemed awfully taken with you."

She grinned at me as she reached the end, but I'd already realized she was teasing me. "When he could woo you away from Niki," she added, "who is even more taken with you. Will he offer for you, do you think? That would solve a lot of problems."

I wanted to tell her he already had. Yet for some reason I didn't. That lackluster proposal, perhaps. Niki had seemed much more interested in me today, but would it last? And if it did ... "You think Igor would accept Nikita's offer for my hand?"

Solomonida shook her head. "Not in a thousand moons, I'm afraid."

"Precisely," I said. "But you didn't tell me. What did Igor say when Alexei asked about his father-in-law?"

"That he's met many powerful men but would appreciate whatever assistance Alexei chose to give. Alexei didn't take the bait, though. He nodded and moved on to something else. So you're probably right. If he didn't come to please Maria, he wanted to see how deeply Koshkin has his claws into Igor and get a hint as to why Koshkin's wasting his time on our cousin."

I giggled, remembering. "Only to discover that Juliana has hers in twice as deep, and with half the effort."

My sister laughed too, her face relaxing for the first time since she entered the room. "And what of you? Did you overhear anything? Between Lord Felix and Nikita, you were surrounded by adoring males. You'll make Juliana jealous!"

"I have faith in Lord Felix," I said in the lightest tone I could manage. "I'm sure he can convince Juliana that she's his one true love."

"But what were the three of you talking about?"

"All sorts of things," I told her. "Life in Poland. Life in Staritsa. How they compare. I'd say that Lord Felix is trying to figure out whether the boyars will seek a Polish bride and whether those rumors of the Vorontsovs' ascendancy are true. That's what he asked about directly. Nikita politely deflected him by pretending ignorance, and so did Katya, but Igor would have blabbed everything he knew if Alexei hadn't shut him up."

"And what of Lord Felix himself? Does he appeal to you?"

What an odd question! But if she thought me smitten with Lord Felix, perhaps she would stop pressing me about my conversations with Niki. "As Maria told us, Felix is charming and immensely well educated. You heard him chatting about music and poetry. But a few hours' acquaintance doesn't reveal much, and I'm not stupid enough to challenge Juliana for her man."

Solomonida nodded at that. "I'm glad to hear you talking sense for once. So we may keep you out of that women's monastery after all?"

My cheeks grew hot, and I released an earth-shattering sigh. "So long as Cousin Igor doesn't follow through on his threat to select my husband. I'd end up with someone as horrid as your Semyon." It was the first time in the nine years since she'd returned home after her state-ordered divorce that I'd ever said outright what I thought of Semyon Kolychev.

"God forbid." She changed the subject, as I'd anticipated she would. "And what of Nikita? Did he have anything interesting to say when he wasn't gazing at you as if he wanted to spirit you away to a distant island where he could have you all to himself?"

So much for her not asking for details. "Staritsa, as I told you," I said. "The princess there runs an embroidery workshop. He's glad to be away from invading Tatars, but he says Staritsa seems rather neglected these days. The young prince is a handful and wants Niki to attend him while he's hunting with his cousin the grand prince next week. They're following that journey with a pilgrimage to various monasteries and hermitages, as I understand. Including Holy Trinity, where I've asked him to search for Father Hilarion. Which, if he succeeds, may in itself solve our problems with Igor."

"Really?" She opened her eyes wide and gave me a delighted smile. "That hideous party may have justified its existence after all."

"Was it hideous?" I said. "I haven't enjoyed myself so much in years. The food was lovely. I had fun talking to the guests—except Igrushka himself, and he can't help being silly. And the house sparkled, even though it seems unlikely that Igor will get the results he wants despite forcing the two of us to work like slaves. Not to mention what he put the poor servants through!"

Solomonida gave a rueful laugh. "Absurd, wasn't it? So much effort, and what came of it?"

"Absurd," I said. But in fact, I thought a great deal had come of it. And I hoped for even better results tomorrow.

Chapter Ten

I AWOKE EARLY THE NEXT MORNING, COBWEBS OF DIMLY remembered dreams clinging to my brain. In them Cousin Igor, cackling like an unholy fool, chased Solomonida and me around the dining area while Nikita barred his way with an ax. Juliana reclined languorously on one cushioned window seat and Tsarevich Alexei watched with magisterial calm from another, while Katya ran after Igor, on occasion catching a sleeve or fold of his robe.

Only when I sat up and clutched my befuddled head did I realize how accurately, in its own weird way, my nightmare had captured the events of yesterday's party. I doubted we would ever again equal that bizarre combination of hostility, humor, and frustrated passion.

I staggered to the window and stared through the panes. The sky was clear but gray; dawn must have broken not long before. I could go back to sleep, but the wisps of dream clung to my brain, and I didn't want to risk another onslaught of nightmare. It was far too early for my promised talk with Niki. And it was Sunday.

I decided to attend church, even though it was also too early for a proper communion service. If I went to the Cathedral of the Virgin's Nativity, next to the women's monastery of the same name, I could attend morning prayers. By the time they ended, I'd have settled my restless soul and could stop by to chat with Niki without worrying that I'd hauled him out of slumber hours before he'd intended to face the day.

I dressed in a white linen blouse and red sarafan, the kind the maids wore on holidays and therefore unlikely to attract undue attention once I left the estate. Unlike my regular robes, the sleeveless sarafan had straps that lay across my shoulders and attached to a tight band above my breasts, then fell loose to my ankles. I covered the shirt with a loose summer jacket to ward off the morning chill, then combed my hair and wound it into a single braid, tied with a red ribbon. I put on a triangular headdress, also simple, also red. With luck, anyone who saw me would think me a merchant's daughter rather than a noblewoman slipping away from her estate without a male escort. I'd press the first female servant I saw into escorting me, and that should safeguard my reputation and my virtue. Two city girls, walking together, wouldn't turn a single head.

On my way out, I remembered I wanted to show Nikita Anfim Fadeyev's map. Now would be a good time to collect it, before my cousin woke up and wondered what took me to Fadeyev's office on a Sunday. I collected the key from Mishka, slipped into the room, and retrieved the map from its pile, then rolled it into a scroll and dropped it into the bag I carried. A quick check of the other papers revealed that, except for the map, the stack now contained only household accounts and recipes—a detail that reinforced my belief that the lists were important in some way.

I returned the key to Mishka, then kept a wary eye out for Laika as I left the office for the courtyard. When I didn't see her, I concluded she must be in Igor's rooms. Good. Much as I loved her, I didn't want her following me to church or even announcing my presence with a series of barks.

I caught my maid Alya leaving the house and ordered her to come with me. We set off right away and reached the cathedral long before the bells ceased to ring. Other than the holy sisters, the number of worshippers was small. I grasped Alya's elbow, and we made our way to the table where the memorial candles were laid out. I left a donation sufficient for both of us, and we bowed before the icons, lighting our offerings and praying for those we had lost. Then I found us a spot close enough to the iconostasis that I could admire it while also studying the frescoes that covered every available surface.

We'd no sooner taken our places than the priest's deep voice rumbled from the back of the cathedral. I clasped my hands in prayer and inhaled the rich, complex scent emitted by the swinging censer as he passed. In the dark interior lit only by flickering candles reflected in gold vestments and icon covers, surrounded by heavenly music and unearthly aromas, carried away on a magic carpet of sound so familiar I could intone the responses without needing to think, I felt transported to another world. A better world, where my petty concerns and complaints had no place. The various discomforts of yesterday and the terrors created by my mind during sleep rolled off my shoulders as rain pours from a branch after a spring shower. My ridiculous cousin, my fears of his intentions, the wisps of my nightmare seeped away.

I don't know how long I stood there, experiencing the service rather than attending to it, before a hand touched my elbow. I opened my eyes to stare in astonishment at Anfim Fadeyev in his Sunday best, a frail elderly man at his side who from the similarity of their features could only be his father.

"I didn't mistake," Anfim said with a dip of his head. "It *is* Darya Petrovna?"

Alya stepped forward then, and he smiled at her with genuine warmth. "Yes, it must be," he said. "For Alya's here too. How are you, Alya?" She crossed her palms over her chest and bowed as if being recognized embarrassed her.

"Well enough, Sir," she said. Even in the dim candlelight I could tell she was blushing. The poor girl was shyer than I was!

Watching them, I realized I hadn't encountered this aspect of Anfim before. I'd often caught hints of amusement on his face, in his eyes, but this was Anfim in control of the situation, Anfim expressing kindness in an attempt to set someone else at ease.

It was like seeing a painting from a new angle. "How surprising to run into you here," I said. "Do you visit the cathedral often? And is this your father?"

"Yes to both questions." Anfim placed a hand on the old man's elbow and drew him forward. "We live close by, so it's convenient for these early services, which my father prefers because fewer people attend them. At this point in his life, crowds unsettle him. Permit me to introduce him. Darya Petrovna, this is Father Faddei." He indicated his companion with his free hand. That was when I recalled Anfim mentioning that he was the son of a priest.

I bowed to Father Faddei and greeted him while Anfim introduced us in turn. "Darya Petrovna Sheremeteva, Papa, and her maid Alya. Darya Petrovna is the younger daughter at the house where I work for Igor Grigorevich."

The long string of names seemed to puzzle the old man. "Pyotr Sheremetev." His brow creased. "Did he not fall ill?"

"He did, Father," I said. "Seven years ago. He died this spring, may he rest in peace. Did you know him?"

"May his memory be eternal." The lines deepened on Father Faddei's forehead as he considered my question. "I met him at his cousin Bezzubtsev's house when I served as priest there," he said after a while. "More than once. But I don't recall Sheremetev having daughters, only a son."

I flinched. I couldn't help myself. Father Faddei seemed to be as muddled as Papa had become in his last years, so I doubted he meant to inflict pain, but that unthinking dismissal of my existence and Solomonida's flicked an old injury into raw, burning life. I found it easy to believe that my father had not mentioned his daughters. Papa adored his only son, spending every moment with Lev from the time my half-brother grew big enough to leave his mother's side.

I saw Anfim watching me. The sympathy on his face told me he understood too well.

"My brother is also with God," I said, with more brusqueness than I'd intended or wanted. "He died at the age of ten, and his mother not long afterward. We grieved them deeply. Especially my father."

"But you are here," Anfim said gently, bypassing the usual expression of condolence. "And from what I hear, you sacrificed a great deal for your father. He must have appreciated the care you gave him during his final illness."

"I hope so." I fought off the sense of aloneness that memories of my stepbrother's and Xenia's deaths inevitably provoked, not least because I saw little of Solomonida during that tragic time. Anna was a baby then, and after losing three boys, one after the other, Solomonida refused to expose her daughter to the slightest hint of infection. I didn't blame her, of course, but with her and Papa both absent for different reasons, I'd felt wholly abandoned by those I loved.

I shared none of that with Anfim and his father. Instead I said, "Alya and I should be getting home." The service was not half-done, but the onslaught of unpleasant memories had destroyed my sense of a connection with the divine. The cries of "Lord, have mercy," repeated forty times, echoed in my brain. I needed to get out of there before the tears started.

Anfim extended his arm, crooked at the elbow. "Come with me, and I'll escort you. A boyar's daughter shouldn't take her chances in the streets. I need to walk my father back to our house first, but as I mentioned, it's a short distance."

I opened my mouth to refuse. We didn't need an escort. With Alya or one of her fellow maids, I visited the cathedral every few months, and no one ever accosted us in the streets, either coming or going.

Anfim's face crinkled in a smile warmer than any I'd seen from him before. "You can meet my children," he said. "My Lara will let you see her embroidery. She's seven, and she misses her mother a good deal. She would like to talk with a woman, I think. You will have little in common with my Tolya, I fear—he is quite the rambunctious boy—but rather adorable at four, if I say so myself."

Hearing the note of pride in his voice, I realized he might genuinely want to show off his children. Even so, I hesitated. My interest in him had been a fleeting thing, quite inappropriate. I should step carefully, lest I leave the wrong impression.

Yet the loss of Xenia and Lev was fresh in my mind. If I could help a child facing a similar grief...

Anfim had treated me with nothing but courtesy and respect. He must understand the social barrier between us—probably better than I, since he was older and more experienced. And Alya wouldn't leave my side.

"Very well," I said. "For your daughter's sake, because I haven't forgotten how I felt when my stepmother died. And for a short time. Alya and I must get home before anyone wakes up and wonders where we went."

We walked slowly down the road that led from the cathedral to Anfim's house on St. Nicholas Street. He suggested that I hold his left arm while he supported his father on the other side, but I refused. It would make for an awkward threesome, and I had no desire to either attract attention or encourage greater closeness, both of which I could avoid by walking alongside my maid.

It worked: no one looked at us twice. We still moved no faster than a group of snails, because Father Faddei set the pace on his unsteady legs, but that didn't bother me a bit. It was early morning on a beautiful late summer day, clear and sunny with a soft breeze and no great heat, and I took full advantage of the opportunity to study the houses as I passed them.

Close to the cathedral the wooden planks that lined the streets remained in good repair, but as we reached the end of Nativity Lane and turned right toward the merchants' quarter ruts showed amid the dust, marking the passage of wagons during the recent rain. Mud didn't suck at our shoes today, but I could imagine how impassable the street must have seemed to Anfim after those day-long thunderstorms that had kept my sister, my niece, and me inside. I was impressed that he'd shown up for work at all.

As we headed down the hill, away from the fortress, the houses became smaller and plainer. Ahead of us, most of the dwellings had the appearance of peasant huts: one-story wooden buildings with two wings opening off a central entryway. But Anfim stopped before we reached that point, at a simple home that although also made of wood—like almost every other house in Moscow, including ours—boasted two stories, a separate building that I guessed held a kitchen and food storage, and some rather pretty decorations on the cornices and around the shutters. Nothing as elaborate as our urban estate but a modest home indicating a family of real if limited means.

I waited with Alya while Anfim ushered his father up the stairs and through a door that appeared to be the main entry to the house. I guessed that the first floor held storage rooms, or perhaps a study.

Once the two men disappeared from sight, I signaled the maid with a brief nod and followed them, stopping at the entrance to ensure I didn't crash into anyone. The room beyond was small and plain, with lines of pegs holding outdoor gear and boots lined up against the wall. Off to the left, another, brighter room beckoned.

Anfim helped me out of my summer jacket and hung it up, then did the same for Alya before extending his right hand toward the open doorway to that brighter space. "Please, Darya Petrovna. Welcome."

I dipped my head toward him and passed through, wondering what I would find. He had already surprised me. The house, although not above his station, was solid and well maintained. Either clerks' salaries were higher than I'd been led to believe or he had some other source of income. Probably the latter—as also indicated by his clothes, which were, as always, good-quality without drawing attention to themselves or imitating aristocratic dress in any obvious way.

The room I entered exhibited a similar style. Discreetly but comfortably furnished, it went beyond the usual benches and table into the land of warm and welcoming. A chair with arms and a seat cushion stood near a beehive stove that emitted no heat at this time of year. Father Faddei doddered over to the chair and settled himself on the cushion with a loud, relieved sigh.

Cushions also adorned the benches that lined the walls, and a carpet woven in broad bands of bright colors that made me think of paint covered the floor. At the far side of the room, where light poured in through an open shutter, I saw a sturdy table just large enough for one person to sit behind. On a shelf above, a pair of carved wooden bears held several books in place, with a sheaf of documents off to one side. An ink well and a collection of quills sat next to the sheaf, but the table itself was bare.

I wondered if the sheaf of papers included the genealogy and other documents that I'd found in Anfim's office, but with no way to find out and no desire to upset my host and his family, I chose not to ask.

Two children occupied the room. A small, pretty girl with long blonde hair, blue eyes like her father, and a snub nose, wearing a simple white dress and bent over an embroidery frame, reminded me of Anna five or six years ago—although Solomonida would have fixed the child's disintegrating plait, wisps radiating out at every twist. The sight wrung my heart, because it underlined the reality that this household had no mother. A younger boy with light brown hair and hazel eyes was racing around the room when I walked in. He skidded to a stop and stared at Alya and me for a moment openmouthed before shouting, "Papa, Grandpa, watch me. I'm a bogatyr, and I've slain a dragon."

"That's not a dragon, silly," the girl said. "It's a cushion, and it can't fight back."

"Can too." The little boy stuck out his tongue. "It was a *fierce* dragon, and I killed it."

He looked so earnest that I had to struggle not to laugh. Again I remembered my little brother Lev, who would not have appreciated being laughed at—especially when a mighty cushion beast lay slain at his feet.

"Enough." Anfim's arm brushed mine as he passed me. "Don't you see we have guests? They came to make your acquaintance. So show them you know how to behave, both of you."

His tone had an immediate effect. I controlled my amusement as the girl dropped her embroidery, jumped to her feet, pressed her hands together, and bowed. Her brother—because who else could the boy be?—didn't respond as fast or with the same level of skill, but he jerked his shoulders forward and kicked something under the chair at the same time. I wondered what mischief he was hiding, but I had no intention of tattling to his father (who had probably seen the kick as well). Instead I returned their greetings. Out of the corner of my eye I saw Alya do the same.

"That's better," Anfim said. "This is Darya Petrovna, children, and her maid Alya." He waved at the children. "My daughter, Lara, and her brother, Tolya." I saw his mouth twitch at the corners. "Who has slain a dragon. He must have known that we would be entertaining a boyar's daughter."

I responded in kind. "How exciting! I've always wanted to meet a real-life bogatyr. The ones in the fairy tales never seem very approachable—always rushing off to commit heroic deeds just as supper is about to start." I smiled at Lara. "And what are you stitching, Lara? May I see?"

Without a word, she held out the frame, and I took it. Small, neat satin stitches formed a central flower in shades of red, set against a black background. But the green stems and leaves extending from the flower were much less even. I looked at Anfim. My thumb pressed against the flower's sun-yellow center, and I turned the cloth in such a way that only he could see which part of the pattern I indicated. "This is your wife's work?" He gave a quick dip of his chin, as if, like me, he sought to spare his daughter's feelings.

"She was a fine needlewoman." I held out a hand to Lara. "And you will be, too." I pointed to the straggling stems. "I see how careful you are, how hard you're trying to keep the stitches even. But this pattern is difficult for someone who's still a beginner. May I show you an easier one? I taught it to my niece Anna when she was your age, and you should see her now! She stitches almost as well as your mama did."

Lara hesitated. Something flickered in her eyes that I didn't know her well enough to read: sadness or concern or fear—of disloyalty to her mama, perhaps? But then she took my hand and let me guide her to the bench where the bag of embroidery supplies lay. I rummaged through the bag until I found a simple piece of white linen and two threads—one red, the other blue. "Can you do a cross-stitch?" I asked her.

She bit her lip and didn't answer, so I showed her, using the red thread and making the crosses big enough for a child to master. "See? You bring the needle up here, then down, then go across and come up again. Make them large at first, so you can get the two sides of the *x* the same size." I gave her the cloth and the thread. "You try it. Take your time and don't worry about the pattern. Once you have the stitch down, you can make flowers and triangles and diamonds—even a bear or a person or a horse."

Lara's eyes grew as round as the center of her mother's embroidered flower. "A horse?"

"Absolutely a horse." I looked over her head, where her brother was staring at us while trying to pretend he had no interest in anything so girly as embroidery. I gave him my best mischievous smile. "Or a dragon."

He cheered. "Yes, Lara, stitch me a dragon, and I'll fight it!" He demonstrated, lunging with an outstretched arm that in his mind must hold a sword.

"You will not!" Lara clutched her linen and thread to her chest. I laughed and pushed the sewing down onto her lap.

"He won't," I told her. "Your papa would have something to say about that. You practice, and I'll ask Papa to bring you to our house one day." I glanced at Anfim then. "Would you consider it? Perhaps even tomorrow, when you come to work? Anna should be back from Tsarevna Maria's by then. She would love to sew with your daughter, and it would be company for them both. Anna would be like a big sister for her."

"Me too!" Tolya said.

"Well, that depends on your papa," I told him. "We'd love to see you, and we have plenty of dragons for you to slay, as well as a friendly dog, but we need to find some boys for you to play with. I'll ask around and see which of the servants have sons your age."

Again I looked at Anfim. "He would like the horses, I think. My brother always did. And he could run with Laika; the grooms would love that, because she exhausts them without even trying. But we should set it up so you aren't stuck keeping him nearby while you're working."

"You're very kind," Anfim said. "I doubt Igor Grigorevich wants noisy boys running around his estate." He made a face at his son that I found quite endearing, and Tolya must have agreed, because he giggled and seemed quite unabashed. "But if you do find him some playmates or a groom willing to put up with him, I'll gladly bring them both. There's little for them to do around here except get into trouble." He gave me a small bow. "In the meantime, shall I escort you home?"

I rose, giving Lara an encouraging pat on the shoulder. "Soon, then," I said to her. "Bring your stitching when you come to see us."

Anfim fetched our outer layers. He handed Alya her jacket and held mine out. As I slipped my arms through the holes, his father left his chair and shambled over to me. Focused on the children, I'd given little thought to Father Faddei since I entered the room.

He stared at me, his brow furrowed and his eyes blurry with confusion. "Is this the woman you're in love with, Anfim?" he asked.

And while I stared at him, stunned—had I misread the situation after all?—Anfim answered his father. "No," he said in the curtest tone I'd ever heard him use. I turned my gaze on him and saw flushed cheeks, clenched hands, and clear signs of embarrassment. "That's long over. I told you, Papa. This is Darya Petrovna Sheremeteva. She lives in the house where I work, and I'm escorting her home. Right now, in fact."

He turned on his heel and marched to the door. I followed, thinking about what his father had said, but I didn't ask Anfim for clarification. It wasn't my business, for starters, and if I *had* misjudged his reasons for inviting me to his house, I might not like the answer. "That's long over," he'd told his father, but his reaction suggested otherwise. And why had Father Faddei thought I was the one?

For the same reason Papa confused me with my stepmother in his final days, most likely. Still, I kept a close watch on Anfim the whole way home and didn't say much. He maintained his usual respectful demeanor and for most of the short walk stared straight ahead, from which I concluded with relief that while he might well be in love with someone, it probably wasn't me. But just in case, I decided to keep a healthy distance between us from now on.

By entering through the first-floor storerooms and climbing the servants' stairs, I managed to avoid attracting the notice of anyone who might look amiss at my early morning excursion—Cousin Igor, mostly. I reached my own bedchamber without incident, changed my sarafan and blouse for the pink robe I'd worn to Maria's two days ago, and added the page of notes I'd taken from Father Job's desk to the map I'd placed in a cloth bag. I wanted to show them both to Nikita and see what he made of them.

My visit to the cathedral—despite the detour to meet Anfim's children—had taken less time than I thought. It was still no more than mid-morning when I gathered my things and descended the stairs. Not so early that I feared waking Katya or Nikita, but still a good two hours before the midday church service would begin.

I thought of taking Laika with me, but as far as I could tell, she was still in Igor's rooms. So I set off alone through the kitchen gardens and orchard, not dawdling today as I had the last time but moving with purpose, eager to see Niki again. Memories of our conversation last night set my insides tingling.

I encountered him, seated on a fallen tree halfway through the Vorontsovs' orchard, even before I reached their house. He alternated between staring at a dovecote set up not far from the fence that ringed the main house and sketching with broad strokes on a paper he held, and I saw no sign that he heard me approach. The grass under my feet muffled my footsteps and even the usual swish of silk as lingering moisture from last night's drizzle wet my hem. I stopped to study him.

Today his clothes were dark and plain, trousers tucked into his boots and topped with a simple high-necked tunic.

His light hair gleamed in the late August sun, and the set of his mouth, the expression on his face—so far as I could judge from his profile—was serious. He didn't look as if he planned to attend church, more like a man intent on riding or some military pursuit.

"Niki?" I said, quietly, so as not to startle him.

He leaped to his feet and whirled to face me, dropping the charcoal, hands raised as if ready for combat. I took two steps back. So much for not startling him, although his reaction shocked me even more.

When he saw who'd spoken, he relaxed. His face creased in the warm smile with which he usually greeted me. "Dashenka," he said. "I'm sorry. Old habits die hard." He crossed the small distance between us and kissed my cheek.

"Old habits?" I didn't understand. Habits from boyhood? I didn't recall him being so jumpy then. On the contrary, he'd struck me as the calm center of our group.

War and disgrace had changed him, I supposed.

"From my time fighting the Tatars," he said, confirming my unspoken thought. "Surprises then were seldom good ones." He took my hand and looked around. "Let's find a place to sit. That log won't do. It will stain your lovely robe."

"It's a beautiful day. Let's walk instead." I hesitated before adding, "You seemed so serious when I arrived. What were you thinking about?"

He sighed. "Whether I should have done things differently. Whether I could have, given the impossibility of foreseeing that the choices available then would later block my path. It's not important. How was your morning?"

I watched him closely as he stooped to pick up the charcoal. I again had the sense he was hiding his face from me, lest I catch sight of an emotion he preferred to conceal. But his words, and even more the intensity of his reaction, spoke of remorse or regret.

Blocked his path to what: the estate, a post, a patron, a bride? Those sounded important to me, especially the first and the last. I understood that he didn't want to tell me, though, because if he did, he wouldn't speak in generalities.

So I refrained from prying. "I had a lovely morning, thank you. May I see what you're drawing?"

Pink flushed his cheeks, but he held out the paper. I glanced down, expecting to see the dovecote, and gasped at the outline of a woman's face, her single braid extending from under a headdress that closely resembled the one I had worn the evening before. I recognized my own features—wide eyes, high cheekbones, mouth curved in a slight smile that contradicted the diffident set of my shoulders. I looked wary but hopeful.

"It's beautiful," I said, still gazing at the drawing. Far lovelier than me, in fact. My stomach tightened as I realized he must care for me to produce such a work of art. "Thank you. How do you manage to convey a whole personality with no more than a dozen strokes? It's astonishing."

When I glanced at him, he shrugged. "It needs a lot of work. I was drawing from memory. So as not to forget, you know, what made the evening so pleasant."

Now it was my turn to blush. While I struggled to find words that could convey my appreciation without sounding girlish, he took the paper from my hand, rolled it into a scroll, and tucked it into his belt. "Now that you're here, I can improve it."

"Let's do that later." I pulled the map from my bag and held it out to him. "As I promised, I brought a couple of things to show you. This one's just for fun. I thought you'd like to see it. I have to return it soon."

He took the paper from me and unrolled it. "Huh," he said, then stared at the map as if he couldn't believe his eyes. "Where did you find this? I haven't seen it in ages."

"Ages? When did you see it before?"

He turned to stand at my side and pointed to the lower right corner, where I had noticed without understanding the image of a white bear against the background of a red shield. "My family's emblem. I drew this map for your father when I was ... seventeen, eighteen? I don't remember exactly. Before I went to Staritsa the first time."

I'd wondered who the artist could be. I'd even named him as the only person I knew with the ability to produce this map. Yet his admission was the last thing I expected to hear. Because of the dog. "*You* drew it?" I touched the romping animal in the center. "But that's Laika."

"Yes, someone added her. Did a good job of it too. But there"—he pointed to the priest I'd thought was Father Job—"is your missing Father Hilarion. And your stepmother's embroidery frame." He touched the picture that marked the women's quarters, then identified the rest of the symbols one by one. "Do you really have to return it? I'd love to keep it. I had no idea your father still had it."

"I do, I'm afraid. For today, I mean. I can get it back later. I took it without permission from Anfim Fadeyev's office, you see. Igor's clerk. I don't think you've met him yet."

"So what?" Nikita had been staring at the map, touching this symbol and that, but he raised his head long enough to look at me as he asked this question. "You're the younger mistress of the house. If you want to take something from Fadeyev's office, that's your right."

"I know." I waved an impatient hand. "But I'd rather keep him off-guard. There's something odd about whatever Igor has him doing. Anfim works from dawn to dusk, and not only on household accounts. I went in there one night and found a list of women's names—probably potential brides for Igor, although Tsarevna Maria says most of them are far too high-ranking to accept him—and another page comparing an Anna and a Ekaterina, with no last name. A Sophia, too, but whoever made the list crossed out her name with great violence, and I have no idea why. Last time I checked, both papers were gone. It's very confusing."

"Anna, Ekaterina, and Sophia." Nikita rolled the names on his tongue as if tasting them. "That's curious."

Now it was my turn to stare at him nonplussed. "Why? Lots of women have those names."

"Because, my adorable innocent, those are the names of King Sigismund the Old's daughters. The youngest is Katarzyna, not Ekaterina, but that's just the Polish form of the name. And that's what got our dear Duckling in trouble with his longed-for patron last night, remember? Igrushka blurted out that the boyars were considering a Polish match for Grand Prince Ivan."

"And Lord Felix confirmed that rumors are circulating in Poland about such a match." I heard the excitement in my voice and sought to moderate it. "What's wrong with Sophia?"

"Nothing, so far as I know. Nothing that would cause someone to scratch out her name with great force, I mean, except that she's twenty-six and Grand Prince Ivan not quite thirteen. It would be like marrying your mother. If the plan founders—and it's a long shot at best, because King Sigismund makes no bones about wanting his daughters to remain Catholic, whereas any grand princess must be Orthodox—the age gap will be one reason. Even Katarzyna is already four years older than the grand prince. He wouldn't have much chance of ruling his own household with her, either." Nikita rerolled the map and handed it to me. "But it's useful information and most clever of you to discover it. I'm quite sure our cousin shouldn't have that document in his house."

"No. If that's what is, I would guess you're right. I wonder why he *does* have it. Fadeyev worked for the government until a few weeks ago, so he may have found it there. I can't imagine why he would bring it to our place, though." A thought occurred to me, and I voiced it before scrutinizing it. "Unless that's what Fyodor Koshkin gets in return for helping Igor. A place to store information he wants kept secret for a while."

"Koshkin's a slippery character, from what I hear," Niki said. "He might try to incriminate our Igrushka by giving him documents he shouldn't have access to, but I don't see what he gains from a Polish marriage for the grand prince."

"Influence." I tapped a percussive rhythm against a nearby tree trunk while working out the possibilities. "A Polish bride wouldn't arrive with a crowd of male relatives the way a Russian woman would. If he can manipulate the grand prince's choice, he might wangle his way into a position of power." That sparked another thought. "Although he has an unmarried daughter. Wedding her to the sovereign would increase his reach even more."

"It's too soon for him to think about making his daughter grand princess," Niki objected. "The diplomats have yet to deliver their proposal. The inner circle at court will wait for Sigismund's answer before making plans for a bride show—if they can even agree to hold one. From what Tsarevich Alexei told me last night, tensions are running high between the Shuisky princes and the Vorontsov clan."

Finding no answer to that, I nodded before dropping the map back into the bag and pulling out the page of notes. I gave it to Niki, then placed my hand on his arm. "This is what I most wanted you to see. Let's walk again. But grip that piece of paper hard. It may hold the key to our future."

We strolled in the orchard, away from the main house. The sun warmed my face, and I heard the hum of the bees who made their hives in the trees. The cherry blossoms had long since turned to fruit, and even the apples were forming as September pressed in on us, but the fall plants grew fast in the kitchen gardens, giving the bees plenty of nectar. Niki and I made our way to a stone cistern at the far edge of the property, where we could lean side by side while I showed him the marks that Father Job had spelled out for me and the entwined NA and D that revealed my father's intentions, at least at the time when those notes were made.

"It's not enough, you understand," I said as he exclaimed over the paper, tracing the letters as I had done. "Igor has a will dated December 1537, and this has no date at all—no clear provisions even. But if you can find Father Hilarion, he may know what happened, whether there is a document somewhere that proves your claim."

Nikita threw both arms around me and kissed me full on the lips. "Dashenka, I love you," he said. "Even if I never secure my right to the estate, I'll always know your father cared about me. Believe me, that means more than a piece of property."

He grinned as he let me go, and I stared at him. "You love me?" I asked after a while.

"Of course." He stroked my cheek. "Why else would I want to marry you? Do you not love me?"

I would have given anything to stay cool and composed, but the warmth in my cheeks had nothing to do with the sunshine. "For as long as I can remember."

"Then shall we wed, as your father wished?" He leaned forward as if he meant to kiss me again, but I stopped him with a hand on his shoulder.

"It's not that simple," I said. "I can't marry without Igor's consent. Even if you control the estate, as head of the clan he still has the right to forbid our marriage. But if we can produce the will and the letter Papa sent you, and those notes, I think we could use that written proof of intent to get Tsarevich Alexei or someone else to twist our cousin's arm."

He eyed me keenly. "And would you agree to marry me if I did those things, or are you politely putting me off?"

"I would like to know you better first," I admitted. "Eleven years is a long time to spend apart. But it's true that I loved you when we were children, so I'm not refusing."

He stepped back and held up the note. "Then I'll look for Father Hilarion. You don't mind if I keep this one? I'll need to show it to him if I do find him."

I took his retreat as expressing respect for my desire to learn more about him and suppressed a stubborn urge to ask for another kiss. A maiden should not entertain such thoughts. "I brought it for that purpose. It belongs to Father Job, and he authorized my lending it to you. He agrees that we need to find Father Hilarion if we're ever going to learn the truth. And he confirmed that Hilarion did go first to

Holy Trinity, although he can't swear that Hilarion stayed there. Nor does he know what his monastic name might be." I touched the edge of the faded paper where it poked between his fingers and thumb. "Take good care of it, as so far it's the only evidence we have that confirms the letter Papa sent you, naming you as his heir. You still have the letter, I assume."

"Naturally." He folded the paper back into its square and tucked it in his belt, then pulled out his sketch once more. "Enough business. You want to know me better, and I'd like to hear more about you. Let's find a dry place where you can sit comfortably, and I'll draw while you talk to me—about this marvelous altar cloth of yours, for example. Didn't you tell me something about peacocks in every corner?"

Chapter Eleven

MY MOMENTOUS MORNING GAVE WAY TO A PEACEFUL Sunday afternoon and evening. Igor had left the estate by the time I returned from Katya's house, and after we attended Father Job's midday service, Solomonida and I spent the rest of the day reading and sewing and in quiet conversation, mostly about domestic matters. Laika joined us, but the grooms had exercised her well, so she too was content to sprawl at our feet. After the tension that had pervaded the house since our cousin first heard about Alexei's planned visit, such serenity made for a pleasant change.

The next day, I slept late—making up for my tossing and turning the previous night, I assumed. When I at last entered the sewing room, I found a small crowd already present. Not only Solomonida but Maria and Juliana clustered in a group at one side of the room. Anna and Lyuba occupied the window seat with Anfim's daughter, Lara, perched between them looking rather baffled. Only when I saw Lara did I recall that I'd asked her father to bring her to visit us today. Clearly he'd welcomed the invitation. I understood then what Father Job had tried to tell me about my own father: that even the kindest of men might not quite know what to do with a young daughter.

Maria and Juliana rose from the bench where they'd been sitting on either side of my sister and came to greet me. "You're better." I put both hands on Maria's shoulders and kissed her cheeks. "I'm so glad. We missed you on Saturday."

"It was quite a party, I hear," Maria said. "I was sorry to stay home, but yes, I'm better now. And Anna never got sick, so I brought her back to you. Who is your littlest guest?"

"The daughter of Cousin Igor's clerk, Anfim Fadeyev. Her name is Lara Anfimova, but you probably know that already. I invited her yesterday after I ran into her father at the early morning service." I greeted Juliana, too, then went to say hello to the three girls.

"I'm sorry I wasn't here when you arrived." I squeezed Lara's hand as I dropped a kiss on her cheek. "Was it scary to find so many people you'd never met before?"

She nodded without speaking, her blue eyes round, and Anna gave her a hug. "I fixed her braid and promised to help her practice cross-stitch, but Lyuba doesn't like to sew, so we'll do that later."

So that explained why Lara's plait looked much neater this morning. "You would make a wonderful big sister, Anna," I said. "That was thoughtful of you. Thank you."

I tugged the closest of our two chairs over so that I could talk to the three women while monitoring Lara. As I watched, Anna pulled her dolls from a bag that lay on the floor next to her embroidery supplies and offered one to each of her guests.

"You ran into Anfim Fadeyev at church?" Solomonida blushed as she said his name. "Why didn't you mention it yesterday?"

The blush pulled me up short. If I didn't know better, I'd believe my sister was attracted to our cousin's clerk. Which didn't in itself surprise me, given that I'd been briefly attracted to him myself. But he was not much more suitable as a husband for Solomonida than for me, despite the undeserved shame of her divorce. I hoped my sister was not setting herself up for further heartbreak. She had suffered enough.

"I woke at dawn," I said, trying to make a light and lively tale of it. "That dinner gave me nightmares—you don't know what you missed, Maria!—and I didn't want to go back to sleep in case they started again. So I dressed and went to morning service. Alya came with me. Anfim Fadeyev was there with his father, and he offered to escort us home. But his father is elderly and rather frail, so Anfim asked us to accompany them back to their house first. I agreed after he promised it wouldn't delay us much. Didn't he tell you when he brought Lara here?"

Solomonida shook her head. Maria said, "You let him escort you. You like him, then."

I glanced at Lara, who'd moved to the floor and sat in a circle with Anna and Lyuba. The doll held Lara's full attention. She touched its eyes and cheeks, probed its elaborate robes with a delicate finger. I doubted she would overhear what I said.

"I like him well enough," I told Maria. "There's no reason not to. He's pleasant and competent and respectful. But I went with him because of the children. They lost their mother a year ago, and I remembered how alone I felt when my stepmother died." I pointed at Lara, who paid no attention. "That's why I invited her here, so she could spend time with women and a girl a few years older than she is. I meant to tell Solomonida to expect her, but I forgot. As soon as I got back, I went to Katya's house. I'd promised the day before to meet Nikita there."

I wondered if Maria would press me further about Anfim, although I had no more to tell her. She didn't, though. Instead she accepted the bait I'd thrown at the end. "Ah yes, Nikita," Maria said. "Alexei told me the two of you got along well at the party."

"Indeed they did." Juliana wasn't carrying her fan today, but she plucked a piece of fabric off a nearby table and waved it before her face with the same languid air. "The heat rolled off them in waves. So you slipped away to meet him in the garden, Darya?"

The three of them laughed at me, but I didn't care. "I did," I said. "But not for dalliance." Although he kissed me ... "Father Job found some notes indicating that Niki is the man Papa intended to inherit our estate and marry me—which is what Niki himself believes. He told me he'd received a letter to that effect, written on Papa's behalf. But this new source goes back at least three years. It's not conclusive, because Igor has the signed and sealed will, but it does suggest that Papa planned for a long time to make Nikita his heir. And that makes sense, because he barely tolerated Igor."

Maria's eyes gleamed, and she leaned forward, as if she couldn't contain her excitement. "So he *is* a fraud, your cousin."

I shrugged. "It seems so."

"And how long have you been hiding this?" Solomonida demanded. "So many secrets! Don't you trust us?"

"Of course I trust you," I said, indignant myself at her tone. "I showed the notes to Niki first because they affect him most. The only person who knows the whole truth is Father Hilarion."

"And Nikita will look for him?" Solomonida continued to frown.

"Yes. I told you that after the dinner."

At this news, my sister stopped scowling. "Juliana's right, then. It's Nikita who has your eye. Good. He's a better choice than Anfim Fadeyev."

How she got there from Father Hilarion escaped me, but I decided to let it go rather than question my reprieve. I glanced at Lara, wondering if she'd react to her father's name, but she seemed preoccupied with the other girls and the dolls. "Of course he is," I said as quietly as possible. "I like Anfim, but he's not for me. Besides, he's in love with someone else." I hoped my sister heard the implicit warning there.

"How do you know that?" Solomonida said, her voice sharp.

I hated to deliver bad news, but I plowed on. Better that she hear it now, from me, than later from Anfim himself. "His father mentioned it. He's forgetful, like Papa, so not very reliable. Anfim denied it, but I could tell he was embarrassed, so I think it's true."

She produced an elaborate shrug, although I saw her bite her lip. "So much the better. You won't do anything foolish."

Nor will you!

I smothered the thought. No reason to upset her further. "I didn't plan to do anything foolish in the first place," I said instead.

"And Nikita?" Maria asked. "Would you marry him?"

You'd think I'd have an answer to that question by now, but in fact I felt as uncertain as when Father Job posed it a week ago. "Probably. I've known him a long time, although his inconstancy troubles me. The bigger question is whether Igor would agree."

"Oh, I suspect we could pressure him into it." Maria sounded as if she'd leap at the chance. "From what Alexei said, your cousin is very eager to please, so long as the right person is making the recommendation."

I hoped she was right.

"We'll hold you to that," Solomonida said with an approving nod. "Speaking of Igor, did you see Katya? Did she comment on Igrushka's idiotic behavior the other night?"

"No, I didn't see her," I said, welcoming the change of topic. "I met Nikita in the orchard, so we talked there. Then I came home. I certainly hope she's having second thoughts about Igrushka as a potential husband. What do you think, Juliana? Will he ever stop making cow eyes at you?"

They started laughing again, and the conversation veered off as Solomonida and Juliana compared notes about the dinner party and regaled Maria with stories about Igor's infatuation. I took the opportunity to go over and check on the three girls, still playing with Anna's dolls.

But as I turned to rejoin Solomonida and her guests, Juliana intercepted me. With a hand on my elbow, she drew me aside and pulled me down to sit next to her on the window seat. "Last time we met, you mentioned joining a convent—if only as a last resort. Today you seem to be open to the idea of marrying your cousin Nikita, which to me seems by far the better choice. Why do you think Igor Grigorevich will forbid it? Your Nikita is of noble birth."

"Yes, he is," I told her. "But you must have noticed that Igor dislikes Niki every bit as much as Niki dislikes him. And marrying me would give Niki access to this estate. Igor will stop at nothing to prevent that. To be honest, I don't think taking monastic vows *is* the right choice for me. But I'd rather do that than accept Igor's candidate for my hand."

"Yes, I understand now." Juliana sighed. "Well, keep in mind that joining a convent would put an end to any hope of wedding Nikita. If your bumptious cousin picks someone obnoxious for you, which I agree is more than likely, we women will think up a plan. Spirit you away, if nothing else comes to mind. I'm sure the Polish court would love you. You'd have King Sigismund Augustus wrapped around your little finger in no time."

While I gasped, stunned into silence by that last outrageous suggestion, she laughed. "You should see your face. I was joking, silly girl. You're far too virginal and proper for dear Sigismund. He already has a wife with those qualities—and look how he treats her."

I was still searching for an appropriate response when she patted my hand. "Don't despair. I'll talk to Maria, and we'll come up with a solution." For an instant, her eyes sparkled and her expression became one of pure mischief. "If need be, I can keep your cousin so befuddled he won't be able to tell one bridegroom from another."

"Then you'd get me in trouble with Lord Felix." I couldn't suppress a giggle. Having already watched her at work for an entire afternoon, I had no doubt she could dangle Igrushka from her fingertips for as long as she wanted. She'd enjoy every minute, too.

"Never a bit," she said. "Felix knows I adore him. And that I wouldn't waste my time on a fool like your cousin. I do have standards."

Solomonida interrupted any response I might have made. "What are you two conspiring about?" She waved a hand in Maria's direction. "It's time to go home, Maria says."

A chorus of protests came from the circle surrounding Anna's dolls.

"Yes, Lyuba," Maria said, her voice kindly but firm. "You spent the last three days with Anna, and she promised to help Lara with her sewing. We told Alexander and Dosya's nursemaid that we'd be back in an hour, remember? So we must go." Alexander and Dosya were Maria's children, aged five and three.

Lyuba groaned, but she gave Lara a brief embrace and Anna a warmer one before standing and coming over to hug Solomonida and me. We said our farewells, and in less time than I would have believed possible, Maria and Juliana were on their way with a reluctant Lyuba in tow. Invitations to visit them floated on the air as they left.

When the three of them were gone, Anna gathered up the dolls and pulled out her sewing bag, and I went to help Lara with her cross-stitch.

The next week was magical. Every day I met Nikita in the orchard or, if rain threatened, in one of the outbuildings at Katya's house or ours. We discussed paintings and music, songs and poetry, historical tales and the world beyond Moscow. He brought his book of miniatures, and we marveled together at the bright colors, the elaborate costumes, the perfectly detailed people, buildings, and animals surrounded by writing in an alphabet neither of us could read that was itself a work of art. I stitched while he sketched me; we exchanged favorite stories and sometimes sat in a comfortable silence. I shared secret thoughts I'd never confided in anyone, even Solomonida, and in return he told me the details of his disgrace and his exile, the despair he'd felt when first his father died in battle, then his mother of grief before Niki could convince his commander to release him long enough to console her. How my father's summons and death revived those bitter memories. As the shadows of mystery thinned between us, my love and desire for him grew.

I told him of Maria's promise to help us marry, if need be, and Niki kissed the back of my hand. "Are you warming to the idea, love?" he asked. "That's the best news I've heard yet."

I laughed. "I'm getting used to having you nearby," I teased. In truth, each day we spent together enhanced the appeal of marriage. The partnership described by Father Job became ever more real in my mind.

"So much the better." He reached out and placed a finger under my chin, tilting my head at an angle. "Hold that pose for a moment."

I couldn't see him, but the scratching of the charcoal told me he was sketching another portrait. He must have created at least a dozen by now. But when I pestered him to explain why he needed more, he insisted he could never have too many. Every mood, every time of day or cast of light, he said, was different.

Laika accompanied our walks from time to time, but most often we strolled among the trees, grasses, and wildflowers. Each moment was precious, precisely because we knew it couldn't last. Any day, Nikita would be called back into service, and then we wouldn't see each other for weeks, perhaps months.

Laika wasn't with us the morning when he told me he had to report to the Kremlin that afternoon. I didn't waste time arguing; I could guess what he would say in response. Instead I clasped his hands in both of mine. We were standing at the edge of the Vorontsov estate, right where their orchard joined ours, a boundary marked by a simple fence and the gate I would walk through once I said my goodbyes. I had my back against an apple tree, and Nikita stood not two steps away. No one else, man or beast, was in sight.

"I wish you could stay. I'll miss you so much," I told him. I wanted to ask him something else, but I wasn't sure that I dared. Suppose he refused or thought me a wanton for asking? He hadn't attempted to kiss me since I first showed him Father Hilarion's notes, although I often had the impression he would like to. And after a week of heart-to-heart talks, I wanted that too. We had rebuilt our childhood friendship and expanded it. If I didn't find out how a kiss would feel with him, would I ever know?

"I'll miss you too, Dashenka," he said in a soft, husky voice. He leaned toward me, and almost without thinking I did the same. I had nothing to lose.

I have everything to lose.

I would not be a coward. Harnessing my courage, I let the words tumble from my lips. "Then won't you kiss me goodbye?" I closed my eyes, so I wouldn't have to see rejection on his face. Suppose he'd changed his mind? "I know I asked for more time, but now I want to find out what it's like."

"Then look at me." He tipped my head back. I opened my eyes to find him gazing at me as if he couldn't quite believe what I'd said. Then he put an arm around my waist, pulled me close, and kissed me gently on the lips. I relaxed, letting him push me against the tree trunk and wrapping my arms around his neck.

At first the kiss was soft, fleeting. I knew he was holding himself back, in deference to my maiden state. But as the kiss went on, it became more passionate, less controlled. For long moments, I didn't think, caught up in the strength of his arms, the pressure of his mouth, the sensation of his body against mine.

Then he pulled away, enough to establish some distance between us. He was breathing hard, and so was I. I said the first thing that came into my head. "I love you, Niki."

He kissed my forehead. "I love you too, sweetheart. If only ..."

"If only what?" A flash of fear ran through me. Did he still have secrets, despite our idyllic week?

He shook his head. "Nothing, sweetheart. Sometimes my past still haunts me. Will you marry me, then?"

I stared at him, troubled. His past again. The something he should have done that blocked his path. I knew without asking that was what he meant. Yet having come so far, I couldn't bear to stop. "I will," I said. "If we can find a way."

"I'll find one," he promised. "Starting with tracking down your Father Hilarion." He kissed me once more and said, as I had earlier, "I wish I could stay, but I can't."

"I know." I hugged him, hard, then let go. I watched him walk away through the trees, wishing that the power of my gaze could work miracles and bring him back to me. Even when I could no longer see him, I stood there, fighting tears.

At last I turned to go home. I passed through the gate and stopped dead on the other side.

Igor stood at the edge of the kitchen garden, Laika at his side, glaring at me.

For a wild moment, I considered turning tail, picking up my skirts, and racing for the Vorontsovs' house as fast as I could go. Even if Nikita had left by the time I reached it, Katya and her brother would bar the gates against Igor until he calmed down.

He bent and released Laika, who dashed toward me at top speed, and I abandoned that notion. Although the dog was as playful and frisky as ever, I had no hope of outpacing her great, loping stride, hampered as I was by ankle-length skirts. She'd probably think it a great game to chase me and knock me down. Although I knew she'd never hurt me on purpose, a tumble would be undignified at best. So, gritting my teeth in anticipation of a battle to come, I made my way toward the house as slowly as I dared. When Laika caught up to me, I petted and praised her so that she would accompany me rather than tear off in another direction. So far, so good: she escorted me back toward her master, whose temper didn't appear to have cooled one bit.

Can I get past him and up to the third floor without a confrontation?

Alas, no. From the way his hands twitched as I approached, I guessed he was already fighting the temptation to shake me. If I ran, he might well grab me halfway—or storm the women's quarters, where he had as much right to enter as he did anywhere else in the house, whatever Solomonida and I pretended to ourselves when we were alone.

So if I couldn't escape, I had to hope that I could talk him down from his mountain of fury.

He stood, hands planted on his hips and a sneer plastered on his face, more irate than I'd imagined possible, waiting for me to reach him. "So, Dashka," he snarled as I came close, "how long have you been playing the whore with that reprobate Nikita?"

"What are you talking about?" I demanded. "He's no more a reprobate than you are. And don't call me Dashka. I'm a boyar's daughter!" It was the most insulting form of my name—not even the familiar Dasha or the Dashenka that Niki used, which expressed affection, but a pejorative reserved for peasants, servants, criminals, and loose women. I had no doubt Igor had used it deliberately.

He took several steps forward until he stood so close that my nose brushed his chest. As I moved away, he grabbed my left arm with one hand and stroked my right cheek with the other. I might have mistaken the gesture for a caress if I hadn't felt the sharp edge of his thumbnail against my face. "Yes, you are, Dashka. So what were you doing sneaking out of the house to meet a man? And don't pretend otherwise, because I saw with my own eyes what the two of you were doing. As if flirting with him throughout my dinner party the Saturday before last wasn't enough. You're supposed to be protecting your purity for a husband. The husband I select for you, no less! Not kissing a traitor in the neighbors' orchard. So the question is what should I do with *you*, cousin, since you've decided to act like a slut?"

I stomped on his toes and hauled my arm out of his grip. "How dare you? I did not sneak out of the house, and I am not a slut. Nor is Nikita a traitor. He's the man Papa chose for me. He wants to marry me, and I intend to marry him."

"Marry Nikita?" Igor stopped pawing my cheek and glared at me. Spittle formed at the corners of his mouth. "You are *not* going to marry Nikita. I don't care what your father wanted, demented old bat that he became. *I'm* the head of the clan now. You'll wed the man *I* choose for you, and you will not roam around the woods fornicating with any man who sweet-talks you."

"I didn't fornicate, you beast! It was a kiss. One kiss with the bridegroom my *father* chose for me." My feet tingled with the urge to kick him.

"A likely story. And even if you're telling the truth, it was one kiss with a man who's not your husband. From now on, you don't leave the house unless I give you permission. You're my most valuable asset, damn you. I've no intention of letting you debase your worth." Igor leaned forward, his face almost touching mine. "And if I find out you're not a virgin, you'll have to pray God to help you, because you can be sure I won't."

I blinked furiously as tears pricked my eyes. "Of course I'm a virgin, you idiot. And I won't marry any man you select. I don't care who he is. I'll take monastic vows first."

He turned so red in the face that I thought he might topple over, as old men sometimes did from an excess of rage. He grabbed me, turned me toward the house, and released me long enough to shove me in the back. "You are *not* going to take monastic vows. You're going to marry the first man I can find to take you, and smile as you accept him. Defy me, and as the head of this household I'll take a whip to you until you agree. Now go to the third floor. Stay out of my sight for the rest of the day. You want to be treated like a boyar's daughter, then act like one. I saw you, you know. You weren't resisting his touch; you were leaning into it, enjoying it. You might as well be a floozy from the stews."

Horrified, I stopped in my tracks. I *had* asked Niki to kiss me. I'd envied Maria and Juliana and wanted to find out more about what they did with the men who loved them. I'd experienced a brief interest in Anfim Fadeyev, too, although I hadn't entertained the notion of kissing him. Was Igor right? *Was* I too free with my affections?

Unable to muster any response in my own defense, I pulled myself together enough to stalk into the house, heading for the women's quarters on the third floor as my cousin had ordered. I didn't know whether he meant his threat to take a whip to me if I disobeyed him, but I had no desire to find out. And his insults had unsettled me, to boot. The whole way up the stairs, I struggled with the question of whether he'd told me something I needed to hear, even if I didn't like it.

However hard I racked my brains, though, I couldn't convince myself that Igor was right. It was true that I'd yearned for Niki's kiss and enjoyed it when it came, but he wanted to marry me—and had my father's approval to do just that. We were as good as betrothed, despite the absence of a formal marriage contract. Was that so bad? Katya had made no secret of her attraction to Igor, and he wasn't calling her a slut. And Igor himself was besotted with Juliana, who'd not only swatted him hither and yon like a cat tormenting a mouse but by all accounts had capped a spectacular career as the mistress of powerful men by falling in love and living with Felix without benefit of marriage. So Igrushka was in no position to call me names.

Which didn't answer the question of how I should respond. And I did need a plan. I refused to stand by and do nothing while my horrid cousin treated me any way that suited him. If he stopped me from going to the Vorontsovs', I'd beg Katya to visit me. I'd ask her to send word to Nikita, and I'd beg him to take me away from this dreadful place. As a last resort, I would write to Mother Elena at the New Maiden's Convent and beg her to accept a novice whose virtue was under siege from her family. I would do everything in my power to foil Cousin Igor's schemes. And if thoughts could kill, he'd be lying deader than Tolya's dragon at my feet.

Papa, how could you give him such power over us?

I'd reached the top step when I ran into my sister. Her eyes widened at the sight of me. "Mother of God, Darya, what *have* you been doing? You have scarlet circles on both cheeks! Did you paint your face, or do you want to punch someone?"

I was not in the mood for this. "Igor," I growled. "I want to punch Igor. He caught me walking in the Vorontsovs' orchard with Niki and had a fit. You wouldn't believe ..." I stopped mid-sentence, unable to speak the words Igor had flung at me. "Niki was called back into service. He's leaving, Solomonida. For how long, we don't know. He kissed me goodbye, and Igor saw it." A huge lump in my throat threatened to choke me, but I took a deep breath and forced myself to finish. "The things Igor called me don't merit repeating. Let's say he assumed that it wasn't the first time. Or the most we'd done."

"He's a villain and a swine." Solomonida sniffed as if the mere mention of Igor smelled bad. "But Darya, what did you expect? Papa would have had a fit too, if he caught you kissing someone, even Nikita."

"It's not what you think. I agreed to marry him." I was too angry and disappointed and scared by Igor's threats to admit that my sister might have a point. I wanted her to leave me alone so I could go to my room and weep. "But Igor swears it will never happen. He's threatened to marry me off to the first man he can find. He told me I couldn't even take monastic vows without his say-so, although I don't think that's true. He'll forbid it if he can, though. I hate him, the monster."

"You can't take vows if you're in love with Nikita. That would be wrong in every sense," my sister said in a matter-of-fact voice that made me want to smack her as well as Igor, but then she put both arms around me and hugged me. "Poor Darya, what a day you've had. You do love Niki, don't you?"

I nodded, sniffing to control the waterfall gathering behind my eyes.

"Then don't worry," she said, compassionate now rather than matter-of-fact. "I'm sure he loves you too. He'll come back."

"One day," I said bitterly. That was unfair, but the loss of both Niki and the dream that we could find a way to be together had my world crumbling around my ears. The temptation to sob into my sister's shoulder was almost more than I could withstand, and if there was one thing I couldn't bear, it was for word somehow to reach my horrible cousin that he'd reduced me to a jellied mess on the staircase.

I had to get out of here, now. I returned Solomonida's hug, so she'd know I wasn't angry with her, then pulled away. "I've been ordered to the women's quarters. And to stay out of our cousin's sight. Which I will do with pleasure. If I never set eyes on Igrushka the Duckling again, it will be too soon."

I pushed past her and stumbled, half-blinded by my tears, through the sewing room, past her chamber and Anna's until I reached my own. If Solomonida replied, I didn't hear what she said.

Chapter Twelve

MY QUARREL WITH IGOR TOOK PLACE ON A MONDAY. ON the Tuesday, I put my plan into action. First I sent Alya to Katya's house with a plea that she visit me as soon as possible. While I waited, I wrote a letter to Nikita, pouring out the story of Igor's threats against us and asking him for help. I intended to give it to Katya for her brother to deliver, since he knew how to reach Niki on his journey and I didn't.

Then I looked at the letter—a blotchy, ragged mess because even recalling my run-in with Igor yesterday reduced me to tears—and tore it up. What was wrong with me? I couldn't ask Niki to walk out on his service assignment for my sake. If he agreed, he might end up back in exile, which would kill any hope of a marriage between us. But even if that didn't happen, we needed him to go to the Holy Trinity Monastery and find Father Hilarion, then persuade the priest to reveal what he knew about Papa's intentions. As a woman, I couldn't travel to the monastery on my own, never mind enter it when I got there. Niki had to take care of that task for both of us, and I had to find a way to resist our horrid Duckling until he did.

I didn't dwell on the possibility that Niki might refuse to leave his prince to help me. If I didn't ask, I'd never have to find out.

As I reached that point in my rather confused deliberations, Katya entered the room in a swirl of silk. I tossed my mangled letter into the tiled stove, running full blast to stave off a chilly wind that had blown in overnight, sinking the temperatures and hinting at the winter snows to come.

There would have been no kissing in the orchard today. I tried to convince myself I'd have been better off if that had been true yesterday.

I didn't succeed.

As I went to greet my visitor, she stripped off a knee-length coat of wool trimmed in black fox fur and dropped it on the nearest bench, then rubbed her hands together before hugging me. "Brr," she said. "That stove of yours is welcome. Who'd believe it's only the first of September? I pity our menfolk, riding to hounds in this weather."

"Dreadful, isn't it?" I opened the door long enough to call for Alya, who came running. "Fetch us some hot cider, Alya, and some of that gingerbread the cook made yesterday." When she left, I came back into the room and sat at the far end of the bench nearest the stove, indicating that Katya should take the closer place. "You're the one who walked here in this chill," I said when she demurred. "Or did you bring your carriage?"

She shivered. "No, I walked. It's a nice, brisk day, but I'll be glad of that cider." She settled herself on the bench and looked at me. "We haven't seen much of you recently. What's going on?"

I blushed. I'd spent more time on her grounds than my own since our dinner party, but little of it visiting her. "I'm in trouble," I said. I explained about Nikita and the kiss. "Igor's demanding I not leave the house unless I have his permission. I expect he'll forget after a while, but he was so furious yesterday I don't dare defy him the very next day." I shuddered, remembering his threat to whip me like a disobedient servant.

My words trailed off as Alya arrived with a tray holding a jug of hot cider, a basket of gingerbread squares, a pair of pottery mugs glazed in blue, and two linen napkins. At my direction, she placed the tray between Katya and me on the bench, then left the room. I poured cider into a mug and gave it to Katya, then passed her a napkin and held out the basket of gingerbread.

She took a piece, bit into it, and sighed with pleasure. "Heaven. Your cook is a treasure."

I poured and sipped cider, took a gingerbread square but didn't raise it to my mouth. Only then did I realize she hadn't responded to my tale of woe. Instead she gazed at me, a thoughtful expression on her face. "What?" I asked. "Have you nothing to say?"

She took another bite of gingerbread. I was ready to shake her by the time she set the rest of the cake aside on its napkin. Cradling the cup of cider in her hands, she said, "Forget Nikita."

"What!" Hadn't she heard a word I'd said?

"Forget him." Katya shrugged, as if she weren't hammering nails into my happiness with every careless word. "He's not for you. From what Dmitry tells me, Nikita's not free to marry anyone. His father promised him to another girl years ago. They didn't marry because of Prince

Andrei's capture and Nikita's disgrace, but now that the government has forgiven him, I'm sure they will. If he told you otherwise, that proves you shouldn't trust him. Your cousin will find you a good husband. He's the one who has your best interests at heart."

My jaw dropped. Whatever I'd thought she might say, it wasn't that.

"You're wrong," I said. "That's impossible. Papa and Niki's father were best friends. If Niki were promised elsewhere, Papa would have known. He wouldn't have ..." I stopped mid-sentence, shocked into silence.

So much had slipped from Papa's mind in the last years of his life. When he decided to send that letter promising his estate to Nikita, could he have forgotten Niki's prior commitment? Was *that* why Niki delayed for so long before responding? The old choice that still haunted him, blocking his path ... to me?

He'd insisted the past wasn't important, when he must know that nothing doomed our chances more than a previous contract. Next to that, my cousin's objections faded into insignificance. Yet Niki had told Dmitry of that old betrothal even as he hid the truth from me. The whole thing was like a knotted thread. I could barely make sense of it, let alone absorb it.

I thought of the last week, the comfort I'd felt in Niki's presence, the depth of my attraction and, I would have sworn, his. I recalled the secrets we'd shared, the laughter, the kiss, and I didn't believe he would lie to me. But according to Katya, he *had* lied, and in the worst way possible. He'd made promises he couldn't keep, knowing that whatever path he chose would dishonor himself and the woman whose trust he betrayed.

No, not woman—women, because whoever that other girl was, she bore no more guilt for this situation than I did. "Who is she?" I stammered.

Katya shrugged. "Dmitry didn't say. Does it matter?"

It didn't, of course. Whoever she was, she had rights, and I had none.

Just the memory of Niki's kiss.

I felt sick. No wonder he kissed me the way he did. He must have guessed he wouldn't see me again.

Katya patted my hand where it trembled on my mug. "Dmitry heard it from Nikita himself," she repeated. "I'm sorry, Darya, but you can't pin your hopes on him. Igor will find you a good husband who will take care of you and give you children."

"Igor will not," I said through gritted teeth. "Whatever happens, you can count on that."

I stopped there. I believed she'd told me the truth about Nikita, as she understood it, but her decision to take Igor's side convinced me to watch what I shared with her, in case she blabbed everything I said to my beast of a cousin. I toyed with the idea of asking her to leave. But precisely because she wanted Igor for herself, I thought that under the right circumstances I had a chance of using her against him, to convince any husband he chose that I was not a suitable bride. That had to become my top priority now: to prevent Igor from marrying me off to one of his cronies. Alone in my room, I could pine for Nikita, knowing it would do me no good.

"You're hurt," she said in a sorrowful voice that I hoped was sincere. "I understand. But remember, you have to marry someday. The sooner, the better. Don't turn away every offer only because it comes through your cousin."

Since I didn't agree and had no wish to get caught up in a fruitless argument, I chose not to answer. Instead, I finished my cider, ate the gingerbread without tasting it, asked if she wanted more, and when she refused, cleaned my fingers on the napkin and moved the tray to one side. Then I picked up my altar cloth and threaded a needle. While she talked, I'd start the next peacock. "So tell me what you've been doing this last week. Has my cousin shown any more interest in you?"

"He hasn't approached my father, if that's what you mean." Katya flicked a completed peacock with her thumb. "Beautiful. Has he mentioned me to you?"

"We're not on speaking terms," I reminded her.

"He hasn't been hanging around that Polish woman, I hope?"

"No." I might as well tell her the truth. It was unlikely to change anything. "She comes here with Maria, but they don't talk to Igor. Tell me what else you've been doing."

She launched into a series of tales about women she'd visited and information she'd gathered. I listened and nodded and made encouraging noises as I stitched the third peacock's body and planned the sweep of its extended tail.

Yet in the depths of my heart I was keening. How could I have been so wrong about Nikita? I'd believed his declarations of love, not even considering the possibility that he'd made the same declarations to others. I'd asked *him* to kiss *me*. What young man would not take advantage of such an easy conquest?

Then I knew what I had to do, no matter what anyone said.

I must write to Mother Elena. Tonight.

That evening after supper, I summoned Mishka the steward and ordered him to bring me paper, a sharpened quill pen, and an ink well. When he complied, I took the objects from him and told him to send a groom before the church bells rang again. Then I swore him to secrecy, let him go, and sat by my dressing table, where I'd swept the usual brush and comb and jewelry box to one side while waiting for him.

Soon I was composing a letter laying out my woes to Mother Elena. I started by reminding her that we had met nine years ago, when I visited the Convent of the Veil in Suzdal with my sister.

You were mother superior there, I wrote. *We came with my niece, Anna, at the command of Solomonida's husband. Even then I felt called to adopt the monastic cowl. You urged me to wait. I was sixteen—under my father's direction, you told me, too young to decide.*

I blinked back another onslaught of tears. So long ago, such different circumstances. How had my life come to this: threatened by a cousin not three years older than myself, convinced he was my guardian and my master?

More important, how could I make Mother Elena understand?

But I am a woman now, I went on. *Twenty-five, an orphan, unwed and disinterested in marriage.* If I couldn't have Nikita, that is. *I yearn for a life of chastity, poverty, and obedience—a life devoted to God's service. I am under siege from a cousin who seeks only to increase his worldly influence and power by selling me to whichever man he believes can best advance his own interests. He threatens me with violence because I seek to devote myself to God, because I wish to preserve my bodily purity as the Scriptures command. Will you not give me succor from this Belial whom the temporal world has inflicted on me by accepting me into service as your novice?*

I await your answer in eagerness and humility,

Darya Petrovna Sheremeteva

I read the letter over. Had I said too much, too little?

No, this was right. Truthful (well, almost), firm. Mother Elena must see that Igor and his schemes imperiled both my physical body and my immortal soul. She would intervene. She *must* intervene, because an abbess cannot leave a fellow Christian wandering in the wilderness of sin when that fellow Christian pleads for salvation.

As I sprinkled sand from the small pot that Mishka had supplied without being asked and blew it from the paper, I heard a tentative knock on the door. I rose to answer it, rather than risk letting Solomonida or Anna, if they were the ones knocking, see my letter.

A groom stood on the other side. The one I'd asked for. The bells rang as I pulled him into the room. I ignored the befuddled expression on his face when he realized this was my bedchamber. Instead I rolled the letter, tied it, and handed it to him.

"Take it to the New Maiden's Convent," I ordered. "Insist that this document be given to Mother Elena in person, then wait for a reply. When you receive one, bring it straight to me."

He looked around, shuffling his feet. "Here?" His voice was a squeak.

"If need be," I said impatiently. "But I will probably be in the sewing room. Bring it there. You needn't tell anyone where you went."

"What should I say if they ask?" He still looked nervous. I couldn't blame him. If Igor could threaten me the way he had, imagine how he terrorized the servants.

"Hmm." I considered that question. I hated to lie—still more to ask someone to lie on my behalf, knowing that he might be punished for fulfilling the task I'd given him—but what alternative did I have?

Then I recalled that most people on the estate couldn't read, including Igor, so barring some extraordinary misfortune I would be safe from discovery. I picked up a treasured icon from the corner table, wrapped it in a silk scarf, and placed icon and scarf in a leather bag. "Tell them the truth. That I sent a gift and a letter to the holy sisters, and they wrote to thank me." It was still not the whole truth, but any remaining guilt would lie on my shoulders.

Relief brought a smile to his face. He dipped his head, tucked the letter inside his shirt, took the bag I held out, and fled the room.

Watching him go, I struggled to keep my fears under control. Cousin Igor would have a fit if he discovered what I had in mind, and I didn't like to think of how he might react. Merely hearing that I'd received a manservant in my bedchamber would convince my cousin that I was the loose woman he'd called me.

But between them, Nikita and Cousin Igor had left me with few options. I couldn't let my cousin force me into any marriage that suited him or meekly tolerate his vengeance if I refused. If my scheme worked, I would confess my sins and fulfill whatever penance the priest set me, even if it meant not taking communion or being banned from the church for years.

For the moment, though, this was war. I'd win or I'd lose. And I was determined to win.

By the time the groom returned, I had joined Solomonida and Anna in the sewing room, taking care to stay well out of my cousin's way. It was difficult not to share with them what I'd done, especially when I knew that if I succeeded I'd be leaving them soon. Only the lump in my throat whenever I recalled Igor's scarlet face, his sneer and the ominous note in his voice, kept me from confiding my secret hopes and fears to Solomonida—that and the desire to spare Anna, who at twelve seemed too young to bear such adult burdens.

Of course, that meant I also couldn't share how Katya had dashed my hopes. But I wasn't ready to reveal Nikita's dishonesty in any case. Even the thought brought a lump to my throat. I'd tell Solomonida soon, I promised myself, when I had the answer to my letter. And when Anna was not in the room. In the meantime, I stitched diligently on my peacock, contributed meaningless pleasantries to the conversation whenever I could, and tried to avoid alerting my sister to my abysmal state of mind.

The groom didn't come himself to deliver the letter. Instead, Mishka arrived unannounced, bearing a tray of refreshments that he deposited on a side table before bending to whisper in my ear. "Lady, I placed the paper you requested in your chamber. You'll find it folded under the pillow."

"Thank you." I tried to act as if his words had no special meaning for me, but I saw my sister's face tense and a slight frown crease her brow.

"It's nothing," I told them. "I sent an icon to Mother Elena, asking her to pray for me." I had to reveal that much, because Solomonida would notice the missing icon the next time she entered my room. "Because of Igrushka plotting my marriage."

When my sister nodded, I gazed at the steward. "It reached her safely, Mishka?"

"Indeed, Lady. The holy sister sends her thanks. I had her letter delivered to your room."

I gave my best unconcerned shrug. "You did well." I waved him away. "I will read it later." He bowed his assent and left.

"That was a good thought, sister." Solomonida threaded a needle. "I hope Mother Elena's prayers prove efficacious. What did Katya have to say? You two talked for quite a long time."

"Oh, many things," I said. "You know Katya. She spent the last week collecting gossip, so she had plenty to share."

Some of which broke my heart, which was why I would soon be a novice at the New Maiden's Convent.

And I will never see Nikita again. Can I go through with it? Really?

Their faces relaxed, which went some way toward relieving my guilt at not telling them my plans. To distract them, I said, "When shall we ask Lara to return? Anna was so kind to her, teaching her to sew. Lara misses her mother, so it would be good to invite her again. I suppose it's only fair to include her brother as well. He's four, so not too old to play here in the women's quarters, but he's very much a boy. He'll wreak havoc on our cushions, slaying them as dragons! Can we find some playmates for him?"

Anna looked alarmed, but Solomonida laughed. "I'll ask Mishka. Quite a few of the servants have young sons. It will be good to hear boys running and shouting again. And they can play with Laika. She'll love the attention—and the exercise." She stopped long enough to sigh. "Although I suppose I'll have to check with Cousin Igor first. He may not agree. What a menace that man is."

"He is indeed," I said, then bent my head over my work, pretending to stitch without making much progress. The letter under my pillow called to me, but I couldn't dash off and read it without awakening suspicion. I had to bide my time.

Why had the groom given the paper to Mishka instead of delivering it himself? Suppose he betrayed me out of fear?

After a moment's thought, though, I realized that it did make more sense to turn over the letter to the steward, who had many better reasons for walking about the women's quarters than a groom could produce if challenged. The man's willingness to consider various possibilities boded well for his capacity to evade detection.

In any case, I was implicated now, so my best chance of keeping my secret was to brazen it out.

I focused my full attention on my work, thinking of nothing but the next stitch and waiting for an opportunity to make my excuses and leave.

At last, enough time passed that I believed I could plead the need for a break. I put my altar cloth away and made my way to my own chamber, closing the door behind me and leaning against it with eyes closed before I could summon sufficient energy to bar it against unwanted visitors. I took a deep breath for courage, then walked to the bed, where my future lay concealed beneath the pillow.

My hands trembled with anxiety. The skin over my cheeks felt hot. I could hear my heart pound, and my knees collapsed under me as I reached my goal. I stopped, not having much choice, closed my eyes and gulped, then opened them once more and reached my hand under the pillow.

The crisp roll of paper caressed my fingertips. I drew the scroll from its hiding place and untied the ribbon that bound it. The same one I had used, which I recognized only now as an incongruous scarlet. Not a fitting choice for a would-be monastic.

I unrolled the paper and struggled to focus my eyes. The black ink swam before my vision, dancing like specks of dust on a sunny window pane. I shook my head to clear it, forced myself to concentrate, traced each letter with my index finger, and mouthed the words under my breath. Usually I could read silently, but when the future course of my life hung in the balance, my only concern was to ensure my own comprehension without speaking loudly enough to be overheard.

Darya Petrovna! the letter said.

All respect to you as a daughter in Christ. I regret to hear of your troubles and wish you success in bringing Grace to your wayward cousin's heart. Alas, I cannot grant your request. A monastery is not a refuge. A life within its walls is a choice best made by women who have already experienced that which the world has to offer and therefore understand what they are giving up for the good of their eternal souls. Without that wisdom, novices are too easily tempted by the pleasures of the life they have left behind.

Test your capacity for obedience by bearing your Cross in the station assigned to you by God, by subsuming your own prideful will to the demands of your cousin and the other members of your family. You can practice chastity and poverty and submission in the world as well as in a monastery. When you have fulfilled your obligations as a boyar's daughter, we will be proud to welcome you. I, in particular, will gladly accept you as a novice ... one day.

Meanwhile, I send best wishes to you, your sister, and your niece. May Almighty God and His Most Pure Mother protect you and guide you in this time of travail.

Yours in Christ,

Elena

I couldn't have read it right. I blinked and tried a second time, then a third and a fourth.

It didn't help. No matter how much I did my best to push the letters into different shapes, the words didn't change.

Mother Elena had rejected my plea. I would not become her novice after all. I would remain Cousin Igor's pawn, a piece for him to play however he wished for his own gain.

The strength drained from my hands, and the letter tumbled to the floor. I fell against the pillow and wept.

Chapter Thirteen

I WOKE LATE AFTER A RESTLESS NIGHT SPENT STARING AT the dark, punctuated with nightmares even more hideous than those that followed Igor's dinner party. At one point, I could have sworn I heard men shouting, but by the time I staggered to my feet, I'd decided that, too, must have been a dream. Eager to avoid questions about my no-doubt-blotchy face and tear-stained cheeks, I washed with water left over from yesterday and dressed without the help of a maid. I even patted powder on my skin to cover the marks, although it took me a ridiculous amount of time to locate the small container at the back of my dresser drawer. Thus fortified, I stashed the letter from Mother Elena in the deepest corner of my clothes chest, then went to look for my sister.

As expected, I found her in the sewing room. "When you left last night, I thought you planned to come back," she said as I entered. "Did you fall asleep?"

"When I reached my room, I realized I was exhausted," I told her. "I lay down, but I had trouble sleeping. I even dreamed that I heard men shouting. That was right about when I woke up."

"Oh, they were shouting all right," Solomonida said. "Cousin Igor and his clerk. Igor must have told him about Nikita and the kiss, because Fadeyev stood up for you, yelling that Igor should wash his mouth out with soap rather than dishonor a virtuous woman by telling such falsehoods about her. Igor shouted back that Anfim should take his pens and papers and go. But when Anfim announced his intention of doing just that, Igor told him to stay. So I think our cousin has relented. He may even apologize, although I wouldn't count on it if I were you."

"Goodness, what a show. How on earth did I sleep through that?" No wonder I'd had nightmares.

Yet a glow warmed my heart. Anfim Fadeyev had defended me—and to his employer, despite the risk of dismissal. Perhaps I *could* consider him a friend. "Anfim's a good man," I said.

"He is indeed," Solomonida said. "A very good man."

I stared at her, struck by the pink in her cheeks and the way she avoided my eyes. I'd thought before that she was attracted to Anfim, and here was more evidence.

Maybe it didn't matter whether they married. If he convinced her that not every man was a brute like her dead husband, she might consider other possibilities. Wasn't that what she'd urged me to do?

Grief stabbed at my heart. I'd listened to her and trusted Nikita, who'd betrayed me. Now I had no prospects, not even the women's monastery.

Anna was not here. I had my answer from Mother Elena, little as I liked it. I should tell Solomonida what I'd learned.

But I didn't, because right then Mishka appeared to announce that Katya had passed through the courtyard gates. I went to meet her, pretending as best I could that I'd taken yesterday's disaster in stride. She seemed to notice nothing amiss as I smuggled her past Cousin Igor—preoccupied with giving orders to Anfim in a biting tone—and into the sewing room. Solomonida greeted her warmly, chatting about this and that. I slunk into a corner and left them to it, interjecting the occasional murmur of agreement whenever their heads turned my way.

As a result, I was the first to react to the unmistakable sounds of riders entering our courtyard. I rushed to the window, Solomonida and Katya close behind me. I reached it in time to see an elaborately dressed nobleman of middle age, his paunch large enough for a man twice his years, dismount groaning from his burdened warhorse and raise a hand in response to Igor's shout of welcome.

"Why, it's Uncle Gavriil," Katya said. "I had no idea he was a friend of your cousin's. What brings him here, I wonder?"

"Isn't he in favor with the grand prince?" I asked. "Igor is desperate to get on the right side of those in power. Although I'm surprised your uncle would deign to visit my cousin. Igor's nowhere near him in status."

"No, he's not," Katya admitted. "Perhaps he's not here to see your cousin."

Alas, I soon discovered she was right.

"Good." Igor stormed into the sewing room not a quarter of an hour later. Solomonida glared at his invasion of our private space, but with his full attention focused on me, he paid her no heed. "For once you look respectable, Dashka," he added.

I scowled at his use of that dreadful nickname, but he paid no heed to me either. "Come along," he said. "I've someone who wants to meet you."

My heart sank, as they say, to the tips of my emerald-hued slippers. Katya's uncle had not left the house, which must mean that Igor was still entertaining him. And I could think of only one reason why my cousin's illustrious guest might want to see me, the younger lady in the household. It would be the same reason that Gavriil Vorontsov had traveled to Igor's house rather than insist on Igor making the journey to his: because Gavriil wanted a bride, and my cousin had nominated me.

"I'm feeling poorly." I touched my head. "I would hate to infect him with illness. The one that kept Tsarevna Maria from your dinner party, perhaps."

Not the complete truth, that, but not wholly a lie either. I did sense pain gathering at my temples. My sleepless night—and the reasons for it—continued to haunt me, even if I suspected that despondency afflicted me more than sickness. But if I could persuade Igor to tell his visitor I wasn't well enough to present myself downstairs, Gavriil might decide my health was too uncertain to risk.

"Nonsense." Igor grabbed my right arm and dragged me toward the door. "You're malingering, you wicked girl, trying to avoid your God-given duty. Gavriil Timofeevich rode over here to get a good look at you, and get a good look at you he will. He'd be a splendid match, and you should be grateful he's willing to consider you at all, given the connections he has."

I shook him off, but I didn't like the idea of him hauling me down the stairs. It would be undignified in the extreme, and there were other ways of discouraging an unwanted bridegroom. So, suppressing the many objections and insults that sprang to my mind, I followed my cousin to the sitting room, biting my tongue the whole way.

Up close, Gavriil Vorontsov was even less appealing than I'd imagined from my glimpse through the window. A massive man in a scarlet wool coat that clashed with those parts of his coppery hair that had not already turned gray, gold braid ties straining across his ample middle, he also wore a fur-trimmed sleeveless overcoat made of brocade, a tall black hat, and high-heeled boots. Given the heat exuded by the tiled stove, his elaborate garb perhaps explained the redness of his face and the beads of sweat that dotted his brow.

Otherwise, I had to admit, he looked pleasant enough—for a man twice my age. His beard spread out across his chest, and when I came in and made my bow, he stroked its tip as if pleased at my cousin's offering. "Well, well, well," he said. "Quite an attractive morsel you have here, Igor Grigorevich." *Morsel?*

"And why is she not married already?" Gavriil went on. "A young lady of noble birth and so fair of face should not reach the age of twenty-five unwed."

Before Igor found his tongue, Katya's uncle lurched forward and gripped my chin with powerful fingers. "Not bad-tempered, are you? No hidden defects? No lack of chastity? My sister-in-law will verify those things."

Bad-tempered? I'll show you bad-tempered!

But as I searched my brain for the brattiest words I could find, I felt Igor's hand twisting my robe from behind, right over my shoulders, as if reminding me that he could, if he chose, whip me into compliance. The horror of that possibility flooded my thoughts, stopping my breath long enough for my cousin to answer first.

"Not in the least bad-tempered, Gavriil Timofeevich," Igor said in soothing tones quite incompatible with the pressure he still exerted on me. "You knew her father. He would never have tolerated misbehavior in a daughter. And no hidden defects either. I'm sure she's still pure." Which wasn't what he'd said to me the day before yesterday, but I had no intention of bringing that up. "Her brother-in-law was disgraced—nothing to do with Darya Petrovna—and then her father fell ill. He had no strength to negotiate a marriage in the last seven years of his life."

Gavriil Vorontsov grunted—agreement of a sort, I assumed.

Igor seemed to take it that way, in any case. "She's pretty and highborn, untouched but still able to bear sons, good at household management and embroidery. Pious, too, and docile." He pinched my back as he said the last. "If you want her, let's discuss the settlement. Her father left her a good dowry, so there's no problem there. Your niece Ekaterina Ivanovna can vouch for her. They're friends. In fact, she's upstairs in my sewing room. We can finish the business right now."

My sewing room? And who gave Igor the idea that Katya and I were friends?

Rage choked me. I'd never experienced such hatred of another person in my life. I wanted to strangle my cousin Igor with my bare hands and throw his inert body in the nearest privy. The gall of him, to shove me at this elderly courtier for no other reason than to give himself influence at court, uncaring what it would mean for me or my sister or even Gavriil Timofeevich himself, stuck living with an unwilling wife and a bumptious cousin-in-law.

Vorontsov wouldn't agree to marry me out of hand. He couldn't, surely. He must have some pride. Ancient or not, he was the grand prince's favorite. He didn't have to settle for the first woman offered.

Desperate, I racked my brain for something I could say in my own defense that would not cause Igor to take out his frustration on me as soon as his guest left. I was about to put my hand to my head and fake a swoon when my unwanted suitor grunted again.

"Not so fast, Igor Grigorevich," Vorontsov said. "You've already half-convinced me there's something wrong with the girl, the way you're pushing her at me as if she were damaged goods and yourself a trader eager to make a sale before it's too late. We'll do this properly. My niece Katya's a flighty piece. I'll ask her, but I'm not taking her word for whether your cousin's the right choice for me. My brother Demid's wife will stop by next week and have a nice little chat with Darya Petrovna. Examine her and all that. Depending on what she tells me, then I'll see about sending a man to discuss the settlement with that clerk of yours."

"As you prefer, Gavriil Timofeevich." Igor spoke through gritted teeth. His fingers dug into my spine. Tempted to embarrass him by crying out, I refrained. I'd escaped for the moment, thanks to Vorontsov's last-minute attack of caution, which gave me time to discuss strategy and tactics with Solomonida. And Katya, if I could persuade her (and trust her) to help me. Juliana, too, if I could get to her. She probably had tricks I'd never even considered. I could only hope that this time I'd manage to dodge Cousin Igor's snare.

But what about next time? Because I had no doubt that if I did succeed in thwarting my cousin's first attempt to get rid of me, he would not delay in roping in a second candidate ... and a third. Sooner or later, one of them would prove impossible to dissuade.

Back in the sewing room, my sister and I discussed the ins and outs of Gavriil's proposal as well as possible escape mechanisms. Katya proved a great help—so much that I concluded she had no more desire to see me in a superior position as her aunt than I did to watch her marry Igor and take charge of our household.

"You know the sister-in-law he plans to send to check on me," I said. "How do I convince her I'm not a good addition to the family? Without causing a scandal, I mean."

"Hmm." Katya seemed to take my question as a challenge. I watched her place one finger under her chin and frown absently at the far wall, as if turning ideas over in her head. "Let me think about that. If only you weren't so pretty ..."

While she pondered, Solomonida said, "I have an idea. You should emphasize your piety. Let Katya's aunt find you at prayer. Cross yourself often. Invoke the saints and the Holy Mother at every turn. It's close enough to the truth not to arouse Igor's suspicions, and if you can keep from going overboard, you'll protect your reputation while giving Katya's relatives second thoughts."

I liked the sound of that. Cousin Igor's accusations and name calling still stung.

"Yes," Katya said. "I can even supply a hair shirt. We dragged it off a maid who went mad and decided she was a holy fool. Only my aunt will see it, and you can pretend you wear it every day instead of throwing it on the moment she arrives. I'll make sure to come with her so that you have time to get into it before she examines you."

That became our first plan.

The weather shifted into drenching rain and gloomy skies—an accurate mirror of my mood. Day followed dreary day, yet Gavriil Vorontsov's sister-in-law did not appear. Each morning when I awoke, I wondered if this would be my last taste of freedom; every night before I fell asleep, I said a silent prayer of thanks that one more segment of time had slid by with my fate still undecided.

At times I wore the hair shirt for an hour or so, at first to test it and then, once I realized how uncomfortable it was, to ensure that my skin had the reddened and chafed appearance needed to convince Katya's Aunt Liza that I mortified my flesh in secret. By the time she at last came to visit on September 7, Katya walking behind her cooing praise of my exceptional capacity for innocent devotion, I was as ready to assume my assigned role as I could ever be. Not to mention determined to burn the hair shirt the moment Aunt Liza left the house.

The discomfort did convince me that Mother Elena had done me a favor by refusing to accept me as her novice. Alas, her decision also meant I had no obvious refuge if Cousin Igor persisted in throwing potential husbands in my path. I couldn't appeal to Nikita. Maria had offered her home, and I would go to her if need be. But that solution would be temporary at best, whereas the monastery would have sheltered me for the rest of my days. Juliana's suggestion of spiriting me away to Poland seemed at once exciting and scary. So rather than spin in circles like Laika chasing her own tail, I decided to trust in God, hope for the best, and focus on scotching Igor's ambitious plans for me by any means available—starting with Katya's ponderous aunt, at present hauling herself up our staircase by brute force.

To honor our guests, Solomonida had insisted that we greet them first in the main sitting room. As soon as I knew they were on the stairs, I dropped to my knees in front of the icon corner with my back to the door, clasped the cross attached to my prayer rope, and launched into multiple repetitions of the Jesus Prayer: "Lord Jesus Christ, Son of God, have mercy!" If I said it often enough, supposedly, I could put myself into a trance—which under the circumstances might be a very good thing.

But it seemed that I was not saintly enough to achieve absorption into God's Light, because at the moment when the door slammed behind me and I heard a horrified gasp, I was thinking mostly about how the hard wood scraped my knees and how much worse the stone floor of a women's monastery would be. I said a final prayer, then pushed myself to a standing position, wincing as I straightened my legs.

Definitely, Mother Elena did me a favor.

I arched and rubbed my back to suggest that I'd spent hours in prayer, then turned to face our visitors.

Aunt Liza might once have been a pretty young girl, but I saw no evidence of beauty remaining. She was as round as her brother-in-law Gavriil, her eyes puffy and her jaw slack. Her headdress concealed every shred of hair, but it did nothing to flatter her, exaggerating the breadth of her cheeks, the lines that bracketed her lips, and the pastiness of her complexion. The prayers I said to welcome her arrival were heartfelt; only I knew that my secret prayer was that I not look like her in twenty years.

I thought of the holy sisters I'd met at the monastery in Suzdal: they had wrinkles on their faces and necks and brown age spots on their hands, infirmities of various sorts, but some retained the bones of beauty, and others exuded kindness and compassion, a certainty of their place in life that to me at sixteen had seemed indistinguishable from God's Grace.

Looking back, I understood for the first time why that life once appealed to me. At sixteen, I was still recovering from the loss of my stepmother and stepbrother two years before. Many girls dislike their stepmothers, but I loved mine. I knew no mother except Xenia. In the years when she cared for me, I felt protected from the world—especially the alien world of men. Lev was her favorite, and my father's too, but I'd never succeeded in mustering any resentment toward my stepbrother. He was too sweet-tempered a child, adorable and funny—in short, my favorite too.

When he died and his mother followed him into the grave, my father withdrew as if I didn't exist. No wonder I'd looked to a world filled with women for succor.

And now I wanted Niki. But that door had closed, and nothing good could result from trying to reopen it. I pushed the thought aside and returned my attention to Katya's Aunt Liza, looming in the doorway.

Solomonida, as the elder sister, greeted Katya and her aunt first. I bowed, thinking of the morning prayer service to put myself in the right frame of mind. "How blissful that the divine powers have sent you to us, Elizaveta

Vadimovna," I said. "I trust that God granted you a successful journey."

"My goodness, child," Liza said. "Katya told me you were devout, but to make such a fuss over a carriage ride that didn't last half an hour! Come here and let me take a look at you."

Solomonida gestured toward the end of the hallway. "Please, join us in the women's quarters. It will be more pleasant and more private, and the light is better there. I will send for refreshments."

My first, uncontrollable thought was that Aunt Liza had probably never met a refreshment she didn't love. Shamed by my own meanness, I murmured agreement and ushered the older lady toward the sewing room.

Solomonida followed, but as we passed the room that had once been my father's private sanctuary, Igor dashed out to bow and scrape in front of his latest visitor. Liza halted in mid-stride, regarding him with an air that again reminded me of the crowds entranced by performing bears in the marketplace. She spoke courteously enough when he stopped to catch his breath, then resumed her interrupted sail along the corridor while he transferred his attentions to Katya, who blushed and flirted, more at ease with him than I'd seen her since Juliana stole Igor's heart with no more than a crooked finger at that infamous dinner party.

My cousin had come to his senses, it seemed, although I had to wonder if Katya's relationship to Gavriil Vorontsov was not the real factor driving Igor's renewed interest. He might see her as an alternative path to his goal, a bride that he could use to achieve the power he yearned for even if I somehow circumvented his plans for me. In that case, Solomonida and I still had work to do.

But I'd worry about that possibility another day. Right now, I had to focus on today's challenge. Determination squared my shoulders as I followed Aunt Liza down the hall, Solomonida at my side. The clicking of Katya's heels against the wooden floor assured me she was right behind us.

The hair shirt tipped the balance. When Katya's Aunt Liza staggered from the house an hour or so later, muttering to her niece about the absurdity of modern girls, Solomonida and I retreated as far into the women's quarters as we could go and laughed ourselves silly.

"Did you see her face?" I gasped, not for the first time. I'd stripped off the miserable shirt the moment I saw Liza retire to her carriage, and it lay across a nearby chest—its ugly brown itchiness on full display. "I thought she was going to croak like a frog when I undid my robe and she saw that dreadful wool."

"And the marks! Did you get those red splotches from wearing it for an hour?"

"No." I told her how I'd practiced in preparation for Liza's visit. Then, because at last it seemed like the right time to reveal the whole, I explained what Katya had told me about Nikita, my letter to Mother Elena, and her response. "And the thing is, I think the reverend mother was right. I'm not strong enough. I couldn't bear the hair shirt for more than a quarter of an hour. Even the praying while I waited: all I could think about was how uncomfortable it was without a cushion under my knees."

"So you'll forget about the monastery for a while?" Solomonida asked after another round of complaints about my secretiveness. "Focus on marriage, even if this story Katya told you turns out to be true, and Nikita's father signed a contract with someone else?"

I apologized for hiding the information from her, then said, "Yes. But I don't want a husband like Gavriil Timofeevich. A young man who would care for me, interesting and reasonably good-looking, someone I could talk to—I'd consider that. Someone like Nikita, if I can't have Niki himself. But not someone selected for me by Cousin Igor to advance his prospects at court."

Solomonida rested her chin on a clasped fist. "Understood. I do believe you'll make a good holy sister one day. And I don't think hair shirts are required of noble ladies who take the veil. But I'd like to believe you're running *to* your vocation, not *away* from an unsuitable marriage. And it's hard to tell which one it is when you have so little experience of life."

"That's what Mother Elena said too. And Father Job. I promise I will stop thinking about monastic vows." I laughed, a rueful sound that well expressed my mood. "Well, I have to, don't I, if no women's monastery will take me?"

"Papa was grateful that you gave up so many years to make him comfortable." Solomonida patted my hand in reassurance and sympathy. "But it does mean that you lost a lot of time. It's too bad about Nikita. He seems like the perfect match for you. Do we know that Katya's right about this prior commitment of his?"

"You think she's mistaken?" Hope stirred in my heart, but I suppressed it. "I don't see how she can be. She got it from her brother Dmitry, who heard it from Nikita himself. That's what she told me, and she seemed sad at having to deliver the news. She said she wanted to keep me from believing in a future that could never come to pass."

"But why didn't Niki tell you himself?" Solomonida asked, echoing my own doubts. "He's not a cad, from what I've seen. And who but a cad would lead on a noble maiden with false promises?"

She had a point. I admitted as much. "Katya sounded very certain," I added.

"Well, she could be certain without being right," Solomonida said. "But either way, I'll ask around, see whether anyone that you and I would like is in the market for a bride. I can't overrule what our cousin plans for you, but I may be able to present him with an acceptable compromise."

"I'd appreciate it." I strove to keep my tone light, although in truth, my mind resisted the idea of another husband. I loved Niki. Who could replace him?

Chapter Fourteen

OF COURSE, WE HID FROM IGOR THE STEPS WE'D TAKEN TO undermine his scheme to advance his interests by marrying me off to Gavriil Vorontsov. The necessity for concealment tormented my conscience, but I decided to confess my sins later. I begged Katya to stop by again the next day, and she arrived in a carriage because it was pouring outside. I met her at the outside door and pulled her into the house before the torrent of water drenched her to the skin, then dragged her up to the sewing room as soon as we exchanged the obligatory double cheek kisses.

"What happened?" I asked while she shed her outer layers and shook herself as Laika had done when she came in out of the rain an hour ago. The dog lay steaming next to the stove, in such a state of bliss that she'd greeted Katya with no more than a thump of her tail and a twitch of her ears.

"Not much," Katya said. "Aunt Liza told Uncle Gavriil that she didn't consider you a good choice. She didn't say why, and he didn't ask."

"He didn't ask? After sending her here? That's odd." This time I'd ordered the hot cider in anticipation of

Katya's arrival, so I poured her a cup and handed it to her as soon as she gave up on her sodden skirts and took a seat next to the stove. Between her and Laika, we could harness enough floating moisture to iron shirts.

"Not really." Katya took the cup with a murmured thanks and sipped. "Oh, that's good. I'm chilled to the bone, and winter hasn't started yet."

"Cold rain is worse than snow, I think. The whole house is damp. I'm wondering if the storms will ever stop." I drank my own cider, enjoying the gentle heat of cinnamon and nutmeg amid the sweet tartness of the apples and warming my hands against the jug as I poured a second round.

"True." Katya set her cup on the floor, then turned sideways on the bench and held out her palms toward the stove. "Anyhow, Uncle Gavriil is preoccupied at the moment. He's convinced young Grand Prince Ivan to appoint my Uncle Demid a boyar as well. The announcement's going out today, from what Aunt Liza said."

"Oh, Cousin Igor will love that," I said, wrinkling my nose in distaste. "He'll be more determined than ever to push me off on your uncle. Two boyars in the same family!"

Katya laughed. "Yes, your cousin will love it, but it could work in your favor too. The higher my uncles rise, the less Gavriil needs to compromise in choosing a wife." I nodded my understanding, and she went on. "Anyway, he can't be bothered with you right now. Your cousin's convinced him that he can have you if he wants you. And if my uncle does remember that you exist and Aunt Liza doesn't tell him about the hair shirt, I'll do it myself."

Which seemed like the best outcome I could hope for, so I let the subject go and moved on to other things.

The very next day, I came downstairs to find Igor buzzing around the house like a bee in a field of clover. His delight in securing the hand of Katya's uncle for me—if only in his own mind—had caused him to relax his strictures on my spending time in his company (somewhat to my regret), although I was still restricted to the boundaries of our own estate. Much as I resented that limitation, which underlined his lack of trust in me, with the weather so foul and no Nikita at the end of a walk in the pouring rain, I had not yet bothered to challenge my confinement.

Today, however, a weak, pale sun peeked from behind gray clouds, and there was almost as much blue sky as I might stitch on my altar cloth. So I would have to tackle my cousin and his silly rules soon if I were not to spend the rest of my life as cooped up as I'd been in the days when I nursed Papa.

"The grand prince has invited me to dine with him at the Kremlin," Igor announced as I entered the room where I'd met him that very first day. A quick glance revealed traces of ink still marring the Turkmen carpet, although Mishka and his minions had done a marvelous job of taking them out. "Fyodor Koshkin sent a servant with the invitation not an hour ago. Your future bridegroom, Gavriil"—Igor leered at me as he said this, and I winced—"will be there, with his brother Demid, Grand Prince Ivan, his boyars, and his associate boyars. My fortune is made. A few more dinners like this, and I can start approaching brides of my own!"

I thought he'd been doing that all along, so this announcement proved something of a surprise. Remembering the list of women's names I'd found in

Anfim's office and the dismissive tone in which Maria had pronounced most of them far too high-ranking for their male relatives to waste a moment considering a potential match with my cousin, it seemed likely that it would take more than a few dinners at the low end of the royal hall to overcome those objections. But that was Igor's problem, not mine.

"Congratulations," I told him, seeing no value in setting up his back. "I hope the experience justifies your every hope. I'll let the steward know not to expect you here for the midday meal."

Preoccupied with his good fortune, he hadn't asked what brought me downstairs. I chose to enlighten him. "Has Anfim Fadeyev arrived? I thought he planned to bring his daughter to stitch with us again."

Igor waved an absent hand. "Not yet. I've no time for such nonsense. I have to attire myself in robes fit for dining with the ruler of all Russia. Off with you. If the child appears, I'll send her to you."

Suppressing a smile, I dipped my head in acquiescence and went to share the news with Solomonida.

With Igor intent on becoming a clothes horse capable of rivaling boyars dressed in cloth of gold, three-foot hats made from the neck hair of black foxes, and soft leather boots, I expected a cousin-free day. But no sooner had Solomonida and I settled Anna with her sewing, assuring her that Lara would appear soon, than Cousin Igor traipsed into our sitting room without so much as a by-your-leave, on what would prove to be the first of half a dozen impromptu visits.

He did look very fine, I had to admit. Katya would swoon at the sight of him in a sleeveless scarlet brocade robe over a charcoal tunic with a collar high enough to prevent him from turning his head to either side. His boots, like the robe, were scarlet trimmed in gold braid. He wore a round cap, also gold, rimmed with sable the width of my hand. Anna regarded him with rounded eyes, as if she'd never seen such finery on a man—which given how young she'd been when she lost her father and even when mine fell ill, she probably hadn't.

"How elegant," I said, because it was true. Whatever I thought of my cousin's brains and character, Katya was right to say that he knew how to dress. "You will do us proud."

"Indeed." Solomonida circled him, inspecting him from every angle. "We can only hope that Gavriil Vorontsov doesn't decide you're trying to put him in the shade."

Igor frowned. "Too much? But I thought it necessary to convey wealth and standing. No one wants a hanger-on." He smirked at me, and any desire I'd felt to appease him with praise curled into a hoop and rolled away. "Especially not the grand prince's favorite, determined as he is to initiate my prim cousin into womanhood, like any fruit ripe for the picking."

I gritted my teeth. "We'll see about that."

"Oh yes, we will." He turned on his scarlet heel and headed for the doorway. "And within a short time. But wait, I have other robes to show you."

"Why is he torturing us like this?" I muttered to Solomonida as Igor shut the door behind him. "Why should we care what he wears to court?"

"He wants to crow, of course." She glared at the closed entrance to the room as if she could pierce the absent Igor by the sheer force of her gaze. "To impress on us how our future depends on him and his success."

She shrugged, laughing. "And because he has no one else to admire him as he believes he deserves to be admired. Come, let's look busy for when he returns."

We'd barely settled into place before a tentative knock heralded Anfim's arrival with Lara. Greetings ensued, and at Solomonida's suggestion Anna swept her new friend off to her own room to braid her hair and practice cross-stitch. I could hear my niece whispering in Lara's ear about Igor and his costume as they went.

"You may as well stay," Solomonida told Anfim, "unless you have paperwork to complete. Our cousin has received an invitation to dine at the palace, and he's caught up in deciding what to wear. He won't have time for anything else."

He had turned to leave, but at this news he stopped mid-step. I saw hesitation in his raised foot, but he soon lowered it and dipped his head in respect. "But I do have paperwork, Solomonida Petrovna, and I shouldn't be in this section of the house. I came only because Lara was unsure of the way."

My sister bit her lip, and I saw a flash of disappointment cross her face. "We shouldn't keep you from your work then," she said in a voice that was not quite level.

Anfim moved toward the door, but he had yet to reach it when it opened once more, and Cousin Igor returned, this time a shade less resplendent in a long-sleeved, ankle-length coat of cobalt brocade trimmed with light brown fur, worn over a forest-green caftan that showed no more than a finger's breadth beneath the hem of the coat and matched in hue Igor's round cap. The scarlet boots remained, their turned-up toes peeking out from under the caftan like shy birds among the reeds. "More appropriate?" he barked at Solomonida.

Then he caught sight of Anfim. "Ah, there you are, Fadeyev. I don't need you today. I have an appointment at court."

"I brought my daughter," Anfim said with another bow. He sounded apologetic, although I couldn't imagine why—at being found in the women's quarters, perhaps. "If you permit, Igor Grigorevich, I will work on those accounts until she is ready to go home."

Igor twirled, the full skirts of his robe billowing like a girl's, and it took every scrap of self-control I possessed not to giggle.

"What do you think, Fadeyev?" Igor asked. "Does this strike the right note?"

The amusement I so often glimpsed on Anfim's face lit his eyes, and he gulped, as if swallowing the first response that came to mind. "Splendid, Igor Grigorevich," he said after a moment. "You look every inch the boyar." He bowed for the third time since entering the room. "If you will excuse me."

"Yes, go." Igor waved a careless hand. Anfim ducked out of the room without another word. I could have sworn I heard chortling from the far side of the door.

Fortunately, Igor gave no sign that he'd heard it too. "Well, Shura?" he asked. "How does this combination compare with the other?"

"They're both lovely, cousin," Solomonida said, her voice tart. I could tell she liked him using her childhood nickname no more than I did. "Either will do you credit, I assure you."

Igor nodded and left. Before long he was back, showing off a cream-colored caftan with embroidered strips down the center and ringing the hem, collar, and sleeves. An amber cape fell from his shoulders, and his rounded cap sported a long feather tucked into its brim.

I thought longingly of lakesides and woodlands—distant, silent, solitary. Anywhere but here.

"What about this one?" he demanded. "Gavriil Timofeevich will think me a suitable client for his patronage now, don't you think?" Solomonida and I murmured our assurances once more, but Igor gave no sign of listening.

Instead he smirked at me yet again, and I clasped my hands together to control the tingle in my palms. I itched to slap that grin off his face. "A suitable cousin-in-law," he said, and then he was out the door once more.

And so the morning continued. Each time Igor stopped by, he treated me to a jab about how his success would benefit me and how brilliant my marriage prospects were as a result of his efforts.

"Why, I may not even give you to Gavriil Vorontsov," he announced during what turned out to be the last of these appearances, with him clad once more in the scarlet robe he'd worn on his first visit. "Once the court accepts me as his equal, I think I should look no lower than a tsarevich."

He bared his teeth at me in what I assumed he considered a smile. The kind of smile a wolf might bestow on a lamb was how I saw it. "Just think of it, Dashka, a Tatar husband. You won't be so prissy then, will you, having to adjust to a brute who'll never tolerate this insane idea of yours about taking monastic vows?"

I bit my tongue to deny him the satisfaction of a retort. I felt certain he knew how much he was annoying me and had used the pejorative "Dashka" to twist the knife. I refused to tell *him* that I'd given up the idea of joining a women's monastery—still less that Mother Elena had turned down my request. In fact, a Tatar convert to Orthodoxy like Alexei would be a vast improvement over any of Igor's patrons or cronies, but the instant of satisfaction I'd get from telling him that wouldn't be worth either the glee he'd experience at having managed to goad me into losing my temper or the risk that he'd start looking for someone worse. I was counting on Aunt Liza and the hair shirt to save me from Gavriil Vorontsov.

So rather than respond in kind, I thought a quick prayer, then lowered my eyes to my hands, and said, "Why, you're far too kind to me, Cousin Igor. A man as high-flying and magnificently attired as you doesn't need to concern himself with arranging marriages for the likes of *me*."

Solomonida, sitting next to me, emitted a choking sound that she quickly turned into a cough. I observed Igor sideways through my lashes and found him gaping at me, as if for once I'd left him speechless.

"What an appropriate sentiment, Darya Petrovna," he mumbled after a while. I'd thrown him off course enough that he'd addressed me with respect, which I counted as a minor triumph.

Within moments, he stormed out, shutting the door rather too hard behind him—a move that forced him to reopen it long enough to release his embroidered hem. Not long afterward, we heard him call for a carriage. We ran to the sewing-room window so we'd have no doubt he'd gone. As we watched from the third story, he raced down the stairs and leaped into the carriage. The coachman snapped the horses' reins, and in less time than we could count, the vehicle lurched into motion, passed through the open gates that linked the courtyard with the street, and disappeared.

I glanced at my sister, still giggling, then went to tell Lara and Anna that it was safe to return to the sewing room. I heard Laika whimpering in the hallway outside my cousin's rooms, so I brought her in to sit with us for a while. Anna, by now completely comfortable with the dog, showed a nervous Lara how to make friends, and the four of us settled down to our embroidery until Laika's caretaker came to collect her for her morning run. By then we were famished, so Alya brought meat and cabbage turnovers in place of the midday meal. As Lara became more comfortable with us, she and Anna chattered about this and that. Listening to them, I realized I hadn't had such a delightfully ordinary morning in a long time.

Best of all, we'd seen the last of Igor for one day.

Alas, we were wrong about that. A few hours later, Mishka arrived with a summons for us to join Igor in the sitting room on the floor below. By then, it was late afternoon. Anfim had long since departed with Lara, his ears ringing with our invitations to bring his son as well the next time she came and to do that soon. Solomonida, Anna, and I had left the women's quarters long enough to ensure that various servants had performed their tasks as instructed, and I'd asked after Father Job, only to learn from Mishka that an illness in the family had kept the priest at home today. We sent good wishes and warm chicken broth and prayers for a quick recovery, then returned to the sewing room.

At the moment the summons came, I was pondering my altar cloth, trying to decide which part of the background to tackle next while deflecting my sister's speculations on whether our cousin had triumphed as he hoped, failed miserably, or faded into the painted walls so far as the young grand prince was concerned.

Of the various possibilities, the last seemed most likely to me, and I said so. However honorable our father's lineage, I had a hard time imagining that Gavriil and Demid Vorontsov, still less the grand prince, would waste time flattering my cousin when the court contained so many men of higher standing. Igor was eager for me to marry Gavriil, but I'd seen little evidence that Gavriil shared that sense of urgency, even if Aunt Liza hadn't yet told him about the hair shirt.

"By the Most Pure Mother, why?" I asked when Mishka finished delivering his message. "Has something happened?"

"Something must have, Lady Darya," he said. "Igor Grigorevich looks crushed—tearing his outer robes off and tossing them on the floor, he was, before dropping onto a bench, rubbing his forehead with both hands, and groaning."

"*Bozhe moi*," Solomonida said. "We must go, if only to find out what's upset him." She patted Anna's head. "Stay here, darling. Auntie and I will be back soon."

"Yes, Mama." Anna looked relieved. One look at her wide eyes and tense grip, and I understood that Igor scared her, even though she sometimes found him as funny as the rest of us did. Perhaps she sensed the savagery he'd revealed the day he caught me kissing Nikita.

My determination to protect her from our cousin and his schemes strengthened. One more reason to resist being married off to Gavriil Vorontsov, which would take me away from this house.

Mishka had not exaggerated: Cousin Igor looked crushed. For once I felt sorry for him, slumped on the window seat and gripping his hair with both hands, as if tempted to rip it from his head by the roots. His fine cap lay on the floor, his outer robe bore a rip near the collar, and he lacked sufficient calm even to raise his head when we stopped in front of him.

Solomonida touched his shoulder, and he shuddered. "By the saints, cousin, what happened?"

Igor pulled farther into himself. I bent to retrieve his discarded clothing, draped it over a nearby small table, then gazed at my sister over his bent head. "He's in shock," I said. "Let's sit on that bench and wait for him to compose himself."

Instead she walked to the far side of the room and poured wine into a cup. She crossed the floor once more and held the cup out to him. "Drink, cousin, and tell us what went wrong."

After a long pause, Igor accepted the drink and downed an enormous swig. He burped and rubbed his stomach. The eyes with which he stared at me were owlish, and I realized that, in addition to his real distress, he must already have imbibed a good deal. I quickly took a seat as far from him as possible and clasped my hands together in my lap.

"You won't be marrying Gavriil Vorontsov," he began.

I blinked. It was the last thing I'd expected him to say. As I understood that he meant it, a song of joy sounded in my head, and I had to fight to hold my emotions in check.

"Why?" Not because of Aunt Liza and the hair shirt, surely. When I saw Katya yesterday, she'd insisted that conversation had yet to take place. Glancing at Solomonida, I saw the same perplexed expression on her face that must show on mine.

Besides, if Igor knew I'd scotched his plans for me, I'd expect fury and scorn, not stunned disbelief.

He swigged the rest of the wine, burped a second time, and dropped the cup on the bench. "He's on his way to Kostroma. With his brother Demid and his son Yuri. He hasn't time to worry about a silly chit who doesn't have the sense to appreciate him."

I blinked again and shook my head. Igor was drunk, I got that. But did he have to be so damnably confusing? "Devil take you," I said in the mildest tone I could muster. "That tells us nothing whatsoever. He wasn't assigned to Kostroma this morning, or you would have mentioned it. So why is he heading there now?"

"Yes, cousin, don't make us drag the story from you sentence by sentence," Solomonida said. "Spit it out. What happened?"

Igor groaned and touched his brow. "Oh, my aching head." Somehow he rallied enough to glare at us.

We stared back, unrelenting. He'd summoned us, not the reverse, so let him explain himself. "We can leave," I pointed out. "If you don't want to talk, why did you demand that we meet you here?"

He picked up the cup and held it out to Solomonida. "Refill it, Shura, and I'll tell you the whole."

She took it, but she didn't stand. "Tell us first, before you fall over, or give us leave to return in the morning when you've slept off the barrel or two you've already drunk."

Another groan. But when we didn't respond, Igor pulled himself together. "Koshkin and I were sitting at dinner, within sight of the ruler, although several tables away from the center—among the lesser members of the Shuisky clan. The Vorontsov brothers were on either side of Grand Prince Ivan, and the boy seemed comfortable with them, laughing and joking. Metropolitan Macarius was there with them, although he mostly observed. The head of the Church has to maintain an appearance of propriety, you know."

"Go on," Solomonida said, an impatient edge to her voice. "None of that had you staggering in here as if you had a demon on your heels."

Curious but bewildered, I watched him. So far, he'd said nothing unexpected. I already knew from Maria that her father sat with the Shuisky princes, and I'd heard enough from my sister to guess that the grand prince's favorites would flank him at the high table. Seating arrangements were among the few ways that Grand Prince Ivan could use to signal whom he favored.

"In the middle of the meal," Igor went on after a while, "Prince Andrei Mikhailovich, the head of the Shuisky clan ..."

"Yes, we know he's the head," I said, tired of his verbal foot dragging. "Just as we know the metropolitan is the most important clergyman in Russia and can't break out into song and dance at a royal dinner party. Do get on with it. What did Andrei Shuisky do?"

Igor's glare returned at double its previous strength. "Shuisky's men dragged Demid Vorontsov into the courtyard outside the Faceted Palace, stripped his robes from him, and started to beat him with cudgels. They'd have killed him if Metropolitan Macarius hadn't intervened. And they conducted the whole attack in front of the grand prince, who's too young to stop them. The metropolitan talked Andrei Shuisky into sparing Vorontsov's life, and the rest of the boyars sent Demid, Gavriil, and Yuri away from Moscow for their own protection."

Solomonida gasped, and so did I. At last I understood what had rattled Igor so badly. I felt pretty shaky myself. Russia had experienced many squabbles between the noble clans in the decade since Grand Prince Vasily died, but this marked a new low. "The Shuisky clan dragged Demid Vorontsov out of a royal dinner and beat him almost to death where the grand prince could see them?" I asked, to ensure I'd heard correctly.

He nodded, staring at his hands, then spoke in a harsh voice. "Because Grand Prince Ivan elevated Demid to boyar rank yesterday, and the Shuisky clan felt threatened. Thank the Lord that Metropolitan Macarius was there. It was terrible to watch."

"It must have been," I said to Solomonida. "Have you ever heard the like? And to commit such a brutal act in front of a child!"

"And the court," she said. "To strip off Vorontsov's robes like that and display him naked in public—they wanted not only to kill him but to humiliate him in front of everyone he cared about." She shivered, and so did I.

"And none of those watching tried to stop them?" I asked. "Have the Vorontsovs no supporters, and the Shuiskys no enemies?"

Did you not try to stop them?

I didn't add that last. I was well aware how low my cousin must rank in that gathering, and how little he would want to draw the kind of attention that might undermine his plans to improve his standing.

"There were protests," he said. "Some of the men of the great clans argued with Shuisky once they got over their shock, but he didn't listen to them. Only Macarius has the religious authority to command Shuisky's obedience."

Much as I disliked my cousin Igor, I could imagine how rattled he must feel having witnessed so dreadful a scene. To show my sympathy, I took the cup from my sister's hand and went to refill it.

I hadn't crossed half the room when his slurred voice spun me around. "So you see, Dashka, you won't be marrying Vorontsov. I'll have to find a Shuisky for you."

He clutched his hair once more and moaned, "Ruined. My plans for advancement ruined."

The cup felt heavy in my hand. It took every scrap of self-control I possessed not to throw it at his thick head. Although the news that I need not fear marriage to Gavriil Vorontsov warmed *my* heart, his family would feel differently about the attack on its leaders.

"You dolt!" I said. "Don't you understand that Katya will suffer for this? And Dmitry and the other members of the clan? These are people we know, our neighbors. Your interests aren't the only thing that counts."

"And what of the young grand prince?" Solomonida asked. "How will he feel, knowing he's lost another pair of counselors he trusts because the Shuiskys care nothing for him and his preferences, only for their own power?"

She was right. Grand Prince Ivan had endured far too much sorrow for a boy who turned thirteen less than two weeks ago. His father dead, then his uncles and his mother—all before he reached his eighth birthday. The Shuiskys had robbed the boy of his mother's favorite, who'd acted as a substitute father to Ivan and his younger brother, and of the nurse who'd cared for him from babyhood. And the Vorontsovs were not the first rivals to fall victim to Shuisky ambition.

And Igor thinks he can marry me off to one of these unscrupulous men?

My cousin was as bad as the warring boyars. I placed the cup on the table and walked out of the room, Solomonida close behind me. Igor called after us, but we ignored him.

Let him pour his own wine.

Chapter Fifteen

IGOR WASTED NO TIME. THE SECOND CANDIDATE FOR MY hand arrived on our doorstep three days later. He didn't even ask to see me in person. This time I watched from the dining-room window as Fyodor Koshkin again rode into our courtyard like a conquering hero, accompanied by an enclosed carriage and a pale, reedy young man on horseback. The two men dismounted at the foot of our staircase and tossed their reins to the groom who came running to meet them. Then the younger man walked to the carriage, opened the door, and proceeded with great ceremony to usher out a taller, thinner, and considerably older woman. Her headdress, which enclosed her hair completely, identified her as a widow or a wife—most likely, the young man's mother or aunt. Their clothes indicated they belonged to a noble clan, but one less affluent than the Vorontsov uncles or Koshkin, who stood preening as Igor rushed from the house to greet the three arrivals.

I left orders for the maids whose dusting I'd been supervising and ran to find my sister. "Quick," I said when I located her in the storeroom at the bottom of the servants' stairs. "Igor's entertaining visitors. Fyodor Koshkin and two people I haven't seen before. A young man and an elderly woman. We need to discover who they are, and as fast as we can. They'll exchange pleasantries for a while, but we should be ready, just in case."

She didn't ask why. Instead she dashed for Father Job's study. I followed her. The priest was still ministering to his afflicted family members, so the study was empty, although Anfim Fadeyev was already at work in the room opposite. I saw him hunched over his stacks of paper as I passed the half-open door. He didn't look up as we went by.

When we reached the window, the three visitors were still standing in the courtyard, chatting with Igor. I guessed that he'd run down from his own rooms to welcome them, because Laika was still descending the last few steps. Soon she sat at her master's feet, swishing her tail gently from side to side while the young man sent her nervous glances. Koshkin and the older woman paid her no more attention than if she'd been part of the woodwork. After a short while, Igor gestured to one of the dog's caretakers, who clapped his hands.

"Come here, pretty girl," the groom said. Laika galloped toward him. As she came close, he caught her collar and led her toward the stables.

"Who *are* they?" I asked Solomonida. I kept my voice down, eager to avoid Igor's attention. Something about the effusive way he greeted these visitors left a bad taste in my mouth.

Solomonida squinted at the visitors, then said, "Why, it's Prince Demian Bledny and his mother."

"Are they here for me?" I didn't want to assume the worst, but it seemed unlikely that a prince, however young and ferret-faced, would bring his mother to conduct routine business with a fellow nobleman.

My sister turned from the window and looked me up and down. "We have to act as if they are. The Bledny family is a Shuisky offshoot, although this particular member is not in line to become a boyar. Or even that well-off, as you can see. But that might make him more willing to accept Igor as an in-law, and his relatives have plenty of clout."

"It's a good thing I wore my plainest robes, then." The dress I'd chosen was simple homespun—clean except for the dust stirred up by the maids and otherwise in good condition, if more typical of a servant than her mistress. "I don't want my clothes to impress them."

"No, but that's not enough. We have to convince the mother to look elsewhere."

"The hair shirt again?" I sighed. More dishonesty. I was sinking deeper into sin with every candidate Igor found.

Although the hair shirt was penance in and of itself. I'd meant to burn it but hadn't, for this very reason: in case I needed it to discourage Igor's next candidate for my hand. "I haven't had time to make it look natural, though." I flinched at the very thought of wearing that horrid wool, but it had worked well with Katya's Aunt Liza.

Solomonida shook her head. "No time. They'll enter the house any moment. We have to get upstairs." Then she stopped. "Oh wait. I have an idea. You run to the third floor. I'll meet you in the sewing room as soon as I can. Don't change your clothes, but grab a proper robe from your chamber and keep it nearby."

"Idea?" I said, but she was already out the door. I picked up my long skirt in both hands and raced to the top floor as fast as I could go.

I was panting like Laika at midsummer noon by the time I reached the sewing room. I grabbed Alya on the way. "How do I look?" I asked her. "Are my cheeks red? Is my hair a mess?"

"I've seen you neater, Lady," she said. Tactful of her. "Should I bring a comb and a damp cloth?"

I shook my head. "Better this way. I'll explain later. Fetch the first decent robe you can find in my chamber. Something I can put on over this dress. Fast as you can." She nodded and ran off.

As I went into the sewing room, I thought of Lara's messy plait, which probably looked better than mine at the moment, but I made no attempt to improve anything. Instead I picked up my altar cloth, folded it in quarters, and tucked it into my sewing bag. Then I pulled out Lara's last effort at cross-stitch, threaded a yarn needle with thick wool, and sat on the window seat, where I stitched a dozen or so crosses every bit as uneven as Lara's before setting the cloth aside.

Solomonida burst into the room. Behind her came our maid Masha, dressed in a robe not much different from mine, and I had a glimpse of what my sister had in mind. "You're going to switch us?" I asked. It was a known trick with brides, but usually in the other direction: when the future mother-in-law came to visit, a beautiful daughter would be switched for the ugly one whose name was on the contract.

Masha was not ugly, but she'd been burned as a child, and the scars covered a good third of her face. It should be enough to discourage any but the most determined prospective mother-in-law. She was holding a small cup, which she held out to me. I took it and sniffed. Vinegar. What on earth?

Alya dashed in, the rose silk robe in her hand. She gave it to me, then waited to see if I had any orders. I looked at my sister, who hadn't yet answered my question.

"We'll switch you if we can," Solomonida said. "We'll use the vinegar in case we can't. Alya, go to the top of the staircase. A lady is coming up the stairs. We need to know if she's alone or with Igor Grigorevich. It's urgent. Come and tell us, then delay her for a few moments if possible." Alya ran off to complete this new errand.

"Masha, go and stand next to Darya Petrovna. If Igor Grigorevich accompanies the lady, take a few steps back and say nothing. If Alya tells us the lady is alone, put the robe on over your clothes and pretend *you* are the young mistress."

"Suppose she asks me questions, Lady Solomonida?"

"Nod and say, 'yes, yes,' as if you don't quite understand." Masha demonstrated, and my sister said, "Exactly. Darya, you have the vinegar?"

I held up the cup in illustration. "What do I do with it?"

"Put a drop in your eye, so it looks as if you have a squint. " I must have made a face—I could imagine the sting—because she added, "You don't want to be the next Princess Blednaya, do you?"

I dipped my finger into the vinegar and touched the fingertip to my left eye. It burned like the devil's own potion, and I scrunched up my face, but I had enough sense left to upend the rest of the vinegar into a jug of water someone had left on the chest where we kept our threads and fabrics.

Alya returned. "The noblewoman's alone, Lady Solomonida."

"Good," my sister said. "See if you can slow her down long enough for me to help Masha into that robe."

"Yes, Lady." Alya disappeared once more while I hid the cup that had contained the vinegar under Anna's embroidery frame. By the time I straightened and could (sort of) see, Masha was attired in my rose silk. Blinking like a madwoman, I took my place behind her, dropping my chin as if I were her maid. I'd wriggled my way into position mere moments before the door opened and the thin woman that Solomonida had identified as Prince Demian Bledny's mother stalked into the room, Alya twittering behind her.

Solomonida went to greet the princess, bowing and introducing Masha by my name before sending Alya out of the room on yet another errand. No one paid the slightest attention to me in my pretense as Masha's maid, but just in case, I took a step sideways, using Masha as a shield. I noticed that she'd tipped her face in such a way that her scars were hidden. Had she not understood that we wanted her to show them, to repel any interest from the princess?

"Hmm," Princess Blednaya said. "Not unattractive."

Masha stared at the floor as if she were too shy to meet the eyes of such an illustrious visitor.

"Pretty dress. Nice hair." The princess reached for Masha's hands. "These could use some work. Do you wash the dishes yourself?"

Masha mumbled something incomprehensible and continued to study the floor.

"How's your embroidery?" the princess asked. I scuttled sideways, swept up the sample I'd prepared, and held it out.

Masha took it from my hands and held it by the corners. I risked a glance at the princess and saw astonishment on her face. "By the saints, girl, is that the best you can do? I've seen six-year-olds who stitch better than that!"

Masha stared at the floor and mumbled.

"Look at me," Princess Blednaya said. Impatience tinged her voice.

Masha raised her head and looked straight at our visitor, turning her head to reveal the scars, inescapable in the brilliant sunshine that lit the room. "Like this, Princess?" she said in a clear, carrying tone. From where I stood near the window, I could see Masha's raised eyebrows, her challenging gaze. I'd underestimated her. She'd known exactly what we wanted and why, and she'd delivered it. It was an inspired performance.

I thought the princess would have a heart attack. She gasped and staggered back. For a moment there was silence. Then she said in biting tones, "I pity your poor cousin. He'll be lucky if he ever finds a husband for you. But that's his problem. I will not accept a dimwitted crone who doesn't know how to sew as the mother of my grandchildren." She turned her glare on me. "Even that squinting maid would be a better choice."

I flinched. Poor Masha. How rude. And when she'd done this to help me.

The princess stormed out, slamming the door behind her. "Are you all right, Masha?" I asked, guilt-stricken. "I'd never have guessed she'd say anything so horrible. I hope she didn't hurt your feelings."

Masha shrugged. "It's not news that I'm ugly, Lady Darya. I was glad to help."

"You'd better get back to the kitchen," Solomonida told her. "Before our cousin comes barreling up here demanding to know what went wrong. But we'll reward you well as soon as he leaves; don't worry about that."

"Cosmetics, maybe," I said. "You aren't ugly, Masha. All you need is something to cover the scars."

"I'd like that." She smiled as she stripped off the rose silk, then left while I pulled it on over my plain dress.

Through the window and my tearing eyes, I saw Princess Blednaya emerge from the bottom of the covered stairs that ran from the second floor to the courtyard. She grabbed her son by the elbow and jabbed a short bow in my cousin's direction. From this distance I couldn't hear what they said, but Igor looked as if he was remonstrating with them.

I could guess he didn't like what they were telling him. There would be hell to pay if he discovered what we'd done.

Moving as fast as I could, I raced for my bedchamber, where I flooded my burning eye with cool water. When I could see once more, I returned to the sewing room. Solomonida and I braced ourselves for our cousin's arrival. I remembered to tuck the bad embroidery away again before he could see it and wonder.

I'd barely had time to stash it in a safe place before Igor marched in. "What did you do, you wicked girl?" he demanded the instant he crossed the threshold.

He raised his arm as if to strike me, and Solomonida said, "Don't you dare. She did nothing."

"She must have," he hissed. "Princess Blednaya grabbed her son and hauled him off to the carriage as if Satan himself was after her. Said she'd never seen an uglier and stupider girl. She told me it would take a miracle to find her a husband."

"How rude." With an effort, I kept my voice level, although inside I trembled at his rage. "I was nothing but polite to her, agreed with everything she said. As for ugly and stupid, do *you* think I'm ugly and stupid, cousin?"

He lowered his arm, although he continued to glare at me, as if he suspected some subterfuge he couldn't detect. Rightly, I had to admit. More sins piling up for that delayed confession.

I set thoughts of my wickedness aside for future contemplation and stared at him, focusing instead on the wrongs he sought to inflict on me.

"No." His tone was grudging. "You're dressed properly. That pink suits you, although your hair needs combing. You're a scourge and a slut, but no one would know that to look at you. And you're definitely not stupid. I'd be better off if you were."

"I'm not a slut," I said, refusing to let him get away with that insult, although I knew he wouldn't believe me.

As expected, he ignored my comment. "I still think you did something," he said. "Don't try it again. Lord Koshkin keeps telling me I should marry you myself. And if you don't accept the next man I find, I'll take his advice. So remember that while you're deciding to interfere with my plans. Meanwhile, I have an obligation to my patron, who awaits me downstairs." And while his threat rang in the air, he took his leave.

The door was getting a lot of hard use today. He too slammed it on his way out.

A couple of days later, on September 14, Solomonida and I again welcomed visitors as they entered the women's quarters. We had a full house, in fact: Maria and Juliana arrived first—with Lyuba, of course, but also with Katya, whom we hadn't seen since the trouble with her uncles. Almost as soon as we had them settled, Anfim Fadeyev appeared with Lara. After a quick greeting, she joined Anna and Lyuba on the floor, watching shyly as they planned a midday meal for Anna's dolls.

"And your son?" I asked.

"I left him in the yard," Anfim said. "There's four or five boys there, playing with the dog, and a groom keeping an eye on them."

"Good idea," Solomonida told him. "They'll wear themselves out, and Laika too. Much easier for the rest of us than having them humming with energy."

Through the window, I identified Tolya, running and whooping amid a pack of boys about his own age. Laika raced alongside them, barking and varying her stride with the occasional leap. The groom strolled after them, close enough to intervene in case of trouble. "They look like they're having fun," I said. "Tolya can come up here if he needs to nap before you're ready to leave. Otherwise, I'm sure he'll be fine where he is. The groom will call for food when they get hungry."

He thanked us and went downstairs. About to turn away from the window and rejoin our guests, I noticed a man entering the courtyard. He wore a dark jacket, charcoal gray or black, covered with a mail shirt. The trousers tucked into his boots were also black, the boots plain brown. His hair gleamed in the late morning sun, and the hilt of the sword belted around his slim waist gleamed as well. I gasped.

Nikita, dressed for war.

Tempted to run to him, I clung to the shutter, questions tumbling through my head. What brought him here? Should I go to him? What about that girl to whom Katya said he was promised? What about *Igor*, who had forbidden any talk of a marriage with Niki?

"What's going on?" Solomonida said. "You look like one of Koshchei the Immortal's stone statues."

"Nikita's here, in our courtyard." My voice sounded strangled. I couldn't help it.

"Then let's go down and greet him," she said. When I turned to stare at her, she raised her hands, palms up to express astonishment. "He's the son of Papa's best friend. What's wrong with you today?"

I didn't know the answer to that myself. Did I want to see Niki or not?

Of course I did. But I didn't want him to confirm that he'd been disloyal to me.

"Yes, let's go and greet him," Maria said. "Or meet him, in my case. Alexei was quite impressed with him. I'd like to know more."

Juliana caught my hand and pulled me toward the door. "You see? It's unanimous. Let's go." So we went.

By the time we reached the bottom of the outside stairs, we could hear men's voices, raised in anger. Nikita and Igor faced each other, noses almost touching, hands clenched into fists at their sides. The five of us stopped to get a clear sense of what had them at each other's throats.

Not that they'd ever been friends, but general dislike doesn't necessarily lead to fisticuffs, as this argument—whatever it was—looked fit to do.

"Do *not* refer to Darya Petrovna that way," Nikita shouted. "She is a young woman worthy of the highest respect, and I will not listen to you disparaging her. And if I hear you refer to her as Dashka again—or even hear that you've called her that while I'm not around—I'll put your teeth through the back of your head."

They were arguing about me. They were arguing about *me*?

And Niki was defending me, in no uncertain terms. A warm glow filled my heart.

"I'll call her whatever I want." Igor flexed and released his hands, but his stance was less pugnacious than Niki's. I even saw a hint of fear. "She lives in this house, under my guardianship. You have no say in what happens to her."

Niki didn't so much as flinch. "I will have a say. I don't know what trick you pulled to get that will written in your favor, but it's a lie and I intend to prove it. Then I'll marry her, and you'll be the one with no say."

"You're dreaming. By then she'll be wed. And the estate is mine. You can't prove otherwise because it's true, whether you believe it or not." Igor plastered a smug smile on his face as he took three steps backward.

Niki roared and lunged for Igor's throat. Laika leaped between them, knocking Niki sideways. I ran forward as he staggered and righted him with an arm around his waist, and he hugged me hard against his chest. Igor swore. Laika growled in defense of her master but—perhaps recalling Niki's petting and those bits of dried beef—didn't attack. I ignored them both.

"I didn't expect to see you again." I pushed the words past a tight throat. "What brought you here?"

He walked me far enough away from the crowd that we could talk without being overheard. "To tell you we're done with the hunting trip. I'm back in Moscow for tonight, but leaving again tomorrow. For Holy Trinity, with Prince Vladimir and his cousins. I'll look for Father Hilarion then. I expected to have found him already, but the hunting party headed in a different direction. I was hoping to spend the evening with you. But what do you mean: you thought you wouldn't see me again? I told you I love you and that I'd get word to you as soon as I could."

"Katya heard from her brother that you've been promised for years." I pulled myself out of his arms, although I couldn't stop the tears trickling down my cheeks. "I can see you've been toying with me. So why would you come back? We can't marry. You should never have asked me. That was dishonorable, whatever Papa wrote to you."

"Well, yes, I have been promised," he said, "but—"

Igor cut him off in mid-sentence. He surged forward, grabbed my arm, and hauled me away, almost throwing me at Solomonida. Then he aimed a punch at Nikita, who sidestepped it with ease before slamming a fist into Igor's chin that sent him flying. The rowdy boys, who had stopped their running at the prospect of a fight, cheered at the sight of Igrushka flat on his back, gasping for air. Their cheers turned to hooting as Laika, in an excess of devotion, straddled her master's shoulders and licked his cheeks. Igor made feeble attempts to dislodge the dog, to no avail.

The whole scene was funny in the extreme, but I didn't feel like laughing. I stared at Niki, who was regarding me with a slight frown between his eyes.

I didn't know what to say to him. He'd confirmed he was promised to someone else. No "but" could fix that. Unless he'd been on the brink of telling me that the woman had died or married someone else in the last two weeks, breaking his promise to her betrayed us all.

Maria walked past me and stopped in front of Niki. "You are Nikita Andreevich Monastyrev," she said, her voice pitched to cut through the furor in the courtyard. Every head turned to stare at her. Even the boys, chortling and pointing at Laika as Igor struggled to free himself, fell silent when Maria spoke. She had the bearing and manner of a queen.

"I am Tsarevna Maria Fyodorovna," she went on. "My husband has told me about you. We need to talk." And without so much as a glance at Igor, still splayed flat against the ground, she placed her hand on Niki's arm and turned him toward the gate.

Solomonida came to stand beside me. "Well, well, well," she said. "That's an interesting development."

I couldn't speak. Tears poured down my face, and every breath came out as a sob.

My sister put her arm around my waist. "Let's go back inside. I'll send a servant to help Igor."

When I didn't respond, she touched my wet cheek. "What is it?"

Her motherly tone destroyed my last shreds of self-control. "It's true, Shura." I dropped my head on her shoulder. "Niki admitted it. He's promised to someone else."

Maria refused to tell us what she'd said to Nikita when she at last returned to the sewing room. By then, I'd recovered my composure enough to realize that the admission that sent me into floods of tears wasn't the only thing Niki had said—or done—during his confrontation with Igor. He'd declared his intention to marry me, as well as his belief that Igor had no claim to our estate. And he had defended me without hesitation. So it seemed likely that Niki did love me, although how he thought we could wed was more than I could fathom.

I said as much. "And the thing is," I finished, "Igor will push even harder now to find me a husband of his choosing."

"Or marry you himself," Solomonida said—less to remind me, I assumed, since the words were seared into my brain like a brand, than to let the other women know.

"That's quite a threat," Juliana said in that cool way of hers. "Should we move her to Maria's house after all? Felix and I have to return to Poland soon; we'd gladly take Darya with us, but getting her back if things work out could be difficult."

Katya had hardly spoken since she arrived, behavior so uncharacteristic of her that I wondered if the mistreatment of her uncles and the disgrace inflicted on her clan had broken her fiery spirit. But now she said quietly, "Did you know that Nikita Andreevich disputed your cousin's claim to the estate?"

She was looking at me when she spoke, but even without that I would have guessed she meant the question for me. Who had spent more time with Nikita than I?

"I did," I told her. "It was the first thing he said to me when I met him that day near your gate."

"Yet you didn't mention it." She sounded calm, even cold. "Although I helped you against my uncle. Are you a friend or an enemy?"

She had a point. I refrained from noting that she had often given me reason to doubt her intentions as well. I took a deep breath and released it, seeking the right words. "You want my cousin. You told me that yourself. And although Niki said he would prove he was the rightful heir, I had—and have—no reason to think he can succeed. Igor's the one with the will. Why distress you with a possibility that may never come to pass?"

She relaxed a little then. "Yes, I suppose. But what happens if Nikita does prove his claim?"

"I don't know." I squeezed her hand, offering what comfort I could. "Since he's promised elsewhere, nothing so far as I'm concerned. But Igor will be even more in need of a noble bride." And I could support Katya wholeheartedly then, since she would no longer threaten my position within this household.

"He will still have a powerful patron in Koshkin," I added, to remind her that his connections might make up in her family's eyes for his lack of property.

"Yes," she said, but she turned her head away, and I knew she hadn't forgiven me. But then I recalled how she'd told me to forget Nikita and realized that I hadn't forgiven her either. Whatever she'd intended, her delivery of that news had shattered me.

Juliana kept silent while Katya and I talked, but at this point she came back into the conversation. "You didn't answer my question," she said. "Should we take Darya Petrovna to Maria's house? You would agree, would you not, Maria? You said before that you would welcome her."

"Of course," Maria said as if this were the only possible response.

"It's up to you, Darya," Solomonida said. "Would you feel safer there?"

A concerted gasp came from the other side of the room. I looked to my right, where the three girls were staring at me with wide eyes and open mouths. I'd completely forgotten their presence. What a show I'd put on. I must have terrified them, weeping and wailing and now this.

I returned my attention to the women, but I spoke to the girls. "I would *feel* safer," I admitted. "But I don't think I would *be* safer. Igor can press me to marry a man of his choosing, including himself. He can sign a contract on my behalf. But noble weddings take time to arrange. With luck, even finding a third candidate won't be easy. Their wives and mothers and sisters will talk. I haven't been out in society for so long that most of them can't have an independent opinion about me. Between the rumors that I'm a religious zealot and the rumors that my face is scarred, that I mumble and can't sew, not to mention the reality of my twenty-five years, I'm probably not the bride any potential mother-in-law yearns for. So I think I needn't throw myself on Maria's mercy yet."

"Good for you," Maria said. "If your wretched cousin signs a contract, then by all means come to me. If nothing else, I can ask Alexei to dissuade him. In the meantime, I have a better plan."

"What is it?" the rest of us asked in chorus. But Maria shook her head and refused to say.

Chapter Sixteen

TWO WEEKS PASSED WITHOUT IGOR FINDING ANOTHER MAN so desperately in need of a bride that he would throw caution to the winds and consider me. As September gave way to October, I stopped running for the window every time I heard hooves in the courtyard due to fear of potential husbands or a vain hope that Nikita would return victorious against the odds. I avoided my cousin as much as possible in the magical, not to say childish, belief that if I stayed out of his sight he might forget my existence. It helped that Igor returned to his prior habit of spending more time away from the house than in it. From remarks he let fall from time to time, I gathered that he had expanded his search for a suitable bride, but also that he no longer included Katya on his list. None of his negotiations, however, progressed to the point where he required Solomonida's assistance in inspecting the chosen candidate—the ordeal inflicted on me by Aunt Liza and Princess Blednaya. As the days piled up and turned into weeks, I relaxed enough to enjoy life, entertaining my friends, working with Anna and Lara on their embroidery, and stitching on my altar cloth, now almost complete.

On this particular afternoon in early October, I'd remembered the map that Nikita drew. I thought it would amuse Anna and Lara, and even Solomonida, since it seemed unlikely that she'd ever seen it. I'd long since returned it undetected to the pile where I'd found it, so I decided to take the direct approach to retrieving it. If things went well, I could find a place for the map in my bedchamber as a keepsake, a memory of those precious days with Niki. If things went really well, I might find a way to return it to him. But the first step was to get it from Anfim Fadeyev's office.

I stopped to greet Father Job as I passed his door and asked after his family's health. With one crisis after another, I'd spent less time chatting with him in the last few weeks, not least because I couldn't imagine sharing with him my duplicitous plans for repelling unwanted mothers-in-law. But I loved and respected Father Job, so I wanted him to know that I still valued his counsel. I did take the time to tell him about my exchange with Mother Elena and my decision not to commit myself to the monastic life yet. He listened with kindly patience, as I knew he would, and nodded in sympathy when I confessed my fears of what my cousin might do next.

"We will trust your sister to find the right man," he said as I rose to leave. "You have done well, my daughter."

"Thank you, Father. I hope she does." I bowed, my hands pressed together, and tried not to think that Solomonida had so far failed to produce a single acceptable candidate—or about the unlikelihood that Igor would agree with her choice. Then I said farewell and moved on to the office where Anfim spent so much of his days.

As usual, when I pushed open the door, he was bent over his paperwork. I cleared my throat, so as not to startle him. The memory of Niki leaping to his feet in the orchard, hands readied for defense, caused tears to blur my vision for a moment. Why had he not admitted then that he wasn't free to marry? He'd obviously been thinking about it, since he talked about choices he regretted. It was the one question that tormented me without ceasing.

"Are you all right, Darya Petrovna?"

I shook my head to clear it and saw Anfim standing, concern on his face. "What's wrong?" he asked.

I heard kindness in his voice and realized he'd misunderstood the head shake as a no. "I'm fine," I said. "And sorry to worry you. I remembered something, that's all."

"May I help you, then?"

I moved into the room, leaving the door ajar, and took a seat on the opposite side of his desk. "I'm looking for a map. Papa told me he had a hand-drawn one of the estate, given to him years ago. Have you seen it, by any chance?"

Would he deny knowledge of it? At one time I'd suspected him of adding Laika to the sheet of paper, in which case he must have seen the map and treasured it as Nikita and I had.

"I'd like to show it to Lara and Anna," I said in the hope that his love for his daughter would overcome any reluctance he might feel.

He rifled through a stack of papers to his left, selected one, and held it out to me. "Is this it?"

It was. Again I smiled at the romping dog and the groom chasing her, the tiny Father Hilarion, my stepmother's embroidery frame, the horses and pictures of food that marked the different storage houses, Niki's seal in the lower right corner. "It's lovely," I said. Then—because why not ask?—I pointed to the running hound. "That can't have been there when Papa was alive, though."

His cheeks crimsoned, and he looked more embarrassed than I'd ever seen him. "Uh, no. I found it early in my tenure here. It was so charming, and that center space was bare. So I added Laika myself."

"She's a wonderful addition," I told him. "How well you draw! I'm sure Papa would have approved."

With my first goal achieved, I pondered how best to tackle the more difficult issue. I wanted to know the origins of the document that Nikita identified as containing the names of Polish princesses and how it came to be in our house.

I decided to ask outright. If Anfim didn't like the question, he would pretend ignorance.

"Do you recall complaining about an intruder in your office, not long after you first came here?" I said. "That was me."

He gasped. "I do. I thought it was you at the time. I saw ink on your hands the next day."

"But you didn't say anything."

I could guess why, so it didn't surprise me when he flushed. "It's not my place to question your movements."

"True," I said. "I came that day because I wanted to see what required so much of your time. I found that map, as well as two sheets filled with women's names. One listed high-ranking noblewomen—princesses and the like. But the second was a chart with entries that I later discovered could refer to King Sigismund's daughters. Why do you have such a document? Is that what you do all day, copy government papers related to foreign affairs? Because I know for a fact that our household accounts don't require this much work. I check them myself once a week."

He blanched, more shocked by the news that I could differentiate among his papers than by my admission of prying. I saw his Adam's apple quiver as he fought for a response. Then he blurted out, "You can read?"

"Yes," I said. I sounded more aggressive than I meant to, because I didn't actually suspect him of wrongdoing. But I decided not to put him at ease just yet. The things I'd been through the last few months—Papa's death, the arrival of Igor and my ongoing conflict with him, the unwanted bridegrooms, my rejection by Mother Elena, the unresolved situation with Nikita, and now Fadeyev's duplicity—had hardened me. I was no longer the deferential girl who laughed at the peacock strutting through her yard and struggled to control her own need to please.

"Answer my question," I said.

"I can't," he told me. "It's not my secret to keep, and it's more than my job is worth to break my employer's confidence."

"Igor took it," I said, making the obvious deduction. If I worked it out myself, he couldn't be held responsible. "Is that where he goes during the day? To a government office?"

Anfim shook his head, a brief but rapid gesture that said everything and nothing. Then I remembered my conversation with Niki, the day he told me about the princesses, and the deduction I'd made then. Igor had a patron, whom I had once described (accurately) as the shiftiest man in Moscow. If anyone had government contacts, a reason to conceal them, *and* an incentive to meddle in a future royal marriage, Igor's patron was that man. Satisfaction warmed my chest as the pieces fell into place.

"Of course," I said. "Fyodor Koshkin. Maria told me her father wanted Lyuba to wed the grand prince, who is nearing marriageable age. Soon the top-ranking nobles will hold a bride show for him—unless they settle on a Polish princess. That's Koshkin's price for serving as Igor's patron: he wants my cousin's support in the forthcoming battle over who gets to be the next royal father-in-law. Perhaps he's manipulating Igor by giving him documents to hold that will get Igor into trouble if they're discovered, and Igor's exerting a similar hold on you, because you both know that you'll never be accepted back into the Treasury if you're found in possession of stolen papers."

To Anfim's credit, he didn't break his employer's confidence by so much as a whispered confirmation. But the quick dip of his chin indicating respect told me I'd guessed right.

Of course, it was too much to hope that Igor would give up on arranging my marriage altogether. I'd come to understand that he was nothing if not determined. A week or ten days after my encounter with Anfim in his office, Igor strutted into the sewing room looking as though he might burst from excitement.

"At last," he said, ignoring the scowls with which Solomonida and I greeted him in a vain attempt to let him know we didn't appreciate his invasion of our private space. "That dinner I hosted months ago has borne fruit. Tsarevich Alexei sent me a most friendly note this morning.

He invites the three of us to visit him tomorrow. He has found a man willing to marry you, Dashka, troublesome piece that you are. Don't even think about trying any of your tricks. We want to keep Tsarevich Alexei happy. So you will accept this man he's found, or you will marry me. And that's the end of it."

He turned, as if to leave. "Wait," I said. My head was spinning with the suddenness of his announcement. "What's this man's name? How does Tsarevich Alexei know him?"

"Prince Alexander Dmitrievich Barbashin." Igor rolled each "r," openly gloating at his own good fortune and my dismay. "A prominent family, related to the Shuisky princely clan. Beyond that, I know nothing about him and care less. He'll get you off my hands, and I'll have Tsarevich Alexei as a patron. What more do I need to know? Be ready after morning prayers tomorrow. I've no intention of letting this boon pass me by."

Watching him strut from the room, even more self-satisfied than when he entered it, I felt my shoulders slump. I waited long enough to be certain he'd gone, then glanced at my sister only to discover that she was studying me in turn.

"Prince Alexander Dmitrievich Barbashin." I repeated the name like the knell of doom, a sound that struck me as more appropriate each time I heard it. "Do you know an Alexander Dmitrievich Barbashin? A Dmitry Barbashin who might be his father? Anything?"

"I knew *a* Barbashin." Solomonida dropped the headdress she was stitching for Anna and tapped her fingers against her palm. "He died a couple of years ago, but he was a boyar and a noted general. Ivan Ivanovich—a good-looking man, a competent soldier, dark hair and eyes, so could be some Tatar blood there. Perhaps that's the connection with Alexei. Ivan Ivanovich must be a relative of this Alexander, although not a father or brother. As Igrushka says, they're an offshoot of the Shuisky clan, a couple of generations back."

I tried to take comfort from the thought that a husband selected by Alexei had to be better than one chosen by Igor. "And if he turns out to be a hundred years old or weaned yesterday or hopeless in some other way? I'm running out of ideas, and I'd rather not end up wed to Igrushka the Duckling. But if he's managed to get Alexei and Maria on his side, my only refuge will be to take monastic vows after all. Assuming I can find a mother superior willing to take me."

"Let's not panic." My sister picked up the headdress and examined it from all angles. You'd think it contained a solution to my problem, the way she stared at it. "I think Igor's making idle threats, although I agree you don't want to push him into carrying them out. But it can't be an accident that Alexei decided to involve himself at this moment. I'm sure it's not because he's developed a belated respect for our Duckling. If the man is completely unsuitable, we'll throw ourselves on Maria's mercy or even send you off to Poland with Juliana and Felix."

I agreed, seeing no alternative, but for the rest of the day and well into the night, I worried about who Alexander Dmitrievich Barbashin was and what marriage to him would be like. I didn't dare think of Nikita, but when I did fall asleep at last, his smile haunted my dreams.

By the time the next morning rolled around and Igor announced he was ready to leave, my nerves were more tangled than the threads in my sewing basket. Igor glowed with triumph, rubbing his hands and muttering, "At last, a patron worthy of my talents," and similarly absurd exercises in self-congratulation as he led the way to our covered carriage and shepherded us inside. Anna followed him, wide-eyed and silent. Solomonida cooed a succession of compliments aimed at our cousin that the twinkle in her eyes told me she didn't mean one bit. I gritted my teeth, longing to kick Igor in his brocade-covered posterior but retaining just enough control to refrain. If the childhood chant "Igrushka the Duckling" echoed over and over in my brain, I hoped God forgave me for that.

Alexei's house was as beautiful as I remembered, but I had little mental energy to admire the elaborate patterns created by turquoise tiles or the brilliant wools intertwined on Turkmen carpets. Even the bright light that impressed me the first time I visited had acquired a vaguely sinister glow because it would reveal with exceptional clarity the face of the man chosen to become my lord and master for the rest of my days, the father of my children. I struggled to remember Father Job's reassuring words about support and affection and partnership in marriage, but facing the reality of a stranger who would acquire full rights to the use of my body from the moment the priest declared us one heart and soul, the idea seemed like sweets offered to a child—comforting but not substantial.

Maria's housekeeper met us as we entered the house. She ushered us three adults into a large room I hadn't seen on my previous visit, then held out her hand to my niece. "Lady Anna, come with me. Lady Lyuba is upstairs." Anna went off with a rapid stride that suggested she couldn't wait to put our tense exchanges behind her. I followed Igor and Solomonida through the door and stopped, confused.

Alexei stood in the center of the room, Maria at his side. Lord Felix and Juliana formed a kind of barrier at the window—bodies turned toward each other, outer shoulders raised and heads facing Fyodor Koshkin, the only other person present besides Igor, Solomonida, and myself. I saw no one who could be the mysterious Alexander Barbashin.

I greeted each person in turn, more or less affectionately as my familiarity with them dictated. We exchanged rounds of pleasantries—inquiries into one another's health, exclamations as to how long it had been since we met, the usual things people say at the beginning of a social gathering. After my initial bow, I stayed as far away from Koshkin as I could, even as I wondered what he was doing here. I chatted first with Alexei and Maria, as befitted their position as hosts, then moved to Lord Felix and Juliana. But the words that came out of my mouth, still less those that entered my ears, evaporated like morning dew as soon as I spoke or heard them, leaving no residue in my mind. My nerves might as well have been stretched on a rack, and my stomach ached with tension. I wanted to ask Maria and Juliana about this man Alexei had found for me. At the same time, I wanted to avoid talking about him. Asking would indicate interest when I felt only dread. It would give him a face and a character as well as a name. It would make him real, when I yearned to pinch myself and wake up, as one does from a nightmare.

After days and weeks that could not in truth have lasted as much as half an hour, Alexei approached me while I sat in a state close to desperation next to my sister, trying to pretend that I understood a word of her conversation with Lord Felix. Igor stood within hearing range, deep in discussion with Fyodor Koshkin, still gloating about having acquired a husband for me with such a distinguished lineage and giving Koshkin credit for the find that even he seemed disinclined to accept.

"Won't you join me?" Alexei said, his voice deep and cool as always. His unflappable courtesy, the kindness in his tone and on his face, calmed my fears enough that I managed to stand and walk with him. Solomonida sent me an encouraging glance as I left. "You must be wondering who it is we've asked you here to meet."

I nodded, too nervous to speak. He led the way to an alcove that contained a side door, which he opened. "Trust us," he said, too quietly for anyone else in the room to hear. "You won't be disappointed."

I turned my head sharply and looked straight into his eyes. He gave me his wonderful smile and indicated the door with an outstretched hand. "I'm sorry we made you wait, but you'll understand why in a minute. Go and meet your husband."

I should have thanked him, but again words failed me. Gripping my skirt tightly to give myself courage, I walked through the door, braced for my first glimpse of Alexander Dmitrievich Barbashin.

The only person in the room was Nikita.

In my shock, I must have swayed, because next thing I knew Niki had his arms around me. I heard the click of the closing door, but dimly, as though from far out among the stars.

"Dashenka, are you all right?" Niki pulled me sideways onto one of the covered benches that lined the walls of every room I'd seen in this house. "I'm sorry for the subterfuge, sweetest girl. Maria convinced me that your cousin wouldn't let me near you unless he thought I was someone else. She talked to Alexei, and we came up with this plan."

I wrapped my arms around his waist and pressed my cheek against his shoulder. The sudden release of fear had me trembling and shivering, and I was glad of the heat emanating from the bench and the warmth of his hold. "None of you could warn me?"

His chin brushed my hair as he shook his head. "I'm sorry, darling," he said. "I'm sure the last day has been dreadful, and I hated to keep the secret from you. But we decided it was best. If you were worried, Igor wouldn't suspect that Alexander Barbashin was not what he seemed." He stroked my cheek. "Forgive me. And marry me?"

I longed to believe him, yet I couldn't force my doubts into the background overnight. "But how can I? Igor will find out soon and forbid it, and what of that girl your father promised you to so many years ago?"

Nikita laughed and pulled me closer. "Ah yes, that girl. Igor has a lot to answer for there. If he hadn't taken a swing at me at the worst possible moment, you'd already know that girl is you."

"Me?!" I heard an astonished hope in my voice. I didn't dare trust it.

"Of course you!" he said, laughing harder. "Who else would it be? Our fathers were best friends. I'm sure they planned our marriage when you were in your cradle and I a mighty toddler."

"But if that's so, what did you mean that day in the Vorontsovs' orchard when you told me your past choices might block your path? After Katya told me about the other girl, I felt certain you were referring to a prior betrothal."

He shook his head. "No, to my support for Prince Andrei. I thought for a long time that my disgrace had ended any hope of wedding you, because your father was desperate to protect you. He'd already seen your sister suffer because of her husband's misdeeds. He didn't want to repeat his mistakes with you. And when he did reach out with his letter, I couldn't keep my promise to visit because I was still in disgrace for having backed Prince Andrei. Serpukhov was a punishment post; that's why the boyars sent me there."

How ridiculous I'd been, how vulnerable to Katya's ... what? I didn't know whether she'd acted from malice or genuine concern. But I myself had noted the date on Igor's copy of Papa's will and wondered whether Niki's connection to Prince Andrei and the abortive rebellion explained what at the time I'd thought was the rupture between Niki and my father.

"I should have guessed," I said. "But I love you so much, and what Katya told me broke my heart. I shouldn't have listened to her."

Tears clogged my throat as I thought of those weeks of anguish, but somewhere in the impending torrent a small flame of anger burned, aimed at Katya. Whether she meant to cause trouble or prevent it, she too had jumped to conclusions and, in doing so, caused me unnecessary grief.

Niki rubbed my cheek with his thumb. "Don't cry, sweetheart," he said. "I understand. We hadn't seen each other for too long. Nor have we spent enough time together since I returned. But I love you too; I always have. And you can trust me. How many times did I tell you your father promised you to me?"

Relief mingled with love and happiness and feelings I couldn't name, obliterating my sorrow and dampening the anger. I gave a deep sigh of contentment. "You did," I said. "Often. And Papa said it too, before he died: that he would find me a husband who would help us with the estate. But Igor won't agree, and he's still the head of the clan—no matter what."

"Igor is making his mark on the contract now," Niki said. "Tsarevich Alexei promised he would take care of that before Igor found out who 'Alexander Barbashin' really is."

I pulled away from him. "But isn't your name on the contract?"

He tapped my nose, again laughing softly. "Yes, of course it is. But you've forgotten. You can read. I can read. Can Igor?"

"No." Awe filled me as I realized how much effort my friends had put into developing a plan to ensure my happiness. "No, he can't."

"Right. But he will believe whatever Tsarevich Alexei tells him is on the paper, just as he believed what Fyodor Koshkin told him about the will—and that chart about the Polish princesses, no doubt. Your cousin is so desperate for an illustrious patron and success at court that it never occurs to him that when people tell him something he wants to hear, they may have reasons that work to their advantage rather than his."

Something about his phrasing caught my attention. "What Koshkin told him about the will," I repeated, testing my vague perception that Niki knew more than he was saying. "But I've seen the will. It says exactly what Koshkin claims."

"It does." Niki was smiling now. "That copy certainly does. But that is not your father's will."

My jaw dropped open. I snapped it shut. "You found Father Hilarion," I said. "Where is he?"

"In Tsarevich Alexei's study, supervising the completion of the marriage contract. He goes by the name Innokenty now. We'll join him soon, but right now I'm going to kiss you, because I've been waiting since the day I turned fifteen to make you my wife."

I pulled his head toward me and parted my lips. It was even more delightful than I remembered.

By the time we reached Alexei's study, he'd made sure the contract was inked, sanded, sealed, and put away for safekeeping. Igor jerked in surprise when Nikita came in, his arm around my waist. Solomonida sent Maria an astonished glance, but after Maria gave a reassuring nod in response, my sister pressed her lips together and didn't ask questions.

I went to Father Hilarion, now Innokenty, and bowed my head for his blessing. I hadn't loved him as I loved Father Job, but I respected him, so I greeted him warmly before returning to stand beside Nikita. I murmured my thanks to Alexei as I passed him, but I didn't look at Igor or Fyodor Koshkin except from the corner of my eye. I did exchange glances with Juliana, who gave me her most impish smile while Felix saluted me with one of his Polish-style flourishes. Then I waited.

It didn't take long. Father Innokenty raised his hand. The smattering of conversation died, and those in the room became completely still. Every one of us focused his or her attention on the priest.

"Nikita Andreevich tells me," he said, "that Fyodor Mikhailovich Koshkin claims that I left Pyotr Alexandrovich Sheremetev's will with him when I left for the Holy Trinity Monastery. That is not true." He reached into a bag lying on Alexei's desk and pulled out a piece of paper. "This is Pyotr Alexandrovich's will. He dictated the provisions to me when he heard that I planned to retire to a monastery, and I drew up the will and had it properly signed and witnessed before I left Moscow in May 1540. I took the document with me only because at the time Pyotr Alexandrovich had not decided which priest he would invite to serve his household. He knew he was starting to lose his memory, and he was afraid that if he kept the will in his house, he would forget its existence. He promised to have a letter delivered to me later, telling me where to send the document, but the letter never arrived, so I kept the testament with me until I could receive instructions from Pyotr Alexandrovich himself or from his heir."

"And what does the will say?" Solomonida asked.

"That your father left most of his property to you and your sister, but his estate to Nikita Andreevich"—Father Innokenty nodded at Niki as he spoke—"on the condition that he and Darya Petrovna agree to marry, so that they can manage the property together with you, Solomonida Petrovna."

"I don't believe you," Igor said. "I'm his closest male relative. Nikita's not even family. Why would Sheremetev let his estate pass into the hands of another clan?"

Father Innokenty, tall and thin, looked down his long nose at Igor as if my cousin were a petulant child. The whiny note in Igor's voice didn't do much to dispel that impression. "Pyotr Alexandrovich saw Nikita Andreevich as a second son. The estate had to pass from his immediate family, because there was no male Sheremetev to inherit. He sought to take care of his daughters while rewarding a young man he loved. What could be more natural in a father? To ensure that nothing interfered in his plans, he inserted the provision that his daughters could remain at the Moscow estate for as long as they wished, assuming it would be only a short time before the marriage of Darya Petrovna and Nikita Andreevich settled matters to everyone's comfort."

"But ...," Igor spluttered. "That's ridiculous. I'm his heir. The man had lost his wits!"

The priest heaved a sigh before continuing. "I had hoped to convince you without saying this, Igor Grigorevich. Pyotr Alexandrovich did not trust your father, and he had no faith in you. Alas, your behavior regarding the will proves that his judgment of you was correct. You took the word of Fyodor Koshkin without attempting to verify its truth, although any sensible person would have questioned his possession of a document that Lord Sheremetev would have shared only with his closest associates."

I heard a moan and risked a glance at Igor, who stared in horror at the priest. As I watched, Igor's eyes flicked to Koshkin, whose face was contorted in anger.

"What have you done?" Igor gasped. "You've ruined me!"

Koshkin turned on him. "What have *I* done? You ungrateful pup! What *haven't* I done for you? I introduced you to every high-ranking nobleman I know. I had a will forged for you. I backed you in every way possible. I even persuaded that miserable Demian Bledny to take your cousin off your hands before the girls figured out what was going on, but you couldn't make it stick." He shook his head, then kicked the carpet for emphasis. "I don't believe it. So much effort on behalf of a fool, and this is the thanks I get!"

"And what did you expect from him in return?" Alexei asked, in a harsh voice I'd not heard him use before.

"Support." Koshkin snarled. "More than I get from the rest of you. Will *you* back me when it comes time for the grand prince to select a bride? Or will you mutter about Lyuba having choices, as if a girl serves any purpose beyond the advancement and continuation of her lineage? The whole lot of you are worthless." He pointed a finger at Father Innokenty. "You especially!"

The priest seemed unmoved by this insult. "You are a sinner, vainglorious and dishonest," he said in lofty tones.

Koshkin snarled again. When Igor gaped, not speaking, Father Innokenty tipped his head at my cousin. "And you need to be less trusting, young man. Or were you in on this scheme from the beginning?"

Igor shook his head, obviously baffled by the cascade of events. "I thought the will was genuine," he said sadly. "That my fortunes had changed."

I almost felt sorry for him, seeing him so overwhelmed by the turn of events. Then I remembered how he'd done everything in his power to keep Niki and me apart, and my flash of sympathy vanished.

"You're welcome to leave," Alexei told his father-in-law, still in that biting tone. Koshkin glowered at him and turned on his heel.

"Wait," I said. Koshkin turned back, a startled look on his face. "I have a question, Fyodor Mikhailovich," I told him. "Why target us? What did my family ever do to you?"

Koshkin hesitated for so long I thought he would refuse to answer. "Yes," Alexei said when the silence dragged on. "Explain. What do you have against Nikita Andreevich? Or do you want me to guess, based on what I know of your past? Sheremetev was already ill when I first met you, but I don't remember any animosity between you. And his daughters have done you no harm. So it must be Nikita Andreevich who has offended you. Somehow you learned of the missing will, and you launched this entire elaborate scheme to ensure he would not inherit. The possibility of support from Igor Grigorevich was an added benefit, not your only goal."

I must have looked as astonished as Nikita. It hadn't occurred to me that Koshkin could hold a grudge against Niki. Why? When had they even met before?

"I've offended him?" Niki put my thought into words. "It doesn't seem possible. I saw him once or twice in Staritsa, but never to talk to. I told you before: I rode with Prince Andrei's majordomo to Kolomna and back, so I wasn't even there most of the time before Fyodor Mikhailovich left the camp."

"But you did see him in the camp, after Prince Andrei made his run for Novgorod?" Alexei asked.

"I did," Niki said. "For a few days here and there, although I didn't connect his name and his face until later. What of it?"

"What of it, indeed. You have to think like a criminal to make sense of it. You saw him somewhere he should not have been. You might not intend to report it, but you could. You can swear that he betrayed the grand prince." Alexei sent his father-in-law a look of disgust. "That's it, isn't it? You've clawed your way back into favor and survived the threat to Shuisky power, so the last thing you want is a young man hanging about Moscow who can attest that you weren't always such a staunch supporter of the throne. You do whatever it takes to protect yourself, no matter who else gets hurt in the process."

"He'd be a fool to attest to anything of the sort," Koshkin said. "It would remind those in power of his own unsavory past."

"No, it wouldn't," Alexei retorted. "Nikita was assigned to Staritsa. He didn't choose the post, but he fulfilled his assignment and defended his prince. He committed no crime. And he has my backing, so no one will dare say otherwise." Igor yelped at what no doubt seemed to him the injustice of that, when he'd so yearned for Alexei's support.

"You're the one who changed sides," Alexei went on, addressing his father-in-law and ignoring my cousin. "More than once, in fact. Moscow, Staritsa, Lithuania, Moscow. You fled wherever you saw a rabbit hole where you could hide and left your family to suffer the consequences. Nikita fought to the end and paid the price. He's earned redemption. You haven't."

Koshkin glowered at his son-in-law. "Easy for you to say. What do you know of hardship and treachery? The son of a khan. You've always had life fed to you with a silver spoon. I've worked for every reward I've received, even when it meant overcoming opposition from people like you."

For reasons I didn't understand, Maria burst out laughing at that, and Alexei, after a moment of stunned silence, joined her.

"No," he said when he could talk again. "I have not always had life fed to me on a silver spoon. My father cast me out when I was sixteen. You must remember how grudgingly he received me when I agreed to marry Maria and enter Russian service. Why else would I have sought an alliance with you in the first place?" He wrapped an arm around his wife, and she rested her head on his shoulder. "She's the only reason I put up with you, and well you know it. And I think we're done, so go pester someone else for a while."

Koshkin scowled, then grabbed Igor by the arm. "Come along, puppy. We're not wanted here. You can stay at my house while we figure out what to do next." He stalked out, head held high, Igor trailing behind him.

"Thank you." I bent and kissed Father Innokenty's hand. "You righted a great wrong today." I went to Alexei, then Maria, and hugged them. I did the same with Solomonida, whispering how glad I was that we had come through this trial together. I heard Nikita behind me, repeating my thanks.

Last I came to Juliana and Felix. "I don't know exactly what your part in this was, but I'm sure you helped. Thank you so much."

"We'll be leaving soon," Juliana said. "It's our great pleasure to see you so well settled before we go. And I'm glad we had a chance to renew our acquaintance under better terms. I wish we could stay for your ceremony, but Felix has affairs to attend to in Cracow."

"I too am glad we part as friends. And to have met you, Felix." I hesitated. But if they were leaving soon, why not ask? I might not have another chance. "Why did you come to Moscow? It wasn't only to see Maria and Alexei, surely."

Juliana's face broke into one of the most genuine smiles I'd ever seen from her. "Well, we do love Maria and Alexei and Lyuba, and we do hope to visit them again. But we also came to find out how people in Moscow felt about a Polish bride—and about Poland and Lithuania more generally."

"And what did you discover?" Her candor surprised me, and I was genuinely curious.

Felix flicked her wrist with his finger and thumb, but her eyes remained riveted on me. "I can't tell all my secrets, Darya Petrovna," she said. "The answer to that question must wait for another day."

"I hope so," I said as I hugged her goodbye. "Because that means I'll see you again."

It was a long road to Cracow, and not always a safe one. And although a few months ago I wouldn't have believed anyone who told me I might miss Juliana, the thought that this could be my last sight of her and Lord Felix made me sad.

"And indeed, you must come back," I added, to lighten the mood. "You never did sing for us, after all."

"I didn't, did I?" Juliana looked thoughtful for a moment, then gave a quick nod of her head. "Well, let's take care of that, shall we?" She walked to the door and clapped her hands. A servant came running, and she ordered the woman to fetch her lute from her chamber, then turned back to us. "A love song to honor your engagement," she said.

The maidservant returned more quickly than I'd have believed possible and handed Juliana an instrument that rather resembled a large pear cut in half, with strings running from the top down the stem almost to the bottom. She ran her fingers over the strings, adjusted a peg or two, then gestured to us to sit. I found a place beside Nikita, who clasped my right hand in both of his. My palm tingled at his touch, and I smiled at him. So twisted a path we'd traversed, yet how pleasant the destination!

Juliana opened her mouth, and the most glorious sound poured out. High and clear and pure, it flowed over me like a waterfall in a forest clearing.

I didn't understand a single word. I couldn't have said whether she sang in Persian or Italian or another language altogether, but I didn't care. Surrounded by love, I let the music sweep me into another sphere, filled with goodness and light.

Tsarevich Alexei was right. Even in church, I had never heard a more beautiful voice.

Chapter Seventeen

THE DAY AFTER THE CONTRACT WAS SIGNED, MARIA ARRIVED at our house in late morning, carrying a large pouch that I at first assumed contained her needlework. Lyuba followed a few steps behind.

I had sewing on my mind, because less than an hour before I had put the last stitch into the tail of the fourth peacock, completing the altar cloth that had occupied so much of my attention for the last year or more. I'd spread it across the desk in what had once been my father's study, and Solomonida and Anna clustered around me, admiring it. Lyuba greeted Solomonida and me with a bow before hugging Anna, then gasping in awe and stretching a tentative finger toward the nearest peacock.

Maria put down her bag and joined us. "Oh, wonderful, Darya," she said. "It's gorgeous. Well done!" She touched a hand to my shoulder, as if that somehow strengthened her praise.

I reveled in their compliments. After so much work, to see the cloth complete was like a gift from Heaven. I had to admit, to myself if not aloud, it was fine. In fact, it was very fine, and pride filled me as I gazed at it: the Mother of

God at the center in her halo and midnight-blue robe, her smile enigmatic and her cheek pressed against that of her infant son; their silk background the color of the sky not long after dawn; borders along the four sides, constructed from scarlet and white flowers that somewhat resembled pansies, connected with long, curving stems; and best of all, the peacocks. At each corner, one sat on a branch, surrounded by scarlet and white roses and leaves the color of jade; the birds themselves turquoise shaded with pink, their brilliant tails sweeping in arcs almost to the gold-fringed edge of the cloth. The roses wound on long stems into the central section, surrounding and setting off the Mother of God.

Even so, as I stared at my work, I wrinkled my nose. "Something's missing," I said.

"No," Anna cried.

"It's the prettiest cloth I've ever seen," Lyuba said. "I could never stitch all that."

"What could be missing?" Solomonida added. "It's beautiful. I wish Papa could see it. He would be so proud of you!"

The thought warmed my heart, yet still I frowned at the cloth. "I don't know," I said. "The peacocks. It's something to do with the peacocks. They're not quite ..." *Quite what?*

Maria's grip on my shoulder tightened. "Aha," she said. "I have just the thing. It means a bit more stitching, but nothing you can't finish in four weeks."

She let go and turned back to the bag she'd brought with her. "Four weeks?" I said. "What's in four weeks?"

"Your wedding." Maria picked up the bag and rummaged through it. "If we don't hold it before St. Philip's Fast, we'll have to wait until after Christmas. That's why

I'm here. I promised Alexei and Nikita I'd take care of the arrangements. I have lists." Before I had a chance to react to that news, she pulled out a smaller pouch, also made of leather, and handed it to me. "I've been waiting for a chance to use these, and those peacocks are the perfect opportunity."

Wait! Four weeks? I would marry Niki in four weeks? I wanted to leap for joy. At the same time, it seemed impossible. Unreal. Even a little scary. It would change my life in ways I couldn't anticipate.

Solomonida and Anna pushed forward. "What's in it?" my sister asked at the same time as Anna said, "Open it, Auntie Darya!"

"You won't believe what's in there," Lyuba said.

"Careful," Maria warned. "They'll fly all over the place if you let them."

I untied the string that held the small pouch closed and gently pulled at the opening. Inside lay tiny slivers of pink gold—dozens of them, each no bigger than a baby's fingernail and pierced with a hole in the center only wide enough to take thread from my smallest needle. "What are they?" I asked Maria. I heard awe in my voice as I reached in and pulled out one of the disks, balancing it on my palm.

"Alexei got them from a Venetian merchant. They come from Constantinople. The Venetians call them *zecchini*. Won't they be splendid as the eyes on your peacocks' tails?"

I hugged her. "Absolutely. But I can't take these. He meant them for you."

"Consider them a wedding gift," she said. "I have more at home, but as soon as I saw them, I thought of you and your peacocks. I didn't think you'd be finished already, but I brought them so you'd have them when you needed them. Have you decided what to do with the altar cloth once it's done?"

"I'd meant to give it to the women's monastery if I entered one, but now that I won't, I'll give it to the church where Nikita and I marry and ask the priests there to use it for the ceremony." I positioned the *zecchino* I held against the cloth, assessing the effect. Maria was right. That flash and sparkle were exactly what the tails needed to complete them.

"Good," Maria said. "You can get started while Solomonida and I talk. Did I mention I have lists?"

"You did," Solomonida said, laughing. "Sit, please." She indicated the closest bench, then turned to her daughter. "Anna, be a darling and fetch the needles and threads from the sewing room. Then you and Lyuba can go and play upstairs."

Anna ran from the room, Lyuba close behind her, and Maria pulled a sheaf of papers out of the bag that had held the pouch of *zecchini*. "Those are long lists," I told her.

"We have lots of arrangements to make, and not much time," Maria said.

"But Niki didn't come with you?" I asked. "I thought we were supposed to visit Father Job. He's going to instruct us on our responsibilities as husband and wife."

"Your Niki will be here soon," Maria said. "Alexei wanted a chat with him. My husband plans to offer him a position, something military enough to satisfy the government but artistic enough to satisfy Nikita himself. I'm not sure what, exactly, but they'll find something."

"Oh, that's wonderful." I clapped my hands. "Niki will be so happy if he doesn't have to fight anymore. He hates war."

"He'll still have to train." Maria studied her lists with an absent frown. "In case he does have to fight. It will be an improvement, though, and less dangerous. Let's get down to business, shall we? Neither of you has living parents, I understand. Alexei and I will take the place of his, so we'll have the bedding ceremony and the dinner the next day at our house. Should we hold it entirely there?"

"No." Solomonida leaned forward. "I'll act as the mother of the bride. We'll ask Father Job to perform the betrothal rite, so we can host that, the wedding banquet, and the feast on the third day." She looked at me. "Will you be comfortable if we invite Katya to serve as your matron of honor?"

I hesitated, but I couldn't think of anyone I'd rather ask, since Maria had already offered to act as Niki's proxy mother and Juliana had left for Cracow. "I suppose," I said. "She did apologize for giving me the wrong information about Niki's prior betrothal, and she swears she never had an interest in him." I rather doubted the assertions, but incidents like these were the reason I would never truly consider Katya a friend. Since she was our next-door neighbor—and would continue to be after the wedding—however, it made sense not to condemn her without proof.

"Your cousin Igor has offered to act as the father of the bride." Maria waved the quill she held in her right hand. "Will you allow it?"

Solomonida scrunched her nose, and so did I. The idea of Igor playing a major role in my wedding didn't thrill me. "I think he wants to express remorse," Maria added. "It was my father who came up with the scheme to defraud you, not your cousin."

I glanced at my sister. "It's true that he let himself be duped. So long as Maria and Alexei control the planning on their side and you on ours, I can live with Igor as proxy father of the bride."

"Good." Maria crossed one item off her lists. "We'll keep an eye on him. Don't worry. My father's a bigger problem. He'll expect to act as master of ceremonies, but Alexei won't stand for that, so we'll pick someone else. Is there anyone on Nikita's side?" Solomonida named several possible relatives.

Maria wrote them down. "My sister Varvara can be the bridal attendant from our side," she went on. "I'll ask my brother Mikhail to act as groomsman. Could Dmitry Vorontsov be *your* groomsman? He and Nikita are friends."

"I'm sure Dmitry will agree," I said. "I'll ask Katya when I talk to her about becoming my attendant. That leaves the guest list."

Maria laughed. "Yes, the guest list. It will be enormous. So fortunate we have large houses! I'll need the names of your father's closest comrades, your relatives, your friends. Is that clerk who worked for your cousin still here? Let's get him to write down the names, then he can negotiate with my housekeeper on the question of food and drink and linens and the six hundred other things they'll need to organize. That will give us an excuse to invite him to the wedding, which I'm sure Darya would like since she's taken his children under her wing. What else?"

"Wedding clothes?" Solomonida asked. "We haven't time to stitch something new. Darya has that gorgeous scarlet robe, but Nikita?"

"We'll take care of Nikita. He and Alexei are about the same size, so if necessary we can alter one of my husband's robes for the occasion. We also have an entire chest of those embroidered hand towels that people give out as mementos. My mother ordered far too many for Varvara's wedding, so half of them went unused. There are at least fifty left over from mine as well."

"We have chests full of those too," Solomonida said. "Papa ordered them made when he planned to marry Darya to Daniil. We need a priest for the marriage ceremony itself, though. Father Job, bless his heart, isn't grand enough to officiate at a boyar wedding."

"I'll ask Alexei to approach the archpriest of the Annunciation Cathedral. He'll probably agree if a tsarevich makes the request." Maria frowned at her lists, turning over pieces of paper one after another. "I'm sure I'm forgetting something. Bride's parents, groom's parents, food, drink, clothes, priests, guests, male and female attendants. What else is there?"

"Candles," Solomonida said. "Sprinkling ceremony, hair combing, bathing ceremonies—"

"Stop, stop!" I stood and kissed her cheek, then Maria's. "Father Job is waiting for me downstairs. I'd better let him know that Niki has been delayed. Should I tell Anfim to visit you here, so he can write down your decisions? I think he's in his office, working hard as usual. Solomonida and I kept him on after Igor left."

"Yes, send him," Solomonida said.

"And tell him to bring lots of paper and ink!" Maria added.

I left them to it and, laughing, walked out the door. I was lucky to have such a sister and such friends.

Somehow, everything got done. On a Saturday in early November—dressed in my scarlet robe and ivory tunic, my single maiden's braid divided into two for the first time, pinned up and covered with a veil to indicate that I would soon be a married woman—I stood next to Nikita in the Annunciation Cathedral. Katya's brother Dmitry held a wedding crown over my head, and Maria's brother Mikhail did the same for Nikita.

Ahead of us, in front of the royal doors, stood a table covered in my finished altar cloth. In the flickering candlelight the olive face of the Holy Mother, haloed in gold, appeared to gaze at me through eyes the color of jet—her smile serene, ineffable. The pink gold *zecchini* glittered like tiny flashing lanterns in the peacocks' tails. On the far side of the table stood the priest who would marry us. Jewels covered his miter, his collar, and his white silk robe. He had a serene face; his spiritual children no doubt entrusted him with their secrets.

I knew that Alexei and Maria were right to pick the highest-ranking cleric they could find to underline the aristocratic nature of this ceremony. But I would have preferred Father Job, whose eyes brimmed with tears while he presided over our betrothal and whose whispered reassurances as he reached the end calmed my nerves. In this tenser atmosphere, surrounded by so many noblemen, my left hand shook as I held the candle. Nikita glanced my way, then clasped my right hand with his. That helped, although I still trembled inside.

The priest I didn't know began to intone the ceremony. Beautiful rolling phrases sung in ringing tones blended with the incense and the darkness, the flickering candle flames, the touch of Niki's hand. Before I had time to grow any more nervous (if that was possible), I heard the announcement that Niki was crowned unto me, saw him kiss the beribboned circle as it was held before his face. Then it was my turn. The priest wrapped a cloth around our outstretched wrists to bind us together as a couple. I felt borne away into a dreamlike state as he led us three times around the table in the Dance of Isaiah, stopping to pray on each side.

It would really happen. It was happening. It had happened. Amid a storm of congratulations, the wedding ceremony ended. Niki pulled me into his arms and kissed me in full view of the company, because that was now his right. He was my husband, and I was his wife. I could hardly believe it.

According to custom, Nikita and I walked hand in hand back to our estate. It was cold but clear, already late afternoon. The sun would soon drop beneath the horizon, but we didn't have a long way to go. A good thing, too, because the wind whipped my cheeks even through my gauze veil and my toes grew numb in my boots.

Yet despite the discomfort, I rejoiced at the chance to stroll with Niki and chat with him, certain that no one could separate us. With a fur hat on my head, one hand in his warm clasp, and the other tucked into the sleeve of my fur-lined coat, I couldn't suffer too much from the chill wind or the snow that covered the wooden planks. All too soon, I saw the gates to my own house as we rounded the second corner from the church. From the moment we reached the courtyard, we would be on display: the center and the excuse for a massive celebration that required our presence and honored our union but at which we were as much spectacle as participants.

As we entered the dining room, so crammed that I could hardly imagine how the servants might find room to serve the guests, Solomonida came toward me, Igor on her heels and Katya close behind him. She removed my veil while Mishka the steward took my outer clothes, then Nikita's, and bore them off to another room, where they would remain until it was time to leave for the bedding ceremony at Alexei and Maria's house. Igor, looking more awkward for once than bumptious, said a blessing as Niki and I bowed our heads. When my cousin finished, he ushered us to the center of the high table. As on the day of the momentous dinner party, Niki and I and our various attendants had individual chairs, even though our guests had to make do with the usual long benches.

Looking out, I saw friends and relatives but also many people I'd never met. Comrades of Niki's, perhaps, or people who'd come to honor Alexei. I whispered a question to my new husband. "I know a lot of them," he said. "Some I've seen only from afar."

I asked Katya, sitting next to me, and she identified a few more. "I don't see Fyodor Koshkin," I murmured. "Did he have the sense to stay away?"

"In a fit of pique, yes, he did. Good riddance, I say." She lifted a goblet of wine and sipped it.

"Because Alexei named another master of ceremonies, I suppose." As the bride, I wasn't supposed to drink wine—or eat, or even talk—but no one would notice or care about my muttered conversation with Katya. My throat felt dry, though. I'd have loved a cup of wine, or even water.

Oblivious, Katya took another sip. "This is good. Your sister did you proud with the preparations."

"She did," I agreed.

"Thank you for including me," she said, not for the first time. "I still feel terrible about the grief I caused you."

"You meant well," I told her. Although I still wondered sometimes, I wanted no disharmony at my wedding.

To distract myself from thoughts of food and drink, I surveyed the room once more. Halfway down, my eye caught a familiar olive-green brocade robe trimmed with twisted braid: Anfim Fadeyev. It would be gauche to wave at him, so I smiled, hoping he would realize I meant to welcome him. It pleased me when he smiled back. Even from my seat at the far end of the room I noticed the light in his eyes and the pride on his face, as if he, too, perceived me as someone whose happiness he valued.

Father Job came forward to bless us and the table, and that was even better. On the women's side I saw his wife, beaming with joy. To her I did raise a hand in greeting.

The wedding banquet, even more than the ceremony, proceeded in a dizzying array of repeated events. I had slept little the previous night, eaten nothing since before the betrothal, and was not supposed to speak so long as Niki and I remained in company.

Igor, pretending to be the father of the bride, raised a goblet. "To Nikita and Darya, now joined in holy matrimony!" he roared with a lack of restraint that made me wonder how many goblets he'd sampled at the betrothal ceremony. "May they enjoy health and happiness and prosperity."

Well, that was nice of him. I smiled to show my appreciation, only to hear him add, "Of course, had it not been for me, they might not have found each other again. May they remember that with gratitude and help those who first helped them."

Might not have found each other? He fought us every step of the way!

While I leaned forward to stare at him—he sat at Niki's far side—he dropped onto the bench rather abruptly. He looked dejected, and I experienced a flash of sorrow for him, but within minutes he'd recovered and bounced to his feet with another toast. "Bitter, bitter," he called, waving the goblet in a way that threatened to splash his fine outfit with red wine.

The guests took up the chant, which I knew from other weddings meant that they wanted Nikita to sweeten the bitterness by kissing me. I glanced at him. My cheeks warmed with the thought of embracing him in front of so many people. A shiver ran through me as I recalled Igor catching us in the garden, how angry he'd been with me that day.

"What do you say?" Niki asked in a voice barely above a whisper. "Shall we oblige them or make them wait?"

I bit my lip. He wanted me to decide? Yet I yearned to kiss him. "Perhaps oblige them this time?" I suggested, my voice as soft as his.

Niki pulled me against his chest and kissed me soundly. The calls broke into roars of approval, and as they died down, a manservant entered carrying a dressed swan on a platter, its shape and feathers arranged to look as if it swam on his shoulder.

Beautiful, no doubt, and traditional at weddings for its association with lifelong fidelity. Yet at that moment I was glad custom forbade me from eating. I hated to watch the bird dismembered and doled out among the tables. I couldn't imagine placing its flesh in my mouth.

I murmured as much to Niki, who was also supposed to refrain from eating until after the ceremony, although everyone expected him to take part in the toasts. He laughed and kissed me again, to more roars of approval. "Are you starving?" he asked. "Shall I slip you some bread under the table?"

"Alas, that won't help," I told him, laughing in turn. "Unless I can eat it under the table, I'm stuck. Besides, I need water more."

"Then let me see what I can do." Before long, he tore a piece of bread into tiny pieces and passed them to me one at a time. He also placed a cup of wine on the arm of my chair. It was a kind thought, so to thank him I moved the cup to where I could reach it unobserved. Taking care not to knock it over, I dipped the bread in the liquid and ate what I could while the company focused its attention on the master of ceremonies, a relative of my husband's whose name I never did quite catch. I could ask Niki later, when we were alone.

"Your new husband is very considerate of you," Katya said, tapping one of the pieces of bread as illustration. "It's good to see." Her eyes strayed to Igor, standing once more. "Would your cousin be as kind, I wonder?"

It was a good question, and I thought the probable answer was no. But I wasn't quite sure how Katya felt about Igor, who had (so far as I could tell) broken all contact with her since the attack on her family. Nor did I any longer have a reason to oppose their marriage. And there were those odd moments when I saw more in Igor than met the eye. So I chose the most neutral yet honest response that came to me. "Consideration is important in a husband, but so is constancy. Igor is not, I think, a bad man, but he worries too much about advancement at the expense of affection and loyalty and other things that last."

She nodded. Maria's sister Varvara, who sat on Katya's other side, asked a question I couldn't hear. Katya turned to answer it, and I went back to watching the company.

Toast followed toast, interspersed with more shouts from the tables of "Bitter, bitter." Niki didn't hesitate to respond, although I knew he would stop kissing me if I objected.

Did I object? Thinking about it, I had to admit that I didn't. That surprised me, because however much I'd grown in the last few months, I still hated being the center of everyone's attention. But I did like the festival atmosphere and the idea that so many people had gathered to wish us well. As during the church ceremony, the flickering candles and the heady atmosphere of scents and sounds wafted me into another world where I became a person different from my usual quiet self. I turned into that magical creature, a bride.

At last we left the table. By then it was full dark, as I could tell from the many-paned windows. Katya, as my chief attendant, would accompany me to the next part of the ceremony, but the next time I saw my sister I would be fully a wife, no longer a maiden.

I walked with Solomonida to the window while Mishka collected my veil and the furs Niki and I had worn from the church. My husband would join us soon, but for the moment his comrades had caught him and seemed reluctant to see him go, even though they would accompany us to Alexei and Maria's house. There the party would continue, moving back and forth over the next two days.

"Now admit it," my sister said as we turned our backs on the noisy crowd and looked out at the courtyard below. "Aren't you glad you didn't join that monastery?"

Although I'd drunk little of the wine that the guests had imbibed with such abandon, I felt light and free, more than I had since Papa first fell ill. "But I did," I said, teasing her. "Join a monastery, that is. As of today, I'm Darya Nikitina Monastyreva. That's monastery enough for me right now."

Solomonida laughed until she almost bent double. "That's true. Do you know, I'd never thought about Nikita's last name meaning 'of the monastery.' Asceticism seems quite unlike him."

"Indeed, although I think he'd prefer it to fighting. He's so happy now that Tsarevich Alexei has taken him on as an adjutant. No one need know that his responsibilities include drawing maps and miniatures for books." I tucked my hand in the crook of her arm. "And I have my sister and my niece and my friends, as well as a loving husband. Life couldn't be better."

"Indeed," Solomonida said. "Who would have thought, that day Igrushka the Duckling strutted into our yard, that things would turn out so well?"

As she spoke, I saw her look over her shoulder and realized she was gazing at Anfim Fadeyev. His cheeks flushed, and so did hers. I didn't see how they could marry, but I decided to help them if I could.

"Next we have to do something for you," I told my sister. "You've lived as a divorced widow long enough."

Historical Note

VERY FEW OF THE EVENTS DESCRIBED IN *SONG OF THE SISTERS* are historical. The attack by Prince Andrei Shuisky and his supporters against the Vorontsovs did take place on September 9, 1543, as portrayed here, although the victim was Fyodor Semyonovich Vorontsov. I used Demid, another name associated with him, to avoid confusion with Fyodor Mikhailovich Koshkin, a fictional character. Russia's negotiations with King Sigismund the Old of Poland-Lithuania, first mentioned in *Song of the Siren*, were still ongoing in the fall of 1543, and the idea of a marriage between Grand Prince Ivan and one of Sigismund's daughters may have been floated in October of that year, although if so, it came to naught for various reasons, including religious differences. And Grand Prince Ivan, later known as Tsar Ivan IV "the Terrible," did leave Moscow with his brother (but not, so far as we know, his cousin Prince Vladimir of Staritsa, although the cousins often hunted and otherwise spent time together when they were young) on September 15, 1543, for a pilgrimage to Holy Trinity Monastery. The story of Prince Andrei of Staritsa's failed "rebellion" forms the backdrop to my earlier novel *The Vermilion Bird*, which also explores

Fyodor Koshkin's fictional part in that conflict and Alexei's difficult relationship with his father, Bulat Khan.

It may seem strange that Anfim Fadeyev, although clearly involved in foreign affairs, works for the Treasury. When I introduced him in *Song of the Shaman*, before I realized how large a part he would play in this series, for the sake of simplicity I described him as a clerk in the Foreign Office. But in 1543, the Foreign Office did not yet exist as an independent entity. Although a group of specialized civil servants like Anfim were already producing diplomatic documents and performing other necessary tasks, the Treasury still had formal jurisdiction over foreign affairs.

With these few exceptions, the plot and characters are entirely my invention. But like the rest of my historical fiction, the situations I portray have a basis in fact. As I mention in some of the historical notes to Legends of the Five Directions, marriages among the Russian nobility in the sixteenth century were arranged for political reasons, since family connections were the primary factor determining alliances at court. Darya's various stratagems for dissuading potential bridegrooms and mothers-in-law are attested in a seventeenth-century work by Grigorii Kotoshikhin, *Russia during the Reign of Alexei Mikhailovich*, translated by Benjamin Uroff, edited by Marshall Poe (2014), and available as an open access e-book or PDF from DeGruyter.

Darya needs those stratagems because the position of women in sixteenth-century Europe was far different from current norms. Obedience was promoted as a woman's primary virtue, and chastity—strictly defined, as Igor's reaction to seeing her kiss Nikita shows—as synonymous with honor. Noblewomen had opportunities to exercise authority not available to those of lower status, whether male or female, but mostly within their own households. Aristocratic women lived in seclusion in an upper story of the main house and were supposed to leave their homes only to visit relatives or female friends, to attend weddings (one of the few social occasions where men and women mingled), or for church services, although even those were most often conducted at home by a priest who either resided on the property or, like Father Job, visited as needed to minister to the family and its servants.

The urban estates themselves were quite large, surrounded by gardens and orchards and including many buildings of different types. Servants—technically slaves, but slavery in Russia differed in certain crucial respects from the plantation slavery of the US South familiar to most readers—could number in the hundreds. The household of sixty maintained by the Sheremetevs is therefore quite small by Muscovite standards, smaller than it would have been before their father fell ill. As shown here, and in contrast to Western Europe, women could own property, but most often landed estates went to men. Women inherited movable property, although individual villages might be assigned for their use—meaning that they collected rent in cash and kind from the peasants who lived in those villages. The specific provision that Darya and Solomonida have the right to remain in the house is more literary than historical; no such terms appear in surviving wills from the period. But as Father Hilarion notes, Pyotr Sheremetev saw the arrangement as temporary: he expected Darya and Nikita to marry and sought to guard the interests of his best friend's son while preventing his daughters' eviction before the ceremony could take place.

Because of the restrictions placed on secular women, the obedience and chastity required of female monastics were not so different from women's everyday lives, although poverty was certainly not characteristic of noble families, who as a rule favored conspicuous consumption. In the sixteenth and seventeenth centuries, wealthy men and women could live quite luxurious lives in monasteries, despite their nominal embrace of poverty and communal living. The attitude that Darya so often encounters—that a young woman should marry and bear children before retiring from the world—is also typical of this period, again because marriage was a political and economic connection in which affection developed after the ceremony, if at all. For a man to leave the court before producing offspring meant taking himself out of the dynastic game; for a woman to do so deprived her relatives or prospective husband of their greatest political asset—the sons she might otherwise have borne. The boyar clans discouraged their younger members from making such choices, although almost everyone accepted monastic vows late in life or immediately before death.

The occasional references to "convent" and "nun" don't have neat parallels in the Eastern Orthodox Church, where monasteries can be either male or female and the same term applies to the residents of both, except that women get a feminine ending (in Russian, *monakhinia* instead of *monakh*). To the extent possible, I have used words that match Orthodox usage, but once in a while the familiar English terms are simply more succinct—or in the case of Juliana, a convert to Catholicism, appropriate.

Last but not least, a word on naming conventions. For the most part, in my novels about Muscovy I strive to avoid the complicated Russian system of nicknames and the yet more complicated custom, still prevalent in the sixteenth century even among the elite, of changing surnames with every generation. I remember too well my confusion the first time I read Boris Pasternak's *Doctor Zhivago* as a teenager and realized only two-thirds of the way through that Antonina, Tonya, and Toniechka were three ways of referring to one person.

These variant forms express emotions, and they can change on the fly in a single conversation. Darya Petrovna is a formal greeting, at the level of Miss Sheremeteva, used by strangers and subordinates. Dasha expresses intimacy and affection, as do Niki, Shura, and Katya; Dashenka points to even greater closeness and love, but Dashka is antagonistic or pejorative. Igrushka, although an affectionate form of Igor, is here used to indicate mockery with its echoes of childhood; his sobriquet Igrushka the Duckling can be made to rhyme in Russian (Igrúshka Utyónushka) and can therefore be chanted, in that way children have of humiliating those they dislike. I suspect that Niki, as shorthand for Nikita, is more characteristic of the nineteenth century than the sixteenth, but the connection is clear, unlike some of the alternatives, so I use it anyway. I minimize the variants here, but in a novel so focused on relationships it seems fitting to hint at this very Russian way of revealing hidden and not-so-hidden feelings.

As mentioned above, family names were not set in the 1540s. So Anfim Fadeyev (the two-part name, in contrast to the three-part names used by Darya and her social equals and by everyone in Russia today, indicates that he is not a member of the aristocracy) is the son of Faddei but the father of Larisa Anfimova (Larisa/Lara, daughter of Anfim) and Anatoly Anfimov (Anatoly/Tolya, son of Anfim). References to married women alternated, depending on circumstances, between identifications based on their father's name (Solomonida, daughter of Pyotr Sheremetev) and their husband's (Solomonida, widow of Semyon Kolychev). Here Solomonida favors her birth name because she was divorced from a husband she hated, and Maria because her first husband died and her second, a Tatar, has a personal name and patronymic but no family name. There are other complexities but none that affect this particular story, so let us leave them for another day.

Acknowledgments

I WOULD LIKE TO EXPRESS MY THANKS FOR ALL THE HELP I have received from my invaluable writers' group and to the members of Five Directions Press for their encouragement and support. *Song of the Sisters* has benefited immeasurably from their comments. I also thank those who read the novel before publication: Ariadne Apostolou, Finola Austin, Kate Braithwaite, Galit Gottlieb, Molly Greeley, Courtney J. Hall, Gabrielle Mathieu, and Joan Schweighardt. A special tip of the hat goes to Ann Kleimola, whose wonderful comments saved me from a number of errors and who took part in the creation of Laika. Andrea Rusnock gave me the benefit of her expertise on Russian embroidery, thus averting another set of potential mistakes. Russell E. Martin generously shared chapters from his forthcoming book on Russian royal and noble weddings, research reflected in the description of Niki and Darya's ceremony as well as those in earlier novels.

To my husband and son—and, of course, the cat, who monitored my progress every day in my office and purred encouragingly while I stared puzzled at the screen—words cannot express my gratitude.

The Author

As a child, C. P. Lesley thought everyone made up stories while falling asleep. It never occurred to her that anyone would pay her for them, and for a long time, she was right—no one would. But after years of producing horrible prose, reading books about novel writing, and pestering hapless fellow-writers and friends to read her drafts, some of the advice stuck, and she finished *The Not Exactly Scarlet Pimpernel*, then *The Golden Lynx* and its sequels: *The Winged Horse*, *The Swan Princess*, *The Vermilion Bird*, and *The Shattered Drum*. Five Directions Press published *Song of the Siren* in 2019 and *Song of the Shaman* in 2020. You can find Juliana's and Grusha's stories, respectively, in those last two novels.

Lesley is currently working on the fourth in her Songs of Steppe and Forest series, *Song of the Sinner*, which explores the developing if star-crossed romance between Anfim and Solomonida, with a little "assistance" from Igor. She has also started a joint project with fellow novelist P.K. Adams, author of the Jagiellonian Mysteries and a duology on Hildegard of Bingen. The new series begins in Muscovy in 1553. The first novel, tentatively titled *The Merchant's Tale*, takes place against the backdrop of Tudor sailors' discovery of a northern route to Russia and their encounter with the young Ivan the Terrible and his in-laws, the ancestors of the Romanov dynasty.

When not thinking up new ways to torture her characters, Lesley edits other people's manuscripts, reads voraciously, maintains her website, and practices classical ballet—an interest reflected in *Desert Flower* and *Kingdom of the Shades* (Tarkei Chronicles 1 and 2). She also hosts New Books in Historical Fiction, a podcast channel in the New Books Network. You can find out more about her at www.cplesley.com.

FORTHCOMING FROM FIVE DIRECTIONS PRESS

Song of the Sinner

SONGS OF STEPPE & FOREST 4

Moscow, December 31, 1543

I'D NEVER REALIZED HOW LONELY ONE COULD FEEL IN THE midst of a crowd. Indeed, I had never *felt* lonely in the midst of a crowd. I loved parties and people, chatter and song, the glitter of gemstones in flickering candlelight, the swish of silk and velvet, the twang of zithers in the background—and yes, the social and political games that masqueraded as idle conversation, rumors, and gossip but in fact determined the ins and outs of everything from war to governance to marital happiness.

Yet as I gazed at this special gathering, aware that I should be in my element, I instead experienced a haunting sense of isolation. The guests at the party—limited to the family and close associates of my next-door neighbors—mingled, for the most part, in pairs.

Perhaps that was what bothered me—the lack of a partner. After seven years of widowhood, I would have sworn I'd grown accustomed to my single state. Indeed, I preferred it to married life. But tonight, watching husbands and wives whispering as they passed me, I knew I missed what I had never had: a man who loved me. A man who would catch my eye as he laughed with his friends, wink at me across the crowded room, mutter in my ear as he moved from one group to the next.

"Solomonida!" Katya Vorontsova, my hostess, bustled over. Vivacious and, at twenty-seven, a few years younger than I, she looked, as always, very fine. Although we both had blue eyes, her dark hair allowed her to wear bright shades that would drain my pale complexion to ashen. I complimented her on her choice of a cobalt silk robe cuffed in cloth-of-gold and a jeweled headdress suitable for a bride—which Katya was not, having returned to her father's home after losing her elderly husband eighteen months ago. It was something we had in common: unsatisfactory spouses, fortunately deceased.

She blushed and gripped my sleeve between finger and thumb. "I wish I could wear that color. Bittersweet suits you perfectly. I'd love to be blonde."

While I searched for a reply, she pointed to loaded tables at the far side of the room. "Supper is served." I let her tug me toward the food, because I had eaten next to nothing since late morning. And because listening to her chatter gave me something better to do than bemoan my own lack of company.

The Vorontsovs had done themselves proud, I saw as we came close. Salmon and sturgeon, cheese straws and caviar, pancakes and turnovers, roast beef and capon and noodles floating in butter, baskets of bread and rolls—these celebratory dishes clustered thick as soldiers on parade. I topped a pancake with salmon and another with sour cream and caviar, then accepted a porcelain dish to hold them and the mushroom turnover Katya insisted I try. Plate in hand, I moved away to let the next hungry diner approach and surveyed the room, waiting to see if Katya would rejoin me or depart to usher more guests to the tables. Taking care not to drip butter or sour cream onto my red-orange robe, I bit into one of the pancakes. It was as delicious as I'd hoped, and for a moment I forgot my distress in the pleasure of satisfying my appetite.

In response to the zithers I'd noticed earlier, as well as flutes and tambourines, a few of the bolder guests had already begun to dance. From where I stood, I saw a nobleman strip off his outer robe to leap and squat with the freedom conferred by trousers and leather boots. Others clapped in time with the instruments and would no doubt join him as the liquor continued to flow. Off to my left, concealed from the sight of those in the main hall but visible from where I stood, several women—girls barely old enough to wed but also their mamas and grandmas—traced sinuous circles with their arms, waving silk scarves. My feet tapped the rhythm, my skirts swirled in response to the sway of my hips, and I yearned to join them. I'd fit right in, more self-assured than the maidens but not yet old and creaky. And to dance, I didn't need a partner. I'd blend into the group, one woman among many.

A clay stove covered in patterned tiles kept the rooms warm enough to discourage much activity, but although it would be unpleasant to end up sweaty and disheveled, I struggled to resist temptation. I hadn't danced in years.

Temptation won. I set my empty plate aside and edged toward them, only to stop when someone caught my arm. I turned to find Katya holding out a goblet, which I took. The rich crimson of the liquid led me to expect cherry juice, but my first sip convinced me otherwise. "Fine Italian wine," I said to Katya. "Thank you. Your father has spared no expense tonight."

"It's a special evening," she said. "If being halfway through the Christmas season isn't reason enough to celebrate, I don't know what is. Walk with me while I check on the other guests. It may be our only chance to talk."

No dancing yet, alas. But I could hardly refuse my hostess, and conversation too would keep my nagging sense of loneliness at bay. I strolled at her side, taking the occasional sip of wine. Katya had a keen eye and a sharp tongue, and she loved to share her acid comments on all and sundry. More often than not, her gimlet gaze led to revelations as accurate as they were entertaining.

A small, dapper boyar in his early forties with dark hair turning to gray crossed my line of sight. "Fyodor Koshkin," I said, unable to conceal a flash of anger. Not long ago he had involved himself in my family's affairs in ways that still made my blood boil.

"Did you *have* to invite him?" I asked Katya, directing her away from Koshkin. "I haven't forgiven him for trying to steal our estate six months ago. If I have to talk to him, I may empty this goblet over his head."

Katya laughed, but she didn't resist the tug of my hand. "Your cousin Igor brought him. So Koshkin can make his peace with my family now we're back in favor at court, I assume. You did hear about the scandal at the Kremlin two days ago?"

I nodded. "Everyone here is buzzing with the news like so many bees. Your uncles took their revenge for the

Shuisky princes' attack on them last September. And Grand Prince Ivan stood by and watched while his boyars ordered the head of the Shuisky clan executed."

"Not just executed," Katya said. "They stripped him naked in public and gave him to the dogs—or at least their keepers. A nobleman, the head of the most powerful clan in these lands!"

The shock I heard in her voice mirrored my own every time I thought about it. "Worse than the beating he administered to your family," I agreed. "Although he would have killed your uncle Demid if not stopped, so I suppose your uncles wanted to make a point about who's in charge now. I do wonder why the grand prince, young as he is, let things get that far."

"Ivan lost patience," Katya said with an airy wave that shocked me with its casual dismissal of judicial murder. "The Shuiskys dishonored him, too, by attacking his favorite. And Ivan blames the Shuisky princes for his own mother's death."

I shivered despite the heat, tormented by memories of Grand Princess Elena's blue face and tragic eyes as she died, poisoned by a concoction of yew delivered as a tisane. I'd served as her lady-in-waiting, and I witnessed the agony of her final hours. More than five years later, the horrors of that day—our desperate and ultimately unsuccessful attempt to save her—still gave me nightmares.

"He's right to do so, from what I've heard." It was another Shuisky prince's wife who had unwittingly delivered the poison at her husband's behest. I did my best to match Katya's lightness of tone, because that detail was not known to those outside the small circle of ladies-in-waiting, but I couldn't disguise the tremor in my voice.

Eager to deflect my hostess onto another conversational path, I tipped my chin toward a rotund middle-aged man, his once red hair fading to gray. It was one of her aforementioned uncles—not Demid, beaten by the Shuiskys, but his brother Gavriil. He stared at us with a fixed expression on his face, like a man struck by lightning. Or perhaps someone behind us had attracted his attention, since I had never, to my knowledge, spoken with him, although I'd seen him often enough at weddings.

"Gavriil Timofeevich seems to relish his return to favor," I said. "Has he settled on another bride now that my sister is taken?"

"Not he." For some reason I couldn't detect, she flushed. "Although I suspect he will after he settles into his new position at court. He got back to Moscow less than a week ago."

I narrowed my eyes at her. "Why does that question turn your cheeks the color of a beet?"

She giggled in a way I'd expect from my daughter Anna, not a mature woman. "I can't tell you yet. You'll find out soon enough. It's a surprise!"

"A surprise? What kind of surprise?"

She shook her head, still laughing. "Soon, I said. Look, there's Aunt Liza. I need to get her some food before she makes a scene. Talk to you later!"

I watched her as she dashed off, leaving me alone once more. I could dance now, if I wished, but the music had stopped during my conversation with Katya. The massed groups of men and women had split into quartets and trios and pairs, husbands and wives together, as if anticipating an announcement of some kind. My stomach knotted at the sight. I might as well be a ghost, gazing on a human realm forever barred to me. At this darkest time of the year, people said, the boundary between the heavenly sphere and our own thinned, and those on the other side could pass through it.

A superstition worthy of slaves and peasants! My dead father's voice sounded in my head, and I chided myself. I had no cause for complaint. In a few months I would turn thirty-two. I had a daughter I adored, home and family, rank and wealth, neighbors and friends. What possessed me to yearn for a partnership I might not want if I found it? I could have remarried anytime these seven years, if that had been my goal.

Gavriil Vorontsov continued to stare, as if he couldn't take his eyes off someone behind me. Glancing around, I saw only a quartet of elderly ladies, deep in discussion of their various ailments. Turning back, I raised my eyebrows at him, asking a silent question. He looked away, but when I moved, I realized that his gaze followed me. So he was watching me. How odd!

And how disturbing. Not only was I alone at the party, but the one man showing an interest in me had grandchildren older than my daughter. Having passed thirty, it seemed, I'd lost whatever charms I once possessed.

Determined to rid myself of melancholy, I decided to seek out my sister, Darya, last seen gazing with adoration into the eyes of her new husband while he muttered secrets into her ear. In their pleasant and undemanding company, I could reimpose order on my rebellious heart before moving back into the party to look for my friends.

Or were Darya and her husband the true source of my misery? My jaw dropped open at the thought, and I hastily shut it again before I attracted unwanted attention.

The truth struck me hard, like a blow between the eyes. I was jealous. Darya, once my closest companion, had found a bliss with her Nikita that I had not enjoyed as a wife. Not that I begrudged them their happiness, of course, but in that moment I realized that witnessing it so often over the last two months had sent my thoughts reeling toward a destination abandoned so long ago that I'd forgotten ever wishing I could reach it.

No wonder I pine for a man of my own.

"Solomonida!" As if conjured from the midst of the crowd, Darya pushed past a pair of large Vorontsov aunts and grabbed my arm. "Look who's here," she said in excited tones. "Anfim Fadeyev! I haven't seen him for months, since before he went back to the Treasury! Let's go and greet him, shall we? He looks very elegant, I must say."

"He certainly does." I followed the line of her pointing finger. At the far side of the room stood a man a hand's breadth above medium height with a mobile, clever face; a body strong and solid but not given to fat; and, as I knew from experience, a pair of dancing light blue eyes and a smile that seldom failed to coax an answering smile from me.

"I've missed him!" The words burst out of me without conscious thought. We were too far away, with too many people between us, for Anfim to hear me. Nevertheless, he raised a hand, as if he spotted us across the room.

"Me too," Darya said. "Who are those men he's with?"

"Nobles who direct government offices," I told her. "I recognize some of them. That's Ivan Tretiakov—the treasurer and keeper of the seal—talking to Anfim, for example. And that tall, distinguished-looking, dark-haired man with them is Prince Alexander Gorbaty. I'm surprised, though. Until now I thought everyone here was friends or family."

"The nobles could be family," Darya pointed out. "In-laws and other relatives. And the lower officials are connected to *them*. Let's go and greet him." She pulled on my elbow, which she had not released, and started toward Anfim.

"Yes, of course." I moved with her rather than lose her again in the mob. And yes, if our path brought us closer to Anfim, so much the better. "The great clans are so intermarried everybody's related to everybody else by now. I should have thought of that."

Thanks to a dedicated effort and a refusal to yield to the many obstacles in our path, we did move forward, but not enough to get close to Anfim and his companions. Dozens of people blocked our way, imperiling our progress with careless gestures and outflung hands, many of them holding goblets. The noise level rose steadily, to the point where I struggled to hear Darya, walking right next to me.

"Do you think one of those men got Anfim his job back?" my sister shouted as she dodged yet another stout noblewoman, narrowly escaping a deluge of red wine that would have stained her apple-green robe. Her hair was darker than mine, matching her hazel eyes, but we were about the same height—a little taller than normal—and had the same slender build. Anyone would recognize at a glance that we must be related.

"No idea." I sidestepped the puddle left by the wine, holding my robe above my ankles. "One day he was at our house, and the next he packed up his papers and left." She'd been away then, helping her new husband move his things from the subordinate principality of Staritsa, where

Nikita had served for a year before Tsarevich Alexei took him on as a resident artist and occasional warrior. "I asked him who put in a good word for him, but he said he didn't know. Like you, I haven't seen him since."

"When did you ask him? I didn't think you spent much time with him."

We pushed our way to a relatively secluded corner, which made it possible for me to lower my voice. A good thing, because her astonished question made my cheeks warm. I had no desire to yell the answer to all and sundry, however small the likelihood they could hear it.

"I saw him often in that month. I had no one else to talk to with you gone," I told her, making light of it. "No one except servants. Even Father Job was busy with his family and stopped by just long enough to perform services and hear confessions."

"Why not tell me, then? It's not shameful to chat with a handsome man, even if he does come from a merchant family. And I've known for a while that he attracts you." She looked at me, her eyes keen, and I realized anew that she was no longer the baby sister who for years clung to me as a substitute mother because her own had died the day of her birth. She was already twenty-five—and married.

"I forgot," I said, which was untrue. I treasured every moment with Anfim and didn't want to dilute the memories with idle chatter. "He'd left by the time you came back, and it didn't seem important."

Darya accepted that explanation with a nod. "Oh look," she said, gazing at Anfim once more. "He's laughing. I haven't seen him laugh like that since the day we told him about pelting our cousin with acorns. Even then, he tried to hide it."

"He's very proper. He would say it's not appropriate to laugh at one's employer." I sighed. "Although he does, and often, whether he tries to hide it or not."

"I'm glad to see him laugh outright," Darya said. "Maybe he'll share the jokes with us now that he's back in the government and his own man again."

"I hope so." From halfway across the room, I studied Anfim. His eyes crinkled at the corners, and he raised his goblet in a toast. I didn't recognize the official who'd amused him, but I liked this new view of him.

Was *he* the man missing from my life?

I was dreaming. Even if I decided to seek another husband, choosing Anfim would create difficulties—and not for me. I was a boyar's daughter with a child approaching marriageable age. I had to put her interests first. Wedding a man from a line of merchants would undermine her chances of attracting a high-ranking nobleman.

Anfim might not want me anyway. Darya had told me last summer that he was in love with someone. For a while, I'd thought the someone might be Darya herself.

Still, people fall out of love as well as into it. And after I found the right husband for Anna, I could please myself. I'd never met a noblewoman who married beneath her station, but I occasionally heard scandalous tales—even one about a girl who fled her estate and took up with a bandit. I was not a virginal bride. So long as I saw Anna settled first, I could choose my own husband.

Watching Anfim from a distance, I felt myself drawn to him once more. His light brown hair gleamed in the light cast by the torches placed at intervals along walls painted in patterns of scarlet and sky-blue; and he was, as always, discreetly but luxuriously dressed—tonight in rich brown velvet with clasps formed from gold braid. Next to the brilliantly clad noblemen and noblewomen he looked like a wren amid a flock of peafowl, but at the sight of him my heart gave a skip.

"I don't think we can get much closer," I told Darya. Indeed, the crowd had become ever more tightly packed as we progressed—and more masculine. Soon we would be lucky to catch even a glimpse of Anfim. "Not until he separates himself from those men."

"Very well," she said with a sigh. She turned back to face me, as if accepting the inevitability of waiting. "I'm sure he'll seek us out eventually. And if he doesn't, I'll ask Niki to fetch him. He promised to join us soon."

Surveying the room, I spotted Nikita and his patron, Tsarevich Alexei, approaching the group of officials. I watched the two of them detach Anfim from his companions with the aplomb of skilled horsemen separating a stallion from the herd and usher him in our direction.

"I don't think you'll have to," I told her. "They're heading straight for us, with Alexei."

http://www.fivedirectionspress.com/song-of-the-sinner

PRAISE FOR SONGS OF STEPPE & FOREST

"In *Song of the Sisters*, against the tense political backdrop of 1540s Moscow, C. P. Lesley brings us into the domestic world of the women's quarters and enchants with a quiet novel about two sisters who wield their limited power to determine their own destinies."

—Finola Austin, author of *Bronte's Mistress*

"From the first page of *Song of the Sisters* I was transported to sixteenth-century Russia. C. P. Lesley's rich prose brings the challenges faced by the young noblewoman Darya and her sister Solomonida to vivid life. Charmed by her humor and ingenuity, I read avidly, rooting for Darya to find her own path beyond the control of her strutting peacock of a cousin, Igor. With themes of love, trust, friendship, and female empowerment, *Song of the Sisters* is an enthralling read that had me turning the pages long into the night."

—Kate Braithwaite, author of *The Girl Puzzle* and other novels

"From Tatar shenanigans on the steppe to the machinations of Moscow's elite, trained historian C. P. Lesley weaves historical facts with a prodigious imagination and a passion for sixteenth-century Russia. In *Song of the Sisters*, the third installment of Lesley's delightful Songs of Steppe & Forest series, she has re-created a world of misogynistic laws, court intrigue, formidable clans competing for power, and women's camaraderie in the face of male domination."

—G. P. Gottlieb, author of the Whipped and Sipped Mysteries

"So rich with historical detail that readers will swear they can taste the foods and stroke the fabrics described, *Song of the Sisters* vividly transports readers to sixteenth-century Russia. C. P. Lesley blends fact and fiction seamlessly to create a sweet tale with more than a hint of intrigue."

—Molly Greeley, author of *The Heiress*

If you enjoyed this book, please consider leaving a review at your favorite online bookseller and/or on GoodReads.

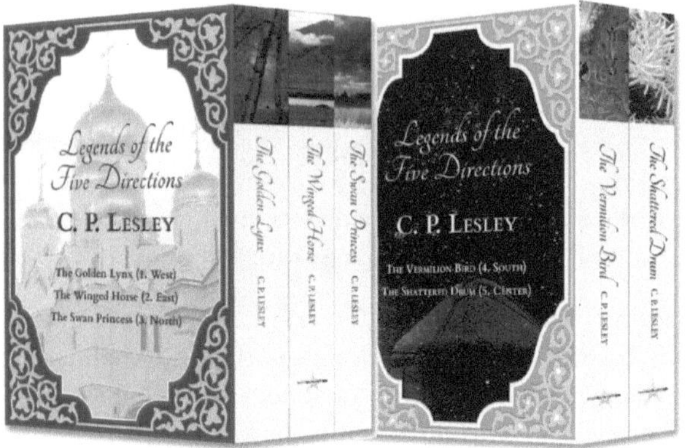

WHO IS THE GOLDEN LYNX?

This question drives the first book in Legends of the Five Directions, a series that will sweep you to the distant world of sixteenth-century Russia, amid the descendants of Genghis Khan and courts that could teach the Borgias a thing or two about political ambition, assassination, and chicanery. Follow Nasan and her kinsfolk as they struggle for power, honor, identity, and love across the steppe and through the vast forests of the Russian North.

"A 'ripping good yarn,' as adventure stories have always been. Enter the exotic, cut-throat world of sixteenth-century Muscovy in the company of a Tatar princess whose skills would have made her equally a heroine on the American frontier. The Kremlin court of the not-yet-Terrible toddler Ivan and his mother-regent Elena Glinskaya, boyar intrigue, arranged political marriages, spirit animals and ancestors pointing the way to restoring balance and order in the universe—what more could a reader want except further adventures, which are heralded by the advent of another animal messenger?"

—Ann M. Kleimola, professor *emerita* of Russian history

Find out more at http://www.fivedirectionspress.com/boxsets.

www.ingramcontent.com/pod-product-compliance
Lightning Source LLC
LaVergne TN
LVHW040827090826
845145LV00001BA/242